THE SUN & HER BURN

USA TODAY & WSJ BESTSELLING AUTHOR

giana darling

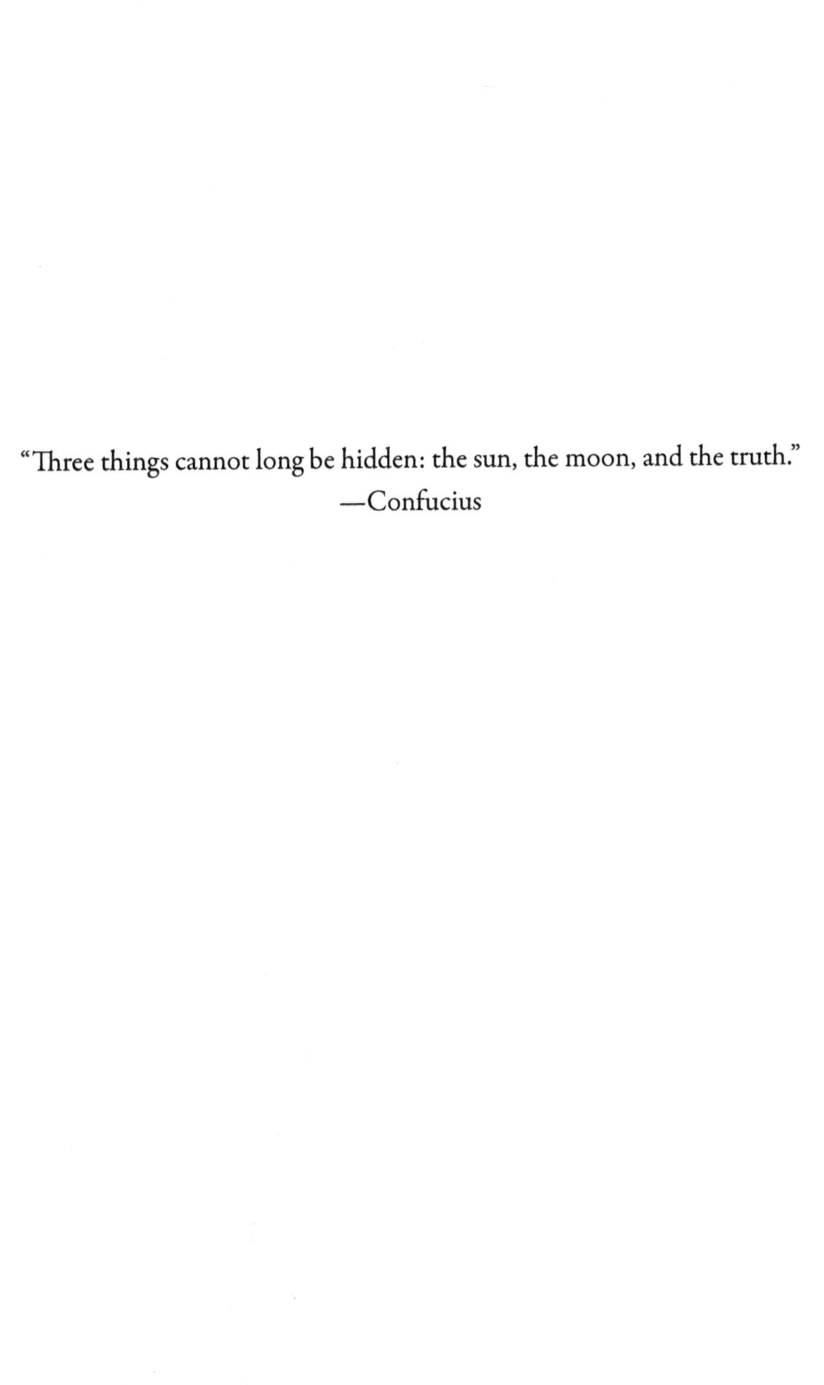

"Three things cannot long be hidden: the sun, the moon, and the truth."
—Confucius

To the dreamers who never stop hoping and wishing even when life kicks them in the teeth.

PLAYLIST

"Down By The Water"—Ocie Elliot

"California Girls"—NoMBe

"Simply The Best"—Billianne

"Summertime Sadness"—Lana Del Rey

"Gold Dust Woman"—Julia Holter

"Ten Years Gone"—Led Zeppelin

"Glimpse Of Us"—Joji

"I Lied"—Lord Huron with Allison Ponthier

"Where's My Love"—SYML

"I Got You, Honey"—Ocie Elliot

"July"—Noah Cyrus

"All the Pretty Girls"—KALEO

"Would That I"—Hozier

"Edge Of The Ocean"—Ivy

"In The Sun"—Aron Wright

"You Put A Spell On Me"—Austin Giorgio

"None Of Your Concern"—Jhené Aiko, Big Sean

"ocean eyes"—Billie Eilish

"Nice to Each Other"—Olivia Dean

"Like Everybody Else (acoustic)"—Lennon Stella

"Feeling Good"—Nina Simone

"Vattene Amore"—Mietta, Amedeo Minghi

"Him.Her"—James Gillespie

"golden thing"—Cody Simpson

"My Silver Lining"—First Aid Kit

"Wish I Was Better"—Kina, yaeow

"People Change"—Mipso

"Golden"—Harry Styles

"Heat Waves"—Glass Animals

"Be the One"—Dua Lipa

"West Coast"—Phillip LaRue

"Surf"—Mac Miller

"Salt And The Sea"—Gregory Alan Isakov

"Worship"—Ari Abdul

"All These Years"—Camilla Cabello

"Hollywood Forever Cemetery Sings"—Father John Misty

"Dancing With Your Ghost"—Sasha Alex Sloan

"You Are In Love"—Taylor Swift

"Fallin' All In You" —Shawn Mendes

"I am not who I was"—Chance Pena

"Bad Love"—RY X

CHAPTER ONE

SEBASTIAN

They were talking about me before I even entered the room.

It wasn't the first time, and it wouldn't be the last.

I knew this mostly because over the past ten years, my name had become a cornerstone of comparison, like the Mona Lisa or the moon, a cultural icon.

But I knew that everyone was talking about me today because *Waking Nightmare* had just premiered and was already generating a tidal wave of Oscar buzz. Despite the glowing early reviews from critics and fans, I had no doubt that I would emerge come March empty-handed yet again. It seemed my famous luck didn't extend far enough to secure me the handsome golden trophy I had lusted over since I was a child. I had received the top accolade as a writer for my screenplay of *Blood Oath*, but never for acting despite being nominated six times.

Still, over the past decade of my career in Hollywood, I had achieved the seemingly impossible dream I'd harbored since I was a child. I had managed to become a household name. Someone who men and women of all ages could recognize by face and name.

The former liked me for my style, the fast cars, the beautiful women, the irreverent charm that made me seem humble despite it all. An affinity for self-deprecation I'd learned from the Brits during my stint in England.

The latter, well, they liked me for the face and the body God and my parents had given me that I worked hard to maintain. They liked the romantic films I'd done, the part of Romeo in the modern mafia adaptation I'd starred in after *Blood Oath*'s success, Diego Rivera in the adaptation of his life and relationship with Frida Kahlo, and most famously, Matteo Rossi in one of the saddest love stories to hit the silver screen in the last two decades.

I was called to my art form like Picasso with his paints and Mozart with his notes, so the success meant something to me. It meant I was doing it well. That I *could* do it for as long as I wanted in an industry where most people floundered after a time, even if they managed to hit it big. After ten years, I had star power that promised longevity.

It should have been enough.

But I'd always known it wouldn't be. Couldn't be.

Not for a soul like mine.

Dozens of romantic roles may have made the world fall in love with me, but no one had touched my own heart since an American expat with pale gold hair and a British aristocrat had taken hold of me like the moon with its tides.

It was this contrast that, ironically, made my fans even more rabid for me.

The elusive bachelor who was not a playboy. *Brooding and mysterious,* they said.

Untouchable, some wrote.

It made me scoff to know how wrong they were.

It was not that I was untouchable but that I had already been so touched by the presence of two hearts that I seriously doubted there was room for any future romance. My heart was a haunted house, empty but for ghosts I had no hope of exorcising.

It was, undoubtedly, one of the talking points that Isla Goodspeed had written on the tablet she held in her hand as she stood to greet me in the lobby of Château Marmont. She was an elegant woman in her early forties with curly brown hair and huge eyes the color of maple syrup. I liked her haughty beauty and professionalism. She reminded me of my eldest sister, Elena.

"Sebastian, it is good to see you again," she greeted me with an extended pale hand and a warm smile. "You look even more handsome than the last time we spoke."

I flashed her my megawatt smile as I raised her hand to kiss her knuckles. "You know how to flatter a man, Isla. You can tell me the truth. I look haggard as hell."

She let out a surprised bark of laughter before covering her mouth with her hand. "We both know that's not true."

I shrugged, indicating she should sit down at the corner table tucked into the murky shadows of the dimly lit bar. Château Marmont was a celebrity haunt in LA because it offered privacy to its guests.

"I jumped immediately from production for my latest project, *Black On*, to the press circuit for *Waking Nightmare*. Perhaps I don't look as haggard as I feel, thanks to the Los Angeles sun," I allowed as I sat down after her, unbuttoning my black blazer as I did so.

Isla's gaze dipped briefly to the tight stretch of the white cotton T-shirt across my pectorals before she locked eyes with me again. I had trained with members of the Navy SEALS in preparation for *Black On* and was consequently in the best shape of my life. The edge of my mouth ticked up in a knowing smirk.

She blushed slightly and turned her focus to arranging her recorder and tablet to her liking on the wooden tabletop.

"*Black On* is your first war film," she started, her tone coolly professional. "What made you curious about the script? You're notorious for only taking projects that speak to your soul, and a war film seems rather…unromantic for you."

I laughed. "Does it? *Certo*, there is nothing romantic about war; the gore and violence, the horrifying waste of human life, and the erasure of dignity. But that is exactly the point of *Black On*. It highlights the despair of war, of wondering what exactly one is fighting for beyond trying to protect one's country and loved ones. The title itself references the military term 'black on' something, as in lacking a resource. In this case, the characters lack empathy. My character, Stefan, does not realize how mechanical he has been about death until he accidentally kills a child and then secretly helps the family in an attempt to make amends. I suppose I enjoy the idea that there are no 'good' or 'bad' guys in the film. War makes those concepts impossible."

"That's quite a shift from your character, West, in *Waking Nightmare*, who critics have described as the consummate villain."

Even now, almost two years after filming, I felt the vestiges of West Lockwood's character like cobwebs stuck to my flesh. He was a psychopath who stalked his victims for years, luring them into his traps with diabolical mind games before killing them. It was all in the name of *love*, love of a woman who did not give him the time of day but whom West had loved since boyhood. The marvelous twist at the end of the movie came when the viewers realized she knew West was targeting people who offended her, and she willingly sent the victims to their deaths.

It was shocking how many critics and fans considered him a

romantic hero, but then, dark romance was a popular genre in books, and many readers yearned to see it on the big screen.

"Yes, he was a villain, but there is enough empathy within his character to draw audiences in. You would be surprised by how willing people are to forgive actions that are proclaimed to be done in the name of love," I said, staring at my bare left wrist as my mind inevitably fell back into the past.

I had not worn a watch outside of filming since the one the Meyers had given me. Even when I had been offered a six-figure deal with one of the top watchmakers in the world, I hadn't thought twice about declining it.

"That's very true," Isla agreed, studying me with a cocked head like a scientist with a specimen under glass. "Well, given the character was a deviation from your usual roles, it must feel validating to know you might be up for Best Actor again with this role in *Waking Nightmare*."

My laughter covered up the pang of insecurity that twanged in my chest. "I have been blessed with a number of nominations, and they never get old, I assure you."

"But a win would be nice for a change, wouldn't it?" Isla asked slyly, gauging my response.

I offered her a bland smile. "Winning is always nice. That is never why I take on a project, though."

"No, I suppose given the movie has already grossed over 200 million dollars domestically in the first three weeks of release, it can be considered a success by any standard. Though I know you are motivated more by your performance than anything else. Does it make you happy to know so many fans are saying it is their favorite movie of the year?"

"Of course," I said with a slight, humble shrug.

"Some reviews have likened your role to Adam Meyers's

performance in *The Devil Cares*. What do you think of the comparison?"

I didn't know why I wasn't expecting the question.

Even though I didn't read my own reviews, my agent, Mali Issah, did, and she always sent me a compiled document of all the best critiques. I'd seen the comparisons to Adam's iconic psychopathic role, the very same one he was filming while I lived with him and Savannah in their London townhome.

Beyond that, I had thought of him when the script first came across my desk. Freddie Bannerman was an ex-convict who took over London's criminal underworld without a shred of remorse, his motivation purely power-based. But the way Adam played his Oscar-winning role spoke of a hidden undercurrent, a desire to be admired because he had never been loved.

It was a similar vein to West Lockwood, who committed atrocities like a cat bringing its master dead mice, as if it would make him worthy of tenderness.

I'd called Mali immediately after reading *Waking Nightmare* to say I would take the role, and I'd dreamt of Adam the entire shoot even when I was desperate not to.

"It's an interesting one," I said with a flippant shrug, stretching my arm across the back of the booth in a way that drew Isla's gaze once more to my physique.

"It's not like you to be so ineloquent," she noted, hardly distracted. "Unless someone brings up Adam Meyers or Savannah Richardson."

Savannah *Richardson*.

She had married Tate Richardson, the media mogul, only ten months after divorcing Adam in a lavish, star-studded ceremony in the Hollywood Hills.

Yet, of the two of them, it was Savannah who was still accessible to me.

It was impossible not to run into each other around New York City, where I kept a residence because Mama, Giselle, and Elena lived there, and Los Angeles, where I spent most of my time shooting or attending press junkets. When you ran in the same circles, both cities became rather small.

And Savannah made it a point, as she had in London before, to be everywhere.

Though she had no discernible career, she had made it her life's work to play the grand puppeteer, connecting people with projects, rubbing elbows with the right financial backers, and introducing up-and-comers to the right casting agents and directors. She might not have held a title at Tate's production company, but she was his right-hand woman.

The first year after everything had happened, I refused to even let myself look at her.

To do so seemed to open a crater in my chest, a seismic degree of pain that stole my breath and inhibited me from carrying on a normal conversation.

By the second year, I started to sneak peeks, my curiosity and longing potent counterweights to my calcifying heartbreak. It felt good, in a strange way, like pressure on a sore muscle, to just look at her after so long. She was aging as I'd always known she would, like a pearl inside an oyster, maturing into her polished beauty, emanating a worldly, covetous elegance that still made me want to bruise her with love bites and pin her down on my driving cock.

Still, the first time she spoke to me at a Fourth of July party thrown by our mutual friend, I had taken one long inhale of that English garden floral perfume and turned on my heel to leave.

It took another year to capitulate to her gravitational pull. She was relentless, orbiting me at social and professional events until one day,

I found myself talking to her about the latest play on everyone's lips, a musical written and directed by the incredible Ryan Gates.

Somehow, that next week, I found myself accompanying her to the Friday night showing.

We developed a…friendship, of sorts.

One where I was deeply and abidingly in love with her, and she allowed me to be.

It was so like Savannah, not to be able to give up that kind of attention while simultaneously being unable to offer me anything genuine in return. We did not speak of my feelings and certainly not her own, but the chemistry between us seemed so obvious, an electric storm in the middle of any room.

Which made it even more bizarre, perhaps, that after a few years of infrequent outings and lukewarm friendship, Tate Richardson asked Savannah to have me for dinner. It was agonizing, watching the small intimacies between them, noting how Savannah seemed content in a way she had not with Adam—and me—if not because of a wild passion for her husband, but because of the life and status he afforded her. He enjoyed social outings and playing the gregarious host alongside her benevolent hostess. Her cutting criticisms made him laugh, even when they were directed at him, and her tendency toward negativity never seemed to impact his natural jubilance. They were an odd pair, but well-suited to each other.

And it hurt like a bitch to witness.

My family, who were too clever and observant not to understand the imbalance in my friendship with Savannah—though only Elena and Cosima knew the true story of our past—asked me why the hell I would put myself through those meals and outings with the Richardsons.

I didn't tell them it was better than no time with Savannah at all, because it would have been too pathetic.

But it was the truth.

No matter how toxic our relationship was, I could not stop myself from longing for her.

Just as I could not stop yearning for Adam.

But I wasn't a nineteen-year-old boy anymore.

On the cusp of thirty, I was pragmatic enough to know I'd never have any kind of relationship with Adam Meyers again.

We hadn't spoken in ten years.

Not even when we'd caught eyes at industry events and parties, my gaze magnetized to his no matter the circumstances. I could find him in a crowd of black and white tuxedos, as if he were under a spotlight. I could find him with my eyes closed and my hands tied, my soul dragged into his orbit like a comet drawn by his gravitational force.

Not one word passed between us.

Just those looks, those green apple eyes hitting me in the sternum with the force of a sixteen-wheeler for the span of a second before they wrenched free and found someone else to grace.

Once, I had been up for a part in an ensemble war movie he was already tied to. Against all hope, I'd considered it. Acting had always been our shared passion, a language we spoke that even Savannah could not quite understand. Maybe, foolish young Sebastian had dreamed, we would share a few comments on set, a handful of lingering looks between takes, and that connection between our hearts would click back into place just like that.

Perhaps then we could be together, even if we couldn't be with Savvy.

The next day, while scrolling through Photogram, I saw his latest post. Adam lounging on a yacht somewhere with water the color of crushed aquamarines, holding Willa Trombley in his arms. She was the actress I met when Adam took me on a tour of Pinewood Studio—the one acting in Andrea Felice's film the first time I met him.

I had deleted Photogram for a month after that. And told Mali I would not take the role in the war film.

I could stand being in the same universe as Savannah, just barely, but I knew in the marrow of my bones, I would not withstand proximity to Adam without breaking into pieces.

So, no.

I did not talk about Savannah Richardson and Adam Meyers.

What words were there to explain what they were and were not to me?

What business was it of anyone else?

I smiled thinly. "I have not seen Adam Meyers in a decade, and Savannah Richardson and I only enjoy a passing acquaintanceship. If you want me to talk about a meaningful relationship, it would be better to ask me about my mother or sisters."

Isla pursed her lips, clearly torn between pursuing what was a sore spot or delving into questions about my only slightly less famous siblings.

As per usual, my sisters won out.

"I hear congratulations are in order for your twin sister, Cosima," she said with a genuine smile. She had interviewed Cosi many times over the years, too, and as was the case with most people who met my sister, Isla held a warm regard for her. "Pregnant, again."

"With triplets. She's due next month, actually," I said, letting the love I had for my family fill the gaping holes in my chest like a cleansing ocean tide over barren rock. "I do not think Xan knows what he's gotten into."

"Xan as in Lord Alexander Davenport, the Duke of Greythorn,"

Isla confirmed, as if hearing such a man referred to by a common nickname upset her sensibilities.

Alexander would have loved that.

"One and the same," I agreed. "Their son, Aidon, is already a little hellion so I cannot imagine what their house will be like. Only that it's a good thing they live in a manor home that has literally endured wars."

Isla laughed with me. "You have a number of nieces and nephews. Do you enjoy being an uncle?"

Joy bubbled in my gut at the additional thought of Giselle and Sinclair's children, Genevieve and Theo, and Elena and Dante's kids, Aurora, Amadeo, and Chiara.

"I have six, soon to be nine, so to say family vacations feel like a circus would be an understatement. Which is why it is a good thing I have always enjoyed the circus."

Isla's smile was warm with interest. Most women seemed to find it wildly attractive that I liked my nieces and nephews, which I thought was setting the bar fairly low.

"Do you want kids of your own someday?" she asked, a little breathy despite herself.

I'd known the question was coming, but it still hit like a dart to the center of my chest.

Did I want kids?

I was an Italian raised in a family that had and would do absolutely anything for each other. A family that had shattered and reformed into something even more beautiful than its original shape.

Certo, I wanted kids.

I wanted them tomorrow.

But I would never have children with a woman or man I did not love to the very depths of my soul.

If I had a romantic heart before Savannah and Adam, I now had proof that the kind of life-altering, soul-ratifying love I had always believed in was *real*.

I saw it every time I was with my sisters and their partners.

The palpable love between Giselle and Sinclair that had given them the courage to upend their lives.

The epic romance between my twin sister, Cosima, and her Lord Alexander that had transcended years and overcome murderous fathers and secret society schemes.

The passion between Elena and Dante that had melted my sister's icy, ten-foot walls and softened her while simultaneously making her the fiercest, most confident woman I knew.

Seeing their love stories play out, witnessing a true happily-ever-after, was almost enough to make me pick up my own pen ten years after I had finished my first and only screenplay, and write again.

Almost.

"Someday," I said. "With the right person."

Isla flushed just slightly when I winked at her.

It was early afternoon on a weekday, so Bar Marmont was empty but for the two of us, so when the door opened, my attention was drawn to it naturally.

A woman walked in, the bright Los Angeles sunlight at her back casting her features in shadow but highlighting her slender form.

As if summoned like the devil by her name, Savannah walked into the bar.

CHAPTER TWO

SEBASTIAN

She wore her signature white—a silk blouse tied in a bow at her throat and a pencil skirt that hugged every inch of her. That cloud of curled, pale-blond hair was the same as ever, and even though she had aged over the last decade, she still maintained that haughty beauty reminiscent of a Victorian-era painting.

Without hesitation, those big blue eyes found me as they swept the space, and her mouth pressed into a firm line.

Because Savannah was with her husband, Tate Richardson, and the young, hot thing in Hollywood these days, Jace Galantine.

No doubt, they were trying to convince him to star in one of their upcoming productions.

He had worked with them on numerous movies over the past five years even though there were whispers in the industry that Savannah was having an affair with him.

My blood turned to poison, sickening me with every brutal beat of my heart.

I was standing before I knew it, offering my hand to Isla with a big smile, hoping its legendary effect would distract her from my discomfort.

"Should we take a walk? This bar is so stuffy, and it's a beautiful day out."

A frown flickered between her brows, but Isla dutifully tucked away her tablet, grabbed her recorder, and accepted my offered hand.

"Stuffy," she asked as we moved toward the party of three still loitering at the doors. "Or crowded?"

"They are often synonymous, aren't they?" I replied mildly as we approached the other group.

"Seb, my boy," Tate bellowed in his 1950s radio announcer voice, a crackling, booming baritone that commanded any space. "What a surprise! It's wonderful to see you."

His sincerity had long ago broken down my bitterness, so the smile I gave him in return was shockingly genuine. "Hey, Tate, good to see you, too. Savannah. Jace."

I nodded at the other two in turn.

Savannah was just staring at me in that way she had, a beseeching look that asked for my forgiveness and my attention. The last time she had phoned me, I didn't answer. Her pride wouldn't allow her to call again until I reached out first.

Jace only nodded back curtly. He was not particularly tall, as most actors weren't, but that was his only shortcoming. Beautiful like an angel descended from heaven with the kind of golden-blond hair that could not be bought in a bottle and features that were finely tuned yet still masculine. He played charming, irreverent characters in action movies and romcoms, the light-hearted, easygoing foil to my darkly brooding, often tragic characters.

We did not particularly like each other, and it only confirmed for me that the rumors of his affair with Savannah were true.

She did, after all, like young, up-and-coming actors.

"Come sit with us," Tate demanded in the way of all old white men, as if my refusal to obey never crossed his mind. "We were going to drink old-fashioneds and talk about this damn movie we're trying to get into pre-production."

"I'm happily tied up at the moment," I said, indicating the woman on my arm. "Have you met my lovely companion, Isla Goodspeed?"

In my peripheral vision, I noticed Savannah frowning at Isla, who was pretty enough to make any woman jealous.

And Savvy, for all her grace and power, was not above envy or possessiveness, even when it was wildly inappropriate.

"You should really join us, Sebastian," she pressed, suddenly stepping closer, her hand reaching out to land as gentle as a butterfly on my arm. "You've played hard to get for too long. It is beyond time for you to take a role in a Richardson Production."

I would rather burn my own eyes out.

"I'm in the middle of an interview," I said, smiling at Isla warmly. "So we should be going. But it was great to see you all."

"I'll call you," Tate said as we moved by them. "We can hit the racket at the club like old times."

We had played tennis only three or four times when I was younger and more prone to that kind of idiocy. I tried to keep my space now even though Tate's fatherly, jovial nature would have appealed to me greatly under other circumstances.

I'd never had someone like that in my life. An older man who genuinely just liked me and wanted the best for me in a paternal way.

Andrea, maybe, but we were co-collaborators even though he was older than me. And his personal life was such a travesty that he was never in any place to give me advice the way Tate liked to do.

"*Bene*," I said anyway, before flicking a hand over my shoulder and then opening the door for Isla.

We walked in surprising silence for a few moments. I was grateful to Isla for giving me the brief respite.

"Tower Bar?" I suggested.

She nodded, slanting me a playful look. "Do you enjoy being such an enigma? You seem like such an open, charming, affable man, but you never truly say anything of substance about your life other than your work."

"I would argue I speak about my family, too." I was proud as hell to be a Lombardi, to count my sisters as both my best friends and family.

"Sure," she agreed easily. "But what about the elusive heart of Sebastian Lombardi? Copies of the magazine would fly off the shelves if I could get that story."

"I would buy my own copy," I joked as I ushered her into the cool lobby and toward the bar.

"Are you implying you don't know your own heart?" she asked shrewdly as the hostess recognized me instantly and silently ushered us into the dimly lit room.

It was busier in the Tower Bar, even in the early afternoon during the week. A few friends tipped their chins at me as we walked by, but I did not linger.

"Do you know why you love what you love and long for what you don't have?" I argued as we stopped at a table in the corner with a view of the glossy, dark wood bar. "And if you do, would you want to talk about it for the world to dissect?"

"Is that why you haven't written a screenplay in ten years?" she pushed while she took her seat.

My smile was crooked. "I do not believe in pursuing anything unless it arrests me. Unfortunately, I have not been struck by the unyielding urge to write in a long time."

My ability to create was something fragile, like a new spring sprout or a castle made from sand, and it had been eviscerated along with my heart after the breakup with the Meyerses. Sometimes something stirred in my chest, a phantom urge to put pen to paper, but I knew it could be years still, if ever, until I was ready to open a vein in order to story tell that way again.

A scent hit me then, aromatic and floral, like spice warmed in a hot pan.

That dark tendril of spicy smoke wafted over me, through me, and brought to mind the thick, fragrant air of a tropical garden, the intimate scent of a woman's inner thigh, the intoxication of Moroccan spice markets, undercut by the salt blowing in on a breeze from the coast. It hooked me by the nostrils and reeled me in, tugging my gaze over my left shoulder to watch as a woman walked by our table toward the bar.

She was tall, her lush curves wrapped in a bright yellow dress, the same color as the sunshine warming the winter skies outside. She moved with a careless kind of sensuality, a physicality usually reserved for athletes or dancers. The long, slightly tangled waves of her blond hair cascaded down her back, brushing the browned base of her spine where it showed through a cutout in the fabric. I watched as her hips swayed, her tanned calves flashing beneath the hem of the dress as she cut across the dining room without a single glance around at the many people who were drawn to her light.

I certainly was. I'd always been a sucker for blonds, and this one with her mass of artlessly wavy hair was a stunner even from behind.

"Sebastian?"

I wrenched my gaze from the gorgeous woman and grinned at Isla, who was watching me with sparkling eyes.

"Would you like me to introduce you two?"

"You know her?" I frowned. If she were famous, how was it possible that I hadn't crossed paths with her before? It could have been arrogant of me, but up until that moment, I was pretty damn sure I knew everyone worth knowing in Hollywood.

Isla shook her head and propped her pretty face in her hands. "No, but I sure as hell would like to meet the girl who made Sebastian Lombardi drool."

"You and me both," I said, looking back over at the girl in question as she finally stopped at the bar, near enough to our table that I could make out the generous swell of her cleavage as she twisted slightly to the side, and the exact pale-yellow shade of her hair. The woman she sat beside was older, with a pinched expression that didn't yield as she turned to look at the blond. However, the bartender immediately spotted her, and they greeted each other familiarly with a kiss on each cheek. I felt my chest tighten with unexpected jealousy and scowled.

It wasn't that I was unused to the feeling. As an Italian, a brother to three beautiful sisters, and a red-blooded male, I was just about as possessive as they came without crossing into unhealthily obsessive. But even I could admit that I had no right to thump my chest over a woman I couldn't even put a name to.

"She's gorgeous," Isla said. "You don't even want to know the things I would do to look like her."

You don't even want to know the things I would do to be inside her.

"I can imagine," I murmured instead.

I watched her cross those endless legs, my eyes tracking the slinky fabric of her dress as it parted at the thigh and revealed a wedge of golden thigh. My throat was dry, and my skin was prickling.

I wanted her.

And not in the polite, civilized way that men were encouraged to desire women now. No, the way I wanted that blond goddess sitting across the room from me was ferocious, a language of the blood that was untranslatable in any language. My muscles swelled with adrenaline, and I had to grind my teeth to keep from stalking over to her like some heathen and claiming her for my own, at least for the night.

"In all honesty, though, Seb, the world hasn't seen you more than once with a woman other than your sisters or Savannah Richardson in years. I'm dying to know why," Isla said, leaning forward far enough that a loose lock of her hair fell over the table and into her water glass. She didn't notice. And even though I liked Isla and she was the only reporter I almost considered a friend, I wasn't feeling generous, given her continued pursuit of information about Savvy.

"I don't talk about my personal life," I said, taking a large gulp of the smooth whiskey. "I've been polite about that, Isla, but you are trying my patience."

"Sebastian, I need something of substance for this article," she insisted, her own pleasant expression souring. "With the rumors swirling right now, this article will have to be pushed if you don't give me something headline worthy."

"What rumors?" I asked, suddenly bored with this game and conversation.

My gaze kept slipping back to the vibrant blond at the bar, hoping to catch a glimpse of her face if she turned in her seat. Something about her called to me, faint as a siren's song buried beneath the rhythm of waves. A recognition.

"About Adam Meyers," Isla said, waiting with a coy smile when my gaze snapped back to her.

My heart lodged in my throat, beating so rapidly I thought I might gag.

Like a shark sensing blood in the water, Isla reached into her purse and retrieved a folded magazine I recognized as a trashy gossip rag. She handed it over like a magician pulling a rabbit from a hat, all smug superiority, waiting with tangible anticipation as I read the headline before dropping the curtain.

"The rumor is that he's gay."

CHAPTER THREE

LINNEA

"**Y**ou still smell like salt."

I accepted my glass of sparkling water from the bartender, a man named Harry who'd taken me on a few dates last spring, hiding my sigh behind the lip as I took a much-needed sip.

"The waves were too good to pass up this morning," I admitted even though Cynthia already knew that was where I had been.

She always knew.

Cynthia Gadon did not like me very much, but she had taken me on as an agency client as a favor to my mother, who was one of her oldest friends. Even though it was obvious she wished she could drop me, she wouldn't. Not now, when this favor absolved her of visiting Miranda in her current state.

"You were late for the audition," she informed me.

I tried not to roll my eyes. "Is that what they told you? Because I was *early*, and the only reason I couldn't get into the room on time was because the casting director's son wouldn't let me through the doors until I agreed to go out with him."

Cynthia bared her veneers at me, pale mauve-painted lips peeled back like a chimp's. "You should have just agreed, Linnea. Why do you always have to make things more difficult for yourself?"

"More difficult for myself?" I echoed slowly, rage curling my fingers into claws around my glass. "How is it that men behaving badly is *my* problem?"

"The Me Too movement is over," Cynthia started to lecture me, as she always did whenever I brought up issues like this at my auditions or on the rare project I landed. "You need to get your shit together and be professional."

I closed my eyes and forced myself to take a deep breath so I wouldn't bite her head off.

"I take it they didn't ask me to come back for a second round?" I asked blandly even though the thought sucked.

It wasn't like I was thrilled to be in a series of commercials for a national burger chain, but Miranda and I needed the money desperately.

As the tabloids had claimed eighteen months ago, "how the gold digger hath fallen."

When my mother, Miranda, was diagnosed with frontotemporal dementia, her husband at the time—Paul, number five, a tech millionaire who was six years younger than Miranda herself—promptly divorced her and left her to care for herself.

Only Miranda had not cared for herself for a single moment in her entire forty-five years of life.

So, when she called panicked and weeping to say she needed my help, what was I going to do? Turn down the only mother I'd ever had?

Dad said I owed her nothing. She had given me half my DNA,

but little more.

I didn't exactly agree. Miranda Hildebrand loved me as much as she had the capacity to love anyone, which was to say, not very much. There was no doubt in my mind that she had a narcissistic personality disorder, so everything in life related to her and her desires. When I was younger, her British husband had decided he wanted them to be a perfect little family, complete with her estranged American daughter. So Miranda had hauled me out of public school in Maui, where I lived with my dad and uncles, to a posh private school in London.

For just shy of two years, she had tried her best to be a mother, but her husband, Wyndam, had actually been the better parent.

When I left in tears the night after my high school graduation, I never expected to see Miranda again, and I was not disappointed by the prospect.

Yet here I was, haggling with a woman who disliked me about a gig in a national burger commercial just to pay for Miranda's bills.

"I really don't know what to do with you, Linnea," Cynthia said, pinching the bridge of her nose as if I'd given her a sinus headache. "Your tits are too huge to model unless you want to do swimwear?"

I made a face thinking of some of the most famous models in the world like Cosima Lombardi and Adriana Lima. There was no *way* I was appealing enough to model in next to nothing.

Besides, I actually liked acting, if I was ever given the chance to do it. I had always been reluctant to follow in any of Miranda's footsteps, but it was a secret desire of my heart to act and do it well in something worthwhile.

"At this point, I have to think I have been more than fair to your mother in representing you when you clearly do not have what it takes to make it in the industry," Cynthia declared, fishing papers out of her Birkin.

They fell to the bar top with an ominous *thawp*.

It was a termination letter.

You would think that at this point in my life, I would be used to life's habit of kicking me in the teeth, but I still felt the blow all the way through to my feet.

"It's just not working out," Cynthia said with saccharine kindness, placing her hand lightly on my arm. "No one is more upset about it than me."

I fought the urge to roll my eyes and won, a minor triumph. The dishonesty of Hollywood never failed to set my teeth on edge.

A slight ruckus behind me drew my attention over my shoulder in time to witness a tall, dark, and handsome man shove back from a table with a snarl.

"I thought you had more integrity than that," he growled at the woman across from him as he buttoned his blazer before turning on his heel to stalk away from her. "If you print that nonsense, I'll use every ounce of influence I have to *bury* you, Isla."

On his way toward the door, his gaze snapped up to lock with mine, and my breath arrested in my lungs.

Sebastian Lombardi.

The man I had first met ten years ago as a petulant teenager on a cold night in London by the Meyers's swimming pool.

We had become friends during the year he lived with the couple in their Chelsea townhome, but when he moved to New York City, our relationship devolved into exchanging postcards. I still had every single one, tied off with ribbons and carefully kept in a box under my bed in Miranda's bungalow. Even ten years on, he still wrote to me.

But I had not set eyes on him in a decade.

And time had been very, very friendly to Sebastian.

Even at eighteen years old, he had been tall and broad-shouldered with the kind of huge hands that set a female mind to fantasizing, but he was a man now, filled out and packed with dense muscle I could see beneath his close-fitting, expensive clothes. His hair was longer, maybe from a shoot, the waves more pronounced as they fell across his forehead into those tiger yellow eyes that pinned me to my seat like a predator's.

Speaking of secret desires of my heart, Sebastian Lombardi had been lodged there since the moment I saw him arrow smoothly into the pool and break through the crust of the water, inky hair slicked back from his tanned face, full mouth parted on a breath I wanted to taste with my tongue.

"Linnea Kai?"

His voice was deeper, his accent the very same as it had been back then, thick and rich as Italian coffee. I had watched him act in films where he pressed those vowels smooth and cut his consonants into hard edges like an American, but I always preferred his voice like this. It was pure music.

"Sebastian," I said, already standing even though I could not remember doing it. "Hey."

Embarrassment burned through me at the trite greeting, but I was still struck dumb by our chance encounter. I knew he still lived in New York City to be close to his family and only came to LA to film or do the media circuit. The odds of running into each other had always seemed so slim that I didn't even think to tell him I had moved to the city.

Or maybe I had, but I was too ashamed to admit why.

The anger crackling around him like an electric storm fell flat in an instant as a broad grin overtook his face. Without hesitation, he changed course to stalk toward me, not stopping until I was in his arms. I laughed breathlessly as I wrapped my own around his neck and he lifted me off my feet, a feat given how tall I was, especially in heels.

"I can't believe it's you," he murmured into my hair, and I thought I might have heard him inhale deeply like he was sniffing my perfume.

I grinned as he set me carefully on my feet, keeping my hands on his chest because I still wasn't sure he was real. I'd dreamed of seeing him again in the flesh so many times, yet the moment was as surreal as a Dali painting.

"I didn't know you were in town!"

"Doing the rounds for *Waking Nightmare*," he explained with a one-shoulder shrug, but his eyes were intense on me as they scoured my face. I had forgotten how unnerving that golden stare was, how much it felt as if he could see through flesh and bone to the very center of you. "Are you busy? Now that I've had the good fortune to run into you, I don't intend to let you go until we have properly caught up."

"Catching up on a decade of life will take a while," I warned him, but the width of my smile ruined the effect.

He winked. "I can make time for my favorite American girl."

"Still full of shit, I see," I said with a raised brow.

His laughter drew the attention of everyone in the restaurant who was not already watching us. It was a rich, melodious chuckle I felt coil warmly in my gut.

The tabloids sometimes referred to him as silly epithets like "Sex God" and "Italian Stallion."

I could understand why.

"You never were charmed by me, were you?" he murmured, his hands still gently grasping my upper arms. "It's good to see that hasn't changed."

"Still irreverent as ever," I promised.

Behind me, someone cleared their throat.

Sebastian's gaze followed the sound over my shoulder, and he frowned. "Excuse me, I'm being incredibly rude. You're here with someone."

"Cynthia Gadon," my former agent said, stepping closer so that she bumped me with her shoulder as she extended her hand to Sebastian. "It's a pleasure to meet you. I must say, I am a *huge* fan of your films."

His eyes sparkled as they slid to me. "Ah, it's good to meet a real fan."

I rolled my eyes at him, and he flashed me that toothy white grin that would have been wolfish if it wasn't so appealing.

"Cynthia is my former agent," I explained to him blandly.

He bit the edge of his grin to keep it contained. "What a shame."

"No, no," Cynthia said, a flustered flush seeping down her pale neck. "Linnea and I were just renegotiating terms."

"Were you?" Sebastian drawled, dropping one of his hands down my arm to tangle his fingers with mine. I could feel my pulse in my fingertips as if my heart had slid down my arm from my chest to get closer to him. "Well, what fortuitous timing."

Cynthia beamed, relieved, thinking no doubt that she had secured the only client she had who was close to such a superstar.

But unlike her, I knew Sebastian. His beauty may have been the alluring flame to draw women into his orbit, but it was his cleverness that made them stick.

"I was just on my way to meet my agent, Mali. I'll introduce you," he declared.

Mali Issah was one of the biggest names in Hollywood. She represented dozens of the world's top stars, including Jace Galantine, Maya Cervantes, and Iona Blake.

Cynthia's mouth fell open.

I hid my smile behind my hair as I leaned across Sebastian to grab the termination letter on the bar. "I'll just sign this, and we can be on our way." I twisted my body so my breasts rasped across his abdomen.

His eyes were lit with humor and maybe something darker, when I looked up at him. "You don't happen to have a pen, do you?"

Suddenly, Harry the bartender was before me, offering one across the counter, but I waited for Sebastian to reach into the inner pocket of his jacket to retrieve his own pen. He dipped down intimately to hand it off to me, the scent of his spicy cologne warm and inviting.

The perfume I had taken to wearing reminded me of a feminine version of that same scent. Having it in my nose again made me wonder if that wasn't why I'd been subconsciously drawn to it.

"Good riddance," he whispered as he pressed the pen into my hand.

It was my turn to wink.

I dashed my signature against the paper and then turned to face him fully, sliding the pen into the inner pocket myself. The beat of his heart was a heavy drum against the back of my hand.

"Thank you," I said softly, not just for the pen but for showing Cynthia just exactly what she was missing by letting me go.

Sebastian's hand came up to cover my own, flattening it briefly to his chest. "Anytime."

"Linnea, really, if you'll just take a moment to talk with—" Cynthia tried again.

"I'm afraid I must whisk her away," Sebastian declared without taking his eyes off me. I watched as he fished out some money from a clip in his pocket and tossed it on the table. Two hundred-dollar bills flashed up at me. "That should cover Linnea's champagne."

"It was sparkling water," I corrected. "I just like drinking it in a fancy glass so I feel included with the drinkers."

Humor creased the skin beside those magnificent eyes.

"You are just what I needed to brighten this godawful day," he told me as he bent to grab my large purse from the ground beside my chair. Instead of handing it to me, he tucked it under his arm.

There was something strangely attractive about it, an assuredness in his masculinity that you didn't often see in men. Without hesitation, he ushered me through the restaurant with a hand on my lower back. The abrasion of his calloused fingertips against the sensitive skin there made my entire body flush with heat.

I wound my arm through his and beamed up at him, warmed by the fact that a decade of separation seemed to have been obliterated as if it had never happened. "The beach always makes me feel better. Should we dip our toes in the sand?"

"We should," he agreed. "And we should eat ice cream."

"Definitely," I said on a laugh, because I had forgotten that Sebastian was always hungry. "Ice cream and the ocean, a magical combination."

"Like this hair," he said, sobering a little as he pushed tangled waves off my shoulder to flow down my back. "And your indigo eyes."

"Charmer," I scolded. "You know that won't work on me."

It was a bald-faced lie. My heart was racing, my palms sweating, my belly alive with a million butterflies. But I must have been a better actor than I thought, because Sebastian threw his head back to laugh and said, "I know. I have never been enough for you despite my best efforts."

I was clever enough not to push my luck and lie again.

SEBASTIAN HAD THE GOOD MANNERS NOT TO COMMENT on my 1991 Jeep, which was held together with a little too much duct tape, when I led him to where it was parked so I could drive us to the beach. He just blinked at it with a slight frown between his thick brows, tongue stuck in one cheek like he was holding himself back from saying something. In the end, he sighed audibly and opened the passenger door in one try even though it had a bad tendency to stick.

I hurriedly moved the cloth swatches off his seat so he could sit down, shoving them into the back alongside an old sewing machine I kept meaning to get fixed and a bag of clothes I'd salvaged from the local Salvation Army to repurpose for my own designs.

He didn't comment on the mess, either.

It made me fall just a little bit more in love with him.

Especially when the only things he did make note of were the two surfboards strapped to the roof rack.

"You still surf." There was a smile in his tone even though I couldn't see him as I focused on pulling out of the tight spot and heading west to the ocean.

"Probably too much," I admitted. "I try to get out as much as I can. It's one of the only things that brings me peace these days."

There was a brief silence where I winced, knowing that Sebastian was observant enough to pick up on the implication that my life was stressful. I didn't want to spend my undoubtedly brief time with him talking about Miranda, so I bit my lip and manifested him glancing over this, too.

A moment later, he did.

"I try to get out when I can, too," he said, adjusting in the seat that was much too small for his frame.

"New York isn't exactly a mecca for surfing."

"No, but Long Island isn't far. Cold as bollocks, though." He shivered, which made me laugh. "It's much better when I can pop out here, but I try to keep my visits short and busy."

"So you can go home to the city," I surmised. "How are the

Lombardi women?"

I slid my gaze to him because I knew the smile he'd have on his face would be worth the effort to see it.

"Amazing," he said proudly. "Mama's restaurant won another award, and even though she's had offers to open others, she says she is happy cooking in Little Italy. Elena is, well, kicking ass and taking names like she always has, but now she's doing it making scads of money and representing some fairly eccentric characters. I think I told you she fell in love with Dante Salvatore?"

I nodded, because he had, but also because I had read about the scandal in the papers along with everyone else. Dante Salvatore was a suspected mafioso who had met his now-wife when she represented him in his murder and racketeering case. Famously, they had won the case and taken down United States District Attorney Dennis O'Malley at the same time. I could still summon the image of Elena and Dante's courtroom kiss from the front page of *The New York Times*. It had even become a popular GIF.

"They have three kids now," he continued. "It's amazing, honestly. All her success, and the thing that brings my ambitious sister the most joy is her family. I never thought I'd see the day."

His voice carried so much warmth that I could feel it heating the air between us. It made me yearn for brothers or sisters myself.

"Giselle actually just accepted a position as a guest lecturer at the California Institute of Arts, so she, Sinclair, and their two kids will be here for the next year." He spoke as if he couldn't believe his luck, having his family so close while he had to be on the other side of the country from them. "I have to be in town for a while to campaign for award season, so it is good to have family close."

"Especially when your twin sister lives in England," I concluded because the way he missed Cosima was evident in almost every letter we wrote to each other.

"*Sì*," he murmured, looking out the window without seeming to see the scenery. "I miss her very much. But we have all agreed to spend next Christmas there because Cosima was too pregnant to join us last month in New York City, and I was too busy with the release of *Waking Nightmare* to visit. I had my manager clear my calendar so that I could spend some weeks there."

I bit my lip as I considered asking the question that bloomed on my tongue, but I had never been a hesitant person, quite the opposite really, and now didn't seem like the time to start. Not when I had Sebastian beside me for the first time in years.

The scent of him, rich and mouth-watering like something you could eat, filled the car like drug smoke, lowering my inhibitions.

"Is it hard to go back there? To England?"

The sound that came from him was a bitter little cough. "You could say that."

"I haven't been back," I offered as I flicked on the signal to pull onto the I-10 West. "But I still see Wyndam sometimes. He comes out once a year to visit me."

Beside me, Sebastian relaxed slightly. "I'm glad to hear that. Though I'm surprised you're in LA. The way you spoke about Maui, I thought you'd never leave once you got home."

Homesickness panged like a discordant note he'd plucked in my chest. My hands squeaked against the steering wheel as I gripped it too hard.

"I thought so, too," I said with a breezy smile tossed over my shoulder. "But the City of Angels has some charm, too. The fashion alone is reason to be here."

"Ah," he exclaimed, reaching over to squeeze my shoulder warmly. The touch sent sparks of electricity showering down my spine. "*Certo,* this is why you are here. To pursue design!"

I winced. "Not exactly."

Between taking care of Miranda, serving at Affaire restaurant, and taking as many auditions as I could to supplement the rest, I did not have much time for design. Oh, I constantly carried around my sketchbook and pens, stopping at Mulholland Overlook on the way home from work at three in the morning to take inspiration from the night lights, or dashing off a loose design at dawn before I dove into the frothing surf with my board. But the illustrations of elaborate gowns, cocktail dresses, and lingerie I tended to gravitate towards were as useless as scattered leaves glued into the pages of a scrapbook left to decay over time.

Sebastian's sun-gold eyes burned my skin as he studied me, but I refused to look over at him. One glance at that beautiful face filled with concern would unravel me completely, and I couldn't afford that.

"I saw a photo of you and Savannah Richardson a while ago," I said, cruelly turning the tables onto him once more so I wouldn't have to talk about my pain. "I was surprised."

"I think I am, too," he admitted, rubbing a hand over his stubbled jaw so it rasped like sandpaper on wood. "Whenever I agree to see her. Nostalgia is a dangerous emotion."

I hummed, reaching out without looking at him to pat his—rock hard—thigh. "Or a comforting one."

"Yes," he agreed, collecting my hand in his as if our friendship had always consisted of holding hands. "It is very good to see you again, *trottolina*."

My hand spasmed in his at the use of the Italian nickname.

Little spinning top, *it meant*.

I could still remember the first time he'd called me that on our tourist date around London the night of the BAFTAs when I was just sixteen. Even though he was only three years older than me, there had always been something powerful about Sebastian Lombardi, an intensity of purpose and purity of passion that made him seem so much older, his aura highly addictive. That quality had only magnified itself in the intervening decade, and I found myself poorly equipped to deal with it.

We had barely started hanging out, and I was already dreading its inevitable end.

"I'm sure it is," I teased with an impish grin that made him laugh. "I'm hard to forget."

"Impossible," he agreed, easily.

He was still holding my hand. In a way, I wasn't even sure he knew he still held it, fiddling idly with my fingers.

It felt good, not just because he was ungodly levels of handsome, but because I didn't get a lot of physical affection these days. Miranda could be sweet and docile sometimes, but mostly, she was either paranoid and angry or lucid enough to be rude and demanding. Even though I'd been in town for a year and a half, I hadn't had the time to make many friends except for Rozhin, who worked with me at Affaire.

I was touch-starved and so lonely that my gut ached hollowly.

"Why do I get the sense you don't want to tell me about your life? You have been very vague in your postcards, too," he said quietly. "Do you think because I am famous or some *cazzate* that I would judge you? You are my friend, Linnea. There is nothing about you that I would not try to understand."

"How do you always know the right thing to say?" I asked, incredulous. "You could give TED Talks if acting doesn't work out for you."

His smile was indulgent because he knew I was just dragging it out, hiding behind my snark. "I'll keep that in mind."

I was saved by the fact that we were pulling into the parking lot by the Santa Monica Pier. It was the closest beach to Tower Bar, though it wasn't my favorite. Even on a weekday in January, it was packed with locals and tourists alike. I grabbed a loose knit sweater from the pile of clothes in the back seat of my car to ward off the cool ocean breeze. We were quiet as we walked down the pier to grab ice cream, but Sebastian stayed close, his shoulder brushing mine as we stepped in tandem down the wooden boards. The ocean was so different here than back at home in Maui, less vibrant and tropical, spreading out like muted blue velvet from the caramel sand, but it still brought me untold comfort to be near the waves.

He smiled quietly to himself when I ordered bright blue Cookie Monster ice cream.

"What?" I demanded, taking a big scoop of the sweet, cold dessert onto my spoon. "I thought you wouldn't judge me for anything, hmm?"

Sebastian's eyes crinkled with mirth, and he lifted his shoulder in a Latin shrug. "That was before I saw you get a flavor named after a blue children's puppet. It's not even a real flavor!"

I took another large spoonful and hummed my delight before sticking my tongue out at him. "It's delicious. You don't know what you're missing out on."

"Your tongue is blue," he noted dryly as he accepted his own cup of chocolate and coffee ice cream.

"Don't judge until you try it," I tsked, waving my spoon at him in condemnation.

The motion flicked droplets of melting cream onto my cheek.

Sebastian chuckled, that belly-deep rumble that made my thighs clench, and reached over to collect the blue liquid on his thumb. I could not have looked away from that golden gaze or those full, sensual lips parting, even if a nuclear bomb went off beside us.

His mouth closed around his finger, and his throat worked as he sucked at it.

A little gasp escaped me at the sight of him.

"Not bad," he deduced with a crooked grin. "But I will stick with *cioccolato* and *caffè*. Though American ice cream is never so good as Italian *gelato*."

I blinked at him, still momentarily struck dumb by what might have been the single most erotic experience of my life thus far, and he hadn't even touched me.

"I wouldn't know," I said, my throat parched. "I've never been."

Sebastian clucked his tongue and shook his head despairingly as he led us back down the pier. A few teenage girls noticed him and tittered behind their hands as he passed by. He flashed them a megawatt grin that would probably fuel their fantasy for years to come.

"I will take you one day," he said conclusively, as if it was that simple and obvious. "You will love it. The people, the scenery, the *food*. It is all a sensory delight."

"Everything is magical to you, isn't it?" I asked, happy to say it aloud when I'd thought it every time I received one of his postcards, filled with cramped, spiky script as if he was in a rush to communicate with me the joys of his life. "Even the bad things."

Sebastian hummed as he sucked ice cream off his spoon, causing a passing woman's mouth to fall open at the sight. I hid my smile behind my own spoon as we took the stairs down to the beach.

Instantly, Sebastian toed off his expensive leather shoes and dug his toes into the sand. I followed suit, the cool, dense sand like heaven against my skin after the high heels.

"Do you want the truth?" he asked as we started to walk down the beach. It was a gorgeous day, so it seemed that everyone was out on the sand.

"Of course."

"I like the bad things just as much as the good," he admitted, angling so that we cut down to the water and he could walk through the frothing edge of the waves. "They remind me not to take anything for granted, not even for a minute."

"Wow, you're scarily well-adjusted," I muttered.

He laughed, throwing his head back to do it to the heavens. Someone sitting on the beach snapped a photo of him, but I couldn't blame them.

He was glorious.

And I was lucky enough to count him as a friend.

"I have my burdens," he told me with a slight shrug. "But overall, how could I not feel lucky? Even now, just at this moment, I am walking along a beautiful beach under a bright sun with one of the most beautiful and interesting women I have ever known."

"I grew into my face a little," I quipped, because I'd never known how to accept a compliment gracefully.

Sebastian stopped suddenly, so I mimicked him. Only then did he reach out and rub his thumb along the thick arch of my ash-brown eyebrow, shades darker than my hair.

"I think you've grown into yourself," he corrected. "You don't seem happy, exactly, but you have this light about you. *Luminosità.* Luminosity. I would like to get to know you better, Linnea. In person, again."

His hand had dropped to my neck, cupping the side of my throat warmly in his big palm. My pulse was probably beating a tattoo against his skin, but I didn't let myself be embarrassed by it.

I tipped my head back to look up into those sunlit-gold eyes and smiled more genuinely than I had in months.

"I'd like that."

"*Bene*," he said with a satisfied grin that edged on smug. He let his hand fall away and started walking again. "Tomorrow, you will show me where you like to surf."

"Oh, will I?" I raised a brow at him. "I'm not sure you could keep up."

He laughed again, and it felt like such a gift to have him here in Los Angeles with me that if I were a different kind of girl, I could have cried.

Instead, I stuck out my tongue at him and smeared the side of my melting cone against the arm of his white T-shirt as I sprinted past him.

"Prove you can keep up!" I hollered.

"You brat," he called out from behind me.

I laughed as I surged through the edge of the ocean away from him, feeling lighter than I had in years.

CHAPTER FOUR

SEBASTIAN

I didn't sleep that night.

The moon, almost as bright as the pale morning sun and full in the sky, was visible outside my hotel window and only fueled the sense of nostalgia that kept me awake. Between thoughts of Adam and his current plight, running into Savannah with Tate and Jace, and finding Linnea in the city of Los Angeles, my brain was too mired in thought to find rest.

Instead, for the first time in much too long, I wrote.

The story came to me the way remnants of a dream did, in snapshots of scenes and blurry colors smeared behind my closed lids.

But it was so vivid, so tangible I could taste the Cornish sea in my mouth as my fingers flew over the keys, could feel the hot stage lights on my face.

The title came to me before anything else.

The Dream, I typed out with one finger while sipping grappa. &

The Dreamer.

When 5:00 a.m. rolled around and it was time for me to get in my car to pick up Linnea from her house for our morning surf, my fingers were cramping, and my eyes were gritty with the sand of exhaustion.

But I had written the rough outline and twenty pages of a new screenplay.

Much like *Blood Oath*, it was semi-autobiographical, with the truth of my life hidden beneath the layers of a story set in the early 1900s in London and Cornwall. It revolved around Emerson Bainbridge, a struggling artist who began to dream vividly about a woman who inspired him to create masterpieces that launched his career. His obsession with the ideal of her was already unhealthy, but when he saw a woman who looked exactly like his dream girl bathing in the Cornish sea while on vacation with his wife and family, his love turned to a kind of madness.

Freud, I was sure, would have had a field day with the parallels, but I didn't care.

I was too awed and bewildered that I had felt so compelled to get a story down on the page again. That I could see it so clearly in my mind's eye, as clearly as Emerson Bainbridge saw his muse in his dreams.

I called Andrea Felice as I stumbled around the hotel room changing into my swim trunks and grabbing my wetsuit.

"*Sebastian, ciao, amico mio,*" he answered warmly. "It is early in America, no? Why are you calling me like this? Not that I am not happy to hear from you always."

I smiled, as I always did when I was talking to Andrea. He was one of the only people in my life who knew the whole of my history, every last sordid detail. Yet he never treated me any differently for knowing about Seamus and his mafia debts, or what happened that year in London between Adam, Savannah, and me.

Andrea was my family as much as Mama, Elena, Giselle, and Cosima.

"I've written something," I admitted, grabbing the keys to the Lamborghini Urus SUV I'd rented for my stay.

Once a driver, always a car lover.

The silence that followed was potent.

"Sebastian," he said finally in Italian. "This is wonderful. Send it to me immediately. I will go to my computer now."

There were signs of life in the background, diners maybe, but it was obvious he was not at home by his computer already.

I laughed. "It's not finished yet. I stayed up all night writing, but I need some more time with it. I finished the treatment, though, which I will send to you. Andrea, I have not felt such excitement about a project in…well, a very long time."

"What prompted this?" he asked, sounding as eager as I felt. "You have said the well is dry for years. I had almost given up on ever seeing a new Sebastian Lombardi screenplay."

I hesitated as I shut the door to the hotel and took the stairs to the lobby so I wouldn't lose the phone connection.

"I ran into Savannah yesterday," I confessed. "She was with Tate and Jace Galantine."

Andrea made a noise like an irritated bear. "Well, this is not the first time you have seen them. Though I do not know why you bother with that woman."

That woman.

The name Andrea saw fit to give Savannah these days.

"I was also doing an interview with Isla Goodspeed, and she told me that there has been gossip about Adam's sexuality again."

"Ah, yes. I had heard something of the sort."

"And you didn't tell me?" I demanded, slamming my car door behind me as I got into the driver's seat. "*Cazzo*, Andrea, you didn't think that was something I should know?"

"No, I did not. Why would I tell you gossip about an ex-lover who wounded you badly ten years ago? One you have not had contact with in that time, hmm? Tell me why I should have told you. So you could protect him? Comfort him? That is not your job anymore nor has it been for many years."

His words slid between each one of my ribs like slim, sharp blades. For a moment, I couldn't breathe through the pain.

The pain of his honesty.

Because, of course, he was right.

I was nothing to Adam Meyers anymore, if I ever had been.

What was I going to do about his plight?

"Yes, well, anyway," I said, pausing to clear my throat and input the directions to Linnea's house in the GPS. "It was a perfect storm. Seeing Savannah, hearing about Adam, and then running into Linnea later that day."

"The girl from Maui," Andrea remembered. "The one you write those ridiculous postcards to."

"They aren't ridiculous," I said automatically because this wasn't the first time he had teased me about them. "Writing by hand is a lost art form. Anyway, I could not sleep because this idea was flourishing like a weed in my mind, and I had to get it all out."

"I want to read everything you have," he demanded, as I knew he would. "Send it immediately."

"I'm on my way to pick up Linnea, but I will send it when I park," I promised. "It's rough, Andrea. I told you, I haven't finished."

"Honestly, Sebastian, I do not care if it's one line written on the back of a receipt. I have been waiting a decade to make a film with you again."

"You've directed me three times since *Blood Oath*. Including *Black On*, which we just wrapped," I reminded him. "The *LA Times* calls me your muse the way Leonardo is for Martin Scorsese."

Andrea made a noise of derision in the back of his throat. He did not like to be compared to any other director. "Send me the pages. And, *fratellone*, be careful, yes? The past always seems prettier through the pink lens of nostalgia."

He hung up before I could respond, which was just as well because I had no response to that.

Probably, he was right.

Still, I knew myself well enough to know there was a large likelihood I would ignore his advice anyway.

No matter how much my head cautioned it, or my gut screamed its concerns, my heart never seemed to listen to either of them.

I was still mulling over *The Dream & The Dreamer* and how surreal it was to have three ghosts from my past crop up in the same twenty-four-hour period when I pulled up in front of a small yellow bungalow in Westwood. Winter flowers bloomed in tidy beds beneath the front windows, and a robust lemon tree gleamed with bright fruit in the early morning sunlight. It was as charming and unpretentious as Linnea herself and suited her to a T.

I parked and walked the slightly cracked asphalt path to the front door to knock because my mama had taught me never to honk for a lady.

A moment later, a little curtain over the square window in the door twitched aside to reveal Linnea, wide-eyed and obviously startled.

It was a long moment before she opened the door.

"Sebastian," she said, slightly breathless, the masses of wavy blond hair mussed into a wild halo around her head. "I thought I said

I would meet you at the beach."

"You also said you unexpectedly had to take your car into the shop. I was not going to make you catch a rideshare. Besides, I rented a Lambo. I like any excuse to drive it," I allowed with a grin.

Her features softened, but she still stood in a narrow crack between the door and the frame as if she didn't want me to peer inside.

"That's sweet of you," she admitted, shifting her weight from foot to foot. "Okay, if you don't mind waiting just here, I'll grab my things."

"I can help—" I started to say, only for the door to be quietly shut in my face.

Okay.

So she was private about her home. I chose to believe something was charming about that and waited with my shoulder pressed into the stucco wall for her to re-emerge.

But a moment later, a rousing scream sounded from within, followed by a loud crash of something unmistakably breaking.

Without thinking, I wrenched the front door open and barreled inside.

There was a small entryway that led to a narrow hallway down the middle and two rooms on either side. The sound of a struggle emitted from the left, so I ran into the living room and paused at the sight that awaited me.

Linnea was on her knees on the ground with water dripping down her face and neck, flower petals caught in her hair. She had her hands shackled around an older woman's wrists, struggling to contain her as she writhed in her worn, blue velvet chair.

"You bitch," the woman shouted, nails curling into Linnea's hands so deeply, blood welled beneath the tips. "You bitch, I told you that part was mine!"

"I know," Linnea spoke so softly, it was almost hard to hear her after the screech of the other woman's pitch. "I know, which is why I'm going to go speak to the director right now and tell him you're the one who is right for the role, okay? But I need you to relax, or I can't fix things. You want the part, don't you, Miranda?"

My breath stuck in my lungs, caught in the web of surprise.

Miranda?

As in Linnea's mother, Miranda Hildebrand?

The once stunning actress who had earned her fame from soap operas and a series of spectacularly failed marriages.

Now that I knew who she was, I could see the fine features under her lank white hair and the vivid blue of her eyes, once her most famous qualities. Otherwise, she was almost unrecognizable, frail in a way I would expect the elderly to be, not a woman who had to still be in her late forties or early fifties. She wore clean loungewear in pale pink, but her face was makeup-free, and her hair was unstyled. The woman who used to associate with Savannah Meyers would have never lounged about the house in less than a silk negligee and glamorously done hair and nails.

What happened to her?

Linnea noticed me then because her mother did.

"About time you got here," Miranda told me with an imperial sniff. "You're lucky you're so handsome, Clark, or I wouldn't agree to go out with a man who was twenty minutes late for our date."

My gaze darted to Linnea, who stared at me with her mouth pressed so tightly it almost disappeared.

"I apologize, Miranda," I said, stepping forward to collect one of her hands from Linnea's loosened grip so I could bring it to my mouth for a kiss. "I know better than to keep a beautiful woman waiting."

"Yes, you do," she agreed, shooting me an unimpressed look even though her cheeks pinked with pleasure. "You could have at least brought me flowers."

I did not mention the shattered crystal vase at the base of the wall behind Linnea or the blooms scattered across the carpet.

"Next time," I promised.

"Freesia," she instructed, sinking back into her chair and clasping her bony hands over her stomach. She seemed suddenly lethargic as if her tirade had eaten up the last of her energy reserves. "Don't listen to Linnea. She'll tell you I like orchids because they're *her* favorites."

Done with our conversation, Miranda turned her head away from us both and closed her eyes.

Silence descended.

"I'm so, so—" she started just as I said, "I am sorry, I should not have run inside. Only, I thought you were in danger."

Linnea was already nodding by the time I finished. Her heavy sigh puffed out her cheeks, and she ran a hand through her soft halo of hair before rocking back onto her heels and standing.

"I'll explain in the car, shall I?" she suggested with a tepid smile. "If you could grab my board from the side of the house, I'll just text Mrs. Ramirez to come over, clean up this mess, and I'll meet you at the car."

She looked so young and small standing in the middle of the tiny, cluttered living room in frayed jean shorts and a tiny white bikini top. So I didn't resist the impulse to go to her, plucking a wilted yellow flower from her hair, dropping it to the ground before I slid my hand under her heavy hair and cupped her neck. She stared up at me with those almond-shaped, violet-colored eyes as if she could not believe I was real.

"I'm going to hug you now," I told her as I pulled her gently by the neck into my chest.

Her heavy exhale warmed my skin through my tee as she pressed her nose into the space between my pecs and wrapped her arms around my waist.

I held her without speaking so I could focus on the infinitesimal way the tension leeched from her muscles as the seconds passed until she was utterly soft and flush against me. She smelled of sea salt and flowers in a way that reminded me startlingly of Napoli. Of home.

When she was ready, I let her slip from my arms and watched as she moved into the back of the house. I took another second to study the room properly, noting the shelf of daytime television awards, the movie posters framed on the walls, and the old-money furniture crammed into the small space. A big life reduced to memories and a tiny floorplan that didn't allow for the grandeur Miranda had once enjoyed.

I had never particularly liked Miranda and Bobbi, Savannah's best friends in London all those years ago. They had brought out the more brittle qualities in my lover, her materialism and haughtiness, her aloof reserve and cutting judgements.

But I would never have wished this for Miranda, whose worst quality seemed only to be a Bambi-like naivety that the world would and should always work out in her favor.

I found Linnea's board around the left side of the house. It wasn't a new surfboard with the latest technology like the one I had strapped to the top of the SUV, but it had been lovingly tended to and was the sunny yellow color I had come to associate with Linnea.

When she got into the car, she dumped her big straw bag at her feet, kicked off her flip-flops, and rested them on the top of the dash before leaning her head back and sighing deeply. It was a posture of familiarity, as if she had been riding in this car with me for years, and it did something strange to the center of my chest. I resolved to think about it later.

"You are too young to look so tired," I told her as I pulled out into the street. It was still only quarter to six in the morning, but we had to make good time to get the best of the morning waves.

"I am too young to feel this tired," she agreed, rolling her head to face me.

"Your mother is sick, *sí?*" I asked softly, glancing at her before I turned left to get back to the highway.

Another long, weary sigh. "She has frontotemporal dementia."

"This is like Alzheimer's?"

"It's in the same family, but FTD specifically affects the personality and language centers of the brain. Some days, she's better than others, but she forgets about personal hygiene and eating, and she has episodes of intense paranoia or anger. She has muscle weakness and a lack of coordination, so someone has to watch her because she can fall or drop things and seriously hurt herself." She paused, turning her face to look out the window before softly admitting, "Once, a few months ago, I left her alone to go to an audition, and when I came home, she'd lost so much blood cutting her foot open on a broken glass that I thought she was dead."

My heart ached with empathy. I could not imagine watching my mother or sisters going through such a sad and frightening disease, not to mention having to deal with it alone.

"What happened to her last husband?" I demanded. "I thought she had married again after Wyndam."

She nodded, twisting the ends of her overlarge, embroidered white shirt above her belly button into a knot. "She was. He left when she was given the official diagnosis."

"What about alimony? Surely that should cover the cost of full-time care."

I did not know why I asked when it suddenly seemed obvious that

Miranda required full-time care.

"The prenup stipulated that she wouldn't get anything if they divorced before two years had passed. He left two months before their second wedding anniversary."

I winced. "*Cazzo*, what a *stronzo*."

Her laugh was brittle, cracking at the edges. "I couldn't have said it better myself."

"So you moved to Los Angeles to take care of the mother who was rarely a proper mother to you," I summarized, looking over to see Linnea twisting one of the chunky gold rings she wore around one finger. "That is incredibly good of you."

She snorted. "Don't make me out to be some kind of saint, please. There wasn't really a choice, you know? Her husband left her, her friends in this cesspool of an industry basically fled as if FTD is contagious, and Miranda needed someone. I was the only option."

"There is always a choice," I said because I had learned that the hard way. Sacrificing came so easily to me that I didn't realize how many pieces of myself I had given away until Adam and Savannah cast me out. I'd given so much to them, so much to my family to make sure they could have a better life, and for what?

For a horrifying moment after the break-up, I couldn't find the answer.

But then I went to New York, and I saw Elena and Mama set up in Little Italy. Elena had enrolled in law school, and Mama was working at an upscale Italian trattoria, as they'd both always dreamed of.

As they had both always deserved.

And I knew what it was all for, all the pain and the perpetual grind and the aching loneliness.

It was for them.

The people who meant everything to me.

"You're a good person, Linnea Kai," I murmured, reaching over to take one fidgeting hand in my own. Without hesitation, she flipped her palm up and linked our fingers together. "She's lucky to have you, even if she doesn't say it."

She laughed again, that hard cough that didn't come from a pleasant place. "She certainly doesn't say it. I think even when she's lucid, she hates me for seeing her like that. She'd hate *anyone* for seeing her like that, but I think it makes it worse that it's her daughter taking care of her. The one she never made time for and not the men or friends she devoted so much of her life to."

"How does it make you feel?" I asked as she pulled our hands farther into her lap and started to trace the veins on the back of my hand and forearm. It was an intimate touch that warmed me through to my bones, especially since she didn't seem to notice she was doing it. She was so natural and unaffected, our closeness entirely unmanufactured.

It made my throat hurt and my stomach ache.

"It makes me feel sad for her," she admitted softly. "It makes me feel lonely, too, I guess. Just the two of us, her so alone and me, too, because even though I take care of her, even though I always wanted us to be, we aren't a team. I just…I don't want to end up like that. More than my dreams of fashion design or acting or traveling the world, I just don't want to end up alone."

My lungs contracted, trapping the air in my chest until it was so full I worried it would burst.

Yes, *I wanted to say,* I understand completely.

Yes, *some inner voice screamed,* my nightmares all find me alone in the cold dark, and when I wake up alone in bed, it is too close for comfort to feel good.

My hand tightened in hers, probably painfully. It drew her gaze back to me, and even though I was driving so I couldn't look at her, I could feel the weight of her regard like sunbeams against the side of my face.

"You won't," I promised. "I'm sorry we haven't seen more of each other the past few years, but I promise you, there will never be a day when you are not loved by me. *D'accordo?*"

There was only silence as I pulled off the highway and navigated the streets of the Pacific Palisades before finally pulling into the car park at Topanga Beach.

When I cut the engine and turned to look at her, Linnea was already twisted my way, her expressive features arranged into a soft smile.

"I missed you, you know," she told me baldly, and her frankness was so different from Adam and Savannah, both so much on my mind after yesterday, that it almost alarmed me. "I've kept every single postcard you ever sent me, but they weren't the same as this. Being with you? It feels as natural as slipping into the sea—a refreshing, comforting embrace."

The effect of her sincerity, combined with her stunning beauty was almost too much to comprehend. How was the woman single? How hadn't she found a good man to sweep away her worries and show her just how wonderful life could be when you were in love?

Maybe because none of them were worthy of basking in her light.

Spending time with Linnea felt like swallowing sunlight, the warmth of her presence brightening the empty, echoing corridors of my lonely heart.

"I feel the very same," I told her solemnly, raising our joint hands to my mouth to kiss her knuckles. "I am glad we have found each other again."

For a moment, a promise hovered in the air between us, a sultry whisper in my ear urging me to lean forward and capture those full lips with my own.

Only one thing held me back.

I wanted to be a source of goodness in Linnea's life. If I gave in to my base urge to strip her out of that little white bikini and taste the sun-kissed skin on the inside of her elbows and inner thighs, I would never want to stop. My desire for her went beyond her beauty to the radiance of the soul shining out at me from those unusual purple eyes. I wanted to devour her, eat her up, and swallow her down like some ancient pagan god swallowing the sun, as if her light could eradicate the dark blemish of heartbreak on my soul.

But that wasn't fair.

What did I have to offer her when I knew in my bones I would never fully recover from the loss of the Meyerses?

So I flashed her my trademark grin and teased, "I hope you are ready for me to kick your ass, *trottolina*. I have improved much in the years since you taught me to surf."

Her laugh was loud and belly-deep, head tipped back so her gold hair streamed over her shoulder, pooling in her lap.

And I thought, Yes, this is enough to fill me up.

CHAPTER 5

SEBASTIAN

"Why were you so angry at the restaurant the other day?" Linnea had asked after two hours of showing me up on her shortboard, carving through the water as if she had been born to ride the waves.

We were mostly just bobbing in the ocean past the break, feet dangling in the cold, wetsuits rolled down to our waists so we could catch some winter sun on our skin. It was hard not to stare at her, the salt crystals and droplets glistening on her tanned skin like jewels. Her hair was darkened to flax and pushed away from her forehead in a way that highlighted her huge eyes and dark brows, her cheeks and lips pink from exertion. Though she was slender, she had large breasts that were barely contained in the small white triangles of her bikini, and it took every ounce of my willpower not to admire them like a teenage boy.

She was so unlike Savannah, or any of the women I had dated since, whose femininity was cultivated beautifully, like a piece of orchestra music, a collection of notes and instruments built together in perfect harmony.

Linnea was just herself, so without artifice that she reminded me of myself when I had first moved in with the Meyerses. It hurt a bit, that constant reminder of how young and foolish I'd been, but it was healing too because nothing about Linnea was foolish. Her lack of airs was deliberate, not a consequence of youth, and she was utterly confident in herself, sitting barefaced on a board or done up in a trendy LA bar. Her beauty was as natural as the sun shining above us in the cerulean bowl of the sky and the glitter of blue water below.

She liked herself, it seemed, and when so many people struggled to feel the same, it was intoxicating to be around.

It made me like myself a little more, too, somehow.

"I was being interviewed by a woman I considered a...friend until she informed me of some rather salacious gossip about an old acquaintance," I admitted.

Linnea rested her hands behind her on the board, tipping her face farther into the sun the way one might do in a shower, to saturate herself in it.

"What was it? You don't have to answer, but you know I have to ask," she paused to dip her chin down and offer me a cheeky grin. "I'm an invasive species. I want to know everything."

"About everyone?" I teased.

"About you," she countered with a slight shrug. "About the people I care for."

I swallowed thickly, surprised by my desire to share with her when I knew my history was better served staying buried six feet deep in the past.

"There is a rumor going around about Adam Meyers," I said quietly. "It was hard to hear."

"Oh." Linnea's brow furrowed as she adjusted on the board,

sweeping her legs back through the water to sit on her knees, her balance so perfect that she barely wobbled. "I'm sorry to hear that. Is there anything you can do to help him?"

I snorted. "He would not want my help. We haven't spoken in… *Dio mio*, ten years."

She cocked her head, squinting at me through the harsh sunlight. "Are you sure? I know that I wouldn't have turned any friend away when I first arrived in Los Angeles, alone and new in a city that overwhelmed me, to take care of a mother who barely tolerated me even when she remembered me."

"I'm sorry I wasn't around for you."

"But you were," she countered. "You sent me postcards every couple of weeks, and they always made my day. Just because someone isn't physically with you doesn't mean they aren't there for you in a hundred other ways that matter."

I swirled my feet through the water to get closer to her, reaching out to catch the edge of her board. She instantly swiveled to sit on her bottom and drag her long legs over my board, effectively locking us together. I reached for her foot without thinking, cupping the high arch in my palm and giving it a squeeze. A little shiver rolled up her spine, a spark of electricity I felt mirrored in my own.

I wanted her badly, with a kind of intensity I hadn't felt in years.

It shouldn't have been shocking, really. She was stunning and inherently sensual, sweet and funny and candid in a way that made me feel both nostalgic and safe.

But even as the realization occurred, I shoved that desire into the deepest recesses of my gut.

There was no way I could fool around with Linnea and risk jeopardizing our friendship.

And the truth was, that part of me that had yearned to love and be loved had calcified around the memory of two people who were inaccessible to me. I had tried to move on for ten years and failed enough to know that it just wasn't in the cards.

The idea of soulmates was so romantic until you realized that there might be one—or two people—meant for you, but you might not be meant for them in return.

There was someone out there for Linnea who could love her without ghosts interfering with the level of worship she deserved.

So I squeezed her foot, then set it down beside me.

"Adam wouldn't want to see me," I repeated. "Just trust me on that."

"Because you had an affair with his wife?"

I startled so badly, I almost slipped into the ocean. When I recovered, I looked up to see her watching me with those purple eyes, wide and knowing.

She shrugged. "Miranda would talk about it on the phone with Bobbi and Savannah. I don't think Savannah ever confirmed it, but it seemed like an open secret between them. The lady and the driver. Miranda used to have a laugh about it."

Linnea rolled her eyes at that, then nudged me in the side with her foot.

"Don't look so scandalized, Sebastian. You're the one who had the affair, not me."

I was startled into chuckling, shaking my head at her. "You never mentioned it back then."

"Neither did you," she countered with a raised brow. "I was always curious, but you seemed so much older and wiser than me even though you were only two and a half years older. I didn't want to scare you off."

"Never," I said solemnly, tugging on her big toe. "I mean that, Linnea."

"I get that now," she said with a roll of her eyes. "But sixteen-year-old gawky and awkward Linnea did not."

"You are certainly not gawky any longer," I quipped.

Her grin was wide and wicked, a knowing gleam in her eyes as she reached up to cup the underside of her breasts. "Karma for being a late bloomer, I think."

I laughed again, undone by her candor. "You can ask, now. If you'd like. I cannot promise to answer everything, though."

"Was it an affair, then? I wouldn't blame you. Savannah has always had this…aura about her. A regality that makes her desirable and unattainable at the same time. The two of you would have made sense together."

I hadn't spoken about the Meyerses in so long that for a moment, I wasn't sure I could find the words even though I yearned for the catharsis.

"I had a close friendship with Savannah," I confessed. "I fell in love with her before I even truly knew her. I'm not sure you could call it an affair because Adam knew about it." *And participated freely*, I thought but did not say. It wasn't that I distrusted Linnea, but in light of the gossip swirling about him already, I didn't want to take the chance when I didn't have to. "We were friends, too, though. I loved him in my own way, and I was devastated when they chose to let me go."

"You miss them," she said, a little surprised. "I can hear it in your voice."

I shrugged one shoulder and scrubbed a hand through my wet hair. "Yes. Nearly every day. Savannah was Savannah, but Adam was the best mate I ever had."

"You should call him," she declared. "Really, Seb, what is there to lose? Worst-case scenario, he doesn't answer or he tells you to fuck off, but you're already *there*. Best case, he's grateful you reached out when so many others are probably scattering like locusts in the face of tabloid gossip. Best case, he misses you, too."

He misses you, too.

The idea of that made my stomach clench so hard, I thought I might vomit.

It seemed wildly outlandish, but I couldn't stop a kernel of hope from taking root in the fallow field of my heart.

"Maybe you can understand what he's going through," she continued. "Honestly, I was pissed when I opened the door to you this morning, but I feel kind of…relieved now that you know about Miranda."

"I could help you, you know," I murmured. "If you'd let me. I would love to do it."

Her fierce scowl was instantaneous. "Do you mean like a handout? Don't insult me, Seb. I won't take your money."

"You're working as a server, going to auditions, and trying to work on your designs, all while taking care of your mother," I countered passionately. "You do not have time to breathe, and you are only twenty-six. You deserve some peace."

"You call me *trottolina* for a reason. I don't yearn for peace," she argued, eyes flashing, chin tipped pugnaciously. "I yearn for love, and success, and adventure. I'm willing to work hard to earn it all."

"And you don't have the time for it," I pointed out. "You could, if I just hired someone to—"

"Don't you dare finish that sentence," she snapped, thrusting her finger at me.

I caught it, using her own momentum by tugging on the digit to pull her forward and unseat her from her surfboard. My free hand caught her by the hip as she tipped forward, catching her and settling her smoothly in my lap, her thighs draped over my own, her hair curtaining us as she stared down into my face with a shock-slack mouth.

I took advantage of her surprise to press my point. "I know you do not want to feel like you are using me, so I will let this go for now. But if I see an opportunity to help you, Linnea, I will do it. If there is an audition I can help you land, a nurse I can pay for, a meal I can treat you to at the end of a long day, I will do it even if you hate me for being high-handed. This is how a man like me loves a woman, you understand? I care for her, even when she refuses to care for herself."

I watched her long neck as she swallowed thickly, my gaze traveling up to that ridiculously full mouth. She licked her lips, and it felt like a dare.

Kiss me, it said.

Madonna santa, I wanted to.

"I won't take a handout," she repeated, this time breathlessly.

I could feel the brush of her hard nipples through the wet fabric of her suit against my chest.

"But you will accept my help if I offer a reasonable solution?" I pushed.

"If you offer a reciprocal solution," she countered, and her hands reached up to play with the hair at the nape of my neck in a way that made me shiver. "But the moment it feels like you are pitying me or I am taking advantage of you, it's over. Your friendship means more to me than anything else."

"*D'accordo*," I said. "Deal."

"I won't be another person in your life who takes from you," she shocked me by whispering.

I was still reeling from the comment and wondering at her insight when she ducked slightly to press a featherlight kiss over my mouth. Before I could respond, she was slipping out of my lap like a seal, smoothly diving into the water to emerge belly down on her surfboard.

I watched as she cut smoothly away from me, timing her escape so she dropped into the bowl of a wave and rode it on sharp cuts back to the shore.

Leaving me oddly aroused and emotionally sore, bobbing on the ocean alone.

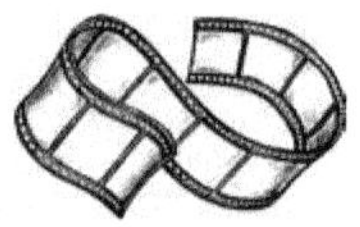

IT WASN'T UNTIL THE FOLLOWING WEEK that the idea came to me.

I was eating at Nobu in Malibu with my sister Elena, and her husband, Dante, who were in town for work, and Dante's pseudo-father, a man named Amadeo Salvatore whom everyone called Tore. I didn't know or particularly like the man, but he had become a staple at family gatherings over the years due to his close relationship with Dante, Elena, and, for some reason, my twin sister, Cosima. Even Mama seemed caught up in his web. I often caught them whispering heatedly in the kitchen at family dinners, but when I pressed her about it, she always evaded me.

Still, I was happy to see Elena. Growing up, we had not been particularly close, but the past ten years had changed her immensely and brought us closer than ever. She had been through more than most people ever survived in a whole lifetime, and it had made her the strongest and smartest woman I knew. She'd cut a man to ribbons with her sharp tongue, and she would protect any of her loved ones until her last breath.

It made me immeasurably happy to know that she had the love and devotion of a man like Dante Salvatore. The infamous mafioso, with a criminal record as long as my arm, was a complete sap for Elena and their children, Aurora, Chiara, and Amadeo.

The kids were with one of Dante's "men" at their hotel so that the four of us could have a late dinner in relative peace.

Or, more accurately, so Elena could grill me about my life.

"I saw a photo of you with some blond woman in the tabloids this morning," she mentioned as Dante served her from a platter of sashimi. "An 'unidentified woman' practically sitting in your lap on a surfboard at Topanga Beach."

I slanted her a cool look. "Since when do you read the tabloids, Lena?"

"She has an alert set for each of her siblings," Dante divulged, ignoring his wife's glare. "She likes to stay on top of what's happening with you in case she needs to intervene."

"Intervene?" I asked with a raised brow before popping a bite of miso black cod into my mouth.

"Legally," Dante explained. "Or illegally, if she asks for my help."

I laughed at him as Elena swatted his shoulder. Dante caught her hand and tugged her in close to kiss her mouth.

"You are the most frustrating man," she told him, but her voice was soft, almost sweet.

"You are the most infuriating woman," he countered through a broad smile before sliding his hand under her hair and kissing her again.

"They're sickening, aren't they?" Tore asked me, leaning closer conspiratorially.

They're all I've ever wanted, *I thought but didn't say.*

"So, who was she, *patatino*?" Elena demanded to know, using my childhood nickname. "She certainly seemed your type. Blond and beautiful."

"She's nothing like Savannah," I said before I could curb the impulse.

Which, of course, made everything worse.

My sister was like a bloodhound. Once she caught a scent, she could not let it go.

"Ah," she said smugly. "So she is not just some other Unidentified Woman. What's her name?"

"Linnea Kai," I muttered. "And we aren't seeing each other. She's an old friend."

"The one he sends the postcards to," Tore noted, to my surprise.

When I shot him a look, he shrugged. "Cosima has spoken to me about this. The girl you write to."

"She shouldn't tell you my personal business," I said, even though it made Tore, a seasoned criminal himself, flinch slightly.

"Sebastian," Elena reprimanded. "Don't be rude. Tore is part of our family."

"Your family," I corrected, even though it was cruel to do so. Something about the Italian had always rubbed me the wrong way and brought out the worst in me. I did not respond well to men who tried to be my authority figures, not after Seamus and the circling mafiosos of my youth.

I did not find crime romantic, not after my childhood. It was a testament to Dante's winning personality that I liked him at all, given his job. Mostly, I liked him because he would raze the earth to ash for Elena, and she deserved that kind of love.

All my sisters did.

"Ours," Elena snapped. "You are the one who always stressed to me the importance of family. Do not disparage ours now when we have all fought so hard for each other."

Only a big sister could make a grown man feel so ashamed.

"I apologize, Tore," I said, facing him even though I did not like the look of him.

Something in his pale brown eyes, a shade darker than my own, unsettled me.

"*Nessun problema*," he said quietly in Italian.

No problem.

He was always too kind to me, always too attentive.

I wished Elena and Dante had not invited him.

"You should ask her out," Elena said, not to be deterred from her mission. "You haven't truly dated anyone since Savannah Richardson."

"I've dated plenty."

"Loved, then," she pressed. "You haven't loved since her. Since them."

"Elena…" I warned.

But she would not be ignored.

"I read that Adam Meyers might lose his part in the new Daventry film because there are rumors he had a sex tape with a male lover," she said baldly.

I looked around on instinct, my heart racing at the thought of anyone hearing the gossip. I hadn't known there was a supposed sex tape, but *cazzo*, of course there was. My chest burned, and for a moment, I thought I might be sick in the yellowfin tuna on my plate.

"Have you spoken to him?" Elena asked softly, reaching to smooth her fingers over my knuckles, white from the strain of clutching my water glass.

"Not in years."

"I've never understood why she deserved your grace and not him." I looked up at her in surprise, because I had never thought of it quite like that. "You haven't told me the whole story, but I've always believed the more something hurts you, the more you try to avoid it. Doesn't it say something that you're willing to see Savannah, but you haven't spoken to Adam in a decade?"

My gaze shifted to Dante, who was kindly engaging in quiet conversation with Tore, to give us a semblance of privacy. I knew both men were listening despite the ruse, but it meant something that they did not seem to care.

"You told Dante," I said, not a question because it was obvious.

"He's my husband." She shrugged elegantly, and it reminded me of Savannah. They had many similarities—both could be aloof, cunning, elegant, and cold—but at the end of the day, my sister was the brave one, always going after what she wanted and trying to better herself even when it was uncomfortable to do so. Maybe that was why I kept nursing this weak flame of hope that one day Savannah would find some courage, too. "Are you worried about him?"

I closed my eyes for a moment because my mind's eye conjured the memory of Adam mid-panic attack when he'd discovered the paps had captured an intimate photo of us on the beach. He had looked so…wrecked. Broken to pieces barely held together by fragile skin.

"Yes," I whispered. "I can't stop thinking about him."

She uncurled my fingers from the glass and threaded them through hers. In the setting sunlight, her hair glowed like a dark flame, her eyes a clear, burnished grey. She was so lovely and so happy settled into her skin, it made something loosen in my chest.

"Call him, then. Help him. I'm not saying he deserves it, but I think you need to do it. You're the most selfless person I know, save for Cosima, and I think it might kill you not to go to him in his time of need."

"How exactly am I supposed to help?" I said, biting off the words in frustration. "Associating with me is hardly going to help when I was the source of the problem the first time around."

"No," she agreed, sitting back in her chair with pursed lips as she mulled over the problem. "What he really needs is a good beard. Some pretty girl who can change the narrative and wouldn't mind being at the center of attention for a moment. I'm sure his publicist can find any number of thirsty starlets to take the part. Whether or not they can be convincing or care about Adam at all is another story of course…why do you have that look on your face?"

"What look?" I asked absently, still stuck on the thought that had cropped up in the wake of her words.

"That look," she said, pointing at my face. "The same one you had before you called Leone Valeria a pig when he pushed Cosima into the mud. The one that preluded you getting a broken finger."

"Worth it," I retorted. "But you're right. I think I have an idea that could help more than just Adam."

"Well, then," she said, crossing her long legs and reaching for her wineglass. "Aren't you lucky to have a wise sister like me?"

I snorted but lifted our joined hands to my mouth to kiss her hand. "*Sono baciato dalla fortuna.*"

I am kissed by fortune, I told her.

And despite the heartbreak I'd experienced in my life, I knew I was the luckiest son of a bitch in the world to have the love of the women in my family and to have experienced the kind of love that changed my center of gravity, even if I'd spent the last ten years trying to regain my equilibrium.

CHAPTER SIX

ADAM

I was running for my life when the doorbell rang.

The thwack of my feet against the treadmill was thunderous, the mechanical whirr loud enough to drown out my thoughts. It was the only escape I had found in the last two disastrous weeks. Run, run, run until the demons fell back, and I was—momentarily—free.

Chaucer was worried about me even though she didn't try to keep me from working out. There were worse outlets, we both knew, than spending too many hours in the gym.

The last time my life had fallen to pieces, I'd dived headfirst into a bottle of whiskey and hadn't emerged for years.

So running was the lesser of many evils.

At least my trainer was pleased.

If I did end up getting the famous role of Anton Daventry, even after the gossip rags had exploded with new conjecture about my sexuality, I would need to be in the best shape of my life. While

I'd always been broad-shouldered and fit, the last few weeks had seen what remained of my body fat melt away to reveal the kind of muscle normally reserved for professional athletes. Some of my shirts were too small, now, a problem Chaucer was happy to rectify by burning a hole in my credit card on Rodeo Drive in service of new clothes for me.

I was annoyed when the doorbell rang once, twice, three times, and then again, a few minutes later when I didn't deign to answer. I thought Chaucer was somewhere in the house, because I didn't remember her leaving after she arrived that morning to check that I was still alive and sober. Certainly, my live-in chef and cleaner, Bruce, was around somewhere.

So why the bloody hell wasn't anyone answering the door?

I hit the stop button on the treadmill when the chiming bell sounded for the fourth time, muttering under my breath about lazy employees as I snatched the towel from one handle and used it to mop the worst of the sweat from my brow. There was no helping my drenched quick-dry shirt, so I peeled it over my head and tucked it into the back of my shorts.

Whoever it was at my door had already been vetted by the guard at the gate from my list of approved visitors, or by Chaucer, who was rung whenever someone else wanted access. I didn't have to worry about modesty with the intruder, and I was too irritated by the interruption—and the general state of my life—to care as I stomped through the house to the foyer and wrenched open the oversized wooden door.

Nothing could have prepared me for the sight that awaited me on the other side.

It was like hitting an invisible force field. Every atom of my body was thrown against an immovable wall, then ricocheted back painfully, recoiling and freezing as if stasis would save me from the revelation of the guest who stood on my doorstep.

My system was overloaded by so many powerful emotions, it short-circuited.

I had not let myself *feel* so strongly in a decade.

Almost to the day I had last seen the man with the golden eyes staring at me calmly as if I wasn't having an internal meltdown in front of him.

"Adam," Sebastian Lombardi said, and oh *fuck*, the sound of my name in his mouth…a song that haunted my dreams and had me waking up with a gasp lodged in my throat, a painful hardon and heartache like a stab wound throbbing in my chest.

Adam, he said as if it had not been ten years since we spoke.

Adam, he said as if we could just…pick up where we left off. Best mates, lovers, the moon and his tides.

Of everything that had happened to me in the past two weeks, the threats of blackmail, the leak to the press about my sexuality, the offers falling through and execs not returning my calls, somehow this was the worst.

To be faced with the only thing you'd truly ever wanted and fucked up too badly to ever be worthy of having.

"Sebastian," I said, like an echo, like I didn't have a choice but to respond to the sound of my name in his mouth with his in mine.

A small, crooked smile bloomed across his face.

Jesus Christ, he was gorgeous. So much more so than he'd even been at eighteen. A decade of living had hardened his exquisitely carved bone structure, packing more muscle onto that tall, broad-shouldered frame so his hips seemed even narrower and his legs endless in their tailored black denim. That boyish charm had rubbed away to reveal a wicked magnetism that was honestly arresting.

I knew because staring at him, my heart stopped beating.

He didn't mock me for my long silence or bewilderment. If anything, he seemed to take advantage, his own gaze—those searing tiger yellow eyes—scouring every inch of my sweaty, naked chest and my bare legs beneath the athletic shorts I wore low on my hips. When his stare found mine again, his lips ticked up even higher.

"You have silver," he murmured, his accent just as thick, and God, I was grateful because nothing about that voice should ever change. He reached forward for a moment as if he was going to touch me, and the thought sent electricity coursing through me so hard I jerked, as if flinching away from him. His hand snapped back against his chest as if I'd hit him before slowly raising to touch above his own ear. "Just here. It's handsome."

I swallowed the sob that rose in my throat, and when that didn't work, I swallowed again, so hard I almost choked.

We hadn't spoken in ten years, and he tells me I'm handsome, *I thought fuzzily.*

It hurt, God, it hurt to know he was still so beautifully honest and unfiltered.

"Are you going to invite me in?" he asked with that same crooked smile, rocking back on his heels with his hands in his pockets.

He seemed almost bashful, which was hard to reconcile with the scenario I had created in my head over the years. I always imagined if we saw each other again in a real way, alone with privacy, that Sebastian would rail at me, shouting and condemning me, rightly so, for the coward I had been back then.

How could you ruin both our lives? *he would say.*

I don't know, *I would answer,* but I've regretted it every day since, even though I don't know what other option there could have been.

It was a self-serving fantasy, anyway. I felt he deserved to be at least half as angry with me as I was with myself, and in saying something like that, it might mean he still wasn't over it.

Me.

That there was, in some fucked-up way, hope for us yet even after so many hurts and years later.

Without saying a word, because I didn't know what the fuck to say, I moved aside to let him into my house.

He stepped inside, immediately looking around and issuing a low whistle of approval at the view, which extended directly to the back wall of windows, offering a glimpse of the green cliff and the sun over the Pacific Ocean. It was setting, spilling thick, syrupy light into the house and over Sebastian, so he looked gilded. His eyes were pure, precious metal when they met mine.

"I like your house," he said.

He'd seen about one inch of the seven-thousand-foot home, but that didn't matter.

Not when I'd bought it seven years ago, thinking only of him standing in almost exactly that spot, bathed in sunlight, smiling at me.

For once in my life, I didn't know what to say, all the words that needed to be spoken tangled in a mass at the back of my throat. So I just smoothed a hand through my sweaty hair and offered an anemic smile.

Sebastian nodded, as if that was an acceptable response. "It's good to see you, Adam. The camera doesn't do you justice. It never has."

I blinked as shock rolled through me. "You still watch my films?"

Seb bit the edge of his grin and rocked back on his heels. "I never could resist watching you act. You do such a damn good job. I can pretend the man who broke my heart doesn't even exist behind each character you play."

For some reason, that struck me like a punch to the gut.

"Sebastian," I said, but I didn't have anything tangible to follow it up with, and suddenly, I was tired again. So fucking tired. I scrubbed a hand over my face. "What are you doing here? How did you even get through the bloody gate?"

"Chaucer and I have stayed in touch," he said easily.

Of course, they had. I'd never asked her, unable to bear the thought that we might only be one person removed. That if I was desperate enough, I could beg Chaucer to give me his number or tell me how to make things right.

"That doesn't explain why you're here," I said flatly.

Seb pursed then flattened his lips, and I was cruelly reminded how lovely his mouth was, pink and full against the inkiness of his stubble.

"Why don't you offer me a drink? And you look like you could use some water," he suggested, already moving through the house as if he were a frequent guest here.

Bemused, still struck faintly dumb by his presence in my home after so long, I trailed him. My eyes found his pert arse, flexing in that tailored denim, before I could find the will to wrench them away.

"Left," I corrected when he made to move the other way.

"Ah," he said, clapping his hands together when the kitchen came into view behind the long expanse of a comfortable living room. "My mama would embarrass herself over this kitchen."

"My cook seems to enjoy it."

Sebastian laughed, and it made my breath thin inside my lungs.

"You never were the chef, were you?" he asked, eyes sparkling as he opened the door to the fridge, peering over his shoulder at me.

I shrugged even though he'd turned back to rummage through the drink drawer. He was quiet as he perused the selection of non-alcoholic beverages and chose one for both of us. I waited as he slid the La Croix across the marble island toward me and watched as he cracked his own open, his strong throat working around a sip.

Jesus Christ, what was he doing here?

This was both the worst and best thing that had happened to me in years.

Seeing him would always conjure remnants of the magic I'd felt during our year together in London, the calm and joy and passion he'd brought to my life.

But seeing him now, when I was in the middle of a media shitstorm, was absolutely *not* what I needed.

His temptation was, and always had been, too strong. I'd resisted him once, but to do it again would take a herculean effort.

Not that he was here to…rekindle anything.

Surely.

My heart beat so hard against my breastbone I thought it might crack in half, the bloody organ falling to the table between us for him to toy with.

"Sebastian," I said, a little too sharply. "What the hell are you doing here?"

He nodded slightly, studying the can of sparkling water like it held the answers. "I heard about the…scandal."

My breath caught.

Of course, he had.

It wasn't exactly low profile, though it hadn't yet exploded the way it had the potential to. Oscar would not make good on his threat to expose me until I had what he termed "adequate time" to fulfill his list of demands.

"I hate this for you," Sebastian continued, his voice low and intimate, the way he once spoke to me in the late hours after making love when Savannah lay already asleep between us. "I hated it then, and

I hate that it is happening again now."

"Yes, well." I cleared my throat. "Obviously, I do, too."

"I'm sure you have a whole team on it."

I did. Chaucer had reached out to Mi Cha Lee, the best crisis PR manager in the business, and my agent Rachel Hoffman, was an absolute gladiator who would go to war before she let blackmail tank my career.

"But I figured," he continued, "maybe you could use a friend who could understand a little of what you're going through."

The words pierced me through the tenderest points of my flesh.

"Pardon?" I breathed, gutted by his kindness.

He shrugged one broad shoulder. "I thought you could use a friend."

My fingers flexed against the marble countertop.

God, I couldn't remember the last time someone had made me such a genuine offer.

It would have been irresistible to a saint.

And I was no saint.

"You know," I said gruffly. "I can't quite remember the last time someone called themselves my friend."

Sebastian's nervous sobriety cracked as his mouth ticked up. "It's hard to make friends, Adam, when you do not let anyone close."

"It's been ten years since we last spoke," I said mildly. "Perhaps I've changed."

He cocked an eyebrow. "Well then, where are your friends in your hour of need?"

His gaze was intensely gold in the honeyed light spilling in through the window. It hurt to look at him the same way it hurt to stare at the sun.

I wrenched my gaze away to look out the window.

"Chaucer is here, somewhere," I said quietly, an admission.

She was my constant, the silver lining in my split with Savannah. My ex-wife acquired most of our social circle in London, our house in Pacific Palisades, and the country home I'd hated in Yorkshire, but I retained Chaucer. Her keen mind and unwavering loyalty had seen me through my years of excess and sorrow. Without her, I would probably have killed myself a long time ago.

But Sebastian was right. Other than her, I only had Arthur and Alasdair, the princes of England, and Iker Ferrera, Europe's beloved soccer star, all of whom could not just fly to California on a whim because I was about to be outed to the press.

"You were always good at evasion," Sebastian murmured before taking a sip of water, his mouth molding around the can. "But I must know if you need my friendship or if it is like…before."

The word echoed in my mind.

Before. Before. Before.

Before when I slaughtered his dream of that impossible universe where we might have ended up together.

Before when I unceremoniously banished him from my home.

"You don't need to be caught up in my shite storm, Sebastian. You've done well for yourself."

His eyes widened before he smoothed over his surprise with a smirk. "How would you know this? Have you kept up with my career, Meyers?"

There was a folder on my computer labeled "The Universe," rather melodramatically, where I kept screenshots and downloads of articles and interviews Sebastian had given over the years. My favorite, which I kept on my phone, was the photo of him accepting his Oscar for *Blood Oath* with a wide, boyish grin.

A small part of me was proud of him, not just because he was preternaturally talented, but because I'd had a role to play in the inception of his rise to fame. I wasn't arrogant enough to think he wouldn't have made it without me, but it felt good nonetheless that I had given him a little leg up in his life.

"You're impossible to escape," I drawled mildly, sitting in one of the barstools and cracking my own sparkling water.

Even with the chaotic memories and the toxic guilt and remorse churning in my gut, Sebastian was doing what he'd always done best.

Putting me at ease despite myself.

He grinned. "Good. I like the idea of you being faced with me wherever you go. Did it make it easier or harder to avoid me all these years?"

"Was it me avoiding you or the other way around?" I quipped. "I don't seem to recall you reaching out to me or crossing the crowd at award ceremonies to seek me out."

If I hadn't once known him so intimately, I wouldn't have noticed the tightening around his eyes, a minute flinch that meant my well-meaning jab had hit a little too close to home.

"Well," he said flatly. "We did not end on very good terms."

"No," I agreed quietly. "A fact which has plagued me for ten years."

Our gazes met, a humming resonance in the air between us. I wanted to go to him as much as I wanted to flee. Instead, I sat very still to avoid either impulse.

"I want to help you," Sebastian reiterated softly, almost the way one would speak to a spooked horse. "If you'll let me."

I'd let you skin me alive if it meant your love and forgiveness, I thought rather desperately.

I swallowed down the words painfully and said, "I'll try."

He nodded, satisfied perhaps because he knew I would have been lying if I gave him an unequivocal go-ahead. I'd always struggled with being transparent and totally committed to anything other than my craft.

"*Bene*," he said with a little smile. "*Bene.* Well, then, as I said, I know you probably have all the best people on it, but I had an idea that could change things around for you. Completely switch up the narrative for the better."

"Oh?" I asked, not expecting much, which was always a mistake when it came to Sebastian Lombardi, who could wring miracles and inspire visions.

"Yes," he declared. "I think you should get married."

CHAPTER SEVEN

LINNEA

"I was worried you wouldn't ever be very beautiful."

I closed my eyes for a moment as I ripped a few weeds out of the garden beds by the front door. It helped to take a second to shore up my shields when Miranda acted out like this. The problem was, she hadn't been the kindest mother before her frontal lobes had started to atrophy, and now that the disease was progressing, she was downright cruel much of the time.

"Life is hard for ugly people like you," she continued blithely from the Adirondack chair I had set up for her in the yard.

It was a hot morning, and I had a few hours between my audition that morning and my shift at the restaurant later that evening, so I thought it would be nice to spend it together in the garden. I didn't particularly like the chore, but I always felt better out in the sun, and Miranda loved flowers, so I tried to keep the garden thriving for her.

"Life isn't difficult for ugly people, Miranda," I said calmly. "And ugliness is subjective. Everyone has something beautiful to offer the world."

She laughed. "You've always been such a funny thing. Savvy always called you the ugly duckling. Where is she? Have you been keeping her calls from me?"

I sighed. Savannah hadn't called in ages. The last time she'd been by to visit, Miranda had accused her of stealing her baby, her film roles, her lovers, and a vintage Prada purse she claimed Robert Redford had given her. Savannah had left ashen-faced and never returned even though Miranda accused Mrs. Ramirez of the same things every week.

"She's been busy, but Bobbi called and she said she would visit you next week. Won't that be nice?"

Miranda sniffed and studied her nails, painted a sunny yellow by yours truly. "Bobbi is a cow."

"Miranda," I said patiently. "She's one of your best friends."

"She can be both things," she pointed out. "Just like you can somehow be my daughter and be so ugly. Clearly, you didn't get my genes." She peered at me. "Though at least you got my breasts. You used to be flat-chested just like a boy."

She devolved into making a series of clicks with her tongue, a tic that came with her FTD. We had a doctor's appointment next week, and I was both anxious and nervous about it. She seemed to be declining faster lately, and I worried about what would happen when she needed full-time care, such as assistance with the bathroom every time. For now, our next-door neighbor, Mrs. Ramirez, was a godsend who didn't mind looking after Miranda, while I worked, for ten dollars an hour, as she ran her sewing business from her house and could easily do it from the guest room I'd converted into my design studio. However, she wasn't a qualified nurse, and despite hours of research on FTD, neither was I.

We just simply didn't have the money to get better care.

Whatever money Miranda had made as a young actress had been spent nearly as fast as she could earn it, and her husbands had the good sense to protect themselves in their prenups. Wyndam didn't know how bad it was. Otherwise, he might have offered to help us. However, I felt bad asking for his money when Miranda had broken his heart by cheating on him.

Dad and my uncles had offered, but they didn't have a lot of money to spare even though their charter boat company was doing better than ever. I knew Dad even considered moving out to help me with her. He and Miranda had never spent more than a few hours in each other's company since I was born, so I couldn't just let him uproot his whole life.

The only thing that made sense was for me to move out and do what I could for her.

Dr. Jamshidi, Miranda's doctor, said that typical life expectancy with FTD could range from seven to twelve years.

We were on year four of her diagnosis even though I only moved in a year and a half ago.

Sometimes, when I was alone at night in bed, exhausted after a day of caretaking and working but unable to sleep, I wondered if I could really sacrifice another four to eight years of my life for her.

"Linnea?"

I startled, turning to see Miranda staring at me with clarity, her hands twisted in her lap, and her mouth twisted with fear.

"What's happening to me?" she whispered.

I abandoned my trowel and gardening gloves to go to her, crouching in front of her chair and gathering her cold hands in mine.

"It's okay, Mom," I said softly, rubbing my thumbs over her knuckles. "You're okay."

"I don't feel like myself," she admitted weakly. "I don't like it here."

"Okay," I said, forcing the words through my tight throat. "Do you want to go inside?"

She clicked her tongue again as she struggled for the words. Finally, she nodded, but when I tried to stand, her hands tightened on mine.

"You won't leave me, will you?" she whispered fiercely, leaning forward to bare her teeth at me. She hated to brush them now, and I had to pay a dentist to visit us at home to examine one of her broken crowns because she refused to go in. "You won't leave me like all the rest of them."

"No, Mom, I won't leave," I promised as I always did, tipping forward to press my forehead to hers.

For a long moment, we stayed like that, her frantic breathing slowing until she was slouched against me.

"Okay, let's get you inside," I murmured, moving to her side and wrapping an arm around her back to help her stand.

"Let me help."

I looked up to see Sebastian on the pathway. He wore black sunglasses, white linen shorts, and a black button-up shirt undone at the top of his chest, revealing a swathe of bronzed skin and oddly sexy collarbones visible in the gap. Even without the celebrity, he would have been extraordinary limned in sunlight, smiling gently at me as if he wanted nothing more than to help me.

My throat went dry.

Taking my silence for acquiescence, he moved forward to Miranda's side and helped us stand her up.

"Clark," Miranda said sharply. "Where are my flowers?"

Sebastian chuckled. "I left them in the car so I could help you in the house, Miranda, but I'll grab them for you."

"Good man," she praised because she always had a ready smile and a compliment for a handsome male.

Miranda shuffled her way into the house with Sebastian and me on either side of her for support, and she sighed wearily when we helped her into her velvet chair in the living room.

"It's too hot," she complained. "Linnea, get me a cold glass of white wine."

I didn't argue with her even though she wasn't allowed to drink anymore. Instead, I moved into the kitchen with a tight smile for Seb and got some cold lemonade from the fridge. When I returned to the living room, he was gone, but Miranda didn't seem to mind, already flipping through the latest issue of *Vogue*.

"They almost asked me to be on the cover in '99," she told me for the millionth time. "Willa Percy couldn't make it last minute, so they asked *me*. But then Francis asked for a divorce, and it got ugly." She pouted. "Why are men never very nice to me?"

"I don't know if some men are ever very nice to anyone," I told her as I handed her the lemonade.

Her fine motor function wasn't great, so she spilled some on her shirt, but I was ready with a napkin to mop it up.

"Some men are," she crowed, spilling even more lemonade as she clapped her hand against the glass.

The happiness on her face so transfixed me that it took me a second to look for the cause of it.

Sebastian stood in the doorway with an armful of flowers—a large bouquet filled with white and pink freesia and lilies—and another beautifully made blue glass vase stuffed with yellow flowers, including a few varieties of orchids.

"A man should always bring a beautiful woman flowers," Sebastian said, as he handed the freesia bouquet to Miranda, who giggled in delight.

But he was looking at me.

And when he handed the flowers off to Miranda, he closed the space between us with a few long strides and brought the yellow flowers up between us.

"Yellow reminds me of you," he said softly, just for me. I watched as he plucked a daisy from the stem, brushed the hair away from my ear with his fingers, and hooked the bloom there. "As warm and vital as the sun."

"Sebastian," I murmured, because it was the only word I knew how to say at that moment, absolutely struck dumb by his sweetness.

"Linnea," Miranda called too loudly. "Put these in water for me. I don't want them to wilt before Bobbi can see them. When was the last time someone brought that old hag flowers, hmm?"

Sebastian bit the edge of his lip to hide his smile, but I gave in to mine, shaking my head slightly as I took my flowers from him.

"Thank you," I said, rolling to my toes to brush my lips along the edge of his jaw because that was as high as I could reach even though I was fairly tall. The texture of his inky stubble made me shiver.

His warm hand found my hip, branding me through to the bone. He tipped his head into the kiss, smoothing his own mouth over my forehead.

"Anytime."

"Linnea!"

I laughed a little breathlessly as I pulled away to grab her flowers, taking both bouquets into the kitchen. Sebastian stayed back with Miranda for a minute, but finally made his way into the back when I had finished cutting the stems and put them into a Waterford crystal vase Miranda refused to sell.

"You didn't have to do this," I told him. "But you've made her month, honestly. She loves pretty things, especially when they come from pretty men."

He chuckled, eliminating the space between us until he was right at my back. I shivered as his fingers traced my ear and the flower he'd set there then trailed down my hair to my lower back where the waves ended.

"I wish I could say I did it for Miranda," he admitted. "But I think I'm becoming addicted to your smile now that I've seen it in person again."

"You're dangerous," I said, sidestepping him because I couldn't breathe right with him so close, and I was frankly terrified by my crush on him.

For the first time in my life, I understood why they called it a "crush" because it threatened to annihilate you under the weight of it against your heart.

"I think you mean charming," he countered with a crooked smile.

"Did you just come over to flirt with my mother, or did you need something?" I asked, slanting him a look that made him laugh again.

God, I loved that husky sound and the way humor lit those sun-gold eyes.

"Actually, I was hoping to chat with you about something. Can you spare a few minutes away from her?"

I frowned but nodded. "Sure, let me just take the flowers in to her and put on the TV. We can talk on the back porch. Do you want a glass of lemonade?"

Something about that made his lips twitch. "Why don't you go to Miranda, and I'll pour us some lemonade? I'll meet you outside."

I swallowed thickly because I liked the familiarity of having him help himself in my house. Even if it was Miranda's, I had made it feel like my own over the years as much as I could, repainting the outside, adding charm to the cluttered, fussy interior. I liked having Sebastian in this space even though he seemed too large and lovely for the little house.

I placed Miranda's flowers on her side table and put on *General Hospital* for her, turning on the baby monitor I'd bought so I could check on her when I wasn't in the same room, and trailed out the back door after Seb.

He sat on the wicker loveseat, staring out at the little yard with its flowering bushes.

"You garden for her?" he asked.

I shrugged one shoulder and took a seat beside him, lifting one foot onto the cushion to hug my knee before accepting the glass he handed me.

"She likes having a pretty garden. In London, Wyndam used to surprise her with all these exotic varieties."

Sebastian stared at me for a long moment, his gaze so penetrating I thought he could see through my skin and bones to the secrets and dreams I had written in invisible ink on my soul.

"You're something else, *trottolina*," he murmured. "Which is why I wanted to talk to you. You promised that if I had a reasonable offer to make your life better, you'd take it."

I blinked. "I believe I said, if you had a *reciprocal* offer that would be good for both of us, I would hear you out."

"I have one, only it's not exactly for me," Sebastian admitted. "Do you remember our conversation about Adam? I told you that he'd recently been the cause of some…speculation."

"Yeah," I said slowly, trying to figure out where this could possibly be going.

"Well, without going into particulars before you agree to meet with him, he could use an image boost in the media. A contractual relationship with someone who would agree to be his girlfriend, be seen out with him going to events and dinners etc. until everything cools down."

I crinkled my nose. "Like a prostitute?"

"*Cazzo*, Linnea, not like a prostitute." His shocked and dismayed expression was so pure, it made me smile despite myself. "Like a fake girlfriend. It would help with the gossip surrounding him, especially when he is on the precipice of securing a role he has always dreamed of."

"The Daventry part?" I asked because while I didn't keep up with celebrity gossip, I did track film news, and it had been all over the news that Adam Meyers was up for the role of the iconic British spy.

Seb dipped his chin. "Yes. He's worked hard all his life, and he's *meraviglioso*, a true generational talent. He deserves not only the role of a lifetime but to be free of this gossip about his sexuality."

"Ah." I was shocked by the idea that Adam Meyers was into men, if only because his marriage to Savannah, and string of girlfriends since had been so well documented. "He needs a beard, then."

"He likes women," Sebastian said firmly, but the words carefully left room for conjecture.

He liked women, but he might also have been attracted to men.

Interesting.

"Do you have a problem with that?" he asked, his voice cooler than I'd ever heard it.

I met his eyes, noting the way his jaw clenched and his eyes went stale.

"Hardly. I hooked up with my best girl friend when I was eleven, and I've been attracted to all kinds of people my whole life. It would be hypocritical of me to judge others, wouldn't it?" I asked with my own sharp smile.

I was used to defending myself. When Miranda found out about my first girlfriend in high school, she had insisted I move to England to live with her and Wyndam. She said it was to better my education, but Dad and I both thought it was to split up Kaleigh and I.

Sebastian blinked at me, obviously caught off guard by my blasé confession.

My smile softened and turned sly. "Are you imagining me with a woman, now, Sebastian?"

He swallowed thickly but returned his usual charming grin. "Would you blame me if I did?"

"Just as long as you know my bisexuality isn't something performative to turn men on," I allowed. "I may be a two on the Kinsey Scale, but I've loved women before, and I could again."

"I do not think I have ever met someone so comfortable with themselves," Sebastian said, a thread of awe in his voice. "You must teach me."

I laughed. "You seem secure enough in yourself."

He shrugged one shoulder, twisting slightly so that his knee was up on the seat pressed into my thigh. "In many ways, not all. I try to be kind to myself, though."

"Me too. Life is too short and too frequently horrible to spend it hating myself for who I am."

"You know, I absolutely agree with you. Which is why I think you are just the woman to date Adam."

It was my turn to blink, so shocked by his proposition, my thoughts turned to static as my brain went offline.

Date Adam Meyers?

Four-time Academy Award winner Adam Meyers.

Once married to Savannah Meyers, with a history of dating

Hollywood's hottest actresses and models.

A man so gorgeous that he'd been voted Sexiest Man Alive twice and his billboard for the movie *Stranded* on Sunset Boulevard had to be taken down because the sight of him shirtless and wet in the Pacific Ocean had caused too many fender-benders.

Not to mention, he was thirty-eight, twelve years older than me and infinitely more experienced.

I may have spent one dreamlike afternoon with him in southern England teaching Sebastian and him how to surf, but it was an isolated incident. I never spoke to him before or after even though we were not infrequently in the same vicinity because Savannah and Miranda were friends.

It was a memory I cherished, evidence that a perfect day could exist.

"What?" I finally asked.

Sebastian bit the edge of his grin at my reaction. "I know it seems unorthodox, but you were the one to encourage me to help him."

"I meant buy the guy a coffee or lend him a kind ear," I spat incredulously. "Not loan me out to him like some benevolent pimp."

"Linnea." His voice was a cross between a growl and a chuckle, as if he was both appalled and amused by me. He took my flailing hands in his, smoothing his thumbs over my knuckles. "This is neither a joke nor some kind of scandalous proposition. This is me seeing two people I care about who need help and providing a solution. You would enter a contractual agreement with Adam to *pretend* to be his girlfriend, to appear with him in public, with the understanding that absolutely nothing sexual would occur between you. And in exchange, he would pay you and, intentionally and incidentally, help you with your career. Believe it or not, this kind of arrangement exists in Hollywood."

When I opened my mouth to protest again, he continued, "This isn't just about the fact that you—that *Miranda*—need help. This is also about your dreams. You are too young to have given up on yourself."

"I haven't given up," I bit out, suddenly furious with him. Wrenching my hands away, I stood to pace along the porch, needing the movement to work out my frenetic thoughts. "Life isn't easy, Sebastian, and sometimes you have to make choices. I made the *choice* to come to Los Angeles and help Miranda. I still go on auditions, even if it's not as frequently as I'd like, and I still work on my designs. We may have been friends for a long time, but only through those letters. Don't pretend you know me or what I most long for, all right?"

I finished, standing before him, the air too hot and fast through my lungs, a vibrating finger pointing in his face.

Sebastian only stared at me placidly, resting his ankle on top of the opposite knee.

"*Bene*, Linnea. Tell me, what is it then that you most long for?"

What an impossible question to answer even though I'd essentially goaded him into asking it.

I wanted to scream at him. I wanted to take him by the neck and shake him.

Love! Success! Security!

But a quiet voice, almost a whisper yet impossible to ignore, said something different.

A witness, it spoke.

Someone to be with me through all the peaks and troughs of life. To see how hard I struggled and strived to be better, to hold me when I needed a hug, to observe even those things I did not want anyone to know about myself and to somehow make me feel better about them.

Companionship was too tame a word.

A lover seemed too shallow.

I wanted someone to stand beside me in this cruel and glorious universe and never stop holding my hand.

I wanted *him*.

And Sebastian had just made it painfully obvious he was so uninterested in me romantically that he was willing to offer me for a fake relationship with a man he barely even knew anymore.

Pain and confusion tangled up in my throat and made it hard to breathe.

When I visibly struggled to find words, Sebastian dropped his foot to the ground and leaned forward on the bench to gently take my hands. He was so tall that even though he was seated and I was standing, I didn't have to look down far to see into those topaz eyes.

"You said to me that you do not wish to be alone," he said softly, his gaze searching my face for what I didn't have the vocabulary to say. "I understand that sentiment very well, and Linnea, no one knows that feeling as well as Adam. He has been alone for too long, and now he is struggling under the weight and scrutiny of a scandal that could take his only dream from him. I do not tell you this so that you will do this out of pity. I tell you this so that you know the two of you have more in common than you might think. That beyond helping two friends out of difficult situations, I am proposing this deal because I think it could help you both heal."

"I'm not broken," I said, an automatic argument because I wasn't.

I was a twenty-six-year-old woman with her health, her beauty, and her brains, a roof over her head, and a family back in Maui who loved her.

Sebastian raised a brow and then slowly lifted my hands between us to showcase the way my nail beds were ripped apart, some stained with blood, the others scabbed over. It was a stress tic I'd developed as a girl, picking at my nails until they were open wounds.

I didn't remember ever telling Sebastian about it, but wasn't that part of his power? That he could look at a person and see through to their underbelly, no matter how layered their mask was?

Wasn't that secretly why I had not told him when I moved to LA?

A part of me had known he would swoop in to save the day because he simply could not help himself from sticking out his neck for the ones he loved.

"He hurt you," I said, as a last-ditch attempt to get out of this deal that seemed both too good to be true and a horrifically bad idea. "I don't know if I can be friends, even fake friends, with someone who could hurt you the way he so obviously did."

Every muscle in Seb's body tensed for a moment before he gathered a deep breath and expelled it in a controlled exhale. "I have thought a lot about that over the years. The truth is, I knew what I was getting into when I agreed to our unusual arrangement. Savannah isn't the kind of woman to take no for an answer, but how was it going to ever end but in agony, hmm? I was an eighteen-year-old chauffeur, and they were married."

He shrugged as if none of it mattered, but his eyes were stale with old wounds. "Honestly, something about helping you both like this feels like closure. Like something good coming out of the bad. Maybe Adam and I can find our way to being friends again."

"Well," I said after a moment, forcing humor into my tone to mask the noxious mix of hope and fear wrapping strong hands around my throat. "You'll have to be if I agree to this. I don't intend to lose your friendship now that we are living in the same city, and if I'm supposed to be…" I wrinkled my nose. "Dating this guy, then you'll be around each other."

Sebastian laughed, a full-bellied movement that erased the unease from his expression. When he finished, his eyes were sparkling, and he used his grip on my hands to tug me forward into his lap, a ploy I was beginning to think was his trademark. I settled easily on his lap, though, looping my arms around his neck and staring down into that happy face.

"You know, most women would be falling over themselves for even the chance to fake date Adam Meyers," he informed me.

I would have fallen over myself to date him, but again, that didn't seem to be an option on the table.

I shrugged. "I grew up around celebrities, the only person I'll ever willingly fall over myself for is Taylor Swift. What I wouldn't give to meet her."

Sebastian laughed again, holding me close enough that I could feel the way the humor moved through his strong body. I watched him, brushing my fingertips through the short hairs on the back of his neck, and wondered how the hell I could ever pull off being in love with another man when I was falling head over heels for the one sitting me in his lap.

CHAPTER EIGHT

LINNEA

Affaire was one of the hottest restaurants in Los Angeles, but tonight was still absolute chaos compared to the norm. An up-and-coming rapper was celebrating his birthday in one of the private rooms in the back, and the daughter of a top Hollywood director was hosting a sweet sixteen in the wine cellar. The main floor, an opulent, French-themed landscape of red velvet seats and chandeliers, was packed with A-list celebrities and quiet money.

I had been gobsmacked when I got the job given that the hotel was part of the world-class Faire Developments Group, and the head chef was Etienne Devereaux, a three-star Michelin chef from New York City. The tips on the first day alone had honestly made me weep, and even though the hustle was absolute insanity each shift, I loved everyone I worked with. Serving celebrities was never going to be glamorous, but most of them treated me with polite indifference or cool disdain, and I'd only had to deal with the odd tantrum.

Besides, it was where I had met Rozhin.

"If Bob Henry doesn't stop staring at my breasts, my hand is going to have a word with his face," she told me as she swooped into the server's station with glittering dark eyes. "The uniform is hardly revealing."

This was true. We were required to wear black dress shirts and tailored black pants with heels, but Rozhin was blessed with a body like an hourglass, so she could make any outfit look indecent.

"Bob isn't a day under eighty-four," I said as I printed a bill and slotted it into a leather folio. "Give the guy a break. He's trying to live a little before he dies."

Rozhin laughed like I'd intended her to, bumping her hip into mine. "Why do I even love you?"

"Because I'm fabulous?" I teased with a winning smile, flipping my hair over my shoulder as I started to walk out of the hub.

"Because you make me pretty dresses," she corrected. "I'm with you for your clever fingers, Nea. Don't forget that!"

I was giggling, staring down at my billfold, when I crashed into someone on the other side of the wall.

"Oh my gosh, I'm so sorry," I gushed immediately, raising my hands to press against a decidedly male chest so I could catch myself from falling into it completely. "I apologize, sir."

I looked up just in time to see vivid green eyes darken, a sharp muscle ticking in a square, clenched jaw dusted with golden stubble.

My breath left me on a long whoosh.

Adam Meyers stood before me—against me, really—staring down at me with an almost murderous expression on his unfairly handsome face.

God, how unjust was it that men just got so much better looking with age?

The last time I'd seen Adam in person was a decade ago, on one of the last nights of his marriage to Savannah when she had called in my mom to soothe her, and Miranda hadn't had time to dump me at home before heading over.

I'd seen Adam in the kitchen at the back wall of windows looking out over the moonlight turning the pool water silver and limning the guesthouse in shadows. He had looked so sad then, I'd almost gone to him.

But who was I to comfort him?

A sixteen-year-old nobody who had only spent one beautiful afternoon with him.

The years had added handsome crow's feet to the corners of those vibrant eyes, a hint of silver above the temples in his golden hair. This close, I could find no fault with his beauty. He was perfectly symmetrical, his mouth wide and firm, his chin strong and slightly dimpled.

The desire to bite it was sudden and fiercely shocking.

"Linnea," he said in that posh British accent that made my name sound like a poem. "I was hoping to run into you."

I lifted my hands between us limply and offered a crooked smile. "Tada!"

His somber expression didn't even twitch.

I swallowed thickly.

"I would like to speak with you."

"Um, well, I'm working right now and we're slammed, so I don't think—

"That shouldn't be a problem," Adam assured me. "I'm seated in your section."

I blinked at him.

"Perhaps you could see me to my seat," he suggested in a way that made it seem more like an order.

I was surprised by the way it affected me because I was a fiercely independent woman raised by a father and three uncles who let me run wild most of my childhood. Male authority figures did not feature heavily in my life, and normally, I would have snapped at someone for ordering me around.

But there was something about Adam's cool-toned arrogance, a highborn haughtiness that made my pulse race with something other than indignation.

Of course, I couldn't let him know that.

"Usually the host does that," I said mildly before shaking my hand holding the billfold. "And I have to drop this bill at a table before I go to the kitchen and deliver dishes for a few other tables. I'll be with you shortly."

"You know, for someone so eager to be my paramour, I expected you to have a better attitude," he had the absolute audacity to say to me before turning on his expensive leather shoe and walking away from me.

A sound of frustration worked itself up my throat without my permission.

Who even said words like "paramour" anyway?

"Was that *Adam Meyers?*" Rozhin asked from behind me on a hiss. "Fuck, he's hotter than sin, isn't he?"

"I didn't notice," I said through my teeth. "You can take his table if you want it?"

When I turned to face her, Ro's mouth was agape. "Are you kidding me? I mean, hell yeah, I will."

I nodded curtly. "Great, have fun."

"I'm sure I will," she practically purred as I walked away from her to get back to work.

After dropping off the bill, I went to the kitchen to grab the entrées for a party of four famous housewives and then took the order for an elderly gay couple who came in to dine with us every Thursday. It was only when I was coming back from punching in their order that I realized most of my section had miraculously disappeared.

The housewives were gone, leaving only the lingering scent of heavy designer perfume in their wake. The newly set table of six was vanished, and three twosomes packed up, with only dirty dishes left to mark their time here.

What the hell?

Only my elderly couple remained, sipping on the champagne I'd popped for them.

And Adam Meyers.

He sat at the most discreet table in the restaurant, partially obscured from the entrance in a little alcove where the walls were studded with cubbies filled with candles. I could see him perfectly from my vantage point, and he was staring at me.

Looking extremely displeased with me.

I pursed my lips and stomped back to the server hub to wait for Ro, who swanned into the space a moment later, murmuring under her breath about fussy diners.

"What the hell, Ro? Haven't you been to see Adam Meyers yet?" I asked.

She pouted. "Oh, I went, but he had absolutely no interest in me. He said the only reason he was in tonight was to see *you*. Do you have something you want to tell me, Linnea?"

Goddamn.

"No," I said on a long exhale that blew a tendril of my long hair out of my face. "At least, not right now. Apparently, I have a bossy celebrity to see to."

Rozhin frowned at me, but I didn't have time to fill her in on the absurd events in my life during the past few days. Not when I had a feeling Adam Meyers would somehow find a way to punish me if I kept him waiting any longer.

He watched me cross the floor to him the way a big game hunter waited for his prey to trip a booby trap, as if he had always known it was only a matter of time before I was his.

That look set my teeth on edge and made something deep in the base of my gut ignite.

I ignored the fission of desire and set my face to granite.

"Did you empty my section on purpose, or was it the dark cloud over your head that made everyone scatter?" I asked, propping my fist on one hip as I stared at him.

"Perhaps you aren't as good a server as you think you are," he suggested mildly. "I've been here ten minutes without any interaction from you."

I wasn't an angry person, not really. When your mother takes up all the oxygen in the room, there is no fuel left to ignite your temper. But I found myself furious, then, staring into Adam Meyers's annoyingly handsome face, knowing that he had the upper hand because he was rich and famous.

"No wonder you need a fake girlfriend if this is how you treat people," I snapped.

"Keep your bloody voice down," Adam growled. "Take a seat before you cause a scene."

"I think you accomplished that when you sent my section away," I hissed, even as I reluctantly took the seat opposite him. "Everyone else in the restaurant is staring at us."

Adam snorted. "They were staring at me before you sat down, at least now they have something interesting to speak about. I paid for everyone's dinner and asked the general manager to pack up whatever had yet to be delivered. No one was unhappy with the arrangement."

A bubble of laughter lodged in my throat despite myself, a giddy giggle because of the surreal nature of the moment.

I was arguing with one of the most famous film stars in the world because he was a grump with no manners who wanted to date me to save his reputation.

And somehow, I was actually considering it.

"Sebastian told me that you were on board with this idea, but you don't exactly seem happy to be having this conversation with me even though you rudely interrupted my shift to speak to me," I noted.

Adam's mouth thinned as he adjusted a silver and gold watch on his wrist. Even though he was dressed casually in a thin, black cashmere sweater and dark wash jeans, there was no escaping his aura of wealth and prestige. Though, even dressed in rags, he would have been breathtaking.

"It's a good idea," he said reluctantly. "It's the 'you' of it that concerns me."

I raised my brows, propping my chin on my hand. "Of course, it is. Go ahead, then, list the ways I'm unsuitable to date The Great Adam Meyers."

I braced myself, feeling every atom close up at the thought of the coming criticism. Just because I was used to Miranda's constant complaints didn't mean I'd found a way to alchemize my heart to stone. I was too emotional, too empathic and raw to deal well with well-aimed judgements, no matter how hard I tried.

Adam's frown faltered for a moment as if he was surprised by my words.

"You're too young," he said and then paused, waiting for my rebuke.

"Or you're too old," I offered sweetly. "I guess it's a glass half full or half empty debate."

Even though I thought I was fairly funny, the Brit scowled at me again.

"You may be Miranda's daughter with some exposure to this world, but being tied to me opens you to an entirely new level of inspection, most of it unkind. I doubt you could last two weeks as my girlfriend."

"Sebastian didn't mention you were such a curmudgeon," I said mildly, trying to defuse the tension because Adam seemed set on convincing both of us that this was not a good idea.

There was an edge of panic and helpless frustration that I could sense lurking beneath his cold demeanor, which made my sympathetic heart reach out to him.

He lifted a thick brow. "Curmudgeon?"

"A bad-tempered person. A grump. Usually an old one," I defined with a saccharine smile.

His glower deepened. "I understood the meaning. I'm hardly old."

"But you agree that you're bad-tempered?"

He stared at me for a long moment. I'd always wondered if they used special filters on his films and photo shoots to make his eyes seem so luminously green, but even in the low, intimate light of the restaurant, they glowed.

Finally, his mouth twitched. Just a tic, but it softened his features and the tension around his shoulders.

"Sometimes," he agreed, leaning back in his chair more comfortably. "When I have good reason to be."

I drummed my fingers on the tabletop. "I hate to continue our argument, but don't forget I've known you for a long time, albeit at a distance. I know you're a brooder, Adam."

Another mouth twitch, one he curbed by biting the edge of his plush lower lip.

"You're not wrong," he admitted. "It's in my nature to overthink."

"It's not in mine," I said with a light laugh. "I'm fairly impulsive."

"So, it wouldn't be hard to convince you to agree to this… arrangement?" he asked, cocking his head as if he was making a study of me.

I shrugged. "You made it sound like I was going to beg you for the opportunity, and now you're saying you'll have to convince me?"

Adam had the good grace to wince slightly. "I was an arsehole. It's a defense mechanism. Perhaps you can understand that, given the current shite storm that is my life, I might be somewhat prickly."

I leaned forward without thinking to place my hand over his on the table. "I'm sorry to hear about your troubles."

He went utterly still under my touch, as if it was something threatening. After a moment, he slid his hand out from under mine and let it drop into his lap.

"Thank you," he said, a muscle in his jaw popping as he clenched his teeth. "What exactly did Sebastian tell you?"

I liked the way he pronounced Sebastian, distinctly British and very posh.

"Only that someone was threatening to out you in the press," I said quietly even though we were officially the only people left in my corner of the establishment.

Adam nodded curtly, his gaze distant. "Yes. While I have absolutely no issue with anyone's sexuality, I'm sure you can understand it would have negative repercussions on my career."

"Like losing the Daventry role," I said. "I imagine it's every British actor's dream to have a shot at playing the iconic spy."

"Indeed," he said. "Even if we start immediately, it might be too late to salvage my connection to the film, but it would shore up my defense in case certain things did come to light."

"I hate that you have to worry about such things in this day and age," I muttered. "It's absolutely ridiculous that who someone could love might affect their career. Why should anyone care?"

"Isn't that the age-old question?" Adam asked wearily, rubbing a hand over his chin. "It has always perplexed me that people are so afraid of anything other when the human mind was meant to be curious about things we do not know. If more people asked questions and were open to learning about the world and themselves, I'm sure we wouldn't still have problems with racism and homophobia and sexism. Tell me, Linnea, do you have a curious mind?"

It felt like one of the most important questions I would ever answer, so even though my reply was obvious, I took a moment to let the question settle, to look into Adam's guarded gaze and write the truth on every inch of my face.

"Yes," I told him. "I've always had an inquisitive nature. It's gotten me into trouble before."

"And will you let it again?" he quipped with a wry grin, opening his hands to reference himself. "I cannot promise this bargain will not be more trouble than it's worth. I can offer you money and fame, but it's a double-edged sword. You will be scrutinized by the public, stalked by paparazzi, and mocked in the media. People will say you are too ugly to be with me, that you are a gold digger or a whore, that I don't really love you, and I'm having an affair with this or that actress on the side."

"You don't really love me," I pointed out.

Adam leaned forward to brace his elbows on the table and reach over to take my hands in his. They were warm, a shocking ridge of callous under the base of his strong fingers as they curled over mine. I was utterly engulfed in his hold, transfixed by those long-lashed eyes as they seemed to unpeel every layer of my skin and muscle and bone to see through to the fabric of my soul.

"If you agree to this, Linnea," he said in a low, husky murmur that made my blood thrum. The way one lover spoke to another in the darkest hours of night tangled in sex-warmed sheets. "No one who ever looks at us would imagine that we are anything less than beautifully, wonderfully, incandescently in love with each other. You will be the sun I revolve around. All the press and the public will ever hear from my lips is that I am the lucky bastard who landed the love of his life."

I couldn't breathe.

Perhaps it was just that Adam was such a good actor that he could deliver the lines with heart-stopping poignancy, or that I had always yearned for a love exactly like he was describing.

Or maybe it was something more elemental—a base magic that passed between our clasped hands and locked eyes, a subliminal message that revealed something of both our truths.

Two lonely souls desperate for connection.

"And if I agree to this, Adam," I mimicked softly, turning my palms up so I could hold his hands right back. "I want you to understand that our love story might be a farce, but our friendship would not. If you want someone to play the part and leave you alone otherwise, I'm not the right girl for you. I can't pretend to love someone I don't know, and I won't defend someone as viciously as I plan to defend you if they won't tell me about the demons we have to fight against."

I paused, taking in the way Adam's lids had shuttered, his mouth a white seam in his tanned face.

"Can you do that?" I asked softly. "Can you be my friend? Or is it too hard to teach an old dog new tricks?"

His eyes flashed as I'd intended them to, and he automatically said, "Thirty-eight is *not* old."

I grinned at him in reply, and he shook his head at me, his mouth softening.

"Why do I have the feeling agreeing to be friends with you is infinitely more dangerous than agreeing to our fake relationship?" he asked warily.

My smile widened. "I can be a lot."

He surprised me then by lifting our conjoined hands to his lips, brushing them against my knuckles.

"That's exactly what I'm worried about," he murmured, not unkindly.

Something in my chest clenched and refused to loosen.

"Just promise me one thing," he said, dropping our hands back to the table and untwining our fingers. He leaned back to cross his arms, leaving my hands curled like dead bugs on the tablecloth.

"What?"

"Promise me, no matter what happens, you won't fall in love with me."

I laughed lightly but swallowed it down when Adam only leveled me with a cool, somber gaze.

"I mean it," he pressed. "Acting is my passion and my profession. It will seem very often as if I love you and am the type of bloke worthy of your love in return. That allusion is a lie, Linnea. I won't ever love again, do you understand?"

My gut soured at his sincerity. How could a man who stressed how young he was not understand how deeply wrong it was to close himself off to love for the rest of his life?

"I have no intentions of falling in love with you, Adam," I said after taking a moment to collect myself.

It was the truth, too. I was currently in danger of losing my heart to an entirely different man with golden eyes and a pure heart of gold.

I might be moved by Adam's blatant sensuality and authority, and intrigued by his broken, brooding nature, but there was no way I would ever get seriously involved in a very fake relationship.

I wasn't an idiot.

"I know you probably aren't used to hearing this, given you're famous and fairly good-looking," I continued with a wave of my hand as if those traits were meaningless. "But you are not actually irresistible." At his look of wary surprise, I grinned. "Besides, I'm not into old men."

"Thirty-eight is not *old*," he snapped.

When our picture appeared on the most popular gossip website, *The Backlot*, the following morning, it captured the moment that followed, Adam smiling faintly at me while my head was thrown back in belly-deep laughter.

CHAPTER NINE

ADAM

It was all over the media outlets by the following morning.

Adam Meyers has a new mystery woman.

No one had the time to figure out her identity, which I was grateful for, if only because Linnea had not yet actually signed the papers. We would discuss the particulars and our game plan when she arrived in an hour, accompanied by her lawyer.

And Sebastian.

My gut had been in knots since the moment I saw Linnea in Affaire last night. She looked nothing like the tall, gangly girl with bushy brows I remembered from a decade ago.

I had stood at the entrance, while the host fetched the manager for me, and watched Linnea Kai as she swept through her section with unconscious grace and a sway to her hips. She smiled easily and often, the expression bright enough to make me blink even from where I stood across the vast space from her. I watched as she laughed with an elderly couple, her thick mass of honeyed waves spilling down her back to the small of her tiny waist, her hands moving fluidly as she spoke. It wasn't merely her beauty that arrested me, but her animation, those large, expressive eyes and mobile mouth, the way she seemed committed to every emotion that churned through her.

Sebastian had a similar quality, a catching kind of passion that infected even the most reluctant soul.

By the end of the night, after surviving Linnea's sass and assertiveness, I knew it wasn't quite the same magic that our Italian friend possessed.

In Linnea, it was expressed as enthusiasm.

A bright, effervescent curiosity about the world and everything in it.

After she playfully agreed never to fall in love with me, Linnea had insisted she get back to work even though the manager had assured me it was fine if she took the rest of the evening off. So I'd remained at the table to eat dinner alone and watch her interact with customers as they filled her section once more.

I couldn't remember a thing about what I'd eaten even though Chef Devereaux was one of the best in the country, but I was left with a lasting impression of Linnea's laugh as she chatted easily with her guests.

A frothy giggle like uncorked champagne spilled from the bottle.

I wondered what might have happened if I had run into her organically. Maybe one morning when I was jogging on the beach and she was out surfing, or a night at Affaire when I went for dinner with Chaucer and Rachel.

But the train of thought hit an abrupt dead end. The brutal truth was that I had lost interest in romance long ago, and one look into those vivid violet-blue eyes would have been enough to tell me this woman deserved a love for the ages.

I had already let down someone like that once in my life, and I wouldn't survive if I did it again.

Despite all of that, I could not stop thinking about Linnea as I paced the kitchen, waiting for my ex-lover and future faux-lover to arrive. I had the terrible premonition that this arrangement was a truly disastrous idea.

"This is a fool's scheme," I declared for maybe the third time that day. "She'll be eaten alive in the press, and I'll be left worse off than I already am."

Chaucer sighed. "It's really not. And I hate to break it to you, Adam, but I'm not sure it can get worse than Oscar actually releasing the tape."

"I still can't believe you were stupid enough to make a sex tape," Rachel, my agent, said with a shake of her head.

"Oh, for Christ's sake, I didn't," I snapped. "If there *is* a tape, he filmed it without my consent."

"Let's get back on track. Linnea Kai is not some thirsty socialite or greedy actress desperate for fame," Rachel had said in her blunt way while spooning a ridiculous amount of beef and broccoli into her mouth direct from the carton. "You already shot down the three actresses Mi Cha suggested for exactly those reasons."

"Sebastian said she wants to be an actress," I argued. "Apparently, she's done a few guest appearances on television series and did a commercial for a soda brand."

Rachel rolled her eyes behind her thick-framed glasses. "Sure, but she's *from* celebrity. She knows what's up."

Chaucer pointed her chopsticks at me when I opened my mouth to argue again. "You know Rach is right. Linnea spent more than a year with Miranda Hildebrand in London, and she was a frequent guest at your parties. I never once saw her swoon over any of the famous and fabulous visitors. She's not fame-struck, and she knows how the industry works."

"Miranda was never exactly an A-lister," I countered, bracing my hands on the countertop to level both women with a cool look. "She might have a sense of things, but going from relative obscurity to being my girlfriend is a bloody huge leap."

"Agreed," Bruce said, the only one eating from a plate like he wasn't an absolute heathen.

I'd hired Bruce Chan when I first bought the Malibu house eight years ago, after coming across his account on social media. He'd blown up for the recipes he shared in short videos and his no-nonsense attitude around life and food. I'd messaged him directly, without passing it by any of my team, and offered him a job as my live-in chef.

He'd agreed immediately, only twenty-six at the time, but already annoyed with his flash-in-the-pan fame. He still made videos, and sometimes I was even a guest star, but he never interacted with his fans and didn't give a fuck about being popular. He was just a bloke who loved food and wanted to share his passion.

Hiring him was one of the best decisions I'd ever made. He might have been younger than me, but he was essentially misanthropic and grumpy, which suited me just fine. I liked having him around for his quiet energy and stalwart loyalty.

"So, we'll teach her," Rachel concluded with an eye roll. She may have been in her early fifties, but she acted like a snarky teen, which shouldn't have been half as charming as it was. "Why else did we hire Mi Cha Lee? We show her the ropes, meticulously plan your relationship timeline, and Bob's your uncle."

"You don't think people would see it as me practically robbing the cradle?" I asked. "She's twelve years my junior, for fuck's sake."

"Welcome to Hollywood," Rachel said with a wide grin, broccoli stuck in her braces.

She was an absolute mess in her personal life, but Rachel Hoffman was one of the best agents in the business, with only the elite of the elite in her clientele. I wouldn't have traded her for anything.

"It's bloody depressing that my life has been reduced to this… faking a relationship," I grumbled, pushing off the counter to continue pacing. I had already worked out for three hours that morning, and I knew Chaucer would literally throw herself across the treadmill if I tried to take another jog.

"Adam," Chaucer said softly, reaching over to take my hand in both of hers. Her riot of red curls was barely tamed by a huge teal clip at the top of her head, and her wide eyes were soft with sympathy for me. She was what I imagined having a sister might feel like, albeit a younger, annoyingly bossy one. "This doesn't have to be forever. You don't even need to marry the girl. A long-term relationship would work just as well."

"It wouldn't," Rachel rebutted instantly. "Weddings in Hollywood are like Get Out Of Jail Free cards. C'mon, people, if we're going to the trouble of staging this play, let's make it an award winner, huh?"

"You want me to actually marry a stranger," I deadpanned, my stomach roiling at the thought.

I had lived without a partner since Savannah left almost ten years ago, and the idea of living with someone now was repugnant. Being the solitary king of my own castle had made it easy to isolate myself from the world. Other than filming and press circuits, I didn't engage in socializing with my peers in Hollywood.

Or anyone, really, for that matter.

"You know Linnea, Adam, don't be dramatic," Chaucer scoffed.

"She was the teenage daughter of my ex-wife's best friend," I corrected. "I hardly knew her."

"She was there that day, though, wasn't she?" she pushed, as she always fucking did. "On the beach in Cornwall with you and Sebastian."

Silence descended at the table.

Rachel and Bruce didn't know the details of my past with Savannah or Sebastian, but they knew I shut down all conversation anytime they were brought up, and that only Chaucer dared to do so.

"She was," I allowed reluctantly, because I had not stopped thinking of that afternoon since I saw Linnea last night. The awkward girl had grown into a gorgeous woman, but that effortless humor and joy for life had remained. I kept wondering if Sebastian and I would have embraced the easy loveliness of that day without her there to facilitate it.

Rachel shoved her tablet across the counter so that Chaucer, Bruce, and I could see the image on her screen. It was a photo of Linnea and I from the restaurant, our clasped hands raised to my mouth for a kiss. Linnea's expression was soft with tender shock, and though the lower half of my face was obscured, my eyes looked kinder than they had in a very long time.

"If you need any proof that this will work, just look at the comments," Rachel suggested, flicking a nail-bitten finger across the screen.

@ADAMMEYERZFANDOM Finally, he dates someone almost as beautiful as him._

@LOWRIDER98 He can do better than some server *smh*_

@ANGELAWHITT Adam deserves happiness! He always looks so sad in his photos._

@BB48E A brooding Adam is a hot Adam, but I admit I'd give anything for him to kiss my hand like that. Lucky B_

@ADAMMEYERZFANDOM Anyone know who she is!? I need the deets of this love story!_

@BUTTERFLIESBETTY He has literal hearts in his eyes! Squeee_

"ADAM MEYERS'S MYSTERY GIRL IS TRENDING on socials," Rachel added. "People are thirsty for more of this love story."

"There is no love story," I muttered, scrubbing my hands over my face.

"There will be," Chaucer said sunnily, and when I looked at her, she only grinned. "Don't be such a sourpuss, Adam. Clearly, Linnea grew into herself if these photos are to be believed."

"She's even lovelier in person," I admitted darkly.

Chaucer and Rachel shared a look and then burst out laughing.

I looked at Bruce, who only shrugged. "Would it really be the end of the world to spend some time with a gorgeous girl?"

Something in my chest turned over at the thought.

Because *yes*, it just might.

I'd always had a weakness for beauty and those things in life that moved me even when I didn't want to be moved.

Linnea seemed threateningly able to do both.

Especially if she brought Sebastian back into my life.

On cue, the doorbell chimed throughout the house.

Rachel perked up, tossing her grey-brown hair over her shoulder. "I'll get it!"

"No way," Chaucer protested, shoving Rachel back down in her seat. "I will."

"Sit," I ordered curtly. "This is my bloody house despite what you two may think. I will greet our…guests. Rachel, please meet me in the office. Chaucer, text Boone Decker to let him know to walk over for the meeting?"

Boone was my lawyer, but also a good mate I'd met when I was shooting a film in Boston. He spent most of his time on the East Coast, but he was the only man I trusted to represent me when the shite hit the fan.

Chaucer nodded, but Rach waved a hand at my outfit. "You're really going to wear that?"

I was wearing a suit, which, granted, might have been a bit officious for a meeting in my home office, but it gave me the illusion of control in a situation that felt wildly outside of my comfort zone. Our lawyers and agents would be present, and Mi Cha Lee was due to arrive any moment. I wanted to strike the right chord so that everyone would understand exactly what this situation really was.

A business arrangement.

I chose to ignore Rachel, leaving her and Chaucer sniggering at my back as I stalked out of the kitchen through the living room and up the short flight of stairs to the entryway.

If I took a moment to breathe deeply a few times the way my therapist had taught me before I opened the door, no one was around to witness it.

My past and my future both stood together on the other side of the door, and truly, I had never seen a more terrifying sight.

"Adam," Sebastian greeted with a chin dip as he pushed his sunglasses up into his shiny black hair, revealing those golden eyes that had always taken my breath away.

"Hey, Grumpy," Linnea teased as if we had been friends for years. She stepped forward without hesitation into my space, planting a hand on my sternum so she could rock to her tiptoes and brush a kiss across my stubbled cheek. She smelled of summer flowers and ocean air. "Nice place."

I blinked as she stepped around me to walk inside, turning my head to follow her swaying hips in the short, buttercup yellow T-shirt dress that hugged her pert arse almost obscenely.

When Sebastian cleared his throat, I snapped my gaze back to his, heat burning across my cheeks at being caught staring like a schoolboy.

A small smile played at his mouth, but he rubbed it away with his hand as if he didn't want to embarrass me.

"May I?" he asked, gesturing toward the interior behind me.

I nodded but didn't step back as he walked through the doorframe into the house. It was a large opening, but Sebastian and I were large men, so our shoulders brushed as he moved by, and electric sparks erupted through me at the contact.

I followed them inside, closing the door so I could take a moment to ensure all my walls were sealed shut and my hatches were battened down.

I would not be charmed by the fresh blitheness of Linnea Kai.

I would not be drawn in by the nostalgia and charm of Sebastian Lombardi.

CHAPTER TEN

LINNEA

Adam sat behind a palatial desk wearing a bespoke navy-blue suit that perfectly complemented his golden-haired handsomeness. His expression was stony, his hands clasped over the leather folio on the tabletop, as if he were an executive about to discipline unruly employees.

It was ridiculously attractive, and I found myself rubbing my thighs together as I sat quietly in my seat across from him.

The room was crowded with Adam's manager, agent, lawyer, and crisis management representative, alongside Sebastian's agent and lawyer, both of whom had graciously agreed to represent me.

Even though the agreement was about me, I had yet to say a word the entire meeting.

The legalese and structure of outings, leaks to the press, and scheduled interviews being arranged were well above my pay grade.

Adam hadn't looked at me once.

Sebastian, on the other hand, had reached for the arm of my chair and dragged it across the carpet to be closer to him the moment the teams started going at it.

"How're you feeling?" he asked me quietly, leaning in to whisper.

"Like I'm hungry because I forgot to eat breakfast after surfing this morning," I whispered back. "And like these guys need to relax a little bit. We don't need every single thing scheduled. It'll be too obvious."

Sebastian nodded as he slid his arm along the back of my chair, his fingers tangling gently in the ends of my hair.

"Adam," he said, and the word had the same effect as a bomb, silencing everyone at once.

Adam, who had done an amazing job of ignoring us both, finally looked over with a coolly raised brow.

"Linnea thinks this is overkill, and I have to agree," Seb continued, gesturing to the women in the room who all had their calendars pulled up on their phones. "There needs to be some spontaneity and casualness to your relationship, or the press will sniff out the lie."

"There will be rumors that she's a beard," Mi Cha Lee agreed. "But they'll be drowned out by the narrative of the love story."

"It won't be a convincing love story if you plan to act like this when you take her on a fucking date," Sebastian snapped.

And suddenly, the tension in the room was a palpable pressure on my chest.

I wasn't the only one who looked between the two men with wide eyes.

Adam's jaw clenched. "Why don't you leave that up to me, mate?"

Mate, he said.

Like an insult.

Mostly because everyone there knew they were not mates

anymore.

They were almost strangers except for the pile of baggage sitting in one corner of the room.

"He's right," I spoke up, sitting straighter in my chair. "On both counts. In every photo or interview you've given for years, you look like some kind of Byronic hero. The brooding and pouting are sexy, sure, but it's not very fitting for a man who is newly head over heels in love."

Adam's scowl deepened. "I'm a rather accomplished actor, if you both did not know. I think I can manage."

"And," I continued as if he hadn't spoken. "I don't think we need all our dates planned out. Remember what you promised me at Affaire the other day? We might not be dating, but we are about to have a relationship that will last for some time…" I looked at his team for confirmation because we hadn't actually discussed the longevity of the contract yet.

"Three years," Mi Cha and Adam's manager, Chaucer, said at the same time.

I swallowed thickly, rocked by the commitment.

"Three years," I echoed. "We are going to be living together for most of that time. I won't be roommates with someone who wears a suit to breakfast."

Chaucer and Rachel Hoffman hid their grins behind their hands, but Sebastian had the audacity to chuckle at my dig.

I beamed at him and then turned it back on Adam, who was staring at me with unnerving intensity. "I understand attending premieres with you, and I'm happy to do that. Some dinner dates at celebrity hot spots, sure. But otherwise, I think we can agree on a set number of dates per week, and we see how we feel at the time about what we want to do."

"It should be public," Rachel protested. "That's the point of this whole charade."

"If she moves in within three months, they won't need to be seen out together as much," Mali Issah, my new agent, countered for me. "Premieres and events, the odd dinner should be good enough. People will be buzzing about the new girl in town, and it will do just as much for Adam's reputation as it will for Linnea's burgeoning career as an actress."

"That's what I thought," I said with a hint of smugness just to watch Adam glower at me. Riling him up was shockingly entertaining. "And I call dibs on our first date."

"Dibs?" Adam echoed, deadpan.

I nodded curtly. "Dibs. It will be public, but I get to plan it." When he remained silent for a moment, I added, "Aren't you *curious*, Adam?"

If I hadn't been looking closely enough, I might not have noticed the twitch of his mouth as he fought a smile.

"Fine," he agreed. "But I want us to get married."

The air whooshed out of my mouth so hard, I started to choke on it.

Sebastian dropped his hand to my back and rubbed my spine as I recovered.

"You didn't have to drop it like that," Sebastian groused.

Adam only smiled slightly, proud that he got me back for my callback to our conversation at Affaire.

"Do we have to?" I asked. "I feel like dating for three years is good enough."

"It isn't when you factor in an adequate amount of time for dating, engagement, and marriage itself without it seeming rudely truncated, and therefore causing even more rumors that could damage Adam's career," Mi Cha explained.

"Hollywood weddings are America's equivalent of royal weddings.

Everything in Adam's history will be effectively erased in the public memory after a big, white wedding to a beautiful up-and-coming actress who is a Hollywood legacy," Chaucer added.

I snorted. "I'm hardly a legacy."

"On that we agree," Adam said, and I couldn't help my slight flinch as the words burrowed beneath my skin.

"Linnea." I looked back at him to see his mouth had softened. "I only meant that you have more talent and drive than your mother ever cared to cultivate."

I blinked at him. It wasn't the nicest comment about my mother, but it was the bald-faced truth. And it felt monumental to have such a comment—a compliment—from a caliber of actor like Adam Meyers.

"Thank you," I said. "But you haven't even seen me in anything."

Adam pursed his lips, but his eyes sparkled. "I may have streamed the four episodes of *Swamplands* you guest-starred in."

Beside me, Sebastian made a noise of surprise that mirrored my own.

"Oh my God." I laughed, hiding my face in my hands for a moment. "Are you serious?"

Adam shrugged. "I already had Bruce hide all the knives."

I burst out laughing. My character in the show was a manic ex-girlfriend determined to kill one of the main heroes. She successfully stabbed him three times with a kitchen knife before he subdued her, and she went to prison.

I looked at Sebastian to share my laughter with him, but he was looking at Adam with such an obvious expression of tenderness that it felt intrusive to witness it.

"It's good to know you can be charming when you want to," I teased Adam, who smiled slightly and tipped his palms up in a modified shrug.

"Charming enough to agree to marry me?" he quipped.

"Not quite. Is it possible to revisit that part of the contract? I'd like to see how spending time with you goes first."

"I don't—" Mi Cha started to say, but Adam cut her off.

"That's only fair. I would still like you to move in within the next three months. Is that possible?"

"My mom is unwell. I wouldn't be able to move in until I found a place I could afford that could take her on."

"Unwell?" Mi Cha asked. "We'll need details about your family situation so that we can be prepared for any bad press."

"Mi Cha," Adam cut off. "Ladies and Boone, I think we can finish off negotiations without you. I will email you the changes to the contract, and Linnea can do the same."

"But Adam—" his lawyer, Boone, started to say.

"That sounds wonderful," Mali Issah said, turning to wink at me as she collected my lawyer, Etta Windsor, and swept out of the room.

Chaucer followed suit, basically dragging Rachel out of the room with a frowning Mi Cha and Boone at their heels.

Only when the door shut did Adam noticeably relax, his shoulders loosening, hands unclasping so he could rub one over his stubbled chin.

"Tell me about Miranda," he said softly.

Suddenly, there was a pit in my throat that I couldn't speak past.

Sebastian reached over to squeeze my hand. "She has frontotemporal dementia. Linnea moved here eighteen months ago to take care of her, but it's taken over her life, and Miranda needs proper supervision."

"Is it terminal?"

"Yes," I said, spinning one of my rings around one finger. "Eventually. Honestly, she's the only reason I even entertained this arrangement. She deserves better than I can give her."

Sebastian made a noise of disagreement in the back of his throat.

"And what about you?" Adam asked softly. "Don't you deserve better?"

I tipped my chin pugnaciously. "I deserve what I work for and nothing more. My dad taught me to be self-sufficient."

"So you won't marry me for my money," Adam said so dryly, it took me a moment to realize he was teasing me.

My mouth curled despite myself. "For Miranda, not for me. I'm happy with my life."

It was the truth. I was busy to the point of exhaustion, sure, but I had access to the ocean, a house to live in, and the love of my dad, uncles, and Rozhin. More than that, Miranda and her life choices had honestly made me wary of affluence. She had eschewed so much in the pursuit of fame and fortune, and now, at the end of her life, she only had a small house filled with stale memories, expensive trinkets, and an estranged daughter to take care of her.

"Well, money and sex are all I have to offer," Adam drawled in that accent that made my toes curl. "It seems you aren't tempted by either."

My mouth went dry as my vivid imagination took over. Those big hands on my body, that cool, authoritative voice in my ear demanding I bend and shape myself to his will, those long-lashed eyes dark with desire.

"Adam." Sebastian's throaty voice cut into my fantasies and changed their tone.

Four hands sliding over my skin. A mouth on my neck, the other on my breast. Two long, thick cocks to worship.

A violent shiver rocked my frame, and heat flared in my cheeks when I realized how obvious I was being about my daydreaming.

"What?" Adam asked innocently even though his grin was anything but. A wolfish expression that made him look capable of swallowing both of us whole. "I am just being honest with my future wife, Sebastian. You're not jealous, are you?"

Sebastian's jaw clenched, the knuckles of his hands white with strain as he gripped the arms of his chair. I wondered for a moment who exactly he was jealous of, Adam or *me*.

"Linnea is a beautiful woman," he said with forced calm. "But don't forget what kind of arrangement you are agreeing to. That's how people get hurt."

An undercurrent of something dark and painful spilled through the room, a ghost that hadn't been properly laid to rest.

"You know, as a condition of the agreement, you won't be allowed to date or sleep with anyone else for the duration of the contract?" Adam asked mildly, but he was looking at Sebastian as if daring him to argue.

Sebastian opened his mouth to do just that, but I didn't need him to speak for me.

"I can be discreet," I offered with a pretty smile.

Both Adam and Seb scowled.

I laughed. "Oh, don't go all caveman on me. I won't lie and say the idea of foregoing sex for the next three years is appealing, but I've been single for a while now. I know how to scratch my own itch."

I almost laughed again when both Adam and Sebastian's gazes grew distant, perhaps imagining just how I tended to that need. It sent a little thrill through me to know that both men might find me attractive, that either might be imagining putting their hands on me just as I had imagined it minutes before.

I was in a closed-door room with two of the most gorgeous men in Hollywood, one of whom I was going to pretend to date and the other whom I was desperate to date even though he clearly didn't want me.

Life could be such a bitch.

Adam cleared his throat. "If you're amenable, I'd like to help you with your career."

"I already introduced her to Mali," Sebastian interjected. "She will represent her going forward."

"Excellent, though Rachel is arguably the best in the business," Adam said, crossing his arms and managing to stare down his nose at the Italian.

On cue, Seb scoffed, "Mali represents the best young actors in the industry."

"There is something to be said for experience," Adam countered.

Laughter lodged in my throat at their repartee even though I knew neither found it funny. Their rapport was so obvious, a half-hidden artifact buried poorly beneath years of neglect.

"Did you have a monetary number in mind for reparation?" Adam's voice broke into my reverie.

I blinked because I hadn't really thought about an actual dollar amount. How much did someone get paid to pretend to date a celebrity?

"Why don't I mock up the contract with a number I think is appropriate, and you can let me know if it's acceptable?" Adam suggested when I was quiet for too long. "Talk about it with your lawyer, your agent, and Sebastian, if you must. But I promise, it will be generous."

"Okay," I said. "Honestly, I just need enough to be able to take care of Miranda."

Adam nodded, but he stepped forward with a calculating gaze to capture one of my hands, the same one with the ring I was twisting anxiously around one finger. I watched as he smoothed a thumb over the cheap collection of jewelry I had adorning most of my fingers.

"I think we can manage a little better than that," he murmured. "Perhaps something pure gold for these beautiful hands to match the gold of your pure heart."

"Linnea doesn't need gold to shine," Sebastian said, suddenly standing from his chair, tense and irritated. "Don't play the charm offensive with her, Adam. She'll know the real you soon enough."

Adam tipped his head to eye his old friend. "I seem to recall you found the real me charming enough."

Sebastian's flinch was so minute it was almost imperceptible, but his mouth slackened with hurt, and his eyes went flat like hammered gold.

"That was a long time ago," he said, his Italian accent especially pronounced.

The hurt between the two men was so palpable it felt like an electric current in the air before a summer storm, the hairs on the back of my neck raised in warning. If I exposed myself to it for too long, I knew I would be caught up in a tempest I might not recover from.

But I couldn't help myself.

Throughout my life, I had been a fixer and a caretaker. This was a consequence of both nature and nurture, given who my mother was, as well as my upbringing by my father, who had me when he was twenty-two and was the eldest of his three brothers, himself just a kid.

Now, faced with the broken connection between two men who had obviously meant so much to each other, I was incapable of leaving well enough alone. Something good could come of this situation for them that went deeper than saved reputations.

They had a second chance at loving each other, and I was going to see to it that they did, even if it meant braiding that broken thread back together piece by fucking piece.

After all, as a seamstress and a designer, I knew how to mend a tear so it would never break again.

"It was a long time ago," I agreed, standing up so that we were all out of our seats and arranged in a tight triangle. "But we aren't talking about history, we're talking about our future. Together."

"You and I," Adam agreed, but his tone held a warning.

Which I ignored.

"The three of us," I countered firmly. "Sebastian is one of my best friends, and he's in town for the foreseeable future to campaign for award season and find his next project. I won't be without him close to me, and seeing as you want me close to you, it seems as if we are a package deal."

"Linnea," Sebastian said lowly. "That is not necessary. I can see you without Adam being involved."

He was looking at me, so he didn't catch the way Adam's mouth flatlined just for a moment.

It only solidified my resolve.

"No, you are my best friend, and you are, for all intents and purposes, my boyfriend. If we want this to work, you two will have to get along." When they both looked ready to protest, I held up my hand. "This is a condition of my agreement. Take it or leave it. Sebastian and I are a package deal. Can you handle us both?"

A series of emotions flickered like a shuttering film reel across Adam's face. He was usually so stoic in person that it was easy to forget that he was such a consummate actor, that each expression could speak a thousand poetic words.

I saw heartbreak and sorrow, temptation and hope so bright it burned my retinas, like staring too long into the sun. Finally, he settled on something like tense resignation as he extended his hand to take mine.

It was warm and shockingly calloused, perhaps from the hours he must have spent in the gym maintaining that fine form. His firm grip shouldn't have been erotic, yet it was. I felt heat crawl up my arm like fire ants, lighting up my nerves in a way that was almost uncomfortable.

"Sebastian, too," I added, somewhat breathlessly.

The Italian man hesitated before stepping closer to slide his big palm over the top of our joined hands.

That heat deepened as my imagination—always a wild, untamed thing—galloped away from me. I watched as Adam and Sebastian stared at their hands—our hands—twin expressions of turmoil twisting their mouths, and I knew I had made the right decision for more than just me.

CHAPTER ELEVEN

ADAM

"Absolutely not."

"Adam," Linnea said with a bright laugh. "Don't be a snob."

"It's not a matter of snobbery, Linnea. It's a matter of safety. You have to be at least ten years younger than this thing."

She shrugged, but did not deny it. Instead, she stepped forward to open the passenger door of the car and gestured gallantly for me to get inside. "Your chariot awaits, kind sir."

There was no way I was getting into the ancient Jeep Wrangler in a truly offensive shade of yellow that Linnea claimed was her "baby."

"I think the number I proposed to give you in exchange for our three-year arrangement was *more* than generous enough to afford to buy yourself a working vehicle."

She rolled her eyes. "Yeah, three million dollars is overkill, don't you think? I told you, I just need enough to make Miranda safe and comfortable."

"A million a year seems about appropriate for putting up with my grumpy arse," I quipped dryly just to see her smile. "So I insist you accept it *and* use some of the funds to buy something roadworthy."

"I'll consider it," she said after a moment. "But for now, we have to hustle so we won't be late. Get in."

"Why don't we take one of my cars?" I suggested, walking backward with one hand in my pocket to press the button on my garage door opener.

Behind me, the mechanism whirred as the panels lifted to reveal the interior of the four-car garage. Inside, my Aston Martin DB6 Volante gleamed in one bay. The other cars within were more practical or flashy, but nowhere near as beloved.

Linnea, mouth open to argue with me no doubt, stopped before saying a word at the sight of the Aston.

"That's the car you had in Croyde Bay."

I nodded, watching as she moved toward the Aston because I hadn't been able to take my eyes off her since she arrived twenty minutes ago in black leggings that clung intimately to her hips and arse, and a tiny pink sports bra that cupped her breasts almost obscenely. Her shoes were the same bubblegum pink and matched the stitching on her high athletic socks. Even in workout clothes, she was stunning with an eye for design that made sense given what Sebastian had relayed about her love for making clothes.

She ran her fingertips along the glossy hood the way someone might touch a lover.

"A much better option than your banana wagon," I declared, moving toward her because I could not help myself.

I was used to being the center of gravity in any situation, both because of my career and because of the force of my personality.

Linnea wasn't forceful or persuasive, but I felt an elemental draw to her, the way a flower grows toward the light. She didn't demand attention, but something about her was magnetic.

"My banana wagon is named Little Miss Sunshine," she countered, bending over the driver's side door to look at the dashboard. "But this is a lovely car."

"You can drive if it means we leave behind your yellow death trap," I offered, surprised by myself even as I said the words.

I did not let other people drive me.

Not since Sebastian.

It wasn't just about control, though that was a large part of it. I simply couldn't stand the idea of looking toward the driver's seat and seeing anyone other than Seb behind the wheel.

I wanted to take back the offer, but Linnea was throwing her long, wavy hair over her shoulder to smile brightly back at me.

Bloody hell, I was fucked.

"Awesome," she said happily, straightening and clapping her hands together before making a grabbing motion at me. "Gimme the keys."

With a weary sigh, I went to the hooks by the door and pulled the key ring off before tossing it to her. She caught it easily, her bra riding up as she stretched overhead, revealing the soft underswell of one breast, starkly pale against the depth of her otherwise tanned skin.

My mouth went dry, and for the first time in ages, a rush of unmanufactured lust sparked through my blood.

Could I really spend the next three years with this gorgeous creature and resist my wicked nature enough not to touch her?

I curled my hands into fists and walked around to the passenger seat.

Linnea was already secured beneath her seat belt, adjusting the rearview mirror and then smoothing her hands over the wheel. There was a little self-satisfied smile on her lips like a cat that got the cream.

I groaned. "You just played me, didn't you?"

She laughed, and I found that I liked when she did that. It almost made me want to smile, too.

I frowned instead, irritated with us both.

"Aw, don't be grumpy that I manipulated you into letting me drive this beauty," she sing-songed, before turning on the engine.

"Where are you taking me?" I asked, ignoring the fact that we had spent a total of four hours together, and I was already letting her disrupt my routines.

No one had surprised me in years, and the sensation was not a comfortable one.

Linnea's grin was wicked as she pulled her sunglasses from the collar of her tee and slid them over her eyes. They were enormous and white, almost retro. They shouldn't have looked good on anyone, but she looked somehow right sitting in my vintage car with her golden hair streaming behind her and those glamorous shades hiding her eyes.

"I hope you aren't afraid of heights," she quipped as she turned the dial on the radio to a familiar pop song station.

"You do know we are meant to be seen out together in public," I reminded her.

"Oh, don't worry, people will see evidence of our date. Besides, I think you could use some loosening up, and if we just go to some fancy restaurant downtown, there is no way I'll get to know the real you."

The real me.

What a concept.

I had not made any new friends or true connections in years, as if my heart had frozen after the trauma of losing my male lover and my wife a decade ago.

Perhaps it had.

And that almost painful sensation in my chest now that Sebastian was back in my life, thrusting Linnea into it too, was the return of feeling to that essential organ.

"I am much less interesting than the characters I play on screen," I warned her, uncharacteristically defensive.

"I highly doubt that. Let's play a game."

"A game," I echoed.

"Yes, it's called questions. I can ask you anything, and you have to answer honestly, but I have to do the same."

"That isn't a game, Linnea. It's an interrogation."

"Po-tate-oh," she said, "poh-taht-oh. You can go first if you're scared."

I wanted to argue that this was a childish game, but I was curious about her, too.

What kind of girl changed her whole life to take care of a mother who didn't deserve her?

What type of woman agreed to a fake marriage with a grumpy celebrity for three years of her life when she was young, and gorgeous, and fun enough to find true love herself?

"If your mother and money weren't obstacles, what would you be doing right now?"

She hummed, drumming her fingers along to the beat of the music as we drove out onto the highway heading south.

"I don't think I've ever really thought about that," she mused, almost a little surprised. "Even before Miranda got sick, I had my dad and uncles to take care of."

"Usually that's the other way around, isn't it?"

She shrugged. "Probably, but my dad was only twenty-two when I was born, and his brothers were all still in their teens. I kind of feel like I grew up with them. They started a boat charter company when I was a kid, and I was helping them out before I needed a training bra."

A surprised chuckle worked its way free from my throat.

She was so guileless it was impossible to guard myself against it. I had spent years erecting walls against the kind of cultivated pressure of personas that abounded in Hollywood and back home in the aristocratic circles of my father, but Linnea's bright personality warmed me like sun through the woodgrain.

"I would be acting," she continued, weaving through traffic like an LA native.

"Television or film?"

"Film," she said instantly, then winced. "Not that I'm some highbrow who thinks one is better than the other. I just like the idea of the versatility, traveling to different places to shoot, and donning new characters every year. There has always been a great deal of sameness in my life, and I developed a craving for change. For excitement."

The words shouldn't have been erotic, but somehow, they made my blood heat. Change? Excitement? Those were things I was capable of giving her in spades.

If only our agreement allowed for a baser kind of understanding.

I thought of Sebastian's uncharacteristic snappishness when I'd flirted with her about that very idea, and my gut cramped.

He was attracted to her. That much was obvious.

Any man with half a pulse would have been. More than her build— her heavy breasts, the nip in her waist, those endless legs caramelized from long hours in the sun, curiously attractive feet ending in toes painted sunshine yellow—she had an innate sensuality that spoke like a whisper in the dark. It begged you to wonder what you might do to her and she to you in the deepest hours of the night with only the moon to witness your shared depravities.

The idea of Sebastian and her together was one I steadfastly did not allow my brain to conjure or else, I knew, it would be all I thought of.

But he was attracted to her and for some reason, he had decided that instead of dating her, he would offer her up on a silver platter to *me*, the man who had wronged him so terribly ten years ago.

Why?

The question plagued me, one of many that kept me up at night lately and left me irascible in the morning.

No matter the reason, I couldn't afford to enter into a sexual agreement with Linnea, even if she was interested, without potentially hurting Seb.

And I had promised myself a long time ago, if I ever had the opportunity to have him in my life once more, I would do everything in my power never to injure him again.

"Which is your favorite film you ever shot?" Linnea interrupted my thoughts. "Will you tease me if I say I loved you as Lord Byron? I'll never forget the way you delivered that line 'And thus the heart will break, yet brokenly live on.'"

A thin smile claimed my mouth as I thought of its relevance to my own life. "He was certainly one of my favorite characters, perhaps because of our shared love of hedonism."

Linnea's laugh was an abrupt cough of disbelief as she side-eyed me. "You? A hedonist? No offense, Adam, but you look like you haven't had a good orgasm in half a decade, and with a body like that, I highly doubt you're indulging in anything sinfully delicious."

She was right, in a way.

I didn't indulge in rich foods very often. I'd mostly given up drinking because of the pit of despair I'd fallen into after Sebastian and Savannah were gone, and for the last number of years, though I'd joined an exclusive BDSM club in LA, even my sexual hedonism had felt rote.

But that didn't mean I had stopped yearning for the pursuit of pleasure.

My attraction to her was a case in point.

"Maybe I'm such a curmudgeon, as you say, because I haven't had enough pleasure in my life lately," I admitted, grateful for the sunglasses obscuring my eyes when Linnea studied me as we waited in traffic.

"Well," she said after a moment. "We'll have to fix that along with your reputation, won't we, Mr. Meyers?"

Fuck, the sound of that—*Mr. Meyers*—was electric.

I swallowed thickly. "Unfortunately, the two cannot comfortably coexist."

"Oh, I'm not so sure about that." Her grin was as bright as the sun reflecting off the ocean to my right. "I think today is a good start."

"What the bloody hell have you signed us up for?"

Her laugh caught in the wind as she accelerated forward, swerving into the fast lane around a slow-moving van. "Tell me which film was your favorite to shoot."

"The Devil Cares," *I said.*

The movie I'd prepped and shot while living with Sebastian and Savannah. It would always be special to me for those moments I'd spent running my lines with Sebastian, Savvy's little feet in my lap while we relaxed in the living room after a long day of work. How Seb would grill me when I was just in the door about every aspect of production while pouring me a glass of wine, running a hand through my hair, or squeezing my shoulders as if he wanted to comfort me after hours of playing an emotionally taxing role. How—for a few sparkling, perfect months—both my wife and my lover had seemed incandescently in love with me.

The shoot itself had been good, with a great DoP and director, top-caliber costars, and, of course, the Oscar I'd received for my performance had been a career highlight.

But it was that collection of little, intimate moments with my loved ones that lived perfectly preserved between the pages of my life like dried flowers.

My attention was caught as we pulled off the highway and almost immediately into a parking lot before a long, low industrial building. To the left and behind the structure, I could see a handful of relatively small planes.

"Linnea," I said, slow and low, a dangerous rumble. "What did you sign us up for?"

When I looked over, she had already taken off her seat belt and was leaning forward to plant one hand on my thigh while the other popped the mechanism on my belt open. Her large eyes were a deep purple-blue, like crushed açai berries. Her lashes were long and curly. For a moment, I forgot entirely about my apprehension and wondered if it would be the worst mistake in the world to kiss her.

"Day one of Linnea's trusty guide to the pursuit of pleasure," she announced, tongue in cheek. "Today's theme? Thrill seeking."

"Hiya, Lins," an Australian man called as the door to the business slammed behind him, raising a hand to us. "It's lookin' like a crackin' day to take a sky dive."

"Fuck *no*," I snapped.

But Linnea was already jumping out of the car and running to the attractive, curly-haired blond man, throwing her arms around him in a way that made jealousy bite the back of my tongue, the metallic taste of it like blood in my mouth.

"She's not *actually* your bloody girlfriend," I muttered to myself as I got out of the car and followed.

But when she stepped back just as I reached them, I let instinct take over and curled a finger into the top of her leggings, tugging until she stumbled back into my side. Ignoring the look she aimed up at me, I slid my arm around her waist, palming the curve of her hip. The skin of her belly was so soft, the scent of her like blooming hibiscus and ocean air.

"Hello," I said, offering my hand. "Adam Meyers."

The man's eyebrows rose almost comically, his gaze darting between my possessive hand on Linnea's hip, her face, and mine.

"Ugh, *right*," he muttered, then seemed to remember himself and shook my hand. "I'm Gary. Sorry, mate, just a bit stunned Lins didn't tell me she was bringing a proper celeb today."

"I brought two, actually," she corrected as a door slammed somewhere behind us and the sound of feet approached.

I swallowed thickly, knowing without having to turn who stopped at my side and pressed slightly into my shoulder as they leaned forward to offer the man their own hand in greeting.

"Sebastian Lombardi," he introduced in that rich Italian accent I would know anywhere across any amount of time. "Pleasure to meet you, Gary."

"Pleasure's mine," Gary assured him, face lit up. "Couldn't'a picked a better day for a dive, I'm tellin' ya. Have you both been up before?"

Fuck no.

"Plenty of times," Sebastian answered. "I actually got my C license a few years ago."

"Seriously?" I asked, incredulous.

The idea that Sebastian and Linnea could find dropping to the earth from a great height *fun* was extremely concerning.

Seb flashed me that movie-star grin, all teeth and parted pink lips. "I had to skydive for my stunts in *Enemies Behind Closed Doors*, and I fell in love with it. You haven't skydived before, right? Not to worry, I can tandem with you, and Gary can take Linnea."

My eyes burned with the intensity of the glare I leveled at him.

"Or I could always take Linnea myself?" he suggested, as he pushed his aviators into his black waves, revealing those precious-metal eyes that seemed to pierce through the center of my soul.

"Absolutely not," I said.

"So we go together," Sebastian declared with a happy smile, turning to share it with Gary, who offered him two thumbs-up.

Fuck no, I thought again.

I didn't have a fear of heights per se, but I didn't fuck with them either.

"Linnea didn't inform me that this was on our agenda for the day," I said, but she cut me off, curling into me, pressing a hand to my chest and sliding it slowly, deliberately down my stomach to curl over my waistband, fingers dipping beneath to scratch lightly at the top of my groin.

A growl lodged in my throat that was painful to swallow down.

"I wanted to surprise you," she said, full mouth pouting, eyes wide with mock sincerity. "You're always surprising me, and I wanted to return the favor."

Oh, the bloody cheek on her.

I dipped low enough to turn my mouth into her ear as if I was giving her a brief kiss. Instead, I whispered, "Careful, brat. You're not too old to turn over my knee."

A shiver rolled through her, pupils dilated as she pulled back to look up into my face. "Are you sure you're not too old to make an impact?"

Without thinking, I leaned forward to nip the end of her nose in a little reprimand.

She scrunched it in response and stuck her tongue out at me. "Come on, sweetums, don't tell me you're scared?"

Yes, I was definitely going to get her back for this later.

"The Great Adam Meyers?" Sebastian asked with a chuckle. "Scared of jumping out of a plane? Now, that's a thought."

Gary, eager to be involved with the celebrities, jumped in, "That'd be hilarious, given you held your breath for like six minutes in the Jonathon Cross series."

Of course, he remembered that.

But holding my breath in the ocean, a place I'd grown up beside during my childhood in Cornwall, was not at all the same as diving into thin fucking air toward a very stationary, decidedly *hard* ground.

Sebastian's arm draped across my shoulders as he twisted slightly to face me. "On the other hand, if you *are* afraid, don't worry. I can take your lovely girlfriend up for a spin and return her to you later safe and sound."

These manipulative arseholes.

I smiled at Gary in a way that was all teeth and, apparently, fairly alarming, because he reared back slightly.

"I've been in free fall all my life," I said, and wasn't that the truth. "A tumble from a plane should be a piece of cake."

Forty minutes later, after we had been through the consent forms and education seminar, I found myself up in the small aircraft with Linnea across from me strapped to Gary's front. Sebastian was behind me, his breath hot against the side of my head as an assistant fiddled with the many straps securing me to him and my own emergency parachute.

Dread was a lead weight in my gut, the back of my tongue coated in acid.

"Adam," Sebastian said low and intimate, nose brushing my ear as he moved closer so no one else could hear us. "I have only seen you so afraid once before, and this is not worth your terror, not like that was."

"It's typically inadvisable to bring up someone's prior panic attack when they may be on the precipice of another," I snapped.

"Always so dramatic." He chuckled, and I had to pin my shoulders back to stop from shivering. "This is meant to be fun, Adam."

"I can't imagine anything less fun than this."

"No? Not even seeing me again?" Seb asked softly.

A noise like a protest emerged from my mouth before I could curb it. "Why would you even say that, Sebastian?"

"Maybe because you haven't seemed at all thrilled to be back in my orbit."

Orbit.

Wasn't that the word for it?

Because Sebastian's impossible universe had the gravitational pull of a black hole, and it was just as potentially destructive to my life.

"I just don't know what to do with you," I admitted, feeling oddly secure enough to confess the truth with the loud thrum of the plane's engine obscuring our voices and the press of Sebastian's body at my back. "I want you to forgive me more than I want my next breath, but I don't know how to make that happen, and I don't know where we would go from there. If I'd even float away after the weight of missing you and agonizing over you was lifted. If we'd even be friends at this moment in time. If I could handle whether or not we would ever be more."

A long moment of silence followed, and I almost laughed darkly because it took a lot to shock the loquacious Italian into silence.

Before he recovered enough to reply, Gary was beside us with Linnea.

"You about ready to drop?" he hollered over the engine and the roar of wind across the open drop zone.

"No," I shouted back honestly.

Gary laughed as if I was joking.

Linnea only reached over to squeeze my hand, strands of blond hair ripping out of her tight braid to whip around her face in the wind.

"Be curious, Mr. Meyers," she coaxed with a twinkle in her eye that might as well have been a gauntlet thrown at my feet. "Be brave. And maybe you'll experience some of that pleasure you claim to love."

I glowered at her, which only made her laugh as she turned to hand off her phone to the assistant.

"Can you take a photo for us?" she asked.

But the assistant was already nodding and taking the photo. We awkwardly shuffled in tandem to face the photographer, and I was surprised when Linnea leaned across to wrap her hand in the chest of my jumpsuit and tug me toward her. She was smiling as she pressed her mouth to mine and the pressure of that happiness sent a zing of electric current down my spine, reanimating me like a corpse under the paddles of life.

Behind me, Sebastian shifted his hand so that it was wrapped around my hip, holding me firmly as I shared a kind of kiss with his friend.

When we broke away, Linnea was still smiling, and Sebastian's grip was still strong.

"Let's go!" Gary yelled, and I was still so disoriented from the moment that I complied with Sebastian's instructions as we moved closer to the opening.

It was only when Linnea lifted her hand in the Hawaiian symbol for hang loose before disappearing out of the plane with a whoop that I realized what was happening.

"Fuck *no*," I shouted, but Sebastian was already moving, his laughter loud in my ear as he turned us and fell backward out of the plane.

If I survived and anyone asked me later, I would tell them I fell in stoic silence.

The truth was, I hollered as we free-fell.

Sebastian kept us horizontal. His body flexed into a stabilizing configuration above me. I remembered to mobilize my own body into position and then allowed myself to look down at the ground rushing toward us.

The ocean lay to our left, a bright cerulean-blue expanse that glittered gold under the afternoon sun, and directly below us was the patchwork of grey, brown, and green that made up Los Angeles.

It took my breath away, and not just because of my fear of heights.

The beauty of the earth beneath me, combined with the rush of dropping like a stone from the sky, alchemized something in my brain: fear and exhilaration morphed into something that felt an awful lot like peace.

No rumors were threatening a career I loved, no trauma or bad blood with the man tethered to me by straps and buckles, no future looming unknown and ominous as dark clouds on the horizon.

There was just this.

The calm at the eye of a storm.

I felt the wind rush past my ears, muting my hearing; the sun on my face and hands warming me in the cool draft; Sebastian's strong frame curled over mine, guiding me the way I had not let anyone guide me since I was a boy and lost my mother.

I closed my eyes, and, if I could have smiled through the force of the drop, I would have.

It felt like hours as much as it felt like seconds before Sebastian pulled the parachute, and there was a sharp tug forcing us upward before it relaxed, and we hung like a dust mote, floating slowly to the ground.

"It's beautiful," I whispered, as if the words had been lodged in my throat all this time and could only now emerge.

My voice sounded strange to me after the roar of the wind. Smaller than usual.

"It is," Sebastian agreed in that gorgeous Italian accent. "*É bellissimo.* It is good sometimes, I think, to see the world like this. To know that we are very small in a very large place."

"Perspective," I agreed because I knew now why Linnea had wanted me to have this adventure.

She was trying to shock me back to life.

Reanimate a corpse that had walked zombified through life for the past decade, numb and unfeeling but for brief paroxysms of remembered pain and passion on set.

"Yes," Sebastian agreed. "Does it help?"

With us? I wanted to ask.

But I wasn't brave enough to do it.

"Maybe," I said instead. "I think so."

"Do you see now, why I wanted you to marry her?" he asked, voice almost melancholy as much as it was firm.

The question surprised me.

"To help my reputation," I said, taking the safe way out.

The silence that followed was tinged with disappointment. The ground was drawing near now, a huge field of long, swaying grass that would be our landing zone.

"To help your heart," Sebastian corrected.

And I didn't know what to say to that.

When we landed a minute later, Sebastian deftly handled it while I lifted my legs and relied solely upon him not to kill us. I was still stuck in my own thoughts, trying to make sense of the state of my life. He undid the clips between our bodies before he dealt with the chute, as if he knew I needed the space now that both feet were on the ground. As soon as we were separated, I took a step away.

So I didn't notice that Linnea and Gary had already landed ahead of us and that Linnea had unhooked herself from the instructor until I looked up to see her sprinting across the space between us. Her yellow-gold hair, released from its braid, streamed behind her like tangled sunbeams, white-toothed, wide smile flashing as she pumped her arms.

She looked like she was running toward something.

A victory. A prize.

But I realized, as she was steps away, she was running to me.

I only had a moment to brace myself before she launched herself into my arms, twining her legs around my waist, laughter erupting at our contact like molten lava from volcanic rock.

I held this laughing, vibrant woman in my arms, her head tipped up to stare at me, and felt as if I were living in a dream.

When she tipped her head down, her violet eyes were still laughing, and her cheeks were pinked from the adrenaline and wind burn.

"Did you feel it?" she demanded breathlessly, long fingers plucking at the latch to my helmet before pushing it off my head, then removing my goggles so that nothing was left between us.

"Feel what?" I asked, my hands propping her up at her bottom.

A few days ago, this woman was essentially a stranger.

The daughter of my ex-wife's oldest friend.

Now, we stood in the center of a field in an embrace like seasoned lovers, and even though I *knew* it was fake, that Gary had Linnea's camera out to capture the moment, it didn't feel fake.

Not Linnea's blinding smile or the effervescence of her exhilaration.

Not the fact that she wanted to share it with me.

Or the fact that nothing existed for me at that moment but this sunshine girl held in my arms.

"Alive," Linnea called out, tipping her head back and raising her arms to the sky before suddenly dropping them to join her hands at the back of my head, fingers in the sweat-damp strands. She leaned close, forehead against mine, nose to nose, her sweet breath over my tongue as if she wanted to secret the words away in my mouth. "Like you've woken up from a very long sleep and it's time to live again. Do you feel that, Adam?"

Behind me, a body shifted, and I knew it was Sebastian's hand on my lower back before he walked away from us.

"Yes," I said on a small gasp as both their touches electrified me. The hairs on the back of my arms stood on end. "I do."

Linnea grinned, the shape of her mouth against my cheek, only her eyes across from mine visibly crinkling from the expression.

"Me too," she told me.

CHAPTER TWELVE

SEBASTIAN

I had started to check the tabloids and gossip sites each morning to see what the media was saying about Adam.

To see if my plan was working.

The morning after we went skydiving, a trending photo appeared on social media and was plastered across Hollywood news outlets.

Linnea held aloft in Adam's arms in the middle of a grass field in black jumpsuits, their golden heads the same shade as the dried stalks waving in the breeze around them. They were both smiling, foreheads pressed tightly together, but their expressions weren't for public consumption. They weren't forced grins after a stilted dinner at some celebrity hotspot like Spago or carefully constructed poses for the red carpet.

It was a real moment of pure, quiet joy between two people.

The public was eating it up with a spoon.

Adam and Linnea continued to feed them by going out five times over the next ten days. I knew, both from the reports and from Linnea, who texted me daily, that they had gone for a hike in Runyon Canyon, to brunch at République, for a walk along Zuma Beach, and twice to shop on Rodeo Drive. Adam bought her a straw hat from Dior when she started to get a sunburn, and the paparazzi captured the moment he took it out of the bag to place it on her head.

Most of the commentary was positive, especially surrounding Adam. People loved him in his films, and they wanted to see him happy in real life, even if it wasn't with them. A few said it was fake and a few more said Linnea Kai, daughter of washed-up actress-turned-socialite Miranda Hildebrand, was a hussy. A downgrade from Hollywood elite, Savannah Richardson.

But mostly it was good news.

So why did it make me feel sick to my stomach?

My plan to save Adam and help Linnea was set, both of them in agreement even if it had taken some convincing. If the skydiving date was any example, they seemed to be getting along well, and the media already had a couple name for them now that they knew who 'mystery girl' was.

Linam.

This is what I lived for, to help my loved ones find happiness, and this arrangement would solve so many problems for both of them.

So why did I have a white-knuckle grip on the steering wheel as I drove to pick up Linnea for our morning surf at Topanga Beach?

I pulled up to the cheery yellow house with something like dread in my stomach because I couldn't help wondering what it would have been like if this were a date.

What if I had been selfish enough to keep Linnea to myself?

What if I had been cruel enough to make her fall in love with me when I was unsure if I would ever be free of the sticky tendrils of a love that had snared my heart in its web at eighteen?

Because I honestly believed Linnea could fall in love with me.

We had been friends for years because we shared many of the same passions—film, fashion, good food, adventure—and there was no denying there was chemistry between us. A crackling energy I felt like a lightning strike every time I looked at her.

It happened then, as the front door swung open to reveal her in a tiny, yellow polka-dot bikini and a crocheted, white mini dress thrown on over top. I knew without asking she had made the dress herself because I'd seen the bundles of yarn when she'd given me a tour of the house the other day, a half-finished blanket for Miranda pooled in one corner. She wore a different set of rings today, always swapping them out to match her outfit. Today, they were chunky silver with the odd piece of turquoise and yellow jade. They clinked as she lifted her fingers to push her thick hair out of her face, blowing an errant piece off her lip-glossed mouth at the same time.

"Sebastian," she said breathily as if she'd run to the door. Her chest heaved dangerously beneath the tiny yellow triangles, and I tried valiantly not to watch. "Sorry, would you mind coming in for a moment? I'm almost finished with this dress, and I need it for my date with Adam today."

I nodded, but she was already moving down the hall back toward her studio.

She hadn't noticed what I held in my hands, which, I was discovering, was a lot like her. Just as she had been as a teenager, Linnea was always moving, twirling, hustling.

Trottolina, my little spinning top.

I closed the door behind me and wandered into the living room to see Miranda sitting in her usual chair, and a middle-aged woman occupying a spot on the loveseat as they both watched *General Hospital*.

"Clark," Miranda said the moment she saw me, opening her hands for the flowers I carried. "Good, the other ones need to be thrown out."

I bent to press a kiss to each of her papery cheeks. It still astounded me that a woman in her early fifties could look so fragile, especially one who used to be as bold and beautiful as Miranda.

"It's good to see you, *bella*," I told her.

She grinned, then shot the other woman a haughty look. "This is my Clark, Luiza."

"Hello, Luiza," I greeted her with a wink.

The woman stared at me, unimpressed. "Hello."

Miranda snickered. "Don't be offended, Luiza Ramirez doesn't go gaga over celebrities the way normal people do. The only one she likes is Adam Meyers."

I had to roll my smile between my teeth at the news.

"Understandable," I said solemnly.

Luiza sniffed and lifted the remote to turn up the volume on the television.

I coughed to cover my laughter.

It wasn't every day someone tried to get rid of me.

"Sebastian?" Linnea's voice called out.

"Ladies," I said by way of goodbye and went to find the woman I could not stop thinking about.

She was in her studio, kneeling at the base of a mannequin that wore a muted leopard print dress with thin straps and an almost corseted top. It was beautiful, especially when I considered Linnea modeling it herself. She was finishing the hem, a needle in the side of her mouth, another darting quicksilver fast in her nimble fingers.

I left her to it for a moment and took the chance to look at the sketches on the walls, the brightly colored outfits she envisioned. There were ball gowns and party dresses, a few more casual dresses, and lots of lingerie. The delicate designs were so complicated, I couldn't believe she would construct them herself until I came across a few samples on one cluttered table in the corner. I lifted a white corset with yellow fabric gathered like petals around the breasts and felt my throat click as I swallowed dryly.

"I'm constantly drawn to the feminine," she said by way of explanation.

I turned to see her standing up so she could remove the dress from the mannequin.

"It's why I mostly make lingerie and dresses," she continued. "I think there is something so inherently sexy and powerful about being a woman, and I love to emphasize that."

"There is," I agreed, a little hoarser than usual.

"Maybe it's because I grew up in a house of men," she said on a little laugh, pausing to smile at the memories. "They were so dirty and plain, I started carving out little female places for myself in the house. My room growing up was fuchsia pink, and the first dress I made when I was six was rainbow print. Hopefully, my designs are a little more elevated now."

"Your designs are beautiful, *trottolina*," I told her soberly so she would understand the truth of it.

She beamed at me, tugging on the end of one little braid. "Yeah?"

"*Si, certo*," I repeated in Italian for emphasis.

"Thank you," she said with a shy smile I had never seen before. "It's more of a hobby than anything, but it keeps me sane at night when I can't sleep and everything seems so impossible."

"If you wear your designs out with Adam, it won't be a hobby much longer if you don't want it to be," I told her.

She blinked as if she hadn't realized that.

"Oh, well…huh. I don't think I have time to act and start a fashion line." She laughed, shaking her head as if the idea of being successful at either was absurd. "But it is wild, the pull celebrities have over people. To want to buy something just because the woman fucking Adam Meyers is wearing it."

Fucking Adam Meyers.

Twin flames of anger and arousal burned in my gut. I didn't know what to do with either of them. The feeling haunted me as Linnea collected her things, said her goodbyes to Miranda and Luiza, and we drove off to the beach. It lingered even when I felt the cold slap of water against my hands and face as I paddled out beyond the break with her and ruined each wave I took to the shore, no matter how well I rode it.

I knew I wouldn't be able to purge the poison of jealousy and confusion until I returned to my hotel room and pulled out a pen or cracked open my laptop. This was the kind of emotional congestion that could only be untangled by writing the words on a page.

Linnea sensed my mood and gave me space for it, only smiling at me as we sat in the pocket briefly before cutting out on our own waves.

The intimacy of her knowing me well enough to leave me be, the quality of that understood silence between us, only made me sink deeper into my melancholy.

By mutual decision, we only stayed out for an hour until the sun was a full golden coin above the horizon and the beach started to populate with more than just morning joggers.

We didn't speak as we waded through the frothy surf with our boards, or when we shucked our wetsuits and rinsed off in the outdoor showers.

But I could feel her eyes on me, though mine were closed under the spray of water. The touch of her gaze at the long muscles arrowing from my hips to groin, where my snug navy swim shorts left little to the imagination. For a second, I turned my body, reaching my arms up to run through my hair so that my muscles flexed and twisted, my abdominals stepping out like ladder rungs on either side of my belly, my biceps swollen.

I was rewarded with a little gasp, near inaudible over the splash.

I had to turn my back to her to hide my mean, triumphant grin.

And it was mean because I felt mean and had all morning.

A greedy, irascible voice in my head kept snarling *mine, mine, mine.*

I wanted Linnea with me.

At my side on a hike in Runyon Canyon, jogging down Carbon Beach, at some fancy dinner at a place like Spago.

And I wanted Adam there, too.

It was as gluttonous a desire as it was an absurd one.

I'd thrown Linnea in Adam's path so he would not be outed as bisexual to the press.

There was no room for *me* in *them.*

In Linam.

I was alone on the outside as I'd always been.

My fists clenched on my towel so tightly I tore the edge with a loud rip.

Linnea watched me, but I refused to look up at her.

I was raw, my skin washed away by the brine of the sea, by the heat of her looking at me and seeing through into what lay inside.

The car door slammed shut behind me after I strapped our boards to the roof, and my fingers squeaked on the wheel as I gripped it too tightly.

She let me stew, singing along softly—poorly—to the playlist she played through Bluetooth as we drove through Los Angeles toward Malibu. I had agreed to drop her off at Adam's and viciously regretted it now.

My finger jammed into the intercom at the gate, and I grunted out my name when the speaker came on, pulling into the opening gate too fast.

Linnea didn't say a word, but I could see her fingers drumming on her thigh.

Adam's big, beautiful house came into view, and I hated that, too, because it was exactly the kind of house I would have chosen for myself. Most of it was pale gold stone, styled almost like an Italian villa but from the modern touches that carved huge sections of the house into unblemished panes of glass and black millwork. It was both modern and classic, gorgeous and sophisticated.

I had been house shopping in Los Angeles nearly every time I came out to film or do a press circuit for years, yet I had never found a house that called to me the way this one had.

Of course, Adam had been the one to find it.

Yet another thing that should have been mine that he had first.

I put the car into park so brutally it ground the gears.

Dio mio, I scolded myself as I raked my hair back through my damp, salty hair, *get a grip*.

Without thinking, I twisted to take in Linnea because I knew she was the perfect anchor.

She sat with one bare foot up in the seat, an arm wrapped loosely around her slim, browned leg, her hair a wet, waving mass around her shoulders. I could only see a sliver of her profile as she stared out the window at the front of the house, the rounded tip of her nose, the ridge of her full, petal-pink mouth, and the thick fringe of her spiky lashes.

Even so, she was beautiful.

Even turned away from me and toward the other man waiting for her on the opposite side of the door.

Stay, I wanted to say with such suddenness I almost gave in to the urge, *stay here with me.*

For the day? she might have said.

Forever, I could tell her.

I had decided too late that this was one toy I did not want to share with others, one part of my life I wanted selfishly to guard for myself.

All my life I'd sacrificed for my family, given everything to my mother and sisters, to Savannah and Adam.

Cazzo, I was tired of it.

Linnea turned her head against the seat to catch me looking at her, but she didn't seem surprised by it.

"Done brooding?" she teased lightly.

I huffed out a surprised chuckle.

"It's not a good look on you," she continued blandly. "You should leave it to Adam."

Another laugh, this one from the belly.

Oh, she could light me up. Every corner. Even the ones that hadn't seen the light in years.

My stomach twisted with regret, a feeling that was alien to me.

Even after everything ended so cataclysmically with Savannah and Adam, I'd had no regrets about any of it. Of course, I would always wish it had turned out differently, but loving them, even for a short time, had fundamentally changed me. I was the man I was today because of that year in London.

If I could go back, I would still flirt with my *duchessa* in the back seat of the Rolls-Royce. I would still follow Adam to the car in the back alley, rife with confused, irritated arousal. I would still give them both my heart in cupped palms.

So I wasn't used to the sensation of sour-bitter regret on the back of my tongue as I thought about arranging for Linnea to date Adam.

Why couldn't I, just once, have someone love me? Want me?

Why did I have to set it up so that was not even a possibility?

Did a part of me—fetid and small, a result of a father who had never loved or cared for me, a childhood full of poverty and uncertainty, of a mother who cried herself to sleep too often—believe I wasn't worthy of happiness?

Did the artist in me trick my mind into thinking I had to suffer to create art?

I startled at the soft press of Linnea's thumb over the crease between my brows. She was up on her knees in the seat, bent at the waist over the console to reach me. Her hair had shifted forward over her arms, close enough to smell the salt of the sea caught in the strands. But it was her eyes that I fixated on, almond-shaped and that unique shade of indigo that seemed otherworldly.

"Hey," she whispered as if she felt the bubble around us, knew that the reality was suddenly very far away. "You're doing it again. What has you frowning like that?"

Words raced up my throat, and I had to glue my tongue to the roof of my mouth so that they wouldn't all tumble out into her lap.

Instead, I swallowed thickly and shook my head slightly.

Her fingers traced over one brow and down the side of my face to cup my cheek. I leaned into the pressure, almost purring when she rubbed a thumb along the rasp of my stubble.

A little smile flickered at the edge of her mouth, but her eyes were questing around my features, searching for answers.

"Sometimes, I could glimpse your heartbreak out of the corner of my eye, but like a ghost, it disappeared every time I tried to look at it head-on. Until today. What happened?"

"You," I said, the one syllable carving up my throat and over my tongue like a blood offering. My hand found her wrist, shackling it so she would not stop touching me.

She was a grounding rod when everything I felt was lightning.

"Me?" she asked, rearing back a little. "Have I done something wrong?"

My throat ached with the need to tell her everything, every chapter of my story, no matter how sad or shameful. I wanted to curl up in her lap like a fucking kitten and have her pet me.

I wanted to kiss her so badly it felt like life or death.

"Nothing," I whispered, because my chest was caving in. "Only making me want you when you aren't mine to want."

Her eyes widened almost comically, the sunlight catching the pupils and turning them to amethysts.

"What?" she breathed, her hand spasming against my cheek.

I held her tighter against my face with one hand while the other reached up to tunnel under her heavy, damp hair so I could palm the expanse of her neck. Her pulse throbbed under my thumb.

"I have not wanted this badly in years," I admitted, my accent thicker than it should be, so I gave in to the Italian bubbling up from my gut. "*Quando ti guardo, ti voglio.* When I think of you, I want you."

Linnea's shaky exhale warmed my mouth. "Why didn't you say anything?"

"I don't have anything left of my heart to give," I confessed, even as I dropped her wrist to swipe a thumb over her plush lower lip. "If I did, I would have asked you to take it."

"Sebastian," she breathed, tipping her face closer, a flower seeking the light.

And I had always had a weakness for flowers, for beautiful things needing warmth and love to grow because I was the very same way.

So I lowered my mouth and met her halfway.

The first brush of our lips was suede against suede, such a soft slide I almost couldn't feel her.

That would not do.

A soft growl worked loose from my throat, and I used the hand on her neck to press her more deeply into me, angled so I could swipe my tongue along the seam of her lips and taste the cavern of her mouth.

Warm, wet, and flavored like the sea.

I groaned, or she did, before our tongues were sliding hotly against each other, curving and rubbing and tasting every inch available to us.

I was so hard so suddenly that it hurt, my cock an iron pole down the leg of the grey sweatpants I'd changed into, only a thin cotton barrier between it and the hand Linnea had planted on my thigh to lean closer.

Rational thought fled like a gazelle chased by a predator until I felt more animal than man. I moved the hand on the base of Linnea's neck up into the damp, silken strands at the base of her skull and fisted my fingers, tugging her head back so I could plunder her more deeply.

Her moan shivered from her tongue to mine, and I swallowed it down.

I wanted to undo the strings of the wet bikini she still wore and lick the sea salt off her heavy breasts until her nipples puckered and reddened. I wanted to suck marks into her long, golden neck and rub stubble burn in the valley of her chest like a map of everywhere I'd touched. I wanted to fix my teeth to the curve of her shoulder and bite hard enough to bruise.

And I wanted Adam to see it all.

To know I wanted her, I'd had her, some part of her was *mine*.

But also, that some part of her could be his.

That some part of me had been and would always be his as well.

What the two of us could do to this golden girl in the velvet fold of night, when the outside world faded away and sins could flourish like creatures in the dark.

"You're intoxicating," I told her, before sucking her full bottom lip between my teeth.

"So are you," she said instantly, pressing even deeper into me so that she was almost straddling the console, one knee on my thigh, her hard nipples rubbing against my chest. "I could get drunk off this. Off you."

I pulled her head back with a sharp little pull that made her mouth fall open on a gasp, showcasing kiss-swollen lips and flushed cheeks. Her eyes fluttered open, revealing blown pupils that spoke even more eloquently than her words.

She wanted me.

Did that make this so much better or worse?

Before I could decide, there was a loud bang from outside the car.

Like guilty teenagers caught necking after curfew, Linnea and I sprang apart. She fell ungracefully into her seat, her long legs akimbo, so that when the passenger door suddenly opened, she fell out backward first.

Only to be caught in the strong arms of Adam Meyers.

Who lifted her deftly to her feet, holding her close as he did so, though his eyes were pinned to me.

And he was glowering as fiercely as I'd ever seen him.

For one crystal-clear moment, it was evident he was on the edge of violence, and if I breathed wrong, he would launch himself at me, looking for blood.

I just couldn't tell if he was angry because I had kissed his fake girlfriend, or if, perhaps wishful thinking, he was angry that she had kissed *me.*

CHAPTER THIRTEEN

ADAM

"Why is this so hard for you to admit?" my therapist, Dr. Eng, asked me. "It's okay to like her, Adam."

"You see, that's not the point of this facade at all," I said, opening and closing my hands fruitlessly as I sought to explain my frustration. "The point is not to *like* Linnea Kai. It's to use her to erase the mark Oscar Hampton tried to taint my reputation with."

"Let's reframe that, shall we?" Dr. Eng said firmly. "Being gay or bisexual is not a 'taint.' It is, in fact, very natural and very beautiful."

"Right," I murmured, properly chastened. We had been working on my language around my queerness, reworking how I viewed it outside of the bigoted context of my father and upbringing, and the fear that had been sown when my uni mate, Gregory, had committed suicide after being outed as gay. "I only meant Oscar was trying to end my career with a sex scandal and force me to come out in a traumatic way."

"Better," she acknowledged kindly.

Dr. Eng was one of the best in the business and was referred to me by Prince Arthur Whitley-Fairfax himself. We met over Zoom once a week, and I didn't mind that the sessions were remote because Dr. Eng's Britishness was essential in helping me understand some of my childhood hang-ups.

"Even if the point is to use this relationship to protect your reputation, is it such a bad thing if you happen to like the woman you are using to do it?" she pressed.

And it felt like that, pressure on a bruise. I wanted to wince but kept my expression smooth.

Yes, it bloody well mattered if I liked Linnea.

Because she wasn't the kind of girl one simply *liked*.

She was the kind of girl you bought flowers for because her beauty reminded you of her smile. She was the girl you went home after your first kiss believing she would be your last.

She was sunlight and laughter and the first smooth dive into cool, clean lake water.

And she was being wasted on a man like me.

Three years of her life shackled to this false love.

Only, she didn't treat it like a prison sentence or what it was—martyrdom in order to give her mother a better end-of-life experience, even when Miranda had been a shite parent all her life. She approached each day with me like an adventure, bouncing over to me with a smile and leaning in close to whisper, "Come on, Adam, aren't you *curious*? Let's go."

And every time she uttered that word—*curious*—I found myself gritting my teeth against the flare of arousal in my gut.

She was so different from Savannah and the hurts I associated with her that it was hard to remember I had sworn off serious relationships with *anyone.*

Even beautiful girls with violet eyes and blindingly bright dispositions.

"Adam," Dr. Eng called, pulling my focus back to her. "It's okay to find some happiness in this shite storm. It's okay to feel happiness at any time in any given situation. As a matter of fact, I thought we spoke about you making happiness a mindful practice."

I fought the urge to roll my eyes and succeeded because I had been in therapy for enough years to realize that self-care wasn't erroneous, even if I'd been raised to think it was self-indulgent laziness.

"Working on it," I agreed.

"Our time is up, but I want you to make a promise to yourself right now. Let Linnea make you smile. It may be cliché, but the best medicine is often good company."

I sat in my office chair after we rung off, staring at the photo I rarely took out from the locked drawer in my desk. It was a photo of Sebastian, Linnea, and me from my twenty-ninth birthday on Croyde Beach, the surprise outing Seb had organized in the wake of a godawful row with Savannah. We had taken the selfie on my phone, and it was only later—much, much later, after Sebastian had left because I'd asked him to, and Savannah had left even though I'd asked her not to—that I'd stumbled upon it. Immediately, I had thought to delete it. Phones could be hacked, and often were. There was no point in risking myself with a photo like that after conjecture about my sexuality started from a photo of Sebastian and me on that very day.

But every time I touched my finger to the small trash bin icon, I found myself paralyzed. As if my body was staging a rebellion against my mind and would not, under any circumstances, bend to the directive to erase the evidence of the greatest love story I'd ever had.

Instead, I printed off a single copy and refused to look at it unless my heart ached so acutely, nothing else would curb the pain.

So I looked at it now. The wide, full-lipped smile on Sebastian's mouth, creasing his cheeks and the skin beside those vivid yellow-gold eyes. Linnea, once the least interesting thing about the capture, now stole my focus with the force of her grin, her eyes almost Crayola purple against the backdrop of the Cornish Sea. The relaxed set of my shoulders as I slung an arm around them both and grinned like a boy into the camera. It was that expression that held me arrested most often, not the look of my lost love, but the look of *me* in love.

It was dazzling.

And I had not seen such a look on my face for a decade until Chaucer handed me the photo of Linnea, Sebastian, and me from the skydiving experience. It wasn't the one they put in most of the papers, of Linnea in my arms, our bodies curved like two sides of a heart into each other. This was the one Gary had taken just afterward, when Sebastian had finished tending to the parachute and rejoined us both. Linnea had slipped from my arms to pull Seb in by the hand, hugging him while still holding on to me so that we were gathered in a kind of clutch that wasn't quite an embrace, but somehow was. I was still breathless with adrenaline and excitement, which was probably why I reached out myself, pulling Seb into my side with an arm around his shoulders, while the other tucked around Linnea's narrow waist to grip her hip and pull her in tight. They both curled into me, light and dark bookends with their faces turned away. Only my face was open to the photographer, and the recognition of my own expression hit me like a fist to the chin.

I was dazzling.

Lips parted over teeth, the dimple in my chin pronounced from the force of my grin, eyes green as the flash before the sun sets on the horizon.

Happiness, they called it.

But happiness could be a poison, just as hope could be.

Both sensations buoyed me for the next week, through my dates with Linnea, where she was vivacious enough to bring me to life, through my nights alone, when I thought of having her in my life, and him.

Always him.

I had something to look forward to outside of work now, and it was strange and beautiful and scary as fucking hell.

So I wasn't braced properly for the sight that awaited me when I pulled open my door after buzzing someone through the gates.

Sebastian's rented Lamborghini SUV idled in front of the house, the passenger side window open to reveal an unmitigated view of my ex-lover holding Linnea with a fist in the back of her rumpled, gold hair in order to pin her at the perfect angle for a luscious kiss.

The sight of it seared down my spinal column like a hot blade, cutting me in two. I could not make sense of the pain, the shock of it blurring all the details. It could have been jealousy, that Sebastian could kiss her like that or that she could kiss him at all, the man who was so totally off-limits to me. It could have been bitterness or betrayal. Some of it had to be self-hatred, the lash-whip of recrimination I inflicted on myself because I wasn't fucking brave enough to take what I wanted and consequences be damned.

I'd seen what the consequences had done to my uni mate, Gregory, and again when the paps released those slightly too intimate photos of Sebastian and me at Croyde Beach to the press. The consequences meant I lost not only Sebastian but also Savannah.

My jaw clenched so hard that all I could hear was the grind of my molars.

As a man who prided himself on cool, rational thought, I was caught completely unaware by the ferocious impulse to stop what was happening by any means possible. I was storming from the house before I even realized I was moving, the door slamming shut in my wake.

The loud noise prompted the kissers—lovers?— to spring apart as if they knew they had reason to be guilty.

Even though, despite the way it burned through me, I knew they didn't.

They were perfectly free to be together.

Maybe not contractually, given that Linnea had agreed not to have any indiscretions while we were engaged in this farce of a romance.

But emotionally? Nothing was stopping them from falling in love.

They'd known each other, been friends, for a long time, and even looking at them together in the clinch electrified me so I could only wonder at the alacrity of passion it set off in them both. They were, admittedly, well-suited in many ways.

So why was I watching my own hand reach out to rip open the passenger door just in time to catch Linnea as she spilled out of the car? Why was I hauling her up into my arms in a bridal carry, her long, smooth legs draped over one arm, her side tucked safely into mine?

And why, even with her secured in my arms, was that ravenous, greedy beast that had taken over my brain not satisfied?

Why did it long to haul Sebastian to me as well?

"Adam," Sebastian said my name in a choked-off rasp, and I noticed his mouth was ruddy from their kiss.

I wanted to kiss those swollen lips, chase the taste of them both on his tongue.

My jaw clicked as I ground my back teeth.

"Come inside," I ordered, shocked by the gravel in my voice.

Seb swallowed thickly but nodded.

I turned on my heel, carrying Linnea easily despite her height. Some part of me was surprised by her silence, and even more surprised by the way she pressed her cheek to my chest and let herself be swept into the house and deposited on one of my hand-tooled Italian leather couches. She was still damp from the ocean, which was bad for the leather, but I didn't give a fuck. Stepping back to see her sprawled across the cushions, long limbs browned from the sun, round breasts spilling preciously from her swimsuit, I was seconds away from taking her where she lay, everything else be damned.

It was a dangerous mix, this Molotov cocktail of jealousy and arousal. I wanted to put both of them on their knees and fuck their mouths to show them who they should belong to. I wanted to spin them away from me, arms draped over the couch, so I could drop to my own knees and eat them out for hours, until they were both dripping wet, Linnea's pussy swollen, Sebastian's cock weeping precum. Only then would I fuck them, first her, then him, and back again. For hours and hours, coming in them both until they were stuffed full of me and leaking. And then I would fuck that cum back into them with my fingers while I watched them kiss.

"Adam?" Linnea's breathy voice interrupted my lurid fantasies.

I could feel the heat of a flush in my cheeks as I stared down into her dark eyes. "I'll get you some water," I practically grunted before turning on my heel to head for the kitchen.

I heard the front door close behind Sebastian but ignored him to focus on breathing through my nose to bring down the rabid pounding of my pulse.

It didn't work.

My grip on the glass I had grabbed from the shelf was white-knuckled, and I punched it into the water dispenser so hard that it shattered the side of the glass. Shards dug into my fingers, blood welling in fat drops before sliding down my palm.

Cursing, I moved into the pantry to throw it in the bin and grab some paper towels.

The door closed behind me with a muted thump.

I spun like a cornered animal, injured hand held to my chest, lips parted in a kind of grimacing snarl.

Sebastian stood before me, only a handful of feet between us, breathing hard like he'd run a marathon. He was bare-chested post-surf, his chest chiseled out of fine gold marble, waxed smooth to show off every tight line and ridge of muscle he worked hard to hone. So much bronzed skin, my mouth watered, and I found it nearly impossible to tear my eyes off his chest to look up into his face.

What I found was somehow worse than his beautiful body.

Desire.

Blazing from his eyes like twin suns, threatening to burn me to ash.

"Adam," he said again, the only word he'd spoken yet.

I wanted him to say it over and over for the rest of my life.

Before I could think or blink or force myself to stop this descent into madness, I was lashing out to grip the side of his neck in a tight hold, thumb over his bobbing Adam's apple, and hauling him sharply into me. He stumbled slightly but otherwise came willingly, crashing into my chest, then we both went crashing into the wall behind me. Glass jars clinked together, and some must have rolled onto their side, then off the wall, shattering to the ground beside us.

I didn't pay mind to any of it.

Because for the first time in ten years, Sebastian Lombardi was in my arms.

In my fucking arms.

Warm and passionate and living. Not the pale imitation I met so often in my dreams that ended in nightmares where I woke up alone.

And God.

God.

He tasted even better than I remembered.

Hot like too much spice, but rich and masculine.

His mouth was so plush against my own, a stark contrast to the rough bite of his stubble rubbing against my chin.

Big hands tugged in my hair, forcing me closer.

A strong, hairy calf curled around my leg so he could press his hard cock against the crease of my hip.

Oh, *fuck*.

At that moment, I would willingly sell my soul to the devil if it meant living in this damn pantry in this man's arms forever.

It had been years since I kissed a man and even longer since I'd kissed *this* man.

My man.

I had no choice but to drop one hand down the back of his thin grey sweatpants and palm his naked arse, the hard muscle flexing as he ground into me. His groan vibrated over my tongue, and I swallowed it down like ambrosia.

My blood, my bones, my very soul felt on fire.

I couldn't breathe or think.

I thought I might actually be dying.

And then there was a little knock on the door that exploded in my ears like a bomb.

I tore myself away from Sebastian with the gasp of a man exploding through the crust of the ocean after minutes of drowning.

He let me pull away, hands dropping into spasming fists, expression so utterly wrecked with longing and passion and malcontent I felt I might be ill.

A moment later, Linnea pushed the door open and appeared in

the doorway. The light from the wide windows in the kitchen behind her limned her in gold light and cast her features in absolute shadow.

What could she be thinking? I wondered wildly as desire curdled into panic.

There was no disguising the sexual tension mottling the air like heat waves between Seb and me, no wiping the beard burn from our cheeks or the swollen cast of our mouths.

There could be no mistake about the fact that we had just been kissing like our lives depended on it.

And for a moment there, it felt as if that was exactly what was at stake.

My whole life for one of Sebastian's kisses.

I wondered wildly if that was a bargain I would be crazy *not* to take.

"You're bleeding," Linnea said finally, softly, stepping forward as if into a bomb zone.

I stared down at my bleeding hand dumbly, having totally forgotten about it.

Linnea was suddenly in front of me, her sandals crunching on a piece of glass from a shattered jar. Her touch was light as she took my hand in hers and clucked her tongue.

"Let's get you cleaned up," she murmured, trying to meet my eyes.

I nodded, unable to look into that knowing violet gaze.

She nodded slowly before dropping my hand and moving to Sebastian. I watched from the corner of my eye as she raised to her tiptoes to touch a spot of blood on Sebastian's neck.

It was my blood, deposited in a gruesome handprint on his throat.

The sight of it made my softening cock kick hard in my jeans.

"You too," she suggested mildly to Seb.

He swallowed thickly and shook his head, looking like a spooked horse seconds from galloping away.

"Hey," she whispered, smoothing a hand over his pectoral—over his heart. "It's okay. Just go into the kitchen and I'll help you, okay?"

He looked down at her, expression softening as if noticing it was Linnea for the first time. One big hand raised to brush a lock of layered hair out of her face.

"I'll clean up at home," he said in a voice that seemed crushed somehow. Like it hurt to speak. "I need to leave."

His yellow gaze found mine over the top of her head, but I looked away before we could make eye contact like the fucking bastard that I was.

"Right," Linnea said. "Call me later, okay?"

He kissed her head without another word and carefully walked past me so that we didn't touch in the close space.

I watched him go with my heart in my throat.

"Adam," Linnea said, jerking my attention away from the empty doorway.

She was smiling, just a soft flex at the edge of her wide mouth.

I watched as she extended her hand to me and wiggled her ringed fingers.

"C'mon," she said. "Let me sort you out, okay?"

I swallowed the razor blades on the back of my tongue and tasted blood.

So I nodded instead of speaking and let Linnea thread her fingers through my uninjured hand and tug me forward into the light.

CHAPTER FOURTEEN

LINNEA

Of course, it wasn't a surprise.

Not really.

To be around Sebastian and Adam was to be torn asunder between the gravitational pull of two planets that were meant to merge as one. Their tragic love story was written in every line of their bodies and every truncated gaze.

But to have actually stood in that small pantry with those two big, handsome men in the throes of animalistic passion had been electrifying. Almost terrifying.

What might they do to a girl if she tried to step between them?

Not to stop that rampant desire, though I had a feeling they might both be grateful for someone to tell them to cease and desist.

But to stoke that fire.

To watch as Adam's square palms skate down Sebastian's V-shaped torso to the taut muscles arrowing into his groin. To witness the kiss they must have shared, a mouth-eating, tongue-sucking extravaganza that would have made me wet in seconds.

Far from shameful, their sexual chemistry was intoxicating.

I could understand that even after ten years, it was not something that could be diminished or changed.

It was a part of this world just like the green grass and the sun above.

So why was Adam acting as if it was only a matter of time before I condemned him to slaughter?

I had cleaned up his hand, happy to find the cuts shallow, and easily tended to, and then pushed him toward the shower while I took the one down the hall to get ready for our lunch date at Nobu.

I thought about the expression on his face as I rinsed off and applied my makeup, going heavier than usual because I knew we'd be in the press the moment we pulled up to the restaurant.

He'd looked so frightened as he watched Sebastian walk out.

As if he were both afraid Seb would never come back and afraid that he would.

It didn't take a genius to figure out there was some internalized homophobia there, and it made my heart break for him.

For the first time since we started this arrangement, I felt like I had seen into Adam's soul.

And the glimpse only made me eager for more.

He was completely composed by the time we met in the foyer forty minutes later. Dressed in a thin, forest-green polo that hugged his muscular torso and black jeans with black aviators covering verdant-green eyes, I knew he had pulled himself together behind his Hollywood armor, and I wouldn't get another glimpse unless I dug for it.

Unwilling to spook him, I'd taken his offered hand and followed him to the garage without commenting on the sleek black Ferrari he chose from his collection to take us into Malibu. The car ride was equally quiet, his gaze frequently touching my face as I tapped my thigh to the music and studied the city rushing by outside the window.

I might have looked tranquil, but I was plotting.

By the time we were seated at a discreet table in the corner of the oceanfront patio, Adam was almost relaxed.

I let him order a drink—sparkling water with lemon instead of hard booze, which I thought he would order to take the edge off—before settling in.

"It seems we both know what it's like to be kissed by Sebastian," I mused blandly.

Adam choked on his sparkling water and coughed into his fist.

I smiled placidly at him.

"What the bloody hell, Linnea," he growled. "We're in public."

I rolled my eyes. "At a secluded table."

"There are listening ears everywhere," he whispered with a glower.

"I'm not judging you. Clearly, I have a weakness for Italians with golden eyes, too."

"Nea," he snapped.

And I liked the nickname, even if he spoke it harshly.

So I beamed at him. "He unsettles you."

"You unsettle me," he grumbled, looking down at his menu.

"Good," I declared. "You need unsettling."

He sighed, closing his menu to lean over the table, his green eyes so bright against his tanned skin and burnished-gold hair. "My life was fine before Oscar Hampton threatened to ruin it."

"By outing you," I said softly.

Adam scanned the restaurant behind me and nodded tersely.

I reached across the table to take his bandaged hand into mine, rubbing my fingers along the backs of his knuckles. Almost reluctantly, some of the tension in his shoulders lessened.

"Why would he do such a thing?" I asked.

For a long moment, I thought he wouldn't answer, his gaze caught somewhere in a distant memory.

"He was an old acquaintance of my ex-wife and myself," he said carefully, leveling me with a heavy glance that said that was a euphemism. "He was…unhappy with the termination of his tenure with us."

I had to roll my lips between my teeth to hide my inappropriate smile. Only, I'd just realized Adam spoke even more formally in that crisp upper-class accent when he was being guarded, and it was wildly endearing.

"It seems you and your ex-wife had an interesting relationship," I mused.

His gaze narrowed, but the server chose that moment to return to take our lunch orders. I was starving after surfing, so I ordered the burger with a side of Parmesan truffle fries.

Adam shook his head slightly at my order, rubbing a hand across his mouth as if he could erase the smile threatening to claim it.

"What?" I demanded. "You're lucky they didn't have horse on the menu because I could eat one. I'm famished."

His laugh felt like a gift, rough-edged with disuse and deep from his belly.

Oh no, I thought, watching the handsome grump soften with humor, *I'm in trouble*.

Why was it so intimate sharing a moment of genuine laughter with someone? Why did it feel as if, every time I won his smile, the threads stitching us haphazardly together tightened into something substantial?

A backstitch.

Something that might last beyond the next three years of our contractual obligation.

"By all means, eat whatever you'd like," he allowed magnanimously. "You have to understand, most women I take to dinner order a salad and leave most of it untouched."

I waved my hand. "Unfortunately, being a woman in this industry is brutal on self-image. Not to mention being a woman in general, in this day and age of social media? I dare you to find a female who doesn't experience moments of self-hatred in their own body. It's horrific, really."

Adam arched a brow and leaned against one elbow, his fancy silver watch glinting in the sunlight, his visage everything noble and haughty. Something about those cool good looks made me want to get on my knees to serve him.

I wondered what "good girl" might sound like in those clipped British tones.

"Yet you suffer from none such insecurities?" he asked, but it wasn't really a question because he thought he knew the answer.

I shrugged one shoulder while I fiddled with one of my rings, a silver band hammered to look like coral and studded with sea pearls that a Hawaiian jeweler friend had made for me.

"Yes and no. I have moments of doubt, but I try not to let myself wallow in them. I'm healthy and young with the ability to surf and do it well. I may not be conventionally beautiful like a lot of women in Hollywood, but I also know the industry well enough to say I probably got the few jobs I've landed because I'm pretty enough and not for any serious acting chops."

"Don't sell yourself short. You were unfairly charming in *Swamplands,* given the fact you were supposed to be a villainess."

The tightly furled bud of confidence that had been underfed and underlit my entire life softened and arched into bloom.

"That's high praise coming from The Great Adam Meyers," I said lightly, but there was no mistaking how deeply that praise resonated within me.

Adam inclined his chin regally and tipped his glass to me. "Raise your glass and let's have a cheers, shall we?"

"To our mutually assured professional successes?" I guessed, mimicking his habitual use of raising a haughty brow.

His full mouth, a pale pink that looked petal soft amidst the bristles of his golden-brown stubble, pursed. "To us, I think. In all our iterations for the next three years."

"To us," I echoed, clinking our glassware together.

His other hand lay on the table, and I nibbled my lower lip for a moment before I gave in to the impulse and slid my fingers over the backs of his, linking them together.

When I gazed up at the Brit, his gaze was warm.

"I thought that was you."

I blinked at the familiar voice, wondering for a moment if I was hallucinating.

Of course, I *had* to have been, given that only someone with truly bad luck would bump into their fake boyfriend's ex-wife on a lunch date.

But really, I should have known something like this would happen.

I'd never been particularly lucky, and from the soured but unsurprised look on Adam's face, perhaps neither had he.

"Savannah," Adam greeted flatly as the woman in question stepped by me to stop beside our table.

I had always found her exquisite, as she meant me and everyone else to. Her grace and sophistication were evident in every lithe line of her petite body, as well as in every item of designer clothing, all in varying shades of off-white. Even her expression, looking down her nose at Adam, small mouth perfectly painted a shade of raspberry that offset her wide blue eyes, was calculated for maximum effect.

In any space, at any age, Savannah Richardson was a queen holding court, and no one, absolutely no one, deserved a place on a throne at her side.

Not even her husband, the first or second.

I suddenly felt woefully inadequate in my handmade leopard-print dress. It was casual enough for a posh lunch with Adam, thanks to the muted colors and the structured corset that gave way to a gauzy, flowy A-line skirt I'd matched with pale designer gold sandals I'd found in my mom's room, but I felt suddenly as if I was a little girl playing dress-up in Miranda's hotel closet while she, Savannah, and Bobbi prepared for a televised event.

Adam squeezed my hand, surprising me back to myself to find him smiling ever so slightly my way.

Buck up, his expression seemed to say.

So I steeled myself before tipping my head back to smile up at Savannah.

The woman who had broken the heart of two men I was intrinsically linked to.

My momentary insecurity crumbled to ash in the wake of the anger that built around my heart.

"Savannah," I greeted, much as Adam had in a pleasant but dull tone.

She did not spare me a glance.

"I telephoned you," she told Adam, smoothing a perfectly coiffed curl back behind her ear. "You haven't called me back."

Adam didn't look at her, his tiny smile stretching into something more like a grin. He lifted our conjoined hands off the table to showcase them. "I have been rather busy the last few weeks. You'll have to forgive a man in love."

I had the deepest pleasure of watching Savannah's eyes widen to dinner plates, their bold color seeming to dim with displeased surprise.

"I had heard rumors you were dating," she demurred, looking at our hands before shifting position to look down at me, gaze narrowing as she took me in. After a long pause, she raised both brows and asked, "And who is the lucky lady?"

"I assure you, I am the one who is lucky," Adam said smoothly, lifting our hands again to bend forward and *bite* one of my knuckles.

I had expected a kiss, maybe, but the shock of his teeth against my skin sent a very genuine shiver through my body.

Adam's smile turned wolfish.

I could feel a blush work its way into my cheeks, but boldly looked back at Savannah with a demure smile.

She was staring at Adam with barely concealed shock.

"I'm surprised you don't remember me," I told her sweetly. "Though, I suppose you haven't been by to visit Miranda in ages, and the one time you came, we didn't interact."

Savannah blinked at me before her mouth fell into a little moue.

"Linnea Kai?" she breathed, doing another scan of my person, lingering at my breasts and the ends of my beachy waves. "Miranda's daughter."

"And Adam's girlfriend, if you want to identify me by relationships only," I agreed.

Adam bit the edge of his smile, trying to hold it at bay, and then, catching my eye, gave up with an exhale of laughter. His eyes sparkled with mirth, a boyish contentment I'd never seen in him before.

It was intoxicating.

"You seem surprised, Savvy," Adam said, the frost thawed from his tone because he was more amused by me than he was irritated by her, and that felt like a wonderful gift. "Did you think I would wait around for you to come back to me?"

It was my turn to blink.

What in the world could have possessed Savannah to leave him?

Sure, he was grumpy, a little arrogant, and more than a little stuffy.

But he was also brilliant, charismatic, complicated, and gorgeous with what I more than suspected was a secret streak of tender loving kindness buried beneath it all.

Savannah seemed surprised by his candor, too, more thrown off-balance than I had ever witnessed before.

It took only a moment for that hard gleam to descend over her eyes, though.

"Of course not. Only, I never suspected you would be the type of man who has a midlife crisis and dates someone young enough to be his daughter," she rejoined coolly, unconsciously rubbing a finger over the enormous diamond ring on her left hand.

"Twelve years old is a little young to be fathering a child, don't you think?" he asked acerbically, all joy gone. In its place was the British Lord, and even Savannah, with all her pretense of nobility, was not blue blood enough to stand up to that.

Savannah's knuckles were white around the grip of her Chanel bag.

"I did not venture over here to fight with you," she managed, each word clipped. "I came because I wanted to say what you obviously did not care to hear over the phone. I am here, Tate and I, if you need anything. I heard about the…unsavory chatter around town, and I wanted to lend my services."

What kind of woman, *I thought,* said something like "lend my services" to their ex-husband?

Staring at them both, I could imagine how the marriage dissolved.

Their defense mechanisms were too similar, their baggage expressed too coldly, to ever bridge that void between them.

"I have no need of your services," Adam promised, dismissing Savannah as if she were no less than a hovering server, turning slightly but obviously in his chair so that he was wholly focused on me. "As you can see, I have everything I need."

"It was lovely to see you again, Savannah," I said kindly, even though I was already leaning toward Adam, enclosing us in a little bubble of our own making.

"Likewise," she said quietly, almost wistfully. I could feel her gaze on the side of my face like a scalpel for a long moment before she finally clipped away on her high heels.

Adam blew out a long exhale when she was gone, but his shoulders were still up near his ears.

I pinched my lower lip between my teeth for a second before saying, "Right. I'm afraid sushi is ruined for me now. How do you feel about fried foods?"

Adam stared at me, his eyes roving my face as if searching for something elusive. Finally, the corner of his mouth curled.

"Favorably. Just don't tell my agent."

I crinkled my nose. "The same agent who had what looked like chow mein spilled down the front of her blazer last time I saw her?"

He laughed, a little smoother than before as if he was starting to understand the practice again.

And I thought once more what an absolute idiot Savannah must have been to let him go.

CHAPTER FIFTEEN

ADAM

Linnea took us to Malibu Seafood, a small, no-frills restaurant and market located along the water, where the freshly caught seafood could be smelled from the parking lot. I let her order for us both, chatting away with the person behind the till as if they'd been best friends for years. In the wake of seeing my ex-wife, I usually felt off-kilter, both irritated and filled with a nostalgic-tinged yearning. I could never quite figure out if I actually missed her, or just how simple life had seemed before our marriage ended and I was left to face my demons alone.

But now, watching Linnea in this unassuming seafood joint wearing a gorgeous dress, her hands animatedly flying through the air as she chatted away with the other girl, I felt oddly tranquil.

Perhaps because, for the first time in ten years, someone other than Chaucer had stood up to Savannah for me.

It was a rare thing to see anyone stand toe-to-toe with the imperial Savannah Richardson, and I had not expected it of Linnea, who was usually so easygoing and bright as an unfiltered sunbeam.

But I could admit that it was wildly attractive, seeing that icy edge of her sharp tongue, the confidence she felt in touching me—claiming me—even though this was all supposed to be a ruse.

It had felt so real in those moments, as if we were a team.

As if to underscore my point, Linnea sashayed over to my side and immediately dug her shoulder under my arm so I was forced to wrap it over her shoulders. The intimacy made something swell in my throat, and I found it difficult to breathe. Noticing the green-eyed looks of several men in the restaurant did nothing to alleviate the surge of possession and wistfulness that locked horns inside me.

"You'll love it here," Linnea declared for the second time, pressing a hand to her flat belly. "Not that Nobu isn't delicious, but does anything beat fried foods?"

"They seem to have other options than the fryer," I pointed out dryly.

She wrinkled her nose. "Just trust me, the fish and chips and fried prawns are worthy of worship."

"I've carried you. How is it you weigh so little when you clearly eat so much?" I teased, slipping my hand down her arm to curl around her side so I could pinch the side of her belly.

She squirmed. "Stop that! I surf for hours every week, which always leaves me ravenous, and to be honest, I'm prone to skipping meals. With Miranda, working at a busy restaurant, and auditioning, sometimes I'm lucky to get in a protein bar."

"We should discuss what you want to do for Miranda," I said, now that she had been brought up. I did not like to hear that she didn't have time to take care of herself. "I had Chaucer look into a few places in the area that come highly recommended. We wouldn't spare any cost."

She nibbled on the corner of one pink lip. "I know it needs to be discussed. It's just…I feel so guilty about putting her away in some home where she won't know anyone. I've read so much about how it's beneficial for people with neurodegenerative diseases to be around the things and people they know. I promised her I wouldn't abandon her like everyone else in her life has."

It had been a long time since I was in a position to give anyone comfort, but Linnea's lack of physical boundaries made it easier. I curled her tighter into my side and kissed her temple. She smelled of desert roses and ocean salt, an undercurrent of spice like pink peppercorns and bergamot that made me want to linger too close until I could decipher each complicated note.

"Then we will leave her in her home until it's necessary she requires more care, but Linnea, I must insist on hiring proper nurses. The onus has been on you far too long. You're a twenty-six-year-old woman with her life ahead of her. It's time to focus on the things you dream of accomplishing."

She made a humming sound, her gaze glazing as she imagined those possibilities.

Our order was called, forcing Linnea to leave my side to retrieve the grease-stained carton of fried seafood. Wanting to stay close, I followed her, gathering the majority of the food myself before leading us outside toward the water, where ramshackle picnic tables sat. I took one side and was surprised, though maybe I shouldn't have been, when Linnea sat on the same bench as me.

Slotting into my side, she arranged the food to her liking, lining up the tartar sauce and ketchup cups, squeezing lemon over the fried fish, and piling the malt vinegar packets beside me. When I raised a brow at the assumption, she grinned.

"We had fish and chips that day in Croyde," she reminded me with a little shrug. "I remember you drenched the fries in so much vinegar they were soggy."

"Hardly," I scoffed, even as I ripped open the packets and began to upend them over a pile of chips.

She laughed, which was the goal.

What kind of magic did she have that, after a day of drama—kissing the man I'd pined over for years, crossing paths with my she-devil of an ex-wife—Linnea could make me feel lighthearted and grateful to be sitting on a splintering bench eating cheap fried food?

"Do you miss her?"

I wasn't surprised by Linnea's non sequitur because I was beginning to understand her. Instead of pressuring, she employed guerrilla warfare tactics—shock and awe—to get people to open up to her.

To stall for time, I took a bite of immaculately fried cod and allowed myself to enjoy the silken meat and crisp exterior. It was a deviation from the careful meal plan I had been implementing in the lead-up to my role of Anton Daventry, but with every day of silence that passed, it became clearer to me that even with Linnea at my side, the production was considering other options for their leading man.

I shoved the grim thought from my mind and savored the good food and good company the way Dr. Eng had suggested.

"Not particularly," I said finally, looking at my empty ring finger. It had felt naked and wrong for a handful of years after our divorce, but now I was used to it.

Savannah had been an essential part of my life for so long that it took me ages to realize she had been more pivotal to my career than to my personal life. We hadn't trusted each other enough to let down our guards completely, even after five years of marriage.

It made me wonder if I'd ever been able to commit my heart fully to anyone else's hands. Maybe I was just born and bred to be alone forever, condemned by the struggles I couldn't seem to stop from defining me.

Linnea lifted her brows as she munched on a crab leg.

"It was lonely without her," I ad`mitted, then, because I owed it to her after what she had stumbled in to that afternoon in the pantry, I added, "Without them."

"The three of you lived together like a couple?" She held no judgement in her tone, just an airy curiosity.

"Yes," I said, and it felt like lancing a wound to speak about it.

The hurt was a bright burst that softened into the dull throb of relief.

"For a time."

"You missed him, though," she said, and it wasn't a question.

It hurt to nod, but I did it anyway.

She knocked her shoulder into mine. "He didn't want to leave. I remember that." A pregnant pause I held my breath through. "Did you make him? It's the only way I can see someone like Seb giving up."

Ah, she knew our Italian well.

"I made him," I agreed. It felt like chewing glass. "I've regretted it every day for the last ten years even though I probably wouldn't change a thing if I could go back in time."

"Why?" she asked.

As if it was a simple question.

As if there was a single answer I could give her.

"If I knew why, I wouldn't have descended into a bottle for so many years," I told her before taking a sip of the sparkling water she'd bought me without asking, forsaking the selection of beer and wine. "I wouldn't still be in therapy."

"Yeah," Linnea agreed on a sigh. "When I was young, I used to think that if you could figure out the problem, it would just fix itself. It took growing up to realize localizing the issue is just the first step, and sometimes you never figure it all out."

"I believe it is the December figure who is supposed to be the wise one in a May/December romance," I lectured her.

She wrinkled her nose at me and stuck out her tongue.

"Much better," I agreed, impulsively biting the end of that scrunched nose.

When I pulled back, there was such a lovely look of tenderness on her face that I forgot to breathe for the second time that day.

"Oh, Adam," she said softly, not pitying but empathetic, as if my hurts were hers. "What are we going to do with you?"

"Ply me with fried foods and play passive-aggressive games with my ex-wife?" I suggested dryly.

She shook her head, golden hair slithering over her shoulder and releasing her heady perfume.

"You could have him," she said honestly. "If you wanted him. Sebastian is not the kind of man who falls out of love, I think."

I blinked at her, suddenly enraged that she would say that.

Both that it *could* be true and that it couldn't be farther from it.

"So could you," I breathed, the words punched out of me.

Her mouth twisted. "If he had wanted something more than friendship, he could have asked me out instead of wrapping a bow around my neck and gifting me to you."

"Sebastian is nothing if not a martyr," I said wryly. "He would always give up his own happiness for someone else's. He thought you needed this more than you needed him."

She cocked her head as if considering it, propping her chin in her hand as she tapped a french fry over her mouth.

"You know, for a very long time, he was all I wanted," she mused. "But now that I am starting to know him better, I get the sense that

I fantasized about a myth, and I want to get to know the man." She slid her gaze coyly to mine, long lashes casting deep shadows on her cheeks, which were painted pink in the setting sunlight. "I feel that same way about you."

"That I'm a man of mystery," I said with an arrogant smirk to deflect that intimacy we were building so tightly around each other.

"That I might like the man much more than I like the legend," she explained solemnly. "That I feel privileged to get to see behind the mask, however exquisitely you've crafted it."

Something icy slid down my spine, real fear, the kind I hadn't felt since Sebastian Lombardi moved into my carriage house ten years ago, and the tectonic plates of my life had begun to shift beneath my feet.

"You don't know the first thing about the real me," I told her baldly, even a little cruelly. "If you did, you would not have such a romantic look in your eye. I may have been bred a gentleman, Linnea, but I am a natural-born sinner. The extent of which would make your innocent ears burn."

"You can't shock me," she protested. "I may be younger than you, but I've been a curious girl all my life. Perhaps some of my exploits would appall *you*."

This was dangerous territory in a way our previous conversation—which I had been so desperate to change—was not.

I did not need to think of Linnea as a hot-blooded creature with curious fantasies and a wealth of experience. Best to let her remain an untainted saint-like figure, too young and innocent to experiment in my infernal playground.

She was already too gorgeous to ignore, the lush curves and long limbs, the perpetually tousled hair that begged for a firm grip so that one could plunder the soft, full set of that sassy mouth.

God, the things I would do to her without even knowing how

many things she might want to do to me in return.

It had been too long since I had a creative bedfellow instead of a rote submissive at the club.

A touch to my thigh drew me back from my fantasies with a jolt. Linnea's hand was sliding up my leg, dangerously high, as she leaned so close I could count the striations in her jewel-toned eyes.

"I've spent hours on my knees," she whispered, voice dropping into a sultry rasp that hooked me through the gut. "Mouth open and aching from use as I sucked a nice big cock. I like to feel like that, though. Used and wet and open. Tied up, held down, fucked full. I've tried so many things, I keep waiting to feel satisfied, but I suspect I might truly be insatiable because I read something in a kinky romance novel at night alone in bed, or think about the handsome stranger putting his hand around my throat in an elevator. I know there is so much more I want to experience." I bit back a fierce shiver as she tilted her head to let her silken lips brush the outer shell of my ear, breath hot on my skin. "I only need the right person to teach me."

Cold air slapped me in the face as she pulled back and grabbed a fried shrimp, snapping off the head before offering me a toothy smile.

And though I was a Dominant through and through, with very few tendencies toward submission, at that moment, I felt utterly in her thrall. It was work to pull myself out of it, ripping apart the sticky web that held me prey until I could remember who I was and why I lived the way I did.

"That would not be wise," I said, barely recognizing the gutturalness of my own voice.

"No," she agreed easily with a flippant shrug. "But most things worth doing aren't."

"You promised you would not fall in love with me," I reminded her, forcefully enunciating my words so they were clipped and cutting.

"Sex might muddy those waters."

"For me or you?" she retorted.

I scoffed. "Did I not just tell you I was a sinner?"

"Did I not just tell you I'm a woman who loves sex?" she countered, suddenly close again, her hand on my thigh, yellow-painted nails digging into my tensed muscle. "Three years is a long time for a sinner to be abstinent, Mr. Meyers. A little stress relief might do you some good. If not with me, then think about asking Sebastian for forgiveness and seeing where that may go."

"Don't be preposterous."

"Don't be a coward," she dared.

Our eyes met and held, hers large, almond-shaped, and unblinking.

The standoff was broken only by the sound of Linnea's phone going off, "Mamma Mia" blasting from the small speaker. She pulled it from her purse immediately, with the haste of someone responsible for a dependent.

"Hello," she said, huskiness gone, all professionalism.

Only the lingering heart in my gut to remind me of the dangerous games we'd been playing.

Because now she'd done it.

Implanted the imagery in the fertile soil of my brain.

Linnea on her knees for me, bee-stung lips swollen from the movement of my cock over her tongue, her hands tied with a ribbon behind her back like a present given to me by the man fucking into her from behind, tall, dark and swarthy and glossed with sweat. The iterations of three bodies tangled together in an erotic dance flittered through my mind like dailies after a day of filming. Seb fucking her as I fucked him. His mouth on her breasts, mine between her thighs. Linnea and I teasing him as he strained against the ropes tying him to my bed, because I thought they both might like that.

I certainly would.

Fuck me.

She had opened Pandora's box, and now I feared I would never be able to stuff those lustful dreams back inside.

"Adam." Her voice, ringing with panic, cut through my daze.

Immediately, I was alert, pulling her closer into the cage of my arms and searching the parking lot for paparazzi who might have followed us.

"That was Chaucer," she said, nails digging into my forearm, her face bloodless beneath the tan. "She couldn't get a hold of you so she called me. Apparently, Oscar Hampton did an interview with Tamara Bridge at the *London Entertainment Herald*. There's a photo of the two of you in a Rolls Royce smiling at the camera. He claims you were in a secret relationship while you were married to Savannah."

The news drowned me like a bucket of arctic water, reminding me why I did not get to have nice things like pretty, sunshiney blonds with wisdom beyond their years or Italian actors with enormous hearts.

Because I may have been born with a silver spoon in my mouth but that was when my luck had run out.

CHAPTER SIXTEEN

SEBASTIAN

I didn't sleep for three days.

That wouldn't have been unusual when I was a teen, fevered with stories that would not release me to peace until I'd purged myself of every last word.

But I hadn't felt so consumed by writing since *Blood Oath*, and quite frankly, I never expected to feel that way again.

I thought my ability to tell stories had atrophied right alongside my ability to fall in love.

Apparently, I had been wrong on both counts.

Because *The Dream & The Dreamer* poured out of me almost brutally, my lifeblood splattering against the keys, seeping into the characters like some kind of black magic.

And I knew what had awoken this slumbering part of me.

True love's kiss.

After a decade of estrangement, Adam Meyers was back in my life.

After years of long-distance friendship, Linnea Kai was gorgeous, grown, and so suddenly an integral part of my daily life that I wasn't sure what I would do when I had to go back to my home in New York.

I'd given the woman I wanted to the man I'd used to love because it would save them both from suffering.

Like the ultimate martyr, I hadn't realized how much suffering it would cause me.

I ignored my phone for all seventy-two hours I worked bent over my computer, and when I emerged on the third day, the printer whirring beside me as it spat out the first screenplay I had written in a decade, the second in my life, I rubbed my eyes with one hand and picked up my cell with the other.

Forty-three notifications.

Texts and calls from my mother and sisters, a few new messages in the Lombardi Men group chat, which I had with their husbands, where we mostly conspired to surprise the women in our lives for their birthdays and anniversaries, a couple from my agent, Mali, and one from Chaucer.

There were three texts from Linnea.

Even one from Adam.

But the top notification had my heart dropping into my stomach and then soaring into my throat, where it choked me with its heavy beat.

Savannah

You missed the last three Sunday dinners, Sebastian. We are away this weekend, but I expect you to be here for the next. The Critics Choice Awards are that Saturday. We can debrief._

I want to see you as much as I can before you go back to New York._

I blinked.

Had it really been three weeks since I last saw her?

I couldn't remember the last time I had missed the opportunity to be with Savannah.

She and Tate lived bicoastal like me, New York and Los Angeles, which meant we crossed paths frequently. It still hurt to watch them together, to see how much Tate loved her and how placidly content Savvy seemed to be with him.

I took solace whenever I needed it by knowing that she shared none of her basest self with him. I knew because I had once made a bawdy joke after too much wine about the beauty of Domination and submission. Tate had roared with laughter at the idea of those "silly sex games." And Savannah?

She had pinned me with those iced-over blue eyes, and I had felt, for the first time, why people in the industry were so afraid of her.

Later, she had cornered me like a hissing cat, nails unsheathed and latched into my forearm as she whispered never to bring up her sexual proclivities again.

A thing of the past, *she had said.*

I never made such a joke again.

It hurt to imagine that she was living inauthentically, to know that something she had *needed* so much had been banished to the past because it didn't suit her ambition. But it also made sense, because she made sense to me.

I had never known two people who seemed so confident as Savannah and Adam to be so secretly insecure.

And a small part of me rejoiced that Tate didn't get that version of her.

He had the lady, but he did not have the wanton who emerged powerful and greedy under a steady hand and filthy command.

Only Adam and I had shared that.

That deep, vulnerable part of her.

So, I reasoned, I could more readily handle that Tate was married to Savannah, the Lady.

It had been years since I forgot about her existence enough to skip a date with her.

And here I had three times in a row.

I knew why.

Adam and Linnea.

They had consumed my mind to the point that I was overcome by the need to write this story.

This love story about a man who fell in love with the idea of a woman before he even met her, and then, upon glimpsing her in reality, began a crazed search that derailed his life in order to find her again.

I swallowed thickly, throat dry as dust, as I stared down at her text on the screen.

It wasn't difficult to realize that Emerson's obsessive search for Hallie Whitehall was a metaphor for my own obsessive vigil for Savannah.

The cell ringing in my hand startled me out of my depressing thoughts, Andrea's name flashing across the surface.

"*Ciao*," I answered in a voice that was creaky with disuse.

I looked at the hotel room around me and winced at the discarded water bottles littering the floor, three trays of room service that had largely gone uneaten and were sitting stale on the rumpled bed linens I hadn't slept in for days.

"Sebastian," Andrea shouted joyfully. "Come downstairs."

I rubbed my gritty eyes again, thinking I had misheard him because Andrea should have been at his home in Tuscany.

"What?" I asked blearily.

"Come downstairs," he demanded again. "*Vieni*. I am waiting at the bar."

He hung up before I could question him again.

I stared down at my grimy white T-shirt and the same grey sweatpants I'd been wearing for much too long and decided, if Andrea was really downstairs, he could wait five minutes while I took a shower.

Afterwards, dressed in jeans so old they were softened to white in some places and a new, clean shirt, wet hair dampening the collar, I made my way downstairs to the hotel bar.

Andrea sat in one corner at a small table nursing a rocks glass of what I was sure was grappa even though it was only eleven in the morning.

He stood when I approached, carting me into his arms to kiss me firmly on both cheeks as if I were just a boy and not a man six inches taller than him.

"Andrea," I said on an exhaled huff of amusement and joy. "What are you doing here?"

"I read the pages you sent," he said, speaking too loudly but in Italian, so I didn't mind. His excitement was plastered across his swarthy features, his hands cutting shapes into the air as he spoke. "I had to come."

"You liked them?" I guessed because if he hadn't, he would have called me to say I had lost the plot.

Andrea was not a man who held back.

"Liked them?" he grunted. "I do not have words in the many languages I know to tell you how much I loved them. Genius, Sebastian, pure genius."

I gaped at him. "You're kidding."

"Do I kid about such things?" he asked, as if joking about art was blasphemous. "Never. *The Dream & The Dreamer* is award fodder. No doubt in my mind about it. With the right cast, this film could be iconic. One for the history books."

"I hadn't even finished what I sent to you," I tried to push back.

He waved my words out of the air. "That does not matter. The bones? They are there, and they are gold. Have you finished the rest?"

I ran a slightly trembling hand through my hair and decided I had low blood sugar. "Yes, just now. I didn't sleep for three days."

Andrea laughed, so deep from his belly that his entire body swayed with the motion. "*Eccellente.* You will give them to me after you've had a coffee, hmm?"

He beckoned a server over and fired off my usual order of a double espresso before asking the kitchen to bring me a loaded breakfast. I was sure breakfast service was over, but the server was probably an aspiring actor himself, and he wasn't foolish enough to say no to one of the greatest directors of our time.

"We will shop this immediately," Andrea continued after the server hustled off. "Artfield Productions would be a good fit, maybe Hightower Studios. We need the budget to do it right and film on location. We could drum up a bidding war, but I'd rather you and I decide which fit is best."

"I promised Tate Richardson I would offer it to him if I ever wrote again," I admitted, staring down at the phone I'd placed on the table.

Savannah's text was still up on the screen.

I didn't know why it bothered me so much, but I felt like it was important somehow. Both the text admitting she wanted to spend time with me, and my own reaction to it. But everything was too tangled up in my gut, more emotions than I'd felt in years, and all through the fugue state of my exhaustion.

"Absolutely not," Andrea said immediately, leaning forward to peer at me with dark eyes. "Why would you do that to yourself? It is bad enough you spend personal time with them. Working with them? And on *this?*"

He said *this* as if there was a connection between the script and them.

As if he knew I was as obsessive about Savannah as Emerson was about Hallie.

The truth was, of course, that he was right.

It would be pure madness to work with Tate and Savannah on any film, let alone this one, which had roots in my own heartbroken past.

But a part of me also thought the making of the film should be as emotionally painful as the writing of it, as the story itself.

It was the artist in me.

I would always be willing to suffer for a good story.

Yet another part of me remembered how validating it had been to share that first screenplay with Savannah and Adam. How they had seen its potential and set both it and me up for the kind of success that had launched a long and fruitful career thus far.

"I've never done this without them," I admitted in a small voice. "It feels wrong to create something like this separate from them."

"You have been creating a career and life without Savannah Richardson and Adam Meyers for the last ten years," he said curtly, but he wasn't totally unfeeling, couldn't be as an Italian or a filmmaker. He stared at me hard for a moment before sighing, rubbing a hand over his salt-and-pepper beard. "I won't work with Savannah. I never liked her."

I had known Andrea for long enough to read the space between each word. My heart kicked in my chest.

"You always liked Adam," I said, forcefully mild.

The server returned with my espresso, opening his mouth on a smile that was immediately dashed when he caught Andrea's glower. He scuttled away.

"Did I?" Andrea asked, sipping his grappa.

"It was he who introduced us," I reminded him unnecessarily. "You once said he was the kind of actor who could convince you of anything."

"That does not sound like me."

I smiled because, of course it did. Andrea was almost as dramatic as Adam.

My old friend sighed. "You wrote the part of Emerson Bainbridge for him, didn't you?"

I stared at my left wrist, still surprised sometimes when I found it bare, without the heavy weight of the watch Adam and Savannah had once given me.

"I didn't write it for him," I said honestly. "But I think I wrote it in part because of him."

"*Certo*," Andrea said, looking pained and weary. "Of course, you did. Just as you wrote it for *her*. *Niente di nuovo sotto il sole*."

There is nothing new under the sun, the expression meant. As in, of course my life still revolved around the same couple it had ten years ago.

I shrugged helplessly because I had, but also because I did not have the words to explain how I had written it because of someone else, too.

Linnea.

In Emerson's imagination, Hallie Whitehall was fully realized as the consummate temptress, womanly, haughty with the kind of arrogance that comes from great beauty and great breeding, elegant and well-heeled. She was something to possess, another treasure to add to his collection of expensive trinkets.

But the reality of the living, breathing Hallie was nothing so cultivated.

She was a whirling dervish of vitality, rough around the edges because she had grown up in lower-class London, but beautiful and talented enough to pull herself out of the slums and onto the stage where she was set to become a sensation.

It was this version of Hallie that Thatcher Radcliff, Emerson's best mate and the private detective he hired to find her, fell in love with.

The dreamer in love with his dream was a very different supposition than two real people in love with each other.

I might have written the screenplay because of my past with Savannah and Adam, and the way it had shaped me, but I wrote it for Linnea and Adam to bring the story to life.

"Does it matter why I wrote it?" I asked a little gruffly. "I wrote again for the first time in years. I thought you would be thrilled."

"Of course, I am," Andrea scoffed. "No one is more thrilled than I am to be able to collaborate with you like this again. I only worry for your heart. When one like you has such a giving soul, it is often taken advantage of."

I huffed out a resigned laugh and ran a hand through my hair. "We are who we are, flaws and all."

Andrea gave me a lopsided smirk. "Just so. Certainly, this is a theme in *The Dream & The Dreamer*. It can be a masterpiece, Sebastian. We will make it so. Just tell me what you need, and we will do it."

"Adam," I said immediately because there was no point in denying that while Emerson and Thatcher were both intrinsically tied to different parts of my psyche, I had envisioned my ex-lover as the posh British star of the show.

Andrea rolled his eyes and flapped his hand through the air. "*Si, si,* I know."

"I want to play Thatcher," I admitted because he was whom I related to the most. The hardworking man who fell in love with a woman, knowing she was not meant to be his. "And I want Linnea Kai to audition for the role of Hallie."

Andrea's wiry grey and black eyebrows shot into his hairline. "The young, untried actress who is best known for being Miranda Hildebrand's daughter and Adam Meyers's current paramour?"

"The same," I agreed a little stiffly. "Though she is much more than the sum of those parts."

"If this is because you want to get into her pants, Sebastian, I am sure there are easier ways," Andrea said mildly.

Even though I wanted to state unequivocally that this part was hers, that I had *written* it for her and that only Linnea could pull off that intoxicating mix of sophisticate and ingenue, I decided to let it rest.

Linnea would prove me right herself.

"Just give her an audition," I suggested. "If you are not happy with her, Andrea, we will cast someone else."

"Someone with star power," he suggested. "Studios would love to attach a big name to a project like this."

"*Blood Oath* starred a no-name Italian," I reminded him. "It won us both Oscars."

"*Te lo concedo*," he granted. "She will audition. Anything else?"

"I have to at least speak with Savannah and Tate before we take it somewhere else," I added, though the idea of doing so was tantamount to torture.

Savannah would not take kindly to the idea of someone else's involvement in producing the film. Both because she would, rightly, think I owed it to her, given what she had done for me on my first screenplay, and because, unfairly, she still liked to think of me as hers.

Andrea finished the last of his grappa in one short gulp, shook his head and wiped his mouth simultaneously, and then slammed the glass back on the table.

"It's your funeral. Just try to survive long enough for us to get this thing into pre-production, hmm?"

"I'll try," I said. "But I make no promises. She's little, but she's fierce."

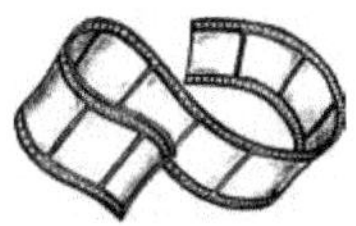

THE RICHARDSONS' ESTATE WAS IN Brentwood, a particularly posh and old-moneyed neighborhood of Los Angeles, where the homes often looked like transplants from Britain. I found it ironic that Savannah had left England only to end up in a proper-looking English country manor home, with the palm trees shading the winding drive being the only incongruent aspect.

I had texted ahead and been told that Tate was at work, but Savannah was home after a charity brunch event, and I could find her in the back garden for a pot of tea.

Again, the American showed her decade in London had given her more than just a British ex-husband.

The butler, Edgecumbe, led me through the Tudor-style home to the back terrace where my *duchessa* sat at a white marble table surrounded by a perfectly manicured array of boxwood hedges and flower beds. In a wide-brimmed straw hat with a white ribbon tied around the center and a white, sheer button-up tucked smartly into wide-legged, white trousers cinched with some kind of brown designer belt, Savannah Richardson looked ready for her centerfold in *House & Garden* magazine.

I loved that about her, though. She matched herself to every aesthetic perfectly, highlighting her surroundings by allowing them to highlight her sense of style and grace. She was a studied thing of beauty, intelligence in every artifice.

I let myself admire her for a moment before she noticed us, thinking back on a time when she had sat with me in an entirely different garden in London.

"Sebastian Lombardi, ma'am." Edgecumbe announced me and then deftly excused himself back into the house.

"Sebastian," Savannah echoed, standing to wait for me to come to her and then opening her arms to brace them on my forearms as I ducked to press a kiss to either of her soft cheeks. She smelled, as always, of freesia and gardenias, an English garden warmed by the hot blood beating beneath her pale skin.

"Savvy," I said, as I pulled away to smile down at her. "You look *bellissima*, as always."

Faint color tinged her cheeks, but she nodded politely and waited for me to move to the seat opposite her before sitting down again.

"You are too charming for your own good," she scolded me without heat, reaching for a Spode china teapot and pouring us each a cup of tea without asking how I took it. "I know you prefer coffee, but this garden calls for Earl Grey, I'm afraid."

I accepted the tiny saucer, worried I would crush it with a single spasm of my thick fingers. Carefully, I put it down in front of me.

"You were not very kind when I last saw you," she started in right away, looking up at me through her lashes as she sipped her own tea.

I raised a brow at her and realized it was something Adam would have done. "Wasn't I? You were clearly in the middle of something with Tate and Jace, and I was in the middle of an interview. It was not the time for casual conversation."

"You were flippant, once again, about working with me," she

noted sharply. "Are you waiting for me to prostrate myself before you? Because that will not happen."

Anger curdled in my gut. "It is a good thing, then, that I have seen you prostrated for me before."

"Don't be crude," she snapped.

"Don't be cold," I countered coolly.

Tension hummed between us.

Not even the birds seemed to sing from their trees.

From somewhere inside, I could catch the faint strains of Bach playing over the speakers.

And suddenly, I was tired. Exhausted, even, with the both of us.

Warily, I rubbed a hand through my hair and rolled back my shoulders to rid myself of their stiffness. "Let's start again, shall we? How are you, *duchessa*? I've missed you."

It was miraculous to watch the way the kind words softened her, water blurring the edge of her carefully painted lines.

Her smile, then, was tiny but true.

"I've missed you, too," she admitted. "It makes me irritable."

A Savannah-style apology.

I inclined my head in acceptance of it.

"What has kept you from me?" she asked casually, though there was nothing casual about her.

I crossed one ankle over my knee and leaned back. "The Critics Choice Awards are the weekend after next, followed swiftly by the Academy Awards. Interviews, podcasts, media events, and any other opportunities to put me in front of a camera for the purpose of winning awards. You know how it is."

"I do," she agreed, pausing for a moment to adjust the stems in a small bouquet on the table. "Are you taking a date?"

Just for a moment, an image of Linnea on my arm appeared in

my mind's eye. In full glam wearing one of her own feminine gowns, I wondered how many people she would stun with her fierce beauty.

I blinked, and the dream dissolved back into impossibility.

"No," I said.

None of the people I wanted to accompany were available to me. Though, to stave off loneliness, I had asked Giselle to accompany me to the Golden Globes.

"I saw a photo of you with some woman on a surfboard recently," Savannah mentioned airily.

"Did you?" I asked with a cheeky grin.

She pursed her lips. "Sebastian, don't be childish. Who is she?"

It was good for my spirit to see her jealous, but I wasn't cruel, so I merely shrugged and told her the truth. "Linnea Kai."

I was startled by her reaction.

Mouth agape, hand froze with the teacup lifted halfway to her raspberry-painted mouth, eyes wide and blue as the saucers on the table.

"Linnea Kai?" she reiterated.

"The very one."

She replaced the teacup without taking a sip, eyes narrowing. "As it happens, I just bumped into Linnea Kai on the arm of my ex-husband at Nobu the other day."

Ah.

I fought my smile valiantly and lost, the edges of my mouth curling deeply.

She thought Adam and I were picking up where we left off.

Only not, of course, with her.

But with another woman.

A younger one.

I knew how much that would burn her and felt both juvenile-like excitement and retribution, and a deep sorrow.

You could have me for as long as you wanted, I felt inclined to remind *her.* You could have fought harder to keep us all together.

But I didn't want to argue.

After finishing *The Dream & The Dreamer* and kissing two of my waking ghosts already, I didn't have it in me to play games.

"Linnea and Adam are dating," I agreed. "I introduced them."

"You did?" she said. There was no outward sign of it, but I knew she was seething.

"You and Adam have been divorced for over ten years and you've been married to Tate for most of that time," I reminded her. "Would you have both of us be miserable forever without you?"

Okay, maybe I did have it in me to play games.

Savannah's small teeth clicked as she snapped her jaw shut at my remark.

"That was unusually rude of you."

I shrugged. "I am tired. I stayed up most of the last three days working. It might have been blunt, but is it true? *Cazzo,* you have never encouraged me with any of the women I've dated. You must know I have been hopelessly in love with you for very many years. Does that seem fair to you?"

She blinked, caught off guard by my candor.

We did not speak of feelings or our past.

When we spent time together, we simply enjoyed the other's company, and we rarely even flirted.

But something about being with Linnea, and Adam again, had left me raw and unwilling to hide from myself.

From her.

"Sebastian," she whispered, leaning forward to place a hand on the table in front of me, almost but not quite an offering. "If that is the case, is not any time we spend together a gift?"

Part of me softened at hearing discernible proof that she was moved by me in her way, too. The other was irritated with her coyness.

I could get drunk off this, Linnea had said when I kissed her, everything she felt shining from those periwinkle eyes. *Off you.*

Savannah, for her part, could not even bring herself to actually touch me, her fingertips curling over the edge of the table instead of the inside of my thigh.

"Having experienced the bright light of true love, how can you expect me to be content to live in the shade?" I asked quietly.

Savannah rolled her lips between her teeth, obviously torn.

I let the silence roll out uncomfortably between us.

When I sipped the tea as a distraction, I remembered how much I disliked it.

"It's funny, isn't it?" she asked finally. "How love isn't everything?"

The words hit my heart like a bat to a piñata, shattering bits of it through my bloodstream so I felt as if I was coming apart at my seams.

"To me, it's everything," I said clearly. "*L'amor che move il sol e l'altre stelle.* Love that moves the sun and the stars."

All at once, I was thrown back to the night she and Adam had given me the Patek Philippe watch.

Savannah had assumed I wanted to be *the man* who moved the sun and the stars.

A powerful force in the universe.

Because she loved power and assumed everyone else did, too.

But Adam and I had both understood the truth.

I wanted nothing more than a love so powerful it moved the sun and the stars, redefined my sense of gravity.

I had thought for a long time that only Savannah and Adam were capable of giving that to me.

But had the beautifully cultivated piece of artwork that sat before me ever been capable of reciprocating that sentiment? Or, like a painting, had her only purpose been to evoke that emotion in others? So she could bask in that adoration while safely separated from reciprocation by glass and frame.

I needed to believe that every mistake Savannah had ever made was because of love. A love so big it overwhelmed her, made her fearful because its sheer enormity threatened to eclipse everything she'd known before it.

I had to believe that. I had to cling to it until my fingernails peeled and bled, until my teeth cracked from the pressure of holding on. Because if I didn't, then what was all of it for?

Why did she have to put us through all of this? The yearning and pain and utterly human suffering.

Why do it if not for love?

The answer to that was not pretty. It was mean and cruel and promised to rip me apart.

Did she even still have the watch I'd returned to her in New York City when I'd first seen her engaged to Tate? I had never asked, but the question burned in my throat.

The ache around my heart moved up into my head and throbbed like tandem wounds. I felt under attack by my own psyche as I tried to fight my way through the thicket of the past and the tangled mess of my present, where, it was quite possible I was on the precipice of loving three very different, very unattainable people.

My mama used to shake her head at me and say of all her children, I was the one who always insisted on choosing the most difficult course for myself.

At this moment, I had to agree with her.

"I do have feelings for you that will never die," Savannah confessed with a wince, pulling her hand back to clasp it tightly in her other one as if she needed to self-soothe. "But believing love is everything is naive. There are other factors."

"Maybe back then," I allowed. "When I had no money or fame. But now? What is stopping you from leaving Tate and being with me the way we could have been all along?"

"Sebastian," she said, a sharp reprimand.

"Savannah," I pushed back. "I'm being serious. If you love me as I have loved you, what is stopping you?"

"I am a married woman," she hissed, thrusting her enormous diamond ring out in front of her.

"That didn't stop you before."

She was out of her seat and slapping me before I could blink, the blow smarting instantly.

I stared at her in shock, disbelieving that she really would have hit me.

It was a passionate thing to do, so wildly unlike her.

Perhaps it shouldn't have given me hope, but it did. I was from a country where people shouted and pushed and went over the line in the heat of the moment. My mother had thrown fish heads at Seamus when he returned from three consecutive nights of gambling and debauchery, Elena had nearly screamed the apartment building down when she found out Giselle and Sinclair were expecting their first child, and Alexander and Dante had quite literally killed men for insulting their wives.

Perhaps this was like that.

An excess of emotion that overflowed from the small vessel Savannah had culled her heart into.

I dropped to my knees on the ground before her chair where she still stood, eyes blown black with her own surprise, hand lifted in horror to her chest.

"This is the second and last time I will ask you this," I told her solemnly, the way one swore fealty to a feudal king. "Leave him and be with me. Choose me this time, as I have to believe you wanted to before. Be brave, Savannah, and pick passion over power. Choose us over anything else. I have held my tongue for the past six years we have been just friends, and I will not do it any longer. That is not the man I am."

A small voice in the back of my head reeled at my proposition.

What if she *actually* chose me?

It seemed like such a pipe dream, but she could shock us both and reach down to clasp my face in her hands and make a decision with her heart instead of her head for the first time in her life.

What then?

Of Adam.

Of Linnea.

Of *them*.

They had each other, though. Even when I had set them up in this Hollywood deception, I had hoped they would fall in love. Two people with hearts like theirs deserved a love that could swallow the world down to nothing, make everything outside of their two twined hearts seem inconsequential in comparison. If anyone could convince Adam—beautiful, broken Adam—to love again and do it fiercely, it was Linnea Kai.

And there was no room for me with them.

I did not fit in Adam's world, his male lover, and I wasn't sure I could love Linnea with half my heart when the other was mired in the past.

Mired in duchessa mia.

I stared up at Savannah, her blue eyes pale but intent on mine. Her gaze scorched me, hot and sharp instead of comforting, as if she was trying to burn away the layers of my skin to see through to my heart.

If Adam had once been my moon, had Savannah been my sun?

How could she have been when the image conjured only violet eyes and caramelized skin, the wide smile of a girl who could never sit still or leave well enough alone? Who tipped her head to the sky to bathe in the warmth spilling from the burning planet we orbited around as if each golden ray was a gift.

"Sebastian," Savannah rasped.

And I knew then, in those three syllables, what her decision would be because she had already made it all those years ago when I stood in a hotel room begging her to leave her first husband for me, too.

No.

"I wish I could," she finished on a weak exhale, hands trembling as one rested on my shoulder and the other pushed through my hair. "If things were different, if I had made different decisions as a young woman, but now… I am sorry. I can't just run away with you."

Was it running away if it was meant to be coming home?

"*D'accordo*," I murmured, rocking back to my feet to stand and step away as quickly as I could. "*Naturalmente. Quando mai sono stato abbastanza?*"

Of course, when have I ever been enough?

I moved to the leather messenger bag I had dropped beside my chair and fished out the stapled pages of the script before I dropped them on the table in front of her. They clattered against the china, the teacup upending from the saucer and spilling brown water across the immaculate white marble.

"I wrote a script," I said woodenly, ignoring her little gasp. "I made you a promise that you could be the first to read it, but you should know, I won't make this movie with you and Tate."

"Seb—"

"You should know," I repeated, the words whipping from my tongue to lash across the space between us so hard she flinched. "We were never just friends, Savannah, and now? Now, you have chosen for us to be nothing."

I walked away then, believing until the very last moment I got into my car and pulled away from the house that she would come after me.

Of course, she didn't.

CHAPTER SEVENTEEN

LINNEA

I hadn't seen Adam or Sebastian in five days.

Not too long, in the grand scheme of things, especially considering that before a month ago, I hadn't seen either of them in a decade.

But five days felt like a lifetime, now.

Sebastian had practically disappeared. Only a single text two days ago informed me that he had been in his writing cave. I tried not to take it personally that, in the wake of our kiss, he was essentially ghosting me, but it was hard not to. Especially when I couldn't exactly talk to anyone about it.

What would I say?

The man I've loved from afar for years finally kissed me, but I'm contractually obligated to date his ex-lover?

Yeah. No.

To add even more confusion to the mix, I also missed Adam.

After our date in Malibu had been cut short, we returned to his place on Carbon Beach for a debrief with his entire team: Chaucer, Rachel Hoffman, Mi Cha Lee, and his lawyer, Boone Decker. They decided that ignoring "the outrageous claims of a disgruntled employee" was still the best overall tactic, though an "anonymous source" close to Adam would offer a reputable publication a quote along those lines.

They decided, too, that enough was enough.

Dating wasn't doing the trick anymore.

"Marriage," Mi Cha pushed. "It's the best option."

"We don't want them to elope to Vegas after this has hit the newsstands," Chaucer argued. "It reeks of guilt."

"True," Boone agreed.

"If my opinion has any bearing at all," I spoke up, unwilling to be swept away on a tide of professionals deciding my future, however well-meaning. "I don't think it makes any sense to get married in such a rush. It will only hurt us both."

My feelings on a marriage of convenience were also understandably complicated. Fake dating was one thing, but to enter into holy matrimony on a pretense? I wasn't religious or even very spiritual, but I was a closet romantic, and I wasn't sure I could stomach the idea of exchanging vows with a man I was only just coming to know and trust.

"Perhaps an increased presence with the paps?" Boone suggested.

"We've been photographed around town countless times in the past few weeks," Adam pointed out. There was such a weariness in his tone even though he maintained a ramrod straight posture and cool gaze, as if sitting at attention would mean that nothing else could take him by surprise.

"You haven't been to a proper Hollywood event yet," Rachel said. "The Critics Choice Awards are in two weeks. It's an excellent opportunity to attend a red carpet event together. Do some interviews, be photographed for all the publications and social media outlets together."

"It was already on the schedule," Adam said, and feeling his gaze on me, I looked over to see he had a raised brow as if to ask me whether it was still okay.

"I'll be there with bells on," I assured him.

His other brow joined the first, high on his forehead. "I assume you don't mean literally. I know you are a fashion designer, so frankly, I wouldn't put that past you."

He startled a bright burst of laughter from me, and I was rewarded with an answering, slightly smug, smile.

"No bells," I promised. "But you don't mind if I wear something I've made myself?"

"Why would I?" he countered. "I assume you've made most of the clothing I've seen you in, including this." His free hand rose to trail a thumb down the thin strap of my leopard-print dress to the edge of the bodice. His pad was rough enough to make me shiver as he paused and then followed the curve of the fabric to the middle of my breasts. He then used that same thumb to tip my chin back up so I was forced to meet his gaze. "You have been utterly bewitching in all of it."

"Mr. Meyers, it would be better for exposure to have her wear a known designer—" Mi Cha started to explain, but one cutting glance from Adam quelled her.

"Linnea will wear what she likes," he declared, once again impervious and completely in control of his domain.

"I'll bring in a team to do her hair and makeup," Chaucer offered, giving me a little wink of solidarity.

I beamed at her.

"Good. Meanwhile, someone call Fitzgibbons and see why the

hell he hasn't been able to locate Oscar. It seems to me that if he is sending emails, we should be able to trace him."

"There are legal means and nonlegal means to track someone," Boone said carefully.

Adam delivered a cool look that clearly stated he expected both to be valid options.

Boone nodded. "I'm on it."

I smothered a yawn behind my hand. The antique clock on the desk said it was nearing ten at night, which was my bedtime, given I was usually up before dawn.

Adam had noticed immediately, insisting on walking me to my car, clicking his tongue in disapproval of my ancient Jeep even as he helped me up into the driver's seat.

"It's been a long day," he told me as he stood in the open door, hesitating even though his team waited inside and I was buckled in and ready to head home. The golden lights mounted on the exterior of the garage cast his face into bright rectangles of brightness and shadow. It was hard to read his expression, but even so, I couldn't look away from the intensity in his eyes. "But I had a good time despite the drama. Because of you."

I swallowed thickly, feeling suddenly shy, every one of my twelve years younger and less experienced than him. The air between us was thick with heat even in the cool February night. I wanted desperately to kiss his weary face, hold him while he tried to sleep tonight, and offer him both comfort and seduction.

But that wasn't my place.

At the most, we could be friends, and I hoped today was a bigger step toward that.

So I leaned forward to brush a kiss along the sharp edge of his square jaw and whispered, "I think it has been a very long time since you were seen instead of just looked at, Mr. Meyers. You've been alone in the dark for too long, and I'm happy to be the one standing beside you now."

"For the next three years, at least," he said. It was meant to be a joke, but it landed unevenly, broken, and ugly.

"For as long as you'll have me," I corrected softly, our noses brushing.

I watched his long, tangled lashes sweep down to cover his eyes, his Adam's apple bobbing hard as he swallowed before he nodded tersely and stepped back to close my door. He turned to walk away, hands in his pockets, shoulders squared as if for battle.

I realized that in the past few weeks, a tenuous anchor had hooked through my heart and linked my soul to his. It tugged as I watched him walk away, urging me to go back inside with him.

Without giving myself time to think, I undid my seat belt, wrenched open the door, and jumped from the car before running to him carefully on my high-heeled sandals. He turned before I reached him, catching me with a surprised *oof* as I threw myself into his arms.

A startled huff of laughter stirred my hair even as his arms went around me in a tight squeeze. "What's this about?"

"You looked like you could use a hug," I whispered thickly, clutching him close and burrowing my nose in his neck where his rich, clean scent filled my lungs.

After a moment's hesitation, he relaxed slightly against me and sighed deeply.

We stood like that for long minutes, pressed together as if sewn tight at the hips, thighs, and chest. When he finally pulled away, there was a phantom sensation of ripping, as if we weren't meant to be parted.

He cupped my cheeks, staring somberly into my face. "What a gift you are," he murmured. "A single sunbeam in my lonely dark."

"Not so lonely anymore," I reminded him.

"No," he agreed softly, thumb sweeping over my cheek before he abruptly dropped his hands and offered me a tiny smile. "Go home, Sunbeam. Text me when you get in safely."

I nodded, my voice lost somewhere in the sensations battling inside my chest.

When he started walking away again, he did it backward, hands in his pockets once more, that little, private smile constructed just for me pinned between his cheeks. I walked backward toward my car, giggling when I tripped over my feet and had to catch myself on the spare wheel attached to the trunk.

When I looked back up at him, I caught the flash of his wide grin before the door to the house closed on his face.

Now, five days later, Adam was on his way back from New York City, and I would finally get to see him again. He had a surprise for me, one he'd teased me about during his absence in a surprisingly boyish way that made me kick my feet whenever I received a text.

I was seeing out my last shift at Affaire, working from opening at eleven until seven. My schedule was too busy to maintain my job at the restaurant now that I was dating Adam and, as a result, finally booking scads of auditions. Mali had told me just that morning I had five lined up for minor roles in some serious blockbusters just next week. The paparazzi, who were always frequent visitors outside the star-lauded restaurant, were also aware that I worked there, and they hounded me whenever I came and went. It had reached the point where my manager had politely suggested I had outgrown my stint with them.

It was sad, in a way. Serving at the exclusive French restaurant was my first job in Los Angeles, and it led me to meet Rozhin, my first and only best friend in town.

So it didn't surprise me when tears sprang to my eyes as I entered the server hub just before my shift was about to end to find Ro huddled with several other servers around a little citrus mousse cake.

"Congrats!" they called out in a muted shout so they didn't disturb the diners.

I laughed as they swarmed me, huddling me toward the cake so I could blow out the single candle and read what the pastry chef had written in dark chocolate on the top.

To the future Mrs. Adam Meyers.

I rolled my eyes so hard they almost stuck that way, making Ro and another girl, Shirley, laugh.

"I told you I'm not leaving to be his stay-at-home wifey," I reminded them.

Dan, a gorgeous gay man who applied makeup like a wizard, batted his mascaraed eyes at me. "Don't be coy, honey. We all know no one in their right mind would resist that future."

"There's nothing wrong with lying around naked all day waiting to serve that fine piece of ass," Mary agreed.

"If we were ever friends, you'll send pics," Paris teased.

"Naked ones," Dan qualified.

I laughed, covering my face with my hands. "You lot are incorrigible."

"Just tell us, is he as well-endowed as I imagine in my dreams?" Mary asked.

I mimed zipping my lips. "No comment."

"That means hell yes," Rozhin translated.

There was a series of longing sighs.

"But in all seriousness," Ro said, slinging her arm around my shoulders to tug me in for a kiss on my cheek. "You'll remember us when you're rich and famous, right?"

"Like I could ever forget you," I promised. "And stop acting like I'm skipping town. We'll still see each other."

She pouted. "It'll be different. It *is* different. You're on the up and up, now."

"Bitch," Paris joked, elbowing me in the side.

"Astrid worked here, you know," Shirley said, referring to Astrid Meeker, a relatively well-known TV actress who starred in a supernatural show. "She literally never spoke to any of us again."

"I'm not Astrid," I pointed out with a raised brow, smiling at myself when I realized it was an Adam mannerism.

"No, you are not." Ro shmushed her face to mine as Mary fed me a piece of cake.

"Okay, okay," our manager, Patrick, said as he came into the hub. "As sad as we all are to see Linnea go, is it too much to ask for you all to get back on the floor?"

There was a general grumbling, but everyone grabbed their things and exited the hub like good little worker bees leaving the hive.

Patrick stopped me before I could follow suit, his hand on my arm, our bodies close in the narrow neck of the hub before it spilled into the hall.

"I'm serious. We will miss you here," he said quietly, his big, brown eyes soft.

I offered him a little smile, a careful one, because Patrick had wanted to get in my pants for a long time, and I wasn't about to give him the wrong idea about the kind of send-off I wanted now.

He was cute and sweet, and, unlike most of the other people at Affaire, he didn't sleep around with back- or front-of-house staff. Rozhin had always thought I was crazy not to at least take him for a spin, but she didn't know the secret desires of my heart.

She didn't know I liked to be put on my knees, bent and folded like intricate origami by a master who was deft enough to handle me.

Patrick simply didn't have it in him to satisfy me in the ways I'd always preferred.

"Adam Meyers is a lucky man," he said, just a little edge of bitterness there.

My smile curled deeper. "Many would say I'm the lucky one."

"Those people don't know you," he said simply.

And I thought it was one of the loveliest things anyone had ever said to me.

I patted his arm and pushed out into the restaurant toward my section to wrap up the last of my tables before Dan took over for the night shift.

Seven plates were carefully balanced in my arms when I looked up from clearing a table to see Sebastian walking towards me. He hadn't seen me yet, so I took a moment to catalogue how gorgeous he looked in black trousers, a knit, short-sleeved button-up, and slick leather loafers. His ankles were shockingly sexy and tanned, exposed between the hem and the shoe in the European fashion of foregoing socks. He had shaved his usual stubble, revealing the strong planes of his face, and his hair was carefully gelled back from his forehead in perfect waves.

It was as if the restaurant took a collective deep breath of appreciation as he moved through the space, all eyes on him.

So it took me a moment to notice who was with him.

A short, curvy redhead in a lavender sundress that swirled around her ankles the way her curls tumbled around her heavy breasts. She looked like some goddess emerged from the ocean, something beautiful and faintly dangerous.

For one heart-stopping moment, I felt rage consume me like the building had crashed over my head, crumbling my bones to dust.

Jealousy, I realized, after struggling to take a deep breath, was what I was feeling.

And completely unfounded, I noted a moment later, when a tall, lean auburn-haired man cut through the restaurant in their wake until he caught up with them at a table in Mary's section. He slid a palm over the woman's lower back as he held out the chair for her, only moving away after she was seated and had rewarded his gentlemanly behavior with a kiss that was slightly inappropriate for public consumption.

The pressure eased from my chest, and I sucked in a relieved breath.

Giselle Sinclair and her husband, Daniel Sinclair.

Sebastian's sister, a renowned artist specializing in provocative paintings, and the French businessman who owned, among other properties, this very restaurant.

Sensing me, or perhaps noticing the woman standing still as a statue in the middle of the restaurant carrying one too many plates, Sebastian looked up from his seat at the table and directly locked eyes with me. I had the pleasure of watching warmth suffuse his features, his eyes the color of the candlelight flickering atop each table.

I quirked a lopsided grin at him before slightly shrugging my shoulders to indicate the plates and hightailed it into the kitchen. It was steamy, too hot, and cacophonous, but it felt like an oasis after the tumult of feelings I had experienced in the dining room.

I had no right to be jealous of anyone Sebastian might date.

Not when I was ostensibly dating his ex-lover and best friend.

Not when he'd had the choice to date me for real and passed it up as if he had never been tempted.

"You okay, Lins?" one of the sous chefs asked as he carefully spooned fragrant butter over a steak in a sizzling pan a few feet from me.

I nodded and gave him a wan smile before heading back through the kitchen toward the locker room. My shirt smelled of seafood sauce and that particular greasy kind of smoke that came from spending too long near a working kitchen. The scent also permeated my thick hair, so I unwound it from its complicated Dutch braids and spritzed with some perfume from my purse before switching out my uniform for the last time. I changed into a delicate, white lace dress that hugged my curves until just above my knees where it flared slightly into a frothy hemline. It was one of the newest pieces I'd finished in the late hours of the night when I was too wired to sleep even though I was exhausted. I hadn't created so many designs in *years* but being on Adam's arm had inspired me.

I wanted to look good, not just for the paps but also for him.

Though, I had originally packed this dress to impress an entirely different man. Adam, who would be picking me up any minute for a date to celebrate my last night serving at Affaire.

I groaned and banged my head lightly against the locker door after I cleared it out.

Was I officially the greediest girl in existence for lusting after not just one gorgeous movie star but two? Was it beyond wild for me to think that maybe—just maybe—if I tread forward carefully, I could have them both?

Or, more correctly, we could all have each other?

Even if being with Adam and Sebastian was a pipe dream for me, I'd do what I could to bring them back into each other's lives. Some people were meant to exist in each other's orbit, and those two were a perfect example of that.

"Buonasera, trottolina mia."

I closed my eyes as I huffed out a laugh.

"Great," I muttered. "Now you're hallucinating him."

A smoky chuckle alerted me to the fact that I was *not*. When I twirled around, Seb stood in the doorway to the locker room, arms crossed over his chest as he casually leaned against the wall. There was a smug, mischievous grin on his face like a teenage boy who had found himself in the girls' locker room.

"How did you get back here?" I asked, a little breathless with surprise and a surge of arousal.

His mouth ticked higher on one side as he pushed off the wall and strolled languidly toward me. My throat clicked dryly as I swallowed hard, frozen in place by the look in his eye as he stood too close and raised a hand to brush a wayward wave out of my face.

"I walked," he teased softly.

"But why? You're here with your family."

"I am," he agreed easily. "My sister and her family have moved nearby, and my mother is in town to help with the children while they get settled. It was my turn to pick the restaurant, and I found I didn't want to waste another day without seeing you."

"Sebastian," I murmured, transfixed by his intensity, the way those golden eyes seemed to burn through to the core of me and light it all on fire. "What are you doing?"

"Being honest," he said with a flippant shrug that was at odds with the way he stared at me. "Is that so hard to believe?"

"Why now?" I asked. "When things are so complicated?"

He looked at the floor for a moment, shoving his hands in his pockets as if to restrain himself from reaching out to me. After a long pause, he looked back up at me through his thick, black lashes, and his expression was ravaged.

"How do you give someone a heart that has already been claimed and broken?" he asked with raw sincerity. "How do you know if the pieces left inside your chest are even good enough to share?"

"Is this about Adam or Savannah?" I asked baldly because even though I wanted to fixate on the "me" part of the equation, his eyes were too haunted to focus on that.

"Both," he admitted with a truncated shrug. "I spoke with Savannah a couple of days ago. After so many years, I think…I think the hope I harbored is finally dead."

I nodded slowly, processing the tangible grief in the room. "Okay. I'm so sorry, Seb. I won't lie and say I think she was ever good enough for you, but I hate that you're hurting."

Absently, he rubbed at his chest as if to soothe the ache behind his breastbone. "Me too, I think."

I chewed on my lower lip, twirled a silver ring around my finger, and took the plunge. "Take your time to mourn. But remember, losing someone can mean you have room in your heart for someone new. Someone who might love you better than she ever did or the ghost she became for so many years."

"I hope that's true," he murmured, finally stalking forward like a runner off the starting line to haul me into his arms.

It was just a hug. His strong arms wrapped around me so tight I couldn't quite breathe, his nose against my neck, his mouth hot on my collarbone. But it was the most intimate embrace I'd ever had. I held him close, hands shifting through the crisp waves of his raven-black hair.

Incrementally, he relaxed into my hold.

It reminded me of hugging Adam, how on guard he'd been at first, how hard it must have been to trust me enough to hold him.

Sebastian and Adam were two very different men, but they shared one vital characteristic. They both felt so much that they often didn't know what to do with it or who to trust with it.

I decided then and there that it would be my life's mission to be that person for them both.

The door banged open suddenly, Rozhin stepping through and

coming to a sudden stop at the sight of me tangled up with a man who was decidedly not the blond-haired Adonis known as Adam Meyers.

My supposed boyfriend.

We locked eyes over Sebastian's back, and her jaw flopped open.

Seb stepped back casually and turned to face her, his charming smile spreading smoothly across his features.

"Hello," he said in that rich, sexy accent. "You must be Rozhin."

Ro, who had never been dumbstruck a day in her life, blinked back at him.

"Linnea has told me a lot about you," he continued easily, stepping forward to offer his hand. "It's good to know she's had a friend in her corner while she's been in town. It's lovely to meet you."

"Lovely," she echoed, swaying to the side to meet my eyes and widen hers comically before she extended her hand to him. "Lovely to meet you too, Sebastian Lombardi."

Seb chuckled. "Sebastian is fine."

"Sure, sure," Ro agreed, still holding his hand. "Uh, what are you doing back here with Lins?"

He moved slightly to angle his body so he could shoot me a wink. "I haven't seen my best friend in a few days, and I missed her. I'm sorry to intrude on your workspace."

My best friend.

Even though that wasn't exactly what I wanted from him, hearing Seb call me something so intimate made my blood warm as if I'd swallowed distilled sunshine.

"Any time," Ro said, finally recovering enough to bat her lashes at him. "In fact, you should come by more often."

"Ro," I murmured, a flash of possessiveness clutching my chest. "Behave."

Ro stuck her tongue out at me, making Sebastian laugh.

"I should get back to my family, anyway," he said. "But I was hoping you might join us for a drink, *trottolina*? I would like to introduce you to my family."

It was my turn to blink dumbly back at him.

"She has a date with Adam Meyers," Ro interceded on my behalf. "He's picking her up."

Something dark and greedy crossed Sebastian's face almost too quickly to notice it.

"*Bene*, I would like to introduce our Brit to my family, too," he announced. "*Andiamo*, Linnea. Let's go."

He reached his hand out for me, and Rozhin's eyes bulged in surprise as I stepped forward to take it. It wasn't wise to show casual affection for another man, let alone a fellow movie star, when I was dating Adam, but I trusted Ro enough to indulge in the need to be close to him.

After nearly a week without seeing him, in the wake of a kiss that had rocked me and left me utterly disoriented, I wanted to hold Seb's hand like I needed my next breath.

The casual affection reminded me that, no matter what, we had been friends for years and would remain so for years yet. Unlike Savannah Richardson, I never intended to let Sebastian Lombardi go.

"You better fucking call me later, girl," Ro muttered as I passed her.

I rolled my eyes at her, but she just lifted a finger to point at me the way a scolding mother might have.

Sebastian didn't let go of my hand as we crossed into the restaurant and weaved through the tables toward the large round-top in the corner where his sister, brother-in-law, and now mother sat.

I tried to pull back, but he held fast.

"*Stai tranquilla*," he murmured to me as he pulled me close to tuck my hand through his arm as we reached the table. "Be still, Linnea.

They will love you."

Daniel Sinclair stood as we stopped at the table, a gentlemanly almost archaic thing to do that made me instantly like him. Miranda would have swooned, and not just because he was gorgeous, with shoulder-length, dark red hair and vibrant blue eyes set in a tanned face.

"Sebastian," he said, his voice faintly French. "Who is this?"

"May I introduce Linnea Kai," Sebastian said, and he did it so… proudly. As if I were famous or important and not just a girl.

To my horror, tears pricked the backs of my eyes.

"Linnea," his brother-in-law repeated with raised brows and a small, enigmatic smile. "Good to meet you. I am Sinclair, Giselle's husband."

"Oh, *Linnea*." Sebastian's mother, a gorgeous older woman with thick, long, black hair with ribbons of silver strands, stood up to grasp me by the shoulders and kiss me on either cheek. "Sebastian has told me about you. You are the girl who loves the ocean, *sí*? You smell of its salt."

I laughed a little weakly, overwhelmed. "Yes, I guess I am."

When I looked at Sebastian, he was smiling widely, eyes glowing like miniature suns.

"You can call me Mama," his mother offered kindly. "Everyone does."

"Or, if that is too familiar, her name is Caprice," Giselle said, standing up to extend her hand across her mother's body. There was crimson and fuchsia paint dried on the inside of her wrist. "My name is Giselle. I'm so happy to meet such an old friend of Seb's."

"I can't believe you told them about me," I muttered, a little embarrassed even though I was also immeasurably pleased.

Dad and my uncles knew about Sebastian, of course, because

they always teased me mercilessly about the postcards and letters I wrote to him, but that was different somehow.

"*Certamente*, I did," Sebastian agreed with a small frown as he ushered me to an empty seat. "You are important to me."

"I love your dress," Giselle complimented as we settled at the table. "It's so delicate, it almost looks like sea foam."

I grinned. "That was exactly what inspired it, actually, so thank you."

She lifted a fine red brow. "You made it yourself?"

"Linnea is an accomplished designer," Sebastian said, sliding an arm along the back of my chair the way a lover might. The press of his bare skin along my shoulder made me shiver. "She is always wearing something new and beautiful."

I blushed and swatted at his chest. "Stop singing my praises. I like you enough already without you being so over the top."

"Over the top?" he repeated with mock outrage. "Me?"

"You are prone to dramatics, *Patatino*," Caprice said with a cluck of her tongue.

"Since he was little," Giselle agreed, grinning at me.

"*Patatino*?" I asked, intrigued by the nickname.

"No," Seb protested strongly.

"It means little potato," Giselle explained.

"He was born with his head shaped like this," Caprice explained seriously.

I looked at Sebastian, who wore a fierce expression of regret, and burst out laughing.

That was how Adam found me, sitting at a table with Seb and his family, the Italian's arm across the back of my chair like a flag staked in the ground declaring his territory.

I felt him before I saw him.

A crackling of energy, a lightning strike at the front entrance.

Sebastian turned at the same time as I did, both of us locked into that familiar abundance of commanding magnetism.

Adam stood beside the hostess stand in a slightly mussed black suit, the top buttons on his dark green shirt undone and the sleeves rolled up, the blazer tossed over one shoulder and hooked by a finger. I wondered if he'd headed to the airport straight from his last interview in the city.

"He does not look happy," I murmured.

"No," Sebastian said, a dark note of glee in the word. "He does not."

"What game are you playing?"

His response was a smoky chuckle.

Adam noted the expression, his own glower tightening. He stalked through the restaurant like a wild cat through the jungle, completely homed in on his prey. Diners tittered as he moved by them, but he didn't seem to notice.

The center of his attention was solely Sebastian and me.

A shiver rolled through me as my blood flashed hot and cold with a curiously arousing mix of fear and anticipation.

The Adam I knew was unfailingly polite, probably due to his upbringing in the peerage and his brief stint in the Royal Air Force, but he eschewed every nicety as he finally approached the table. Instead of greeting the diners, or even acknowledging them, he kept his eyes trained on me.

I swallowed thickly as he stopped at the side of my chair, braced a hand along the back of my neck under the thick sweep of my hair— nestled tightly against Seb's arm—and used the other to grip my chin to tip my head back.

His eyes were hard, glittering emeralds, almost inhumanely

beautiful as they dominated my vision.

"Sunbeam," he rasped in a possessive growl a moment before he bent to claim my parted mouth.

He plundered without hesitation, sweeping into the cavern of my mouth with his hot, dexterous tongue. A breathy moan wrenched from me as heat scored down my throat and unfurled in my belly like a growing inferno. He kissed me so thoroughly, nipping, sucking, thrusting, that, in the end, I would have been happy to have him bend me over the table right there in the middle of the restaurant.

It was our first real kiss.

A public claiming so comprehensive that when he finally ripped himself away from me, his name escaped my lips like a revelation from God.

"Adam."

At the sound of his own name, something animal shone back at me in his gaze. A primal satisfaction that I was left so ravaged by his kiss. Instead of stepping away immediately, he gazed down at me with that intense focus and brushed the rough pad of his thumb over my kiss-stung lips.

"I've missed you," he murmured, and that confession seemed just for me.

A whisper in the dark.

"I missed you," I admitted, reaching up to link our fingers around his grip on my neck.

It was only then that I realized the entire restaurant was silent, only the faint din from the kitchen peppering the dense quiet.

I blinked to clear my vision of Adam and felt a blush rush like a bushfire across my skin.

"Well," Sebastian drawled, his accent thick as cool molasses poured from the tin. "That was quite the greeting. I don't suppose you intend to meet the rest of my family with a similar response, Adam?"

Across the table, Giselle tried unsuccessfully to swallow her giggle.

"I hadn't thought to, no," Adam said easily, straightening so that he stood pressed against my side, his hand still curled into mine around my neck. "Though, not because there is a lack of beauty at this table."

Giselle laughed fully this time, a bell-like chime that made me smile too.

"You are dangerous," Caprice said, pointing at Adam the way a parishioner might point accusatorily at a sinner.

Adam let a slow, sinful smile spread across his full mouth. "I have been accused of much worse things."

"I'm sure," Giselle murmured, her expression absolutely delighted.

She laughed when she caught my look, which must have been a mix of shock and wariness. Her hand lifted from beneath the table to showcase how it was linked with her husband's.

"I caught a charmer myself, Linnea, so I have a special appreciation for how wicked they can be."

Beside her, Daniel Sinclair's expression turned arrogantly lazy.

It was wildly attractive.

Adam seemed to notice because his hand squeezed my neck.

"I hope you'll excuse the interruption, but Linnea and I have plans to celebrate her last night of work here," he explained politely, but I could feel the tension in him vibrating at my back.

He wanted to get out from under the Lombardi spotlight. I could admit to feeling the same way. They were keen-eyed predators who saw more, I thought, than they should.

"You should both stay."

My head snapped to look at Sebastian, who was affecting such a pose of faux casualness that I almost bought it. Only the tightening of the skin beside his eyes spoke of the gauntlet he'd thrown at Adam's feet.

It was a dare.

Don't run, it said. Be a man, take a seat, and play me for the ultimate prize.

Only, I wasn't sure if Adam was the prize or myself, or perhaps— my heart kicked like a horse at my rib cage—both of us together.

Seb was looking at me, his eyes glittering in the low, yellow light spilling through the romantic restaurant, but I knew it was Adam he spoke to. I could have gotten involved, but I figured this was between them.

Adam needed to be goaded more anyway.

After a tense moment, Adam spoke, and I could tell it was through a clenched jaw. "I intended to take Linnea dancing."

I perked up at the thought and the surprise of it.

Adam did not seem like the type to take a girl dancing. He was so proper and suave that the image of him cutting loose on the dance floor was faintly humorous.

Sebastian was surprised too, if his raised brows were any indication. "Dancing?"

I tipped my head to watch Adam frown, haughty as ever. "I was forced into many dance lessons as a boy. I can assure you, I'm quite adequate on the dance floor. Regardless, Linnea's friend, Rozhin, told me that she loves to dance."

"You spoke to Ro?" I asked on a breath, tipping my head back even more so it rested against his hard belly.

The left corner of his mouth curled just a fraction, and his thumb swept over my pulse point. "A man uses every weapon in his arsenal, Linnea."

"Are we at war?" I teased, but the effect was somewhat ruined by the fact that I was still breathless.

Adam arched one brow, and though he didn't look at Sebastian, he might as well have. "Seduction can be a kind of battle."

"Hopefully one with considerably less blood and pain," Seb quipped dryly.

"Blood, certainly," Adam agreed on a throaty rumble.

Both Sebastian and I paused to suck in a steadying breath.

Beneath the cover of my heavy hair, Adam's hand slipped from my neck to Sebastian's forearm and shackled it briefly before returning his hold to me.

A faint ruddy flush stained Seb's tanned cheekbones.

"I own a club downtown." The cool French-accented words hit me like a bucket of cold water, and I shivered slightly as I dropped my head back down to look at Daniel. "We will go dancing after we eat. I already informed Chef Dev that we have extra guests and he's adjusting our meal accordingly."

"When did you manage that?" Giselle asked him, leaning in close to kiss the square hinge of his jaw as if she couldn't help herself.

In answer, Daniel raised his free hand to show his phone.

"It is settled," Caprice announced, every ounce the matriarch. "Sebastian, get Adam a chair, *dio mio*, he has nowhere to sit. Linnea, you must eat everything on your plate, *ragazza*, you are too thin."

Sebastian rolled his eyes playfully at me as he stood to do his mother's bidding and whispered, "You are perfect whichever way you come."

"Even gangly and awkward as I was at sixteen?" I countered with a grin.

He stopped behind his chair to reach forward and touch two fingertips to my cheek. It was such a little gesture, but it lit me up like a lightning rod.

"Whichever way you come," he repeated, smiling softly at me before glancing up at Adam and then going off to retrieve a chair.

When he was gone, Adam shifted to press his hips against the table beside me so he could cup my face and tilt it for his study. In the dim glow of the lamps, his eyes were dark as the night forest, hiding so many secrets I wondered if I would ever understand them.

"We can leave," he said quietly, shutting out the others for a moment so I could be honest with him. "We had a date."

A date.

For some reason, those words hit me like a slap.

Because I wanted it to be *real*.

A date with a man like Adam. Not because he was rich and famous and in need of a beard, but because he was queer and handsome and lonely and kind, and I wanted to be his girlfriend.

It was a good reminder that what we were doing was *staged*.

This, having dinner with Sebastian and his family, would be a good reminder to both of us that we were just playacting.

Only the stakes seemed so much higher than simply playing pretend.

Because somewhere along the line, I had forgotten this was an acting gig.

I'd thrown *myself* into Adam, and Sebastian, and the strange, dark currents between them without holding anything back.

It was only me who would get hurt at the end of three years, and I wasn't sure I could afford to lose Adam, Sebastian, and most likely Miranda all within that time.

So, I smiled widely, hoped the expression touched my eyes and said, "Dinner would be nice."

A little thrill of secret pleasure zinged down my spine at Adam's put-upon expression. He'd wanted to take me out.

He'd missed me.

His huge hands cupped nearly the entirety of my face, a rough thumb dragging over my cheekbone. The scent of him made me feel fuzzy-headed.

"Your lips were swollen from our kiss," he muttered, his gaze fixed on my mouth.

My tongue darted out nervously. "They're sensitive," I explained.

His eyes flashed, fingertips tightening just slightly at the image that must have conjured for him. For a moment, he let his hands sink into the sides of my hair and clench just a little, the way he might have done if he was urging me to suck him off.

"Be careful with the imagery you feed me, Nea," he growled, almost subvocal. "I am a man on a very short leash."

"I've already offered to help with that," I declared lightly as his hands dropped, and Sebastian returned with a chair he slotted in front of Adam.

Sebastian, attuned to the chemistry snapping through the air, smiled rakishly. "I am always ready to offer my services if either of you needs my help."

"With what, *caro mio*?" Caprice called.

"Running lines," he said smoothly, as he clasped Adam on the shoulder and me on mine so we were connected through him, a closed circuit of humming power.

"Ah, Linnea, you are an actress as well as a fashion designer?" Giselle asked, sweeping us back into conversation as Adam and Seb settled into their chairs.

"An amateur at both, I'm afraid," I said with a little shrug.

Sebastian and Adam both went to put their arms around my chair. With a single cold look from Adam, Seb dropped his but it found its way, neatly, onto my thigh beneath the table. He gave it a squeeze and winked surreptitiously at me.

"She's brilliant," Adam corrected. "It's just a matter of time before you see her face on a movie billboard over Sunset Boulevard."

"Gigi, she was in the last season of *Swamplands*," Sebastian said. "Tara Trevena, who tried to murder Eddie."

Giselle's mouth dropped open, and Daniel laughed as he explained her expression. "She had a few nightmares because of your performance."

"Seriously?" I asked, so pleased it made my toes curl.

Giselle nodded. "Seriously. I have a history with a psychopathic stalker, and the way you played her was chilling."

"I'm sorry to hear that," I murmured.

She waved her hand through the air, silver bangles chiming. "I meant it as a compliment."

"Of course, she did," Sebastian said with a toothy smile. "The Lombardis recognize talent wherever we see it."

"And Linnea is brilliant," Adam repeated firmly, as if to close the file on the subject irrefutably.

To my horror, tears pricked small needles at the backs of my eyes.

My father and uncles were supportive of whatever I wanted to do in life, but they were men's men, in love with fishing and surfing and out-belching each other using the alphabet. They didn't know enough to compliment me on my skills beyond blithely wanting to support me.

Miranda, on the other hand, lived to berate me and remind me I was a failure as an actress. At my age, she liked to say, she had already spent five seasons starring on the long-standing soap opera, *The Beautiful & Damned*.

So this?

Praise for something I had worked hard at and loved to do but never felt validated for?

It was a very poignant tool in Adam's arsenal.

And Sebastian's.

I hastily took a sip of water after a server, Shirley, poured it for me with a wink, but for the first time in a long time, I wished for something stronger.

Because I was fairly sure my traitorous, greedy heart was beginning to fall in love with two men who were not mine to want.

CHAPTER EIGHTEEN

ADAM

I had often imagined meeting Sebastian's family properly. What kind of people had helped form such a man, such a masterpiece? It was a question that had kept me awake at night many nights in the wake of his leaving me—of me demanding he do so. He had spoken of them so often, the women in his life, and with a ferocity of love and loyalty that often left me feeling slightly, even childishly, jealous.

I wanted him to feel that way about me even though the idea also petrified me.

Of course, his entire family wasn't present at the table. His twin sister, Cosima, was holed up in England, about to give birth to triplets, and his eldest sister, Elena, was at home in New York City with her husband and three children.

But meeting Caprice, Giselle, and Sinclair was wonderfully insightful.

They teased Sebastian playfully but mercilessly about his stardom, a cowlick in his hair that caused a lock to fall constantly across his forehead, and his unique ability to state the year a film had been made and its director, from blockbuster to totally obscure. I had read somewhere that teasing was a sign of love and intimacy, but this was perhaps the first time I understood how that could be true.

Linnea joined in as if she had been born into the family.

She had that magical ability to be at ease in any situation, so comfortable in her own skin that it did not occur to her to doubt herself. I wondered if it was a result of growing up with a famous mother who had also mostly abandoned her, in contrast to the wild love and stability she had experienced in Maui with her father and uncles. By the time Chef Devereaux brought out dessert—a citrus confection of lemon meringue, raspberry coulis, yuzu mousse and dark chocolate curls—Linnea was even bantering with Daniel Sinclair, a man known professionally to be as cool and aloof as they came.

I was, unfortunately, ridiculously charmed by the entire evening, but particularly by the two people who had so quickly become the center spokes of my life.

Sebastian and Linnea.

So, after Sinclair tried to pay for the bill only to discover that I had taken care of it on a trip to the toilet and then tried to argue with me senselessly about it, I found myself agreeing to go with the group to Sinclair's night club, Temptations.

We all piled into an enormous SUV Sinclair had ordered after saying goodbye to Caprice, who declared herself too old to party into the wee hours of the evening, and suddenly, I was pressed tightly between Seb and Linnea.

My throat went dry at the feel of them lined up against either side of me and the spicy, ocean salt taste of them both on my tongue.

After so many inventive experiences in the back of the Rolls-

Royce in London, cars had become a strange aphrodisiac for me, not to mention the two people beside me.

The savagery of the desire that barreled through me was almost terrifying, a bloodlust, a ravening that called me to rip into their clothes like a beast and rut until they both felt and smelled like mine.

"All right?" Sebastian asked in a typically British manner that reminded me of our time together in London.

We were so close that his nose brushed the hair over my ear as he spoke, and a shiver bit into my spine and shook it like a rabid dog.

I clenched my hands on my thighs.

Why had I agreed to wine with dinner?

I almost never drank anymore. Maybe a celebratory glass of champagne or a very cold lager on a hot summer's day, but mostly I was sober. Alcohol had been my crutch in those bleak years after Savannah and Seb had left me, and when I pulled myself, with Chaucer's help, out of that dark place, I had resolved never to let booze derail my life again.

Yet here I was, buzzing just slightly but still enough to crank up the volume of the wicked fantasies whispering in the warm dark of my subconscious.

"Perhaps I should take Linnea home," I said carefully, the words clicking against my teeth like ice cubes.

Seb reared back as far from me as he could, and I realized I wasn't the only one who had been lulled into a false sense of security by the lovely evening.

"You can leave," Linnea said lightly, but her hand curled around my thigh, yellow nails digging just shy of painful into my flesh. "But I am going dancing with Sebastian, Giselle, and Sinclair."

"By all means," Sebastian said, changing tactics to align with hers, his voice dropping into a smoky tenor. "Leave Linnea with me, *Adamo.*

I am happy to see her home and to bed safely at the end of the night."

Visions of their long, lean bodies tangled in sheets erupted like fireworks behind my closed lids. Linnea was so curious, and Sebastian had always been adventurous, an eager student himself. What had he learned in ten years that he might apply to a night of sin with her?

I swallowed thickly.

"Very well," I said. "Though I should warn you, I am a very good dancer."

Linnea's laughter lit up the car, drawing Sinclair's and Giselle's attention momentarily before they went back to their own private conversation.

"I will believe it when I see it," she teased.

Teased.

The affection was so clear it burned like the touch of unfiltered sunlight.

"I believe it, though I've never seen it," Sebastian murmured, drawing my notice. His lids were low over those tiger-yellow eyes, his mouth parted so his tongue could touch the rim of his lower lip as if tasting a sense memory. "You've always moved well for such a big man."

It was stifling warm in this infernal SUV, but I didn't yank at my collar as I so wanted to.

"What else do you remember about the way I move, Sebastian?" I drawled, just to affect him the way he had me.

The hitch in his breath felt like an Olympian victory.

This is a very bad idea, I told myself, and found, much to my horror, I did not possess the willpower to care.

We pulled up in front of Temptations to find the entryway packed with paparazzi and fashionably clad Angelenos, but the moment we alighted from the car, the bouncers converged to make a path for us.

"Adam," someone yelled over the chaos. "Are the rumors about you and Oscar Hampton true?"

It took every single ounce of experience as an actor not to flinch from the question. A moment later, Linnea was pushing up under my arm, wrapping her own around my waist so that we were pressed intimately together.

She shot a megawatt smile at the arsehole who'd hollered at me and responded blithely, "Should I be jealous you aren't asking about me?"

A few of the paps laughed at her, and one obeyed her unspoken requested by asking, "Linnea Kai, are you and Adam in love?"

Behind me, Sebastian pressed a hand to my back even though he was turned away from the cameras to fade into the background as we paused to address the question. Giselle and Sinclair were already ahead of us, waiting at the door.

"What do you think, Mr. Meyers?" she practically purred, turning into me and running both hands up my torso, around my neck, and into my hair in a blatant act of possession.

In the sparkling lights of the camera flashes, her eyes seemed iridescent.

"Do you love me?" she asked me, smiling through the words.

I palmed her throat, letting that bestial side of me show for a moment. Both because the media would love it, and because I wanted to mark her and show them—show her—just how much I wanted her to be mine.

"How can someone resist loving the sun when it shines so brightly down on them?" I asked before I bent down to kiss her.

It was our second kiss ever and tonight.

Both performative.

But I had never, in all my years acting with dozens of costars and handfuls of love scenes, felt so moved by my own demonstration.

I wanted to pour myself down her sweet, citrus-flavored lips until she was claimed inside and out by every inch of me. It wasn't just about possession. It was about feeling safe.

Linnea had given me a safe haven in the shite storm of my life, a place so free of judgement and constraints it made me free to hope again. Free to feel.

So I kissed her for the cameras, and I kissed her to escape them.

And in the end, I forgot why I was kissing her at all other than to keep feeling those lips on mine, the long line of her curves against my own.

Sebastian's hand on my back shifted and dug into the muscles at the base of my spine.

A reminder that I was not at all alone.

The flashing lights of the cameras madly clicking away left me half blind as I pulled away from Linnea and tucked her back under my arm.

"I guess that answers that, eh, Meyers!" someone shouted.

The smile that curled my mouth was thin and curved like the edge of a dagger. I hated these vultures, but they served a purpose. By morning, Linnea and I would be all over the place, and Oscar's trite interview about his time as my chauffeur and that smiling selfie would be half-buried beneath us.

We caught up to Giselle and Sinclair, following them inside the dark mouth of the club and through a series of doorways until we emerged into a cavernous hall that must have once been a warehouse. Now, it was transformed by massive chandeliers that tinkled and swayed with the bass of the heavy, pulsating music, and the black velvet fabric that hung in swathes across the walls and ceiling. Everything was sumptuous. The floor reflected back in the antique mirrored bar. The servers all wore sultry uniforms of black hot pants or trousers with suspenders and sleeveless white button-ups.

"Wow," Linnea said, blinking owlishly.

Sinclair chuckled. "My clubs are about excess."

I watched a lower-level VIP section balcony where a rapper I admired was surrounded by a coterie of women dancing for him while he drank from magnum-sized gold bottles of champagne. Another scene was a buffet of desserts glinting like jewels as a bachelorette party feasted, toasted, and shimmied together in shades reminiscent of a summer sunset.

"Quite the place you have," I said, tone rich with admiration.

Sinclair shrugged modestly, but his expression was all arrogance. "Let me show you to the private VIP section I enjoy when I drop into the city. I think you will find it to your tastes."

Without another word, we followed him through the hot masses of churning, drinking bodies and to a curling staircase manned by two huge security guards who merely nodded at Sinclair before unclipping a red rope to let us go past.

We climbed the stairs past one level, then two, then three.

"The levels of sin," Giselle explained as she dropped beside Linnea and took her arm. "Gluttony, Greed, Sloth, Lust, Pride, Envy, and Wrath."

"Wrath?" Linnea asked, wide-eyed.

"In the basement," Giselle explained. "It's where fights are held sometimes."

"Clever," I muttered.

"Sinclair is that," Seb agreed, appearing beside me. "He knows how to indulge better than anyone I've ever met."

I must have made a face because Seb laughed, and for a moment, I stopped walking because I forgot how.

God, he was bloody gorgeous.

"The 'Lust' floor is a private sex club on the top floor. He only seems buttoned-up," Seb whispered conspiratorially. "Much like someone else I know."

"It's been a long ten years," I said, because I had a special ability to self-flagellate. "I could have changed."

Seb's mouth thinned, but he shrugged one shoulder. "*Sì*, I think you have. But under the layers of ash, I still see the burning heart of you."

And do you like it? *I wanted to ask*. Do you still want it?

But I didn't because I couldn't.

Finally, we stopped before an ornate wood-carved door with a brass plaque that labeled it "The Den." Sinclair opened it without fanfare, exposing a large room open to the four-story drop below, where bodies writhed like coiled, brightly flashing snakes. A sweep of heavy, black velvet curtains had been pulled back from the opening and tied with gold tassels, much like in a theatre, giving the entire space a dramatic, voyeuristic quality. The music was funneled up here, too, thrumming through the speakers with a bass beat that shook the floor. Velvet booths and opulent furniture decorated the space. To the right and left were a small stage and a bar, where a team of two bartenders was ready for service.

"I thought we could invite some friends," Giselle said as she tugged Linnea, and by extension me, toward the bar. "I already called some of mine and Sin's. Just write down their names and they'll be let in at the door."

"Wow," Linnea said, more breath than sound, eyes wide as she took in the VIP space, the ease with which Sinclair took off his suit jacket and tossed it over the end of a booth before rolling up his shirtsleeves. Sebastian was already on the phone, hands moving animatedly as he spoke to someone even though they couldn't see him.

"I'm not sure this is a good idea," I protested again, my stomach tightening at the idea of the celebrities that would no doubt flood this space in the coming hour.

It was one thing to play pretend as Linnea's boyfriend for the paps and strangers, for the Lombardis who didn't know any better. But I had been in Hollywood a very long time, and there were people who could ferret out my secrets and lies.

"You mentioned," Giselle said, a little tease accompanied by a genuine smile. "Don't worry, our friends keep their business to themselves. This is a safe place for you to let your hair down."

I hummed, not agreeing with her but reluctant to pull Linnea away from what would undoubtedly be a night of fun. She deserved to let loose and forget her responsibilities for a moment.

Maybe so did I.

"What's your oldest scotch?" I asked the male bartender.

He grinned. "An eighteen-year-old Laphroaig."

I nodded to confirm my order and slid a sidelong look at Linnea, who had propped her elbows on the bar to face me. The position propped her breasts in the corseted top, richly tanned skin spilling temptingly over the delicate white lace.

I wanted to tear it apart with my teeth and discover the color and taste of her nipples. Would they be pale or a rich raspberry? Were they sensitive to the mere flick of my tongue, or could they stand to take some abuse with my teeth and strong fingers?

"Adam," she called, and her voice was clearly affected by the same lust coiling serpentine in my belly, hissing at me to act. "I thought you didn't drink."

"I'm not an alcoholic," I explained as I accepted my neat scotch from the bartender and stepped closer to Linnea. Her dress had a slit in the back so the fabric gave as I pulled her against me, her feet straddling either side of my thigh. "I simply don't drink often because it leads me to make bad decisions."

"Mmm." Her eyes glittered as she walked her fingers up my chest and slowly undid two more buttons so that the top of my chest was bared to her gaze. She pulled teasingly at the chest hair she found before looking up at me with her bottom lip caught between her teeth. "Bad decisions like dancing with your girlfriend?"

My gut cramped with longing.

The door to the suite opened, and a few men and women trickled in to greet Giselle and Sinclair. I recognized one of them as the rock star, Cage Tracey, and pulled Linnea a little tighter to me.

"I think that would classify," I agreed.

"Drink up, then. You'll need both hands if you want to handle me," she goaded, swaying her hips to the music as she walked backward away from me toward the dance floor.

I watched as she let her eyes drift to half mast, her hands raising to collect her masses of gold hair and lift it off her neck. She was perfectly content to be the only person dancing even as more people filtered into the space and conversation began to undercut the music.

I let myself study her for a while as I sipped my scotch, relishing the burn down my throat, the little bubble of isolation around me that subtly repelled the newcomers from approaching me, even though I knew many of them, as I stood at the edge of the bar.

Under the multihued lights, Linnea twirled and swayed with innate grace and sensuality despite the fact that I had also witnessed her become clumsy and ungainly at times. I found the contrast oddly endearing.

"*Trottolina mia,*" a rich Italian voice spoke so close to my ear, it almost made me jump out of my skin.

Only, I knew the voice better than I knew anyone else's because it had haunted my thoughts for ten years.

So I didn't flinch or even blink as Sebastian settled just a little too closely beside me. The heat of his hip against my side was a brand that sizzled down through my bones.

"Little spinning top," he translated for me. "Always moving, always shaking things up."

I hummed. "It suits her."

"So does Sunbeam," he approved.

It was a strange way to acknowledge the fact that we were both wildly attracted to and sort of courting the same woman.

"There is a famous Italian song," Seb continued, and I looked over to watch him sip from his own crystal glass. I didn't have to ask to know it was grappa. "'*Vattene amore.*' The last line is known by all Italians." He shifted into a low, smooth singing voice that was surprisingly lovely. I didn't understand the Italian, but when he was finished, he translated again for me. "'We'll wonder how it is the world knows everything about us. Maybe I'll call you, *trottolina amoroso*…and your name will be the name of every city….your name will be the name on a billboard that does advertising for me…and your name will be the cold and the darkness, a curled tomcat who will scratch me…your name will be a month of drought and in the sky there is no fresh rain for me…and I will lose my head.'"

Sebastian finished paraphrasing the song and laughed lightly to himself, staring into his glass as if it were a scrying mirror and he was capable of divining the future.

When he looked up to snag my gaze, his eyes glowed like polished gemstones. "It's funny that the nickname I gave Linnea so long ago came from a song that so perfectly encapsulates how I feel about you."

My throat was so dry it ached. I had to swallow twice, cough, and swallow again before I could find my voice. I raised my glass to obscure half my face so he would not see so much of the feeling I couldn't hide.

"Have you hated me so much?" I asked.

Sebastian's black brows rose. "Hated you? No, Adam. I have never hated you. Longed for you? Pitied you? Wanted to hit you, even? *Si, certamente.* I am a man with big emotions." He shrugged in that Latinate way that seemed casual but expressed much. "Perhaps it is better to say you have haunted me, and now that I am faced with your ghost, I do not know whether to exorcise you or pray you come back to life."

The VIP section was getting busy. Someone bumped into Sebastian, pushing him firmly up against my side. He didn't move away, locking eyes with me the way mountain goats did horns.

"I feel as if I am coming back to life," I admitted, sliding my gaze back to the dance floor, toward the warmth I could feel like sun on my skin emanating from Linnea.

She was still dancing, laughing with some women who had joined her, including Giselle, who twirled under Linnea's arm.

"However reluctantly," I added with a rueful smirk.

"I knew she would be good for you," he said smugly.

I should have kept quiet, but the wine at dinner and the scotch combined to make me say, "It's both of you. I forgot so many of the things I enjoyed in life. Enjoyed about myself, even. It hurts, like sensation coming back to a sleeping limb, but most days, I think it's a good thing."

"You may have forgotten yourself, but I never could," Seb replied with forced casualness, but his body was a tense line against my own. "I'm happy for the opportunity to remind you."

"Not much has changed," I agreed, but it was a warning to us both.

I am still the same man with the same fears, *I meant.*

My old lover nodded slightly, his mouth tight. "I know. Unlike you, I have changed much over the last ten years and grown past childish fantasies. The moon? It is meant to stay far above me in the sky."

I turned from him, closing my eyes against the flare of pain his world weariness caused me.

I did that to him.

Stripped him of that romanticism and hope that had been so elemental to his beauty.

It was probably why, *I thought with dawning horror,* he had given me Linnea instead of dating her himself.

He no longer believed in a love that moved the stars and the sky.

At least, not for him.

Fuck, not all monsters had claws and fangs.

I had never felt crueller.

"Don't beat yourself up too badly," Sebastian drawled, almost teasing me. "You were always good at that. I knew what I was getting into back then, Adam. And I know what I'm hoping to get myself into now."

I shifted to look over my shoulder at him to see the pugnacious angle of his chin and the resolution in his honeyed eyes. It made me feel better to know that he could still be a gladiator when it came to defending his passions, however foolish they might have been.

He noticed the way my shoulders relaxed slightly and smiled a little as he bumped his hip into mine.

"I wish I could dance with you both out there," Sebastian said in a low voice. "It's been so long since I felt a man against me."

My throat went dry in an instant.

"You haven't been with any other?" I asked, but it was all breath and no sound.

Happily, Sebastian understood, and he shrugged. "How could I have fallen in love with any other man? Even the memory of you surpassed the reality of any of them."

What was a man supposed to say to something like that?

The words punctured the armored walls around my heart, cutting me straight to the soul.

"Sebastian," I said, and it throbbed like a wound with longing and angst and the pain of new hope mingled with old fears.

"I've dreamed of you so many times," he continued as if he hadn't just broken my heart and then brought it back to life again with a handful of words. "Touching me again. Tonight, I cannot stop thinking of it."

I swallowed thickly as warmth swept away some of the anguish.

"Tonight, I don't want to talk about feelings," he admitted, very uncharacteristically. He laughed shortly when I raised a skeptical brow. "I want to focus on this moment instead of the past or the next. I want to tell you that I wish I could drag you onto the dance floor and tangle our bodies with Linnea's.

"I want to feel your big hands on my hips as you move me to the rhythm you set, Linnea between us and writhing. I know you've thought about the three of us together." His chuckle was wood smoke, rich and heady. It made my eyes sting and my throat ache. "She wouldn't be like Savvy, cold but politely submissive, a tight restraint on her need to be a good girl for us."

"No," I agreed, because I had thought about it. Linnea made it impossible *not* to. Just watching her move her hips hypnotically to the beat, her own hands like a lover's trailing over her curves, was enough to tempt a much better man than I to sin. "She is so curious. She would be…enthusiastic."

"*Sí*," Seb almost hissed, adjusting his weight beside me so that the hard length of his erection pressed into my hip. It shocked me like a cattle prod. "I think she would beg and beg for more until she could no longer take any more. But oh, she would try."

"Maybe she would even cry for us," I added, lost to the fantasy his Amaretto-soaked voice was feeding me. "Pretty tears as she struggled to come again, to take as much of our cum as we could give her. To please us both because it would please her so much to do so."

We locked eyes, heat crackling between us. I loved that we were the same height and a similar build, though he was narrower through the waist. It was *work* to bend him to my will, and the satisfaction of a job well done was always that much greater because of it.

"Do you think she has thought about it?" Sebastian asked softly.

"Oh, I know she has," I muttered, thinking of the filthy things she had whispered to me about her own desires, about her own insinuations. "She may look like pure sunshine, but our girl has a dark side."

"*La nostra ragazza,*" Sebastian murmured. "Our girl."

I stiffened as I realized my slip, but his happy grin was impossible to take umbrage with.

"I like the sound of this very much," he admitted.

I did, too.

Fuck, I was in a world of trouble.

A muttered curse in Italian alerted me to Sebastian's glare. I followed it over my shoulder to the dance floor and saw an actor I recognized as Jace Galantine, twenty-something American sweetheart, dancing very closely with Linnea.

Our Linnea.

I was moving before I could think to curb the blazing impulse.

Sebastian was so tight at my back, he almost stepped on my heels.

Jace was pressed into Linnea's back, one hand on her hip, holding her close while their hips moved to the music. Linnea's eyes were closed as she tossed her head languidly to the liquid beat, almost as if she was so caught up in the music, she didn't even know she wasn't dancing alone.

A growl lodged in my throat.

"Jace." Sebastian's voice was a whip cracking across the bodies between us as we neared them.

Immediately, the younger actor's eyes widened as he took in the sight of us. He was fit, as most leading men were, but shorter than both of us by a significant margin.

Good, I thought grimly, fists clenching.

"Step off," I ordered him, the words sharp enough to cut my own mouth coming up. "Unless you have been living under a rock, I presume you know the beautiful woman you're grinding against is very much taken."

Linnea had stopped dancing, mostly, only her hips slightly swaying as if she couldn't help the movement. Her head was cocked, though, mouth pursed as if we were curiosities in a zoo.

"We were just dancing," Jace said, holding his hands up in surrender, but the grin on his mouth was wicked. "No crime against that, last time I checked."

"Maybe not," I agreed. "The crime would come later when I knocked you out for touching what's mine."

I was watching her so closely, it was the only reason I noticed her delicate shiver and the way she involuntarily licked her lips.

Far from being disgusted by my admittedly outrageous machoism, my Sunbeam was *aroused*.

Lust cut my possessive rage off at the knees.

Without sparing Jace another look, I offered my hand to Linnea, who took it immediately and let herself be pulled into my arms, her back to my front. I banded an arm around her waist, used my other hand to push the sweat-dampened hair off one shoulder, and used my teeth against her neck instead of a kiss.

"Did you forget who owns you, Linnea?" I asked darkly.

She raised one hand to my neck to pin me to her fluttering pulse point. The scent of her was enriched by her racing heart and warm body, blossoming like a night-blooming garden.

"You left me alone on the dance floor," she said, staring up at me through her long, painted lashes. "And I left my 'look but don't touch' sign at home."

"Perhaps we should get you a new one that says 'property of Adam Meyers,'" I suggested.

She pouted playfully. "But then what would Sebastian do?"

I hissed as she canted her hips back into my groin and swiveled them at the same time that provocative statement sank in.

My hands gripped her hips to still her, only I found them pulling her impossibly closer instead. "Behave."

"No," she countered, swirling out of my arms toward Sebastian who caught her even as he continued to exchange biting words with Jace Galantine.

I hadn't known they were closely acquainted enough for Sebastian to uncharacteristically dislike him, but the set of his jaw and the way his free hand—the other loosely wrapped around Linnea—cut through the air spoke of his animosity.

"She's hurt," Jace said as I stepped closer again to listen. "Both Tate and I have noticed she's not been herself the last few days, and Edgecumbe mentioned you had been by to visit. When I confronted her, she told me you'd said some things you didn't mean."

Seb scoffed. "Oh, I assure you, I meant them. Savannah is just very skilled at wishing away the things that cause her discomfort."

"She's uncomfortable now that you're fighting."

"What does my relationship, or lack thereof, with Savannah have to do with you?" Sebastian asked, and I was momentarily proud of his haughty demeanor.

It seemed likely he'd learned it from me.

Jace shrugged, but it was a stiff expression and he shoved his hands in his pockets. "She's been good to me."

Seb's laughter was bitter. "Of course, she has. Why don't you worry about your own relationship with Savvy. As you can see, I have my hands full."

It was a well-aimed retort, except for the fact that Linnea was in his arms, and I was the one who had just made a claim on her.

Something cruel twisted in Jace's corn-fed handsome face. "You seem to have a thing for other men's women."

"And you like to live dangerously," Linnea cut in, stepping out of Sebastian's hold to snap the words at the other man. "If you're done causing trouble, I think it's best that you leave. You can either do that like a gentleman, quietly and with grace, or I can ask Sinclair to send a bouncer to escort you. Which would you rather?"

He seemed shocked by Linnea's temper, and truthfully, so was I. That she had a backbone had been obvious since the start, but the fierceness of her loyalty was unusual in this town.

Especially given who her mother was.

A woman who had five husbands in her lifetime.

God, she deserved only the very best, and here she was bookended by two men with enough baggage to fill LAX.

Jace rolled his lips between his teeth, something Savannah was prone to do, and I realized that he was most definitely one of her playthings.

No wonder Seb didn't like him.

To his credit, he nodded and turned on his heel without another word, disappearing through the crowd and then reappearing before he left the section altogether.

"Good riddance," Linnea declared as we all stood still on the dance floor in a tight triangle. "I think he has a bit of a Napoleon complex, don't you?"

She held up her pointer finger and thumb to indicate something very small.

Both Seb and I stared at her for a moment and then shared an incredulous look before we burst out laughing. As if the laughter broke the dam of stiltedness between us, Seb and I surged forward to pin Linnea between us, falling into a natural rhythm between all three bodies. It was foolish to dance together, but I stubbornly refused to think about it and took some solace from the fact that these people had been vetted by the Sinclairs and Seb who were notoriously private.

Seb smiled at me, that wide, boyish grin I'd once fallen in love with on a face that had weathered into something even more gorgeous. Linnea planted one hand on my chest, curling it into my opened shirt and hooked the other over her head around Seb's neck, her back resting against his chest, her hips against mine.

I recognized some of the faces around me, enough to know gossip could and would spread based on my behavior.

But how could I resist?

Him and her.

Together.

And both within my reach.

As if sensing the change in mood, the DJ dropped a sultry mix that had everyone rushing the dance floor around us. People clung to each other, writhing and sweaty, hands in the air, hips thrown from side to side.

The tide of humanity carried us farther down the dark stream of temptation.

I bent my head to watch as Sebastian's dusky hand moved from Linnea's belly up, up to the lower swell of her breast, his thumb rubbing the curve. I could feel his hot gaze on me as I watched him touch her.

Never one to shy away from a sexual game, I picked up his thrown gauntlet and hitched her thigh up around mine, the split in the back of her dress giving me access to her bare skin.

Linnea's eyes were almost slumberous as she undulated between us, a high flush on her cheeks, lips swollen as if they had already been kissed savagely.

I took the cue, rocking forward to claim that parted mouth with mine. She groaned against my tongue, hauling me closer with the hand in my shirt.

I groaned when I realized Sebastian was palming her throat, tipping her chin higher for my kiss with his thumb.

"That's it," he crooned, voice lower than the thrumming bass so that only we could hear the Italian-soaked words. "Let Adam take care of you with his talented mouth."

Linnea sucked in a sharp breath and went languid against us, meltingly soft.

I wanted to lift her into my arms and slide into her right there on the dance floor. Fuck her back and forth on Sebastian's cock and my own like a metronome set to this sexy beat.

"Fuck, you taste like sunshine and sin," I said after wrenching myself away from her mouth, trailing my lips down her neck to where Sebastian's hand held her throat.

I nipped my teeth around his knuckles and watched his grip spasm.

Rearing back, I looked at them both, panting hard, eyes blown to black with arousal and thought for the first time in way too fucking long—*fuck the consequences.*

"Meet me in the bathroom in five minutes," I demanded, my own voice filled with gravel.

Linnea roused herself enough to straighten and arch a brow in a mockery of me.

"Meet *me* in five minutes in Sinclair's office down the hall to the right," she amended. "Giselle told me I could borrow it earlier. Boys bathrooms are gross."

And then she tossed her wavy mane over one shoulder and glided off the dance floor toward the exit.

Sebastian and I both watched, captivated, until she had disappeared from sight.

In her wake, we were left only with a crackling tension and a sense of imminent danger, as if we stood on the edge of a high precipice in a lightning storm just waiting for a fork of electricity to land.

It was, it almost embarrassed me to admit, *terrifying*.

Because I was experiencing true, brain-melting, soul-crushing desire when I had not wanted for anything in years.

I had forgotten how it impacted the body, setting every atom buzzing, every thought blinking in and out like static so I couldn't bloody think straight.

"*Adamo*," Sebastian said in husky Italian.

This was new, the Italian way of addressing me, and I found I had a weakness for it as I always had for the way he muttered both filthy and beautiful things in his native tongue.

Sebastian's *Adamo* was a different man than I had been and even than I was now.

He was who I would desperately love to become.

"I have been drinking tonight," I said, a little woodenly.

Because it was an excuse.

A shameful, idiotic excuse.

I watched as the words hit Seb like a blow. He absorbed it, rocking backward and forward slightly, putting his hands in the pockets of his trousers with his shoulders raised slightly in a tense, defensive line.

"*Bene*," he said. "Okay."

Absolving me. Always absolving me of guilt.

"Will you come?" he asked, not looking at me.

Look at me, *I wanted to shout, everyone else be damned.* Devour me whole so I have no choice but to be consumed.

"I will," I said quietly, almost drowned out by the music.

Someone bumped into Sebastian as they danced and he nodded once without looking at me before following Linnea out of the room.

For a moment, just a single second, I felt the cold weight of pragmatism on my shoulders. It smelled like my father, it reminded me of the minutes after my mother died beside me, when I discovered Bryce had been killed in action, and Gregory had taken his own life.

If you do this, *I thought,* you are absolutely fucked.

I raised my hand to rub across my weary mouth and caught the scent of Linnea and Sebastian lingering on my fingers, the spice market and ocean brine of them so delicious blended together.

I was walking forward before I could process my own movement.

Sod it, *I thought,* it's been too bloody long since I was properly fucked.

CHAPTER NINETEEN

SEBASTIAN

The soles of my Italian leather loafers echoed through the surprisingly quiet hall as I stalked away from the VIP section toward Sinclair's office. It was a fitting soundtrack for the lonely walk, a hollow ring like the beat of my heart.

Cold sweat beaded on my brow that I wiped away with the back of my hand, and I had to force myself to take a deep breath before I entered the office because I felt almost sick with anticipation.

That I might be able to touch and taste both the people who had come to haunt my dreams and waking hours was almost too much to bear.

My hand shook as I reached for the doorknob, and even when I shook out the nerves, I felt weak as I turned the handle and pushed inside.

I had expected to find Linnea waiting, but the masculine office was empty.

Unease thrummed through me as I walked deeper into the room, stopping at the large antique French desk dominating the back wall of the space. There was something about the old European furnishings and dark, warm colors only illuminated by a red glass desk lamp and a dimmed overhead chandelier that set the stage for salacious fantasies. There was a silk privacy screen in one corner that begged for some kind of strip tease, a leather ottoman Linnea would look beautiful bound to by her wrists and ankles, a deep velvet sofa I could imagine sinking into with the weight of both lovers pressing into my body.

I planted my over-warm palms on the cool desktop, leaning into them even as I spread my legs slightly, closing my eyes to imagine Adam ordering me into the position so he could touch me again.

Maybe he would have Linnea on her knees in the small space between my hips and the table so I could fuck into her mouth while he reminded me what it was like to be spread open on his fingers.

Cazzo.

It had been so long since I had been with a man in any kind of way, I almost felt like a virgin again at the thought of doing something—anything—with Adam.

As if summoned by my dark thoughts, the door opened and, after a brief pause, closed behind me.

I did not turn around.

A little shiver ripped down my back like a ghost had taken hold of my spine.

The ghost of the many, many nights I had spent in Adam's thrall a decade ago.

I was so fucking weary of the distance between us, of the time that had passed and the awkwardness that remained. I longed to have things simplified just for a moment.

I longed to submit as I once had into the strong, sure arms of a lover who would ply me with pleasure until I was weak-kneed and empty-minded.

So I stayed facing away from the predator even though the hairs on the back of my neck and arms raised with apprehension. My position was subtle enough that he could construe it as weariness instead of a sexual proposition, but after the closeness we had shared on the dance floor, and the fact Adam had already admitted he was going to blame whatever transgressions he made tonight on the alcohol, I had hopes for more.

The sound of the lock catching on the door was as loud as a gunshot in the heavy silence.

He didn't make a noise, yet I was so aware of him that I could feel him come toward me on slow, measured strides. The touch of his gaze on my body was a physical caress and, as if I was eighteen again, my cock was an iron bar in my trousers.

It felt good to be studied and measured. I wanted to pass muster more than I wanted my next breath.

"What a pretty gift Linnea has left for me," Adam said finally in that cold as iron voice that never failed to make my heart rate kick up.

I made a questioning noise in my throat but did not speak. I thought, however foolishly, it would break the spell between us.

Suddenly, his hand was between my shoulders, pressing hard enough to push me into a deeper lean over the desk, my ass canting toward him as a result.

"I received a text that Linnea was held up, but that she left something pretty for me in this office," Adam explained as that hand moved slowly down my spine to the small of my back and around to my hip. I sucked in a sharp breath as he clamped his fingers around my side to steady me while one foot kicked between my spread feet, urging them wider.

I obeyed without thought, thighs burning slightly at the strain.

"And pretty you are, Sebastian." His voice was a low, throaty rumble as if he had left his humanity on the other side of the locked door. "What should I do with such a present?"

Open it, I thought with an edge of desperation even though a part of me was unused to submitting, especially to a man.

There had been none since Adam. The very idea of being with a male other than him made me break out into a cold sweat, even though I still found men attractive and often longed for the kind of intense, masculine-edged sex I had only ever experienced with another cock in my hand, in my mouth, stretching my ass.

Those were memories sacred to my time with Adam, very much like threesomes and polyamory, which I had also eschewed for years.

Some things were too holy to recreate, like religious ceremonies without the proper props and relics.

And now, here I was in an office that felt like a sanctum with the only man I had ever worshipped.

My pulse hammered, echoing in my ears.

"I think I'll open it, shall I?" Adam mused, reading my thoughts as he had always been able to do in these situations.

I shivered almost violently as his hands came around my front and smoothed down my chest, mapping the contours and tracing the ridges of muscle with heavy strokes as if he wanted me to feel the difference between him and any of the many women who had touched me too.

The petting was possessive and just shy of demeaning, a way to reacquaint himself with his property.

"You've filled out." His voice was still cold, but jagged. "Every inch of you hard and sculpted. Did you know how much I might love to feel the curve of your biceps—" His hands found the muscles as he spoke of them—"the swell of your pecs above the hard grooves of your abdominals and the arrow of your obliques as they narrow into your groin."

I hissed as his hands followed that arrow and just ever so gently brushed over the straining bulge in my trousers before trailing back up my torso.

He had barely touched me and already precum was leaking from my cock, staining the placket of my pants. I was breathing as if I'd run a marathon, yet I hadn't even moved.

Slowly, agonizingly, Adam began to undo the buttons of my shirt while he spoke to me almost conversationally.

"It has been so long since I touched you," he mused. "I am almost at a loss about what to do first. My mouth is watering at the thought of baring all this olive-tanned skin to my gaze. Perhaps I will borrow some of Sinclair's brandy and make a game of tasting you."

I groaned affirmatively, which made him chuckle a sinister sound.

"Very well," he agreed as he sloughed my opened shirt off my shoulders and down to my wrists, unable to remove it completely because of my palms on the table. "Just indulge me in this and I will give you so much pleasure you'll be coming all over yourself before you can help it."

Merda, I had forgotten how incendiary his filthy mouth could be.

"Turn around, keep your hands on the table and rest your hips on the edge of the desk. There, what a sight," he praised, moving his hands over my exposed torso, tweaking my dark nipples, scratching lightly down the rippled expanse of my abs and then tugging lightly at my treasure trail in a way that had my cock spitting precum.

"Isn't he pretty, Linnea?" he asked in a low, dark coo.

It took my overheated brain a moment to realize who he was speaking to and then to search the room for her.

She sat on the velvet couch by the private screen, and I realized she must have been hidden behind it when I first entered the room.

Her legs were crossed, one elbow propped on the arm of the seat, a glass of liquor dangling from her fingers as she watched us with heavy-lidded eyes and parted lips.

"Very," she agreed in a husky murmur. "He looks like an idol worthy of adulation."

"Doesn't he," Adam confirmed, stepping back slightly to study me in a way that made me shiver.

I was an actor, it made sense in small way that I would like to play the exhibitionist. Still, there was something that squirmed inside me to be put on such display by two people I adored but had no idea how to label in regard to our relationships.

This was a new frontier.

And an old, archaic part of my brain was embarrassed to have Linnea witness how utterly undone I was by another man. It had been too long since I indulged, and old Italian prejudices flared under my skin.

Movement pulled my attention to Linnea, who slowly unfolded herself from the couch and came toward me, hips a slow pendulum hypnotizing me with every step.

She stopped beside Adam in front of me, sipping from the glass as her eyes traveled thoroughly and languidly up my body.

"I think," she said softly, a wickedness in her eyes that almost alarmed me, "he would look even better kissed silly. Don't you, Adam?"

Adam hummed, rubbing a hand over his stubbled chin as he considered me, head cocked like they were viewing art in a gallery.

"Yes, I think you're right. Would you like to do the honors?"

"No." The word sparked between us. "I want to see what happens when you kiss him. He is almost *shivering* with want for you, Adam. Put him out of his misery."

Cazzo, I thought, almost woozy with desire.

Adam did not hesitate for a moment, stepping between my spread feet to palm my throat the way I had done to Linnea on the dance floor, canting my chin up to just the right angle for his kiss.

"Kissing you undoes me just as much as it does you," he murmured against my parted lips a second before he sealed them with his own.

And I lost myself to him.

He tasted of peaty scotch and something rich but undefinable that was pure Adam.

I groaned as he held me still, totally in control of the depth and pace of the kiss. At first, he ravaged, rubbing his tongue along mine, sucking and biting just shy of painful at my lips. Then, when every inch of my mouth was sensitized to him, he teased me. Feathering flicks and licks, tempting nips and hot breath.

"Adam," I said, and it was the first word I had spoken since we entered the office.

A benediction, a plea for the man who controlled me like the moon with the tides.

"You're so fucking sexy," Adam growled against my mouth as he pressed his entire body against mine. I could feel the heat of him scorch me through to the bones and the hard length of his cock sliding along the length of mine.

I shuddered so violently that I bit my own lip.

Adam licked up the drop of blood that formed and hummed with pleasure before he stepped back.

I was left breathless and aching against the desk, my hands still fixed to the tabletop, my shirt around my wrists. My cock was trapped painfully beneath my zipper, but I didn't dare adjust myself.

"That may have been the most beautiful sight I've ever been lucky enough to witness," Linnea said in a throaty voice.

A heavy flush spilled from her cheeks down her neck and chest, breasts heaving as she breathed heavily, nipples hard beneath the thin lace.

The sight of her, and the praise, was like gasoline on the already raging inferno in my belly. Whatever shame I might have wrongly felt went up in ashes, and I felt only proud that they both found me so tempting.

I twitched as I fought to keep from going to them.

"He does look bloody gorgeous, doesn't he?"

Adam's words built the fire higher.

"He looks seconds away from coming in his trousers," he continued blandly, reaching forward to grip my erection through the fabric, giving it a rough fondle that was just shy of too much.

The moan ripped out of my throat, and my hips chased his hand when he pulled away.

"Sebastian," he said firmly. "Are you ready to play my game?"

"*Si, per favore,*" I said in Italian before realizing it was the wrong language. "Yes, please."

He nodded curtly, then turned his attention to Linnea, rubbing a thumb over his bottom lip as he studied her. She held still for him, but the flush on her chest deepened.

Something was inherently erotic about being under Adam's powerful scrutiny. The wicked intelligence in his eye spoke of all the ways he could take someone apart.

"Did you mean what you told me at the beach the other day?" he asked, finally stepping up to cup the side of her neck and press into the pulse point that was visibly fluttering. "How you like to get on your knees and be used until you are wet and open and aching?"

Linnea's eyes dropped until they were almost closed, but she breathed, "Yes...sir."

"Oh, good girl," he praised emphatically, dipping close to brush his mouth against hers. "I think you are going to like the kind of games Sebastian and I play."

"I do, too," she said eagerly.

If I had been less aroused, I might have been ridiculously charmed and a little smug about that enthusiasm.

"Then be a good girl for us and get on your knees," he coaxed, taking the tumbler from her and then pulling her forward by the grip on her neck until she occupied the space between my legs.

We locked eyes, her pupils blown wide with arousal as she licked her lips in anticipation of what Adam might have her do to me. I watched as she dropped gracefully, sinuously to her knees, palms softly placed on top of her thighs like a proper submissive.

"Have you done this before?" I asked, the words punched out of me with shock.

Adam's chuckle was wicked as he stepped up behind Linnea, legs pressed to her spine so that when he pulled her back, her cheek rested against his own erection. Instinctively, she mouthed at it through the fabric.

"Our Linnea knows what she wants," Adam said, and that cool calm was fractured by a groan as Linnea opened her mouth around the head of his cock and sucked hard through the fabric.

"And what she wants, Seb, is you." He pulled Linnea off him with a grip in her hair, her head canted back to look at him. "Don't you, gorgeous?"

"Yes." The word was like the hiss of steam escaping a boiling kettle.

"Then have him," he suggested, using his hand in her hair to direct her forward until her cheek was now against my cock. "Put on a show for me and I might let you both come before we leave here tonight."

With Adam's hands in her hair, Linnea took her lower lip between her teeth, looked up at me through her lashes, and started to undo my belt and trousers. She took her time, making it almost methodical.

Why was it blisteringly sexy?

I could tell how much the teasing was turning her on because she was panting, but even when I pushed my hips forward, she avoided touching my dick.

The little minx.

Eyes sparkling, she looked up at me as she tugged the zipper down with her teeth.

I sucked air in so sharply it hurt.

I had been on edge for what felt like hours now, and I worried the first brush of her pouty mouth against my bare skin would ruin me. So I held my breath and gripped the desktop until my knuckles ached as she finally pulled me out through the gap in my boxer briefs, her touch delicate around my shaft.

"Look at how wet he is," Adam noted darkly.

And I was.

Precum had soaked through the cotton and drooled obscenely from the head of my flushed, slicked cock.

Linnea hummed as she lifted me and lapped up the precum like a kitten with cream.

"*Oh cazzo!*" I swore savagely as pleasure burst through me and I thrust forward seeking more.

"Be still." Adam's order was like ice water, giving me the control I needed not to thrust into Linnea's mouth as she slapped my head against her tongue a few times and then slid it seamlessly into the back of her mouth.

I trembled and failed not to hump slightly against her chin to lodge more of myself into that tight, wet heat.

"This won't do at all," Adam declared, but there was a smugness there that said he knew I would fail. "Here, Sebastian. Hold this steady or Linnea will be forced to stop her ministrations."

He reached forward to balance the glass of alcohol Linnea had been drinking on the slope of my clenched belly. The angle was just enough that—if I held very still—it wouldn't fall. Otherwise, the booze would spill all over me and it would probably sting.

"Can you be good and hold that there for me?" Adam asked and, at that moment, I would have agreed to anything to get him to touch me the way he was, sliding a thumb across the top of my groin and down the crease of my inner thigh.

"Yes," I declared, even though my gut clenched, dangerously swaying the glass as Linnea's tongue reached out to touch my balls when I bottomed out in her throat.

"Look at how much she loves to suck your dick, Sebastian," Adam crooned, crouching behind Linnea so he could reach around and cup her breasts. "Her nipples are so hard they could cut glass. Would you like to see them?"

"Please," I gasped as Linnea pulled off my shaft with a hard suck and then lapped at the head again, swirling her tongue.

I had known she was a good actress because as soon as she told me she was acting, I had watched everything she had ever been in, even the commercial for nontoxic toothpaste. I hadn't known, though, just how much she could put on a show.

Her full mouth was painted in my precum, glistening and pink as it opened obscenely around my girth and swallowed me down. Cheeks hollowed, eyes watering with effort, she looked up at me as she was filled with my cock, and I thought, quite honestly, I might die then and there. Or that I had already, and this impossible scene was my sinner's version of heaven.

"Only because you're being so good holding still for us," Adam allowed as he pulled down the lace cups of Linnea's dress so that the gathered fabric propped up her heavy breasts.

Dio mio, I had never been a big chest man until now, seeing Linnea's breasts, pale and stark against the tan of her body with nipples the pale pink of the inside of a seashell.

My mouth watered.

Adam plucked at her hard nipples and tested the weight of each breast as I longed to while he pressed bites and sucking kisses along Linnea's neck and shoulder.

Linnea moaned around my cock as she shuttled it into her throat before swallowing, once, twice, three times, and pulling off.

"Jesus Christ," I cursed in English. "I would sell my soul if it meant you never stopped."

Linnea laughed against my cock as she pumped it with one hand. When she spoke, her voice was roughened from taking my dick so deep down her throat.

"I think it's Adam you would have to sell it to," she teased.

My gaze snapped to Adam, who watched me with burning green eyes.

"I think the price of your soul deserves more than just an exquisite blow job," he surmised after a moment. "But why don't we start with that? Linnea, should we let him come all over your pretty tits?"

"Yes," Linnea and I groaned at the same time.

"Only when I give permission," he warned me before addressing Linnea. "Take him as deep and hard as you can, I want to see you both wrecked."

I had never witnessed a woman who loved to give head as much as Linnea seemed to at that moment. She threw herself into the task, fucking her mouth on my cock and working her throat muscles around the head. Moaning and panting as she licked up the shaft, twisting her hand in the mess of drool she left behind on my length.

I was so close to coming, I thought I would die if I didn't release, but Adam still hadn't given me permission.

He was too busy, I realized through blurry eyes, tending to Linnea.

Her hips were lifted off her heels now, dress rucked up around her waist, and Adam's wrists disappeared beneath her. In a moment when Linnea was silent as she rocked my dick back down her throat, I heard the telltale wet slap of a pussy being played with.

"Yes," Adam told me as he fucked her with his fingers. "She's absolutely drenched just from taking you in her mouth. And so fucking tight." A muscle ticked in his jaw as he fought for control.

"You should fuck her while I fuck her mouth," I suggested, almost babbling because the sight at my feet was too erotic to process.

Adam's laughter was a harsh bark. "This isn't about me. You focus on using Linnea's gorgeous mouth and not coming until I tell you."

Linnea pulled off on a cry as Adam did something with those fingers I knew were dexterous and wonderful.

Her eyes were wet and running from the way she'd already sucked my cock, mascara pooling beneath her lids, making her purpled eyes smoky.

"You're so gorgeous," I told her, giving in to temptation to reach down and hold her cheek as I slowly pushed back into her mouth. "Especially when you are filled with my dick."

She groaned her agreement and closed her eyes as if savoring the weight of me on her tongue.

I hunched forward just slightly, and the glass tipped, cold liquid splashing over the lid onto my abs and racing down my thighs.

"Clean up his spill," Adam told Linnea, who immediately licked up the excess, sucking my balls into her cooled mouth, too.

I dug my fingers into the edge of the desk to ground myself and closed my eyes to focus.

The glass was moved from my belly, prompting me to open my

eyes to watch as Adam fed a sip to Linnea, who immediately took my cock back in her mouth.

I hissed in preparation for the sting of booze on such sensitive skin, but it wasn't alcohol.

My eyes blew wide as something effervescent tickled and cooled my cock.

"*Che cavolo?*" I gasped, hunching over at the mix of sensations, the heat of Linnea's tongue contrasting with the cold, bubbling liquid.

"Linnea doesn't drink," Adam explained with a rakish grin. "She only has sparkling water. Does it feel good?"

"*Merda*, yes," I agreed, throwing my head back as she finally swallowed the liquid, and me, down her throat.

"I thought so," Adam declared arrogantly. "You've both been so good. Sebastian, you can come when you're ready."

"Thank God," I grunted as Linnea picked up her pace, sucking and slurping wetly around my length again and again until I lost sense of all time and space.

Everything, except them.

Adam, my moon, and Linnea, the sun, both at my feet, lavishing me.

Both, for the moment, were entirely focused on *me*.

The orgasm barreled through me almost painfully, gathering every single atom and then exploding through my core. My cock kicked viciously in Linnea's mouth once before she pulled off. Adam reached forward to cover her hand partially with his, and together, they jacked me off onto her breasts. I forced myself to keep my eyes open so I could see the stunning sight of them working me like that, ropes of my pearlescent cum painting Linnea until she was covered in me.

Even emptied, my dick twitched valiantly, trying to unleash more cum to add to the tapestry.

Linnea leaned forward to suck the last drops off my head and then gave it a tender, closed-mouth kiss.

Then, shocking us both, she held my still hard cock up for Adam, raising her brows until he leaned forward and kissed me too, the abrasion of his stubble making me shiver. Not done with him, Linnea tugged Adam forward with one spit-wet hand in his shirt and fixed her mouth over his, sharing the remnants of my cum with him. I watched the flash of their tongues through their parted lips, listened to the grumbling moan from Adam, and seriously wondered if I had died and gone to heaven.

Nothing could beat this, *I thought.*

I had always wondered if the eroticism and completeness I'd experienced in the bedroom with Savannah and Adam was sacred only to them as people, but this has proved differently.

I was a bisexual man who equally enjoyed sex with both genders. They lit up different parts of my brain and body so that the pleasure felt…whole.

But it was more than that.

Linnea had enjoyed this in a way I couldn't remember clearly if Savvy ever had.

She had enjoyed *us*, not just for her, but together.

And I thought, maybe, that was new.

New and addictive.

Only there was no space for me between them, not really.

I couldn't dance with them at a club, go to dinners with them in the city, or attend award shows and premieres with them. I was the plus-two, the addition that didn't make sense and didn't fit into the carefully constructed world Hollywood made people subscribe to.

I closed my eyes under the pretense of recovering and wondered if I would ever stop falling for dreams that had no basis in reality.

CHAPTER TWENTY

LINNEA

"We aren't finished here." Adam's voice was a collar around my throat, the leash in his firm hand along with one that tied me to Sebastian.

It was utterly erotic, putting myself in his hands, watching the way he wrote the script for our play. I had known being with them would be incendiary, but I couldn't have prepared for the heat of its reality.

Sucking off Sebastian while Adam conducted us was officially the hottest thing I had ever done.

And it wasn't over yet.

It had been a risk to lure them into Sinclair's office and hide from Seb. To send the text message to Adam.

Yet it had paid off so beautifully.

Seeing them together, the tension, the joy that transcended the corporeal and shone from their souls as they finally came together again. It felt profound to witness it. Old love and battle scars soothed by lust and a new, burgeoning friendship.

Knowing I had helped to facilitate that was a reward.

"I think Linnea deserves a reward for her efforts," Adam declared, and I almost laughed with how the words were along the lines of my thoughts but perverted.

Sebastian stared down at us with hungry eyes even though he should have been satiated by the brutal orgasm that had left my breasts dripping in his cum.

"Help me clean her up," Adam said, the word low and smooth as whiskey and just as heady.

Sebastian dropped to his knees immediately, hauling me almost into his lap as he started to lick his cum from my skin. I shivered at the intimacy of it, clutching his hair in one hand to hold him tight as he laved my sensitive nipples.

"Don't be greedy," Adam admonished, coming closer and sitting on his own heels beside Sebastian before maneuvering me easily to straddle each of their thighs, sitting me between them. "You know I love the taste of you."

We both watched as Adam traced a path of seed up the inner curve of my breast and then clasped Seb around the side of the neck to pull him close for a kiss. They shared the cum as I had with Adam. One dark, the other light, both tall, well-built men eating ravenously from each other's mouths.

Nothing had ever been so scintillating.

I pouted when they finally broke apart. "Don't stop on my account."

Sebastian laughed, a happy, almost dopey grin on his face, but

Adam only shook his head at me in mock indulgence before bending to suck at my nipple.

"Ah," I gasped as Sebastian bent to the other to do the same.

Their heads at my breasts, clever tongues working, was almost enough to take the pulsing beat between my legs over the edge. I had always had sensitive nipples, but the keenness of this pleasure shocked me.

Then again, most women would orgasm having Sebastian Lombardi and Adam Meyers play with their breasts so reverently.

But it wasn't about that.

Their celebrity, their personas, or their pasts.

We were just three people connecting in the most primal way, and I didn't let any thoughts encroach beyond that because there was too much acting against us.

For now, we could be this new, strange, and beautiful *us*.

Slowly, Adam planted a hand on my chest and pushed me backward, my abs controlling the descent, until I lay with my shoulders and back against the floor. My hips were raised on their thighs, but Adam and Sebastian worked in voiceless tandem to lift their hands under my ass so I was level with their mouths.

And then they passed me back and forth.

First Adam, because he was in charge and led the way. He pressed his nose to the crease of my thigh and breathed deeply, moaning at the scent of my arousal. It was so shameless, so decadent and intimate it made me shiver, and more wet trickled from my pussy. His eyes were dark as he tilted his head to trace the leak all the way up to my center.

"Fucking ambrosial," he growled against my folds before he ate me in earnest.

I thrashed against his mouth as he sucked and swirled at my clit, but Sebastian helped hold me steady, his hot gaze on my cunt like an extra tongue.

"My turn," he said, but it was a question voiced in a begging rasp.

Adam wrenched himself away, his full mouth glistening with me.

Instead of letting Seb have his turn, he tugged him back in for another luscious kiss, sharing the taste of me.

My nipples were so hard they ached, the pressure at the base of my clit throbbed, and my walls clenched around nothing, hungry for more.

I whimpered before I could help it, and Adam tore himself from Seb with a wicked smirk. With his golden hair disheveled, and ruddy, flushed cheeks, he looked like a god of depravity and he was just as merciless.

"Don't let her come," he told Seb before draping my thighs over Seb's shoulders.

The Italian didn't hesitate for a moment before opening his mouth over my wet core and lashing it with his strong tongue. I cried out, but his fingers merely tightened around my hips.

"Let him eat you," Adam told me, cold and authoritative.

It was almost a mean tone, but astoundingly arousing because it threatened punishment if you did not do as he said.

A moment later, fingers pressed at my entrance.

I bowed my back at the sensation, then looked down my body to see it was Adam's fingers inside me, parting my swollen walls to rub at my front wall in a way that made heat sluice through me.

I cried out again, my blood roaring in my ears.

More fingers. This time I checked, Sebastian's curling in around Adam's so they were both finger-fucking me in tandem.

My mind whited out, hot sensation crashing every system until I short-circuited. Vaguely, I was aware of convulsing in their hold, shaking apart as I came and came and came so hard it almost hurt.

For a long moment afterward, I merely floated without thought, everything warm and languid.

When I came to, my head was in Adam's lap, and one of his big hands was stroking my hair. My hips still rested on Sebastian, but he had tugged down my dress slightly in case I was modest, and he was rubbing his hands lightly up and down my thighs.

"Hi, Sunbeam," Adam murmured, smiling down at me with genuine tenderness. "How do you feel?"

"Um," I said when I could unstick my tongue from the roof of my mouth. It was dry from calling out so much through my orgasm. "Like I'm floating?"

His chuckle was supremely self-satisfied and echoed by Sebastian's. "That's good."

"It can be hard to come down from a play," Sebastian added, then gave me a curious look. "But you've done this before?"

"This?" I repeated with wide eyes. "Definitely not."

They both laughed again, and that felt almost as good as the orgasm, to see them both so relaxed in each other's presence and with me.

"But I had a boyfriend who liked to play the Dom. I don't know if he was particularly suited to it after experiencing this, but I liked it," I explained.

"And you liked this?" Adam asked.

"Couldn't you tell?"

"Communication and consent are important with this kind of play, Linnea. I won't assume you like something unless you tell us." I liked his sincerity and seriousness. That "play" was structured with consent and rules so that no one would get hurt.

At least physically.

Emotionally was yet to be determined.

I bit my lip and looked between them, noting that Adam had tensed beneath me as if he realized the implication of his words.

"Does this mean we'll do this again?" I asked.

The mood crashed down over our heads. In seconds, the warm intimacy had transformed into an almost hostile tension.

"You know I cannot afford to do anything stupid," Adam said carefully, not looking at either of us.

"Stupid," Sebastian repeated quietly.

I felt his hurt and my own.

"This wasn't stupid," I countered, holding his hand where it lay on my chest. "It felt…" I sucked in a breath. "It felt almost necessary."

"You know it's stupid," Adam argued, carefully slipping out from under me so he could stand and pace. "Anyone out there could have taken photos of us dancing like that and given credence to Oscar's campaign against me."

"Is it really so bad if it comes out that you're bisexual?" I tentatively asked.

Until now, I hadn't felt he would talk with me honestly about it.

His laugh was bitter. "Do you know Liam James?"

I frowned. "No?"

"No," he agreed with a curt nod. "He was a talented young actor who starred in *Young Bucks* and had a handful of huge projects lined up. The paps caught him in a back alley with one of his childhood buddies. A man. The studio dropped him the next day."

I opened my mouth to argue, but Adam was on a roll. "Rupert Everett has openly discussed how coming out impacted his career in Hollywood. He stopped getting juicy roles and leading characters."

"Wasn't that in the '90s?" I asked. "Times are—"

"Don't say times are different," he snapped. "People in the LGBTQIA+ community are three times as likely to commit suicide."

His voice cracked, and his hands clenched so tightly they went white. "Mississippi passed a law in *2016* that made it legal for businesses, doctors, and government officials to deny service to LGBTQIA+ people. Almost one in four experience online bullying. The annual report the FBI releases shows that hate crimes against us are still at record-breaking high numbers. I *know* someone who killed themselves because they felt they could not belong just because they were queer. You want to tell me things are different? Yes, sure, they get better all the time, but is better ever going to be enough?"

He was breathing so heavily, I wondered if he was on the edge of a panic attack. I'd never had one before, but one of my uncles was a war veteran, and I'd been there for a few of his episodes.

"I'm on your side, Adam," I said softly, rolling to a seated position so I could face him with all of my earnestness. "I know it's hard, and it's unfair that you have to think of how your sexuality might impact your career. But how is your career impacting your mental health? Your happiness?"

"God, you're naive," he bit out, but he looked like a cornered animal.

There was a knock on the door. It exploded through the room like a grenade.

Adam, already spooked, immediately put himself to rights.

Sebastian and I stood to adjust our own clothing more slowly, and by the time we were passably presentable, Adam was already striding toward the door. I couldn't find my torn underwear, but I caught a flash of white lace in Adam's back pocket and felt a flare of hope that he'd taken them out of some kind of sentimentality.

He opened the door briskly, nodded at Giselle, who stood there with Sinclair, and then brushed past them as he left.

Giselle winced as she looked after him and then over to us.

"I'm sorry," she said softly. "I didn't mean to disturb, but Sin and I have to get home to relieve the babysitter, and I wanted to say goodbye…I should have texted."

"Nonsense," Sebastian said with a wide grin, that movie-star smile that charmed everyone who saw it.

I knew him well enough now to notice how it didn't touch his eyes.

He strode forward to take Giselle by the shoulders and push a kiss into her head instead of exchanging the normal cheek kisses, probably hyperaware of the fact that his face smelled like me.

"Thank you for a lovely evening," he told her, tucking her into his side as he reached out to shake Sinclair's hand.

"I'm sorry if it's ended badly," Giselle ventured with a curious glance at me.

"Not at all," Sebastian insisted with another blindingly bright grin. "Come, I'll walk out with you." He hesitated, looking over at me with a crack in his mask that spoke of yearning and frustration. "Linnea, do you need me to call you a ride home?"

"No," I said a little woodenly. "I'll get Rozhin to pick me up, she should just be finishing up work right now."

He pursed his lips but nodded and, after waiting for me to thank his sister and her husband, he escorted them out, leaving me more alone than I had felt in a very long time.

CHAPTER TWENTY–ONE

LINNEA

I organized the papers in my lap with sweaty palms as the aide called my name to enter the audition room. Even though I had memorized the sides, the short scenes from the script the casting director sent to actors who were auditioning for a role, and pored over the character notes, adding my own idiosyncrasies in the margins, I was still incredibly nervous.

I had been on dozens of auditions in the last nineteen months since moving to Los Angeles, but this was the first major production I had scored an invitation to, and it was being directed by Georges Gallegos, whom I happened to adore. He had created some of the best action films of the last two decades, and as a woman who grew up in a household of all men, I had seen my fair share of action flicks, so I had a discerning eye.

The character I was auditioning for was not particularly complex.

man, a woman who appeared on screen mostly to kick ass and, occasionally, to fight and kiss the hero. It wasn't exactly a meaty role, but I was excited about the prospect of learning how to "play" fight with choreography, and it certainly beat the guest appearances and commercials I'd booked thus far.

The problem was, after Thursday night's emotional roller coaster with Sebastian and Adam, I was still psychologically exhausted. Adam had texted to say he needed space before our date in a few days to go to the Critics Choice Awards, and Sebastian had been helping Giselle and Sinclair move into their new house in Pacific Palisades and spending most of his time with family while he wasn't doing the media circuit to campaign for his Oscar. He had texted, agreeing that we needed to talk and that he regretted nothing, but I had the distinct feeling he was avoiding me too.

Men.

Jeez.

I sucked in a bracing breath and headed into the audition room, shoving the two men at the center of my life into the back of my brain so I could focus on *me*.

I was considerably less frustrating.

Fifteen minutes later, I emerged from the room feeling slightly shaky with hope.

"Why did you play it like that?" Georges had asked, cocking his head as he considered me.

At first, the panel had seemed mostly disinterested, but when I started Carmen's monologue about her tortured past, the four men had come alive.

"Well, I don't think Carmen is a victim," I explained. "Yes, she was orphaned and abused by her mentor even as he trained her to be a killer, but I don't think she feels badly for herself even for a moment.

The only reason she would bring it up is to manipulate Zachary into softening toward her. It's all part of a game. Carmen likes games, and she's good at them."

"Does she?" Georges asked in a thick Spanish accent, almost to himself.

Beside him, a skinny Black man wearing glasses grinned at me. "She would. Life is a game with very high stakes for Carmen."

I beamed at him, happy to be validated, given that he was the screenwriter, Zeke Ryan.

They'd had me read the scene again and then do another one they handed me cold from a new series of sides.

"Well done," Georges had said when they dismissed me. "We'll be in touch."

Zeke had winked at me.

I'd never gotten a wink before.

I was still trembling with excitement when I got in the car. I wanted to call Sebastian and Adam to tell them the news, knowing they'd be proud of me, even if I didn't actually get the role. However, my car didn't have Bluetooth, so I drove home a little faster than usual, tapping on the wheel with restlessness.

The traffic was crazy leading onto my residential street, and I tried to remember if a block party or something was happening.

When I turned onto my street, I realized it was much worse than that.

News trucks and paparazzi vans had pulled up in a tight grouping around the front of our little yellow house, and people crowded over the front yard.

Around Miranda, who was in her pink sweatsuit, curlers in her hair, shouting and pointing at the cameras.

"Oh my God," I breathed, horror eclipsing every other thought in my head. "Oh God."

I pulled over as close as I could get to the house and pulled my phone out of my purse with a shaking hand.

Adam was the first person I called.

It rang for so long, I was about to hang up when the line clicked and his cool voice said, "Hello."

It was strange that the simple sound of his voice could center me a bit.

"Adam, the paparazzi are at the house. Miranda is having an episode in the front yard. I-I just arrived, and I have to get to her, but I don't know what to do about the cameras, and oh God, Miranda will be so horrified when she's in the papers and media like this…"

I choked on a sob as it came up.

"Linnea," he said so firmly it was like a wakening slap to my face. "Take a deep breath for me. Good. Another, please. Okay, listen to me. I'm twenty minutes away, so I'm going to call some people, and they'll be there to help you before I arrive, but Nea, I *am* coming. We'll get this sorted. Do you trust me?"

I didn't even have to think about it, which was absurd because I'd only known him for a month, and during most of that, he had been emotionally closed off.

But I knew the shape of his heart, even if I couldn't yet map the details of its topography.

Adam Meyers would never let anything happen to the people in his life if he could help it, and he was capable enough to make that so.

"Yes," I breathed on a shaky exhale.

"Good girl," he said tenderly, and the words pulsed inside me. "Now, I would rather you wait for someone to join you before you enter the fray, but is there any hope of you waiting in the car?"

"No," I said, already shaking my head, eyes fixed on Miranda as she wailed. "I have to help her."

I spotted Mrs. Ramirez at the front door, hiding partially behind it with something obscuring her face. It looked like an ice pack or a rag, and I wondered if Miranda had hit her to get outside, and Mrs. Ramirez didn't want to set off the sharks with cameras when they saw her bleeding.

"Get her inside as quickly as you can, then lock the door and close all the blinds. I'll be there soon, Sunbeam. I promise."

"I know," I said before I hung up the phone.

I hesitated for just a moment as I considered calling Sebastian too, but someone shouting pulled my attention back to the scene on my front lawn, and I knew I couldn't delay any longer. I shoved the cell into my overstuffed tote and started running in my wedge-heeled flip-flops. Only Miranda's tutelage walking in heels for hours until I was proficient, while I lived with her in London, ensured I didn't fall on my face as I sprinted to the crowd, then elbowed my way through.

It took the photographers and media hounds a second to realize who I was, but as soon as they did, they parted to let me through.

They probably thought this would be gold.

I cursed under my breath at them before shoving them to the back of my mind.

Miranda needed me.

When she was having one of her paranoid episodes, she could become frantic and violent. FTD caused incoordination, too, so even when she wasn't trying to hurt me, she occasionally did.

The flash of lights, noise, and general chaos were not a good recipe for calming her, and I wondered if I was up to the task and if someone had been thoughtful enough to call the paramedics.

"Miranda," I said softly as I approached, my steps much slower now. My voice was a little unsteady from the run and stress, but

Miranda's wide eyes swiveled to me instantly.

"They don't understand," she insisted in a low, almost growling shout that ended in a scream. "They are trying to take everything from me."

"We won't let them," I assured her. A local FTD support group had taught me that it was a better tactic to agree with the paranoia and get on their "side" of the conflict than it was to tear down their illusions. "We'll make sure everything is safe."

"No, no." She shook her head, the ponytail I'd given her this morning loosened so much that the scrunchie dangled from a tiny lock of hair. "No, you don't understand. They keep coming for me."

A reporter behind me called out, "Linnea, is your mother having a psychotic break?"

The grind of my teeth and the flare of pain in my jaw helped ground me.

I didn't understand how they had found us *now*. It had been weeks since the press realized who I was, but our phone number was unlisted, I had been careful not to let any paparazzi follow me home, and the deed to Miranda's house was listed under a shell corporation Wyndam had set up for her. If they'd found us, it was because someone had tipped them off.

I ignored the anger burning in my belly and focused on Miranda, moving a little closer even though she scuttled away from me. It was, at the very least, taking her nearer to the house and its relative privacy and safety.

"Why don't we go inside the house and talk about it?" I suggested mildly.

It was the wrong move. She shuttled sideways to the edge of the lawn, darting a look at the house and shuddering. Her hands were white-knuckled as she hugged herself around the middle.

"They're in the house," she cried out, softer this time. Tears bubbled in the trough of her lower lids, and my heart ached for her. "They're everywhere."

"I'll protect you," I promised, as I always did. "I'm right here and I won't leave you, I promise."

She stared me down with those vivid blue eyes she'd once been famous for. It would kill her to see the image she cut now, unkempt hair, clad in a soft velour track suit because certain fabrics could set her off and slippers I bought her for Christmas with bunny ears. Once, she'd walked red carpets in vintage Dior and custom Marchesa. Once, she wouldn't have left the house for even a moment without doing full glam hair and makeup.

I always wondered if that was what she was bemoaning during these episodes, that the disease had robbed her of everything she'd worked so hard to collect: money, fame, and beauty.

Even though she was left with family who would, and had, done everything for her, that wasn't enough for Miranda Hildebrand.

Suddenly, I felt like weeping myself.

But I could do that later, after I got Miranda into the house in a familiar environment and locked the house down.

My mother stared at me now, as if she were the child, with wet eyes, a trembling mouth, and a suspicion that I might not be who I said I was stamped in her expression.

"Mom," I said in a low croon as I took a few steps closer and held out my hands palms up. "It's me, Linnea. Do you remember?"

She shook her head tightly and hugged herself so hard, her hands disappeared around her back.

"I'm your daughter," I told her patiently, still moving and smiling slightly as I touched my hair. "You always told me I got my good hair from you instead of Dad. You named me Linnea after your mother, do you remember? She was Swedish."

Something flickered in her eyes, and she dropped to the ground as if her strings had been cut, curling up tighter. "No," she said. "I don't have any children."

I crouched before her and gently ran two fingers along the back of her hand, cupping her knee. "You used to sing me a song when I was too little to remember, but we sang it together sometimes when we lived in London."

This was the ace up my sleeve. Dr. Jamshidi, Miranda's physician, had sent me studies that the part of the brain that most types of dementia attacked was entirely separate from the area that stored musical memories. Sometimes I sang this song we'd shared together, and others I tried from the soundtracks of her favorite movies like *Mamma Mia* and *Kinky Boots*.

I started singing "Feeling Good" by Nina Simone in my passable alto. My entire focus remained on my mother as I sat on my bum across from her and gently took one of her hands in both of mine.

There was blood on the back of it, and I wasn't sure if she was hurt somewhere I couldn't see or if it was from Mrs. Ramirez.

I was only a few lines in when Miranda's face lost some of its abject terror and softened into something closer to confused wonder. By the time I sang the first line of the chorus, she was humming brokenly along with me.

"'*I'm feeling good*,'" a rich tenor joined with mine, startling me so badly I nearly jumped to my feet.

Only the scent of spice and warmth my subconscious instantly recognized as belonging to Sebastian kept me still. Instantly, the panic that had twisted my lungs into a knot loosened enough for me to take a shaky breath.

Adam had called in the cavalry.

Seb's heavy hands found my shoulders as he crouched behind me, shielding me from the cameras at my back as we finished out the song together.

The crowd was quiet in the wake of the last notes.

So was Miranda.

Her lids had drooped considerably, and her hand was lax in mine. Exhaustion often followed these events swiftly.

I decided it was worth the risk to get her inside.

"Mom," I murmured, still stroking her hand. "Why don't we go into the house? You can show Clark your Soapie."

She brightened a little at the idea of showing off her Soap Opera award, or because she finally noticed Seb hovering behind me.

"Clark," she said, her voice dry and cracking in the wake of her shouting match. "You didn't tell me you were coming. I would have put on something special."

"You look marvelous just as you are," Sebastian said solemnly, and there was no doubt in my mind that he meant it.

A sob lodged in my throat and made it difficult to breathe.

"We're going to move slowly," I whispered to Seb, because Miranda could go off again in a heartbeat if she caught sight of the crowd or the flashes started going wild again. "Let's try to keep her focused on the house."

Seb squeezed my shoulders in acknowledgment and gently grabbed Miranda's other arm so we could both help lift her to her feet. As we were doing so, the low growl of an expensive engine preceded the screech of tires on asphalt and the slam of a car door followed by another punctured the quiet.

It prompted the crowd to start taking photos and videos again, a low murmur building into excited chatter.

I tried to move Miranda a little quicker toward the house.

A moment later, the crescendo reached a peak as a name was passed around the ranks of paparazzi.

Adam Meyers.

I could have closed my eyes in relief, but I focused on steadying Miranda as we hit the path that cut through the middle of the yard and started up it.

"That is *enough*." Adam's voice cut through the cacophony like the clang of a cymbal. It took two seconds for silence to descend, and the quality of it was almost reverent.

This was *gold*, and the paps fucking knew it.

"This is private property," Adam said in that crisp British accent that cut the words into bullets and fired them cleanly into the crowd. "You have sixty seconds to get off Mrs. Hildebrand's lawn or you will not like the consequences. In case you doubt me, this is my lawyer, Boone Decker. He would be happy to speak with any of you about breach of privacy, private property, and taking advantage of someone who is ill without their consent."

We had hit the steps in front of the house, and Miranda swayed, almost asleep on her feet, as Sebastian half lifted her over the threshold.

"Can you take her into her bedroom for me?" I asked quietly because there was something I had to do before Adam cleared the way completely.

Seb nodded, his eyes dark with empathy as he pulled Miranda close and murmured sweetly to her in Italian she had no hope of understanding. It seemed to soothe her because she didn't object when I stepped away to face the music.

The cameramen had mostly taken Adam's orders to heart and moved off the lawn to huddle at the edge of the curb, but some of them were walking a little slower, lenses raised to catch the last moments of Miranda before I closed the door on the house.

The flashes were bright, even in the late afternoon sun, but I tried not to blink as I lifted my chin and walked to Adam, who stood beside his lawyer with his arms crossed and legs braced, like an admiral used to being obeyed.

"We have called the police," he said mildly, glaring in particular at a man who was still on the lawn, one foot crushing the pansies I'd taken pains to plant along the cracked concrete path. "If you're still here when they arrive, I will do my best to see you are arrested. You have crossed a line, Mr. Talbot, even for you."

"How'd ya know it was me who started this?" the reporter asked with a crooked smile, still filming.

Adam's voice was a tundra. "It stinks of a rat, and you are king of the Los Angeles sewers, Hank."

Hank grinned but didn't argue, maybe because I hit Adam's side. Literally.

I pushed into his torso, leaning in so heavily he didn't have a choice but to raise his arm and curl it around me to keep me from falling. Pressed against him, it was easy to feel the thrum of barely leashed anger coursing through his body.

If he could have, I thought he might have beaten every single person there.

He turned his head to me, kissing my crown before whispering just for me, "You can wait inside. I'll stay here until the cops arrive."

"I want to say something," I said, not whispering.

He stared down into my face for a second, his eyes so green they seemed almost unnatural, a bright and clean color like freshly cut and watered grass. For a man with so many demons, they were wonderfully pure.

"Okay," he said, squeezing me closer.

I could tell he didn't want me out there, that he would have had me secure myself in the house and, maybe, never even be seen by the paparazzi again. So it meant a lot that he gave way to my needs.

"I know most of you don't think celebrities are real people with real feelings," I started, taking strength from Adam at my side and Sebastian caring for my mother inside. "As if fame and money turn people into soulless automatons. Or maybe you think gossiping about them, raking them over the coals, *lying* about them is simply the tax they should pay for being more successful than you. I don't know, and I don't care. What I do care about is my family. Today, you've taken advantage of a woman with frontotemporal dementia, which is a serious and sometimes ignoble disease. What you witnessed today was the way it can rob a wonderful woman of her reason. What you've done by documenting it with the intention to sell it to the highest bidder is rob her of her dignity. That is on you. Everyone deserves to be treated with basic human decency, and today, you've failed in that. I hope you can live with yourselves."

I rocked to my toes to kiss the square hinge of Adam's locked jaw and then peeled myself off him with a slight nod of thanks to Boone before I turned my back on the paps and headed inside.

I had just closed the doors when the sirens came from a distance.

My eyes were closed as I leaned against the front door, struggling to breathe through the emotions clogging my throat. So much pain and sorrow and relief and hope all knotted like hair in a drain.

"I am sorry, Linnea," Mrs. Ramirez said quietly.

I pried my eyes open to see she was sitting on the couch. It was a rag she had been holding to her nose, but it was curled in one loose fist, drying and bloody as was the skin under her inflamed nostrils.

"It's me who should apologize," I said, the words kind of slurred because I was coming down from the adrenaline. "She hurt you."

Mrs. Ramirez was one of the best, steadiest women I knew. If it hadn't been for her, I would have drowned a long time ago. She stood and came toward me. At five foot one, she was a good eight inches shorter than me, so she had to reach up to tap her palm to my cheek affectionately.

"You are a good girl," she murmured. "She is lucky to have such a good *mija*."

"I am lucky to have such a good neighbor," I admitted a little wetly.

She smiled and corrected me. "A good *amiga*."

A good *friend*.

"Yes," I whispered through the mass in my throat. "Thank you for everything."

"You have been alone in this too long," she said with a click of her tongue against her teeth. "I am happy to see not one, but two strong men come to your aid. That Adam Meyers…" Her eyes went glassy with admiration for a moment before she shook herself out of it. "I have always wanted to meet him. I did not think it would be in circumstances such as these."

A giddy, almost hysterical laugh escaped me, and Mrs. Ramirez laughed softly with me.

"I'll introduce you properly when you don't have a bloody nose. Both of them are good men," I said, as if it was a secret.

What I meant to say was they're the best men I've ever known, and I want to be with them both.

Mrs. Ramirez tapped my cheek again, consolingly, so maybe she read in my eyes what I couldn't say aloud.

"A good girl," she repeated before moving away to grab her purse by the entry table. "Miranda is getting worse, not better. You and I are not enough for her anymore."

"No," I agreed, chewing my lip until the skin broke. "I know. I'll figure something out."

She nodded brusquely, and without another word, she moved down the hall toward the back door so she could reach her own house without encountering the last of the mess in the yard.

I moved down the hall too, but took the jog in the floor plan that led to the big bedroom to the right. Miranda's bedroom door was ajar, so I pushed it open silently to see Sebastian sitting on the edge of the bed with one of Miranda's hands in his. My mom was tucked in neatly, the sheets tight around her body so the effect was almost a swaddle. She seemed more than content in the tight comfort, her head lolled to the side of a stack of pillows, her eyes closed and mouth slack with sleep.

"Mrs. Ramirez gave her some medication, but Miranda wanted me to keep holding her hand," Seb explained as he looked over his shoulder at me. "I have to admit, I am afraid to let go."

My heart skipped a beat, then pounded out a rapid two-step.

God, he was lovely.

It seemed impossible that such a man could actually exist outside of film and fantasy. My dad and uncles had taught me that there were good men in the world, but their love lives left a lot to be desired, given that not one of them was in a long-term relationship. To know that there was a man—men—who could love the way Seb did, yearn and caretake the way Adam did, changed something in my worldview for the better after years of witnessing Miranda's hopeless marriages and Dad's endless bachelorhood.

"Sometimes I spend the whole night just watching over her," I admitted. "It's…scary each time she has these episodes. I worry she won't come back."

"But she does," he said, half question and half soothing me.

I nodded. "For now. They're happening more frequently, though. She has a re-evaluation next week, and I have a few interviews with homes that have experience with FTD. It's different enough from

Alzheimer's and other forms of dementia that she needs nurses with experience."

"*Certamente*," he agreed.

He still hadn't let go of her hand.

I didn't think my heart could stand it any longer, so I moved forward to lean over his hip and carefully fold my hand over his, helping him let go.

Miranda didn't stir.

But Sebastian turned his hand up in my grip and laced our fingers.

I didn't think I could look at him without crying, so I just squeezed back and tugged him lightly from the room.

When we reached the living room, I collapsed onto the couch and buried my head in my hands, one of them still linked to Seb's.

He didn't complain about the awkwardness of his position. Instead, he leaned into my side like a protective bracket.

We sat in silence for an interminable amount of time until the front door opened and closed. I didn't open my eyes or straighten to see who entered because only one person would let themselves in and stride with authority into the living room even though he had never been here before.

The couch sank on my other side, and the other end of the bracket clicked into place the moment Adam's arm went around my shoulders.

Both men urged me gently to pull back from my hands and sink slowly into the couch.

Into their protective embraces.

The sigh that escaped me as soon as I was settled was like a gust of wind in the wake of a tornado, filled with debris.

"I am so sorry that happened," Adam said in a low, furious voice. "It is because of me that those…vultures attacked you and Miranda."

"I was the one who suggested your arrangement," Sebastian

countered in a slightly more measured voice, though his accent was thick enough to eat with a spoon.

"It would have happened one day," I said with a tired, unenthusiastic grin. "If I was ever successful as an actor. I know you both tend to martyrdom, but there's no need for it today."

"It happened today because of us," Adam insisted. "Someone tipped off Hank."

I sighed. "That's what I figured. Do you think we can find out who did?"

Adam's face was carved from granite, haughty and furious like the sculpture of an ancient Greek god. "Oh, there is no doubt about that. Boone's investigator is already on the task."

"Good, thank you. But honestly, your matching scowls, while oddly adorable, are unnecessary. I told you, this was only a matter of time, due to *my* selfish need to pursue acting. Even without my connection to you throwing me into the limelight, I like to think I could have made it to this level without you," I teased lightly, knocking into their shoulders to try to alleviate the pressure in the room.

I could feel their agitation and laughed a little at them. "You feel like you failed me? The truth is, you both rode in like knights in shining armor to save me."

"You saved yourself," Adam disagreed.

"And Miranda," Seb added.

I patted them both on their hard thighs. "Sure, but knowing I didn't have to endure that alone? I hate to sound like a VISA commercial, but that's priceless. Thank you for being here for me." I paused and then emphasized. "*Both* of you."

"Anytime." It was amazing how one simple word from Sebastian could sound like an oath avowed from a serf to some feudal king. As if he would die for me even if he wasn't called to do it.

It made me shiver.

But it was Adam who shocked me, because he was such a mercurial, hard-to-read man, and I was never exactly sure where I stood with him.

He gripped my chin lightly in his thumb and forefinger to tip my head his way so that I could witness the implacable resolve in his face.

"Anytime," he echoed in the same tone Sebastian had used.

"For the next three years?" I dared to venture.

I'd always been a fan of "nothing ventured, nothing gained."

Adam was a man who demanded a brave lover, and I would be no less for him. Even if he wasn't courageous enough to accept me that way.

"For the next three years," he agreed, long, tangled brown lashes sweeping over his cheeks before lifting to reveal those green eyes. "And any time after it. No matter what you are to me in the future, Linnea Kai, you have become my friend. The first one I had made in a very long time, and one I will never let myself be foolish enough to lose. I made the mistake of letting someone good and kind go a long time ago, and I've lived with those painful consequences. I'm a smart enough man not to make the same mistakes twice."

I closed my eyes as they burned, and my nose itched. Beside me, Sebastian shifted and let out a small sigh.

"You're going to make me cry," I warned them. "I'm not a pretty crier either. I get splotchy and snotty."

They both chuckled just a little, but it felt like a feat nonetheless.

"Booth is dealing with the cops. They want to speak with you, but I told them they could call tomorrow and you'd arrange to go in if you want to press charges. What Hank orchestrated was essentially assault," Adam said darkly, a muscle in his jaw ticking.

I shivered, both because the situation called for it and because that cruel current prompted a muscle memory of the way he'd ordered

Sebastian and me into our pleasures at the club the other day.

"I don't know if I have to go so far as to press charges…"

"You absolutely should," Adam rebutted. "To show them that you will not be pushed around. This is just the beginning of a life filled with scrutiny, Nea. Do not let them think you are an easy target, or they will never leave you be."

"He's right," Seb agreed, squeezing my hand.

I sighed, the gusty exhale stirring the little braids that hung over each cheek. "Fine, but you're both bossy."

They did not have the same smile. Sebastian's was broad enough to cut creases into his cheeks and beside his yellow eyes, his lips darkly pink and stretched wide over white, almost wolfish teeth. Adam's was a small thing, restrained to a tipping of full lips that revealed only a sliver of square, straight teeth and a sparkle in his green gaze. But the shape of both those smiles defined the same thing in response to my comment: smug satisfaction.

They were the kind of men who enjoyed being high-handed if it meant keeping their people safe and happy.

And somehow, I had become their person.

"Speaking of bossy, we need to do something about Miranda," Sebastian said, a gentle question in his voice. "However you think is best, but something clearly has to change. You are running yourself ragged, *trottolina*. I know you have an abundance of energy, but even you have your limits."

"Yes," I agreed, sagging even more deeply into the old couch. It smelled faintly musty and unpleasant, but the mingled scent of Adam's and Sebastian's colognes overtook it. "I guess I'll have to pick one of the homes for her next week. A lot of them have waiting lists—"

"I'm sure we can figure something out," Sebastian said silkily, and I knew he meant to use his fame or money to grease the squeaky wheels.

"Actually," Adam said. "I had a thought about that some time ago. The surprise I teased you about on the phone while I was in New York?" He waited for me to nod that I remembered. "I had the guesthouse set up for Miranda. There is a private nursing service with three highly qualified aides who have worked with patients who had FTD before. One of them even included end-of-life care."

He paused to gauge my expression, but I couldn't be sure of it myself because I was fuzzy with shock.

"You told me you didn't want to abandon her like everyone else in her life has done," Adam explained quietly. "If you aren't comfortable with having her on the property, that's perfectly fine. It just seemed prudent, given that you were supposed to move in soon and, now obviously even sooner, given I will not leave you so vulnerable to the paparazzi. This house is too exposed, and it could be unsafe for you. I know you value your independence, and this is ahead of schedule, but—"

Adam Meyers was uncharacteristically babbling because he was nervous I would be cross with him for doing something so unexpectedly lovely I had no words to express my gratitude.

So, instead, I kissed him.

It started as a hard punctuation. An exclamation mark of thanks. But then it morphed into something else as he caught my chin again, tipped my head at a better angle, and softened his lips, coaxing me to do the same.

He hummed into the kiss, stroking into my mouth in a lazy, almost proprietary way that made my thighs clench.

Sebastian stroked his thumb along the ridge of the knuckles on my hand as he held it, as if praising me for kissing Adam.

Between them both, safe and touched with a kind of tender,

protective understanding I felt some of the colossal weight I'd been carrying for months ease off my shoulders.

Whatever I was to them, as individuals and a unit, they cared for me, and they didn't want me to be unhappy or unsafe.

It even seemed, just a little bit, like love.

When Adam pulled away, he cupped my cheek and rubbed his thumb through a tear streak. I hadn't realized I was crying at any point until then.

"You'd like that?" he confirmed.

"Very much," I agreed, pressing my hand over his on my face. "Thank you, Adam."

There was a deep-seated satisfaction in his gaze, an almost smugness. If I hadn't realized it before, I would have known then that both of these men had the kind of hearts that were happiest taking care of others.

"We'll move you and Miranda in tomorrow," he declared, shifting away slightly to dig his phone out of his pocket so he could make the necessary arrangements. He paused, frowned at something, and then shifted one of my legs so it was draped over his thigh as if he couldn't bear the fact that we hadn't been touching anymore.

I swallowed thickly and turned to Sebastian to find his eyes soft as melted butter as they gazed at Adam.

"That's him," he said softly to me. "The man I loved."

I could more than understand why.

"We'll stay with you tonight," Adam declared after he sent off a few texts.

"Here?" I asked, eyebrow raised as I gazed around the little living room. "But there's no spare bedroom. Just my double bed."

"Not ideal," Adam agreed, then shared a sly look with Sebastian, something flirtatious and *easy* that made Sebastian grin. "But I don't mind sharing with the right crowd."

"We can finagle something, *cara mia*," Sebastian agreed, winking at Adam. "You leave the setup to us. Why don't you take a bath or a shower? I'll see what I can make for dinner in the kitchen, and we can settle in for a little movie marathon."

I blinked at the two superstars sitting on Miranda's nineteen eighties velvet couch and wondered dazedly what my life had come to.

"What's your favorite film?" Adam asked as he stood to take off his blazer, laying it carefully over the back of Miranda's chair before he set to work unbuttoning his cuffs to roll back his shirt.

He was getting comfortable. Why that was so sexy and profound to me, I couldn't exactly be sure, but I thought it had something to do with the fact that Adam Meyers never seemed comfortable.

Not unless he was with Seb…and *me*.

"*Casablanca*," I admitted, then frowned as Sebastian laughed at me.

"Of course," he replied to my look and slid a hand under my hair to cup my neck. His eyes were dancing as they swept over my face before lingering on my mouth.

He kissed me, then. Just a soft, open-mouthed press of lips that lasted for a handful of seconds.

But it slid through me like a knife, cutting me to the quick.

I could feel Adam watching with some kind of primal approval and felt Sebastian's own pleasure against my body. When he pulled back, he got to his feet as if kissing me in front of Adam was an everyday occurrence.

He clapped Adam on the shoulder and grinned, "Let's get to work."

CHAPTER TWENTY–TWO

SEBASTIAN

I wasn't the type of man to get or stay angry very easily, but in the wake of the paparazzi staking out Miranda's house, I felt electric with it as if I might spark against the velvet couch and set fire to the house.

It helped to have a purpose.

I took a few deep breaths as I surveyed ingredients from the old, humming refrigerator and decided to make a lemon, parmesan pasta with chicken for dinner. The Hildebrand/Kai house did not include something as fancy as a pasta machine, but I could easily make hand-rolled orecchiette using a rolling pin and my thumbs.

There was a small portable speaker on the windowsill over the sink, beside a row of potted herbs, that I connected to my Bluetooth so I could play some familiar songs from home. It made me slightly homesick, for Napoli or my family I wasn't entirely sure, as I dug my

"I recognize this song," Adam said from behind me. "I think you used to play it in London."

"I did," I agreed without looking over my shoulder. "I'm surprised you remember it."

There was an easiness between us that came, I thought, from having someone other than our history to focus on. We were joined not only by our time in London, but also by our mutual attraction and friendship with Linnea.

And the rapport I hoped we were establishing together again, too.

After our exploits at Sinclair's club, I was uncharacteristically nervous like a shy teen confronted with his crush. My breath hitched slightly when I felt Adam come closer, his hip just barely brushing mine as he leaned against the counter to watch me work the dough.

"There is not a single thing I forget about the time we spent together," he admitted with faux casualness. "Those memories have haunted me and I would not exorcise them even if I could."

"Adam." I said his name because it was the only word that would encapsulate my frustration and longing. "What is it you want from me?"

He hummed. "That is a question I have asked myself since the moment I saw you standing at Finborough Theatre, shining brighter than any actor on the stage, enchanting me with your golden eyes. I wanted you with a ferocity that stole my breath and made me go back on my vow not to allow Savannah and me to have any lovers for a time."

"Look at how that turned out," I muttered, not bitterly, because I would never be bitter about my time with them.

But maybe I was a little tired.

A little weary and broken like a man returned from war who forgets why he fought in the first place.

Savannah was not brave enough to be with me still even though she had to have known what she was doing by befriending me again over the years, towing me along like a fish on the line.

Was this Adam doing the very same thing?

I closed my eyes as I pounded the pasta dough into a ball and then began to wrap it in plastic cling so it could rest in the fridge.

"I will not survive if you cast me out of your orbit again," I told Adam baldly, sweeping aside the thin layers of dirt over the fossilized pain at the heart of my soul so he could see the truth. "Do not take me where you do not want me to follow."

Adam considered me for a long moment, his expression implacable even though something worked in his dark gaze. I appreciated that he took me seriously even though I couldn't breathe through his silence.

"No matter what happens," he said finally. "I do not think I could find happiness in this life without you in it. You are as elemental to me as the sky above us, as beautiful and illuminating as the stars in the night. We will be friends, always, Sebastian, if you would have me again."

Part of my heart soared, giving me a sense of vertigo so profound, I had to curl my fingers over the laminate countertop.

"Just friends?" I managed to rasp, my gaze falling instinctively to that pale pink mouth in the golden stubble I wanted to scrape with my teeth.

I watched that secret, sly smile curl his lips and felt my heart pound.

"I will take whatever you are willing to give me," he said, sincerely if not earnestly, a coyness in his tone that made my toes curl. "Your mind, your spirit, and your body are all of interest to me. But I appreciate that I am not what you deserve and might very well never be."

He paused to grip the back of my neck in that way that made me want to drop to my knees and please him until my mouth ached.

"I do not think you have quite forgiven me, no matter that you say otherwise," he noted, seeing into me so keenly it cut like a knife. "Until then, I think it best if we are friends. Don't you?"

"*Sì, d'accordo,*" I agreed, even though my mouth was watering and my knees were soft like they *wanted* to buckle until I was prone before Adam.

"Do not mistake me," Adam said, suddenly stepping so close that our bodies were sewn together shoulder to thigh. "I want you so badly that I can imagine the taste of you on the back of my tongue and the shape of your cock in my mouth. The way you smell drives me absolutely mad, and when you look at me with heat in your eyes, I feel I will burn up to ash."

My breath stuttered and died in my lungs.

It was not just the incendiary words that painted a salacious, intoxicating image in my mind's eye, but the feel of him against me. He was so utterly masculine, hard-bodied like a professional athlete or a body builder, someone whose job it was to maintain peak physicality, because it *was*. The demands of Hollywood and this career were less so for men than women, but they still existed, and Adam Meyers was nothing if not a perfectionist when it came to his craft.

Heat surged through me as if I had been doused with kerosene and lit with a torch. All from the simple press of his hips into mine and the brutal honesty of his husky confession.

Friends did not affect each other in such a way.

I knew this because Linnea had the same impact on me.

Some part of my brain that had not turned into a beast noted that with Savannah, things had always been arranged differently. I had lusted after her first, loved her like a worshipper at an altar, but we had never had the same sense of equality in friendship that I had fostered with Adam or Linnea.

In the wake of the revelation, fear surprised me by burning metallically at the back of my throat.

Something in Adam's eyes flicked and cooled.

"Ah yes," he said quietly, rubbing a thumb along the side of my neck where he still held me. "There it is. The anger."

He had misread me, but it accomplished the same thing so I didn't correct him as he squeezed me once before letting go to step away from me.

"And Linnea?" I asked, my voice rough-edged as I tried to regain my equilibrium.

I'd asked the question without really knowing what I meant by it.

Adam raised a dark blond brow and leaned his hips against the counter again to cross his arms over his—distractingly broad—chest.

"She is in the shower having a wee cry I think," he admitted with a little frown. "But if you meant in regard to us, do you think it's best if we ask her what she wants?"

It was my turn to raise a brow. "Usually, you operate more as an autocracy than a democracy."

He shrugged a shoulder. "Usually, things do not work out very well for me. Perhaps this time will be different."

I swallowed down the hope that burgeoned in my throat so hard it made me wince.

"She wants us both, I think," I confessed as I gathered myself enough to start on the pasta sauce. There was a bag of lemons in the fridge, and I knew Linnea loved citrus-flavored anything, so I started making a simple sauce with lemons, garlic, butter, and parmesan. There was Italian parsley in one of the small plants on the windowsill, which I pinched off to use later as a garnish.

"Yes," Adam agreed. "I think she's made that clear."

The silence made me uncomfortable only because it was filled with so much unsaid that I could not, uncharacteristically, find the words to say.

"Do you want us both?" I found the ability to say, the vowels scorching my tongue as they came out.

Adam's laugh was a bitter little cough. "Never doubt that I want, Sebastian. It is never from lack of wanting that I hold myself back."

"So you want us, then, but you won't let yourself have us," I corrected.

Or let us have you, I followed up with a flare of fury that scorched up my spine.

It was so wildly frustrating to deal with a man who had the best of intentions but the horrible habit of falling on his own sword. He believed that anything bad that could happen would happen to him and his, and I wasn't sure he was entirely wrong.

But I knew life kicked you in the teeth, it was almost the only guarantee.

Love was what happened when you fought through pain and adversity to reach the other side. It was what made life worth living, even when it hurt.

But ten years of separation and yearning had left me tired in a soul-deep way I wasn't sure I could battle back from without something more tangible from Adam.

Or Linnea.

I wasn't willing to play games of the heart as recklessly as I had when I was just eighteen. At twenty-eight, I was all too aware of the stakes and the tolls it could take.

Adam didn't respond to me. Instead, he moved into the living room to set up for our impromptu movie night, leaving me alone as he was so apt to do.

LINNEA EMERGED FROM THE BATHROOM A long forty minutes after she had disappeared into it with flushed cheeks that still retained the heat of the shower and wet gold hair that dripped down the back of her oversized *Romeo in Blood* T-shirt I had sent her in the mail years ago. It had the poster for the Shakespeare adaptation I had starred in on the front of the black fabric, my silhouette with a rose and a gun stylized so that, at first glance, you couldn't tell one from the other.

She smiled at me when I made note of the shirt and hugged herself as she walked barefoot into the kitchen from the back hall.

"It's my comfort shirt," she explained as the fabric slid off one slim shoulder and the hem flashed around the very tops of her long thighs, turning the faded old shirt into something unspeakably sexy.

The sight of her like that combined with the knowledge that something I'd given her years ago had brought her comfort, the sexiness of that intimacy, made my cock twitch in my jeans.

Even though I had just finished agreeing with Adam's summation that the three of us should remain only friends, I found myself opening my arms to her.

She stepped into my embrace with a relieved sigh and planted her face in my pecs as her arms twined around my waist.

"Thank you," she breathed.

I kissed the top of her head and held her for a long moment until the chicken frying on the stove started to spit. Adjusting her so that I didn't have to break our hold, I turned back to the stove to flip the chicken, and satisfied with its sear, I flicked off the heat. She stood quietly against my side as she watched me assemble everything I had organized by the side of the stove. First, the fresh pasta in each bowl, then a few pieces of chicken, finished with the fragrant, creamy yellow sauce, and garnished with a sprinkle of flat-leaf parsley, freshly grated parmesan, and a generous crack of black pepper.

"It smells incredible," she told me as I handed her a bowl and took two more into my other hand carefully before we walked in tandem to the living room.

"In Italy, we have the pasta dish separate from the meat dish," I explained. "But here, you have condensed it because it is not very American to eat courses. Even though Mama would cluck at me, this is more efficient."

She smiled, as I'd meant her to, though I'd been hoping for laughter. Linnea liked to laugh, and I loved to hear her do it. But the day had taken its toll, and she was soft, almost pliable as we went into the living room to see what Adam had come up with.

By the way we both froze, it was safe to say that he had surprised us both.

The cluttered living room had been transformed, and I wasn't even sure how he had managed it.

The velvet couch was still against one wall facing the television, but the rest of the furniture had been taken out so that a wide space was left before the couch. In that place, he had added a mattress, maybe even two, along the floor and draped them with a collection of a white duvet and colorful, crocheted blankets that Linnea had probably made herself, as well as an array of pillows. Above it all, he had managed to string up some fairy lights I knew Linnea used on the back-porch railings, and a few of Miranda's vibrant silk scarves to create a kind of glittering canopy.

It looked, quite simply, magical.

"Mr. Meyers," Linnea said on a breath. "What have you done?"

He stood beside what was essentially a whimsical pillow fort with his hands clasped in front of him and feet braced in a military stance he'd habituated from his time in the Royal Armed Forces. But Adam had always been better at lying with his body than his eyes, which were low-lidded as if to hide the vulnerability in them.

I wondered when the last time before he met Linnea that he had taken care of anyone.

Even himself.

"It seemed like something you would enjoy," he said a little stiffly.

And I thought he was speaking to both of us.

Linnea moved out from under my arm to walk straight across the mattresses to him. Even though he didn't open his arms, she plunked her head in the center of his chest as she had done with me and looped her arms around his waist, one hand still clutching her dinner bowl.

"Thank you," she whispered just loudly enough for me to hear the thick words.

Adam stared down at her head, her hair wetting his expensive shirt, and softened into her embrace, wrapping his arms tightly around her back so that she snuggled even tighter to him. His eyes connected with mine over the top of her head, and the smile he gave me was one of camaraderie and shy satisfaction.

We were taking care of our girl.

I lifted my chin at him, feeling my own smile play at the corner of my mouth as I got onto the mattress fort and sat down to one side.

"Come eat before the delicious food I labored over goes cold," I directed them, lifting Adam's bowl in offering.

Linnea pulled her face from Adam and whipped around to beam at me as she tugged the Brit with her free hand up onto the cushions with her. When she plopped down between us, her shoulder bumped into me, and she made sure Adam was that close on her other side.

She propped the bowl in her lap, crossed her legs so that an indecent amount of tanned leg was showing that drew both Adam's and my regard, and happily stabbed her fork into the pasta.

"Who has the remote?" she asked.

A moment later, Adam dragged his gaze from her legs, caught me doing the same, and winked at me before he lifted the remote and hit play on *Casablanca*.

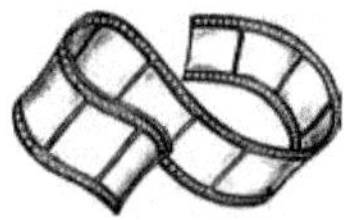

AFTER INGRID BERGMAN CHOSE THE wrong man in *Casablanca*, both Adam and I were subdued, probably because it too closely mimicked the moment I had asked Savannah to leave with me in London and she had chosen to stay with Adam only to divorce him less than six months later.

So Linnea suggested we watch Adam's favorite film.

Which was Alfred Hitchcock's *Vertigo*.

I'd known it was his favorite because we had watched it together more than once in London all those years ago, but until we sat together watching the story of obsession, madness, and love, I didn't realize how much the film had influenced some of my own screenplay in *The Dream & The Dreamer*. There was the shared sense of love as an illusion, of trying to force someone into a role they were simply not meant to play.

It made me reflective, as *Casablanca* had, but not in the same melancholy way.

Instead, it reminded me that I had not told Adam and Linnea about my screenplay.

Or the fact that they were my unwitting muses.

"I wrote something," I said as Adam queued up our last film for the night. My own favorite movies were an impossible tie between *Inception* and *Call Me By Your Name*. As Adam hadn't seen the Andre Aciman adaptation, Linnea insisted we watch that one.

I could tell by the cast of Adam's mouth that he was not in the mood to watch two men fall in love in Italy, but he did not say no to her.

"What?" Linnea asked from the kitchen where she was assembling popcorn drenched in honey and sea salt.

Adam didn't ask me to repeat myself.

His face was broken open with genuine—happy—surprise.

"You wrote something?" he repeated with boyish enthusiasm, leaning forward as to be closer to me as if drawn by a hook through his smiling mouth. "I would kill to read it."

"No need for murder," I demurred, but something bubbly was happening inside my chest that made me feel light and dopey. "I would love to have you both read it."

They both waited as if they knew my pause was just a stepping stone to more.

I carefully sucked a deep breath through my teeth, telling myself it was foolish to be nervous. If I could present awards before my peers at award shows, charm late-night hosts and star in feature films, surely I could pitch a movie concept to these two people who had become my…friends.

"I wrote it for you both," I said, the words raw. I cleared my throat and tried for more casualness. "That is, I had you in my mind's eye when I wrote this story, and if you like the script, I had thought you might do me the honor of starring in it."

Linnea blinked owlishly at me, her mouth dropped open in a little o of shock. Adam's grin widened impossibly. I thought, if he had been a less restrained man, he might even have jumped up and down.

"Give it to me," he demanded, holding out his palm as if he expected me to drop the screenplay into it that moment. "I'll read it now."

I laughed, scrubbing my hand through my hair. "I don't have a paper copy with me as I obviously wasn't intending to spend the night with you both. But…I could email it to you."

"Do it," Adam pressed, standing up to corral Linnea, who was still frozen in the doorway. He cupped her elbow and brought her forward to sit down in her place between us. "Do you have a computer or tablet, Sunbeam?"

The nickname stirred her from her stupor, and she nodded, "I bought one for Miranda to help with her cognitive and occupational therapy. It's plugged in beside the fridge."

Adam nodded curtly before heading into the other room.

Meanwhile, Linnea twisted herself to face me fully, her expression very somber.

"Are you serious about this?" She spoke quietly, as if a loud noise might scare my proposition away.

I nodded slowly and reached out to take the bowl of popcorn into my lap so I could hold her hand. "Very. I do not joke about my art. It's a flaw, I admit."

Her mouth flickered with a smile before falling flat, and her eyes were wide and darkly purpled like gathering storm clouds. "Why me? I told you once before, I won't take handouts, Sebastian."

My laughter took me by surprise, but it eased the last of my nerves, so I gave in to impulse and hauled my blond beauty into my lap with one hand, using the other to move the popcorn up onto the couch. She looped her arms around my neck without complaint, and I loved that she settled so familiarly into my hold. As if she had been born to sit within my embrace.

"Oh, *trottolina*, if I could hand the world to you on a platter, I would. Don't doubt that and don't hate me for it as it's a sign of the man I am and the woman you are to inspire such devotion, *lo capisci?*"

Her expression softened and she ran her fingers gently over my cheekbone and around the curve of my ear.

"That's very sweet," she murmured. "I would do the same for you. Do you know that?"

"*Sì*," I said, because I did.

Linnea was the first person in my life who let me see all of her without much hesitation. *Here I am*, she said that night in London by the pool, *if you are interesting enough, I will shine all my light on you until you won't let me anymore.*

Loyal and brave and loving, our Linnea.

I wasn't sure when I started to think of her as *ours*. It could have been that night at the club when Adam and I watched her blossom under our orders and shared pleasure.

But in my heart, I thought it could have been even earlier than that. The seed planted when I first conceived of Linnea dating Adam to help him out with his scandal, a bridge between our gap that had turned us into a unit of three that felt much more stable than the one before, even though I had no idea of our future.

"I wrote *The Dream & The Dreamer* because I could not stand to have the story inside me for one more moment," I explained, leaning against the couch as I settled with her draped over my lap. When Adam came back with the tablet, he didn't hesitate to sit beside me, our shoulders touching, Linnea's legs in his own lap. I thought, if she hadn't needed the physical comfort so much, he might have hesitated. But Adam was nothing if not a provider who thrilled when someone depended on him. It was powerful enough to make him forget his own hesitations.

"I have not written more than ten words in ten years, Linnea. That I could not stem the tide of this story speaks to the strength of what inspired it. Seeing you again, resuming our friendship in real life." I paused and looked at Adam, who was watching me with a predatory regard that made my gut burn. "Seeing Adam again. I don't know if I was cognizant enough to realize it while I was writing it, but the moment I was finished, I knew there was no other option for this film than to have you both play the leads."

"Email me," Adam said almost as soon as I had finished speaking.

His eagerness was a balm for my nerves, and I laughed softly as I dug my phone out of my pocket from beneath Linnea's lovely ass and emailed the script—filled with my life's blood—to one of the only people whose opinions I cared about.

Adam's fingers tapped impatiently on the side of the tablet as he waited for his email to load, and the moment the note landed in his inbox with a little jingle, he was clicking it open.

"Come here, Sunbeam," he murmured, and Linnea slid across my lap into his own seamlessly. He adjusted so that she sat in the bowl of his lap, her back propped against his chest, his arm around her, allowing him to hold the tablet propped against her raised knees so that they could both read the script.

Before I could protest, Adam said, "Hush, Sebastian. This is a moment we will only get once. I still remember the first time I read *Blood Oath,* and it is a sacred memory."

I tried to sit still while they began to read the treatment, which was a summary of the film, before they delved into the spec script, but anxious excitement prickled under my skin, as if fire ants had infected me.

Finally, Linnea reached over with a little smile curling her mouth and grabbed my hand firmly in hers.

That helped.

I pressed play on the film to distract myself, surprised that it worked even though watching the Italian-set love story always transported me back to my homeland.

It was with a start that I realized, sometime later, Linnea was crying.

I paused the movie and turned my whole body to face the duo who had been quietly absorbed in my screenplay. Linnea smiled at me as tears streamed down her cheeks, a wet little laugh escaping like steam from a kettle, an obvious release.

When I quirked an eyebrow at her, she only laughed louder and shook her head.

"I think," Adam said drolly, "what Linnea means to say is my God, Sebastian."

"*Dio mio*," I repeated in Italian. "This is good or bad?"

"Brilliant," Adam said with a shrug, but his stoicism broke around that wide, genuine smile that had always been able to bring me to my knees. "Bloody fucking brilliant. This makes *Blood Oath* look somehow like child's play, which we both know it very much is *not*. This…"

"This hurt." Linnea picked up the thread of thought and started to speak with her hands as if she needed props to explain herself. "This hurts and it heals and it explains how fucked up and crazy and intoxicating love can be. It's perfect."

I had to close my eyes for a second, or else I might have embarrassed myself by bursting into tears like a small child. My skin felt too tight, my bones too frail under the weight of the joy expanding through me.

"*Davvero?*" I asked. "Honestly, you feel this way?"

"Honest to Christ," Adam swore. "Studio heads will fall over themselves to option this, Seb. You must know that."

"Andrea seemed to think so," I admitted. "But you know the

vecchio is biased."

"I'm biased," Adam acknowledged. "I have also worked in this industry for almost two decades. I know what works, I know what sells, and I know art when it is put before me. This"—

he lifted the tablet and wriggled it—"this is marvelous, Sebastian. If you had not told me you had a part for me in it, I would beg you on my knees."

"I wouldn't hate to see that," I teased, and had the great pleasure of watching his green eyes darken like shadows on the forest floor.

"Neither would I, come to think of it," Linnea bantered back, smiling at me. "But who did you have in mind for Adam?"

"Emerson," I said at the same time he did.

We shared a look that I felt in my chest, an understanding of each other that was fundamental and harkened back to London. In this, in art and film, we had always spoken the same language.

"I thought so." Linnea grinned. "The haughty Brit with false ideals."

"And Linnea as Hallie," Adam continued. "Inspired."

She frowned, picking at a hangnail. "I'm not entirely sure I could do Hallie justice."

"No?" I asked mildly, but my heart was galloping.

This was *it*.

This was the combination of the creative medium I loved with two people I cared for more than I could properly express without writing them a screenplay to illustrate it.

Heaven, I thought, wasn't so much a place you went after you died but a moment in time that reminded you why life was worth living in the first place.

"Why not?" Adam asked.

"Oh, Thatcher's Hallie I can play beautifully," she admitted with a tiny grin. "It's Emerson's Hallie I wonder about. She's meant to be cold and classy when I'm…" She gestured to her oversized T-shirt and damp, rumpled waves.

How she could be so oblivious to the beauty of herself at that moment, unguarded and honest, was almost beyond comprehension.

"Why don't you try her on for size, *trottolina mia*?" I suggested, nodding at Adam who handed her the tablet and gently pushed her off his lap.

She went willingly, settling at our feet on her knees with the tablet on her thighs, one hand nervously tucking her hair behind her ear.

"Which part?"

"Which part spoke to you?" I countered.

She nodded almost to herself and flicked through the pages, which I could see were often highlighted in yellow from the upside-down view. Finally satisfied, she spoke to herself under her breath and then looked up at me.

"Do you have any other notes on Hallie?"

I scratched my stubbled chin as I considered. "The only shared truth between Emerson's Hallie and the reality of her is that she can be haughty and cool when she feels threatened."

She hummed slightly, sucked in a deep breath, and then exhaled it loudly. "I'm nervous. I feel like I'm naked standing on stage before two of Hollywood's biggest names."

"You could take off your clothes if it would make you more comfortable," Adam drawled.

Her head fell back with the force of her laughter, and I grinned at Adam for easing the tension. He reached over and squeezed my hand.

The moment he dropped it, I flexed my fingers against the tremors he left behind.

"Okay," Linnea said, "I'm ready."

We both settled back against the couch, our shoulders and thighs pressed together like seams.

Linnea tipped her head down so her hair curtained her face, but I could see that her eyes were closed and her mobile features were blank.

A moment later, she lifted her chin, and her entire carriage, from her posture to the way she held her expression, was completely changed.

Instead of the elastic mouth with a wide range of smiles, her full mouth was slightly pinched; the angle of her chin was tilted almost pugnaciously, the way my sister, Elena, used to hold herself when she was angry with the world. Her shoulders were pinned back and straight as a ruler, her lids just slightly lowered as if she was bored with us, the same Hollywood royalty she had espoused about just seconds before.

It was arresting.

"You do us both a disservice," she began in a cool, lightly enunciated voice that was American but somehow moneyed. "I am a woman and an actress, yes, so by both counts I invite the male gaze to paint me in with whichever colors suit them best. But I am also unchangeably, irrefutably myself. You do not know me, and quite frankly, if you did, I think you would not wish to. The person you think you want is only a very pretty daydream."

"I know you," Adam said, prompting the line even though he had only read the script once. "I know you even when I close my eyes."

"And if I close mine?" she countered, not quite combative, but something close to it, almost condescending. She closed her eyes as she spoke, "What color are my eyes, Mr. Bainbridge?"

"Blue," Adam replied immediately. "As the sky."

"Violet into indigo," I murmured as Thatcher. "The color of the sky the moment sunset fades into twilight."

Linnea opened her eyes, the very same color as I had described in the script, and smiled at me with acute tenderness. She looked like a different person, *my* person, the girl I had known at sixteen and twenty-six.

"Violet eyes do not exist in nature," Adam argued as Emerson, ruffled and indignant both because he wasn't used to being corrected and because his best mate was interfering in his pursuit of the woman he had been hired to track down. "It's a trick of the light that they might look purple sometimes."

Linnea slid an icy glance his way before fixing her gaze back on me with a tiny, secret smile that flexed one side of her mouth. "Love at first glance is a trick of the light, too. If you want to love a girl, Mr. Bainbridge, you have to do it without sight. It is easy to love with the eyes and less so with all of the other senses."

"You would rather a blind man?" he blustered.

"I would rather someone with soul," she returned archly, sharing a surreptitious look with me because Thatcher and Hallie were, at this point, engaged in an illicit affair. "You may call on me again if you find one."

The silence that followed was a tribute to the scene.

I was the one to break it. "How did that feel?"

Linnea sucked in a deep breath as if she had been holding it underwater before she smiled, a cat-got-the-cream kind of grin.

"Good," she said, flexing her fingers as if shedding Hallie's skin. "Right."

"I couldn't agree more," I said, lifting my phone and opening the recording app. "Do it for me again."

In the scene, Hallie was meant to be donned in an extravagant 1920s-style dress with diamonds at her throat and ears and long silky gloves on her arms. But even in her *Romeo in Blood* tee, with her wavy, wet-tipped hair, Linnea managed to bring her wealth and posterity to life in such a way that captivated both Adam and I.

I had known she would be talented, but seeing her occupy a character in such a way was one of the most erotic moments of my life.

I knew Adam felt the same way because his body was tight with strain pressed against mine and the pulse in his neck thrummed visibly.

When I sent the video clip to Andrea without a caption, I did not expect him to respond until the morning.

Thirty minutes later, I got a response.

Andrea

Chiodo scaccia chiodo. If you are sure, I am sure. She is magnifica.

The expression meant "one nail drives out another," no doubt in reference to Linnea driving out the pain of losing Savannah. I wasn't sure one had anything to do with the other. I had loved them both for a very long time in very different ways, and I was just coming to understand now—watching as Linnea batted dialogue from *my* script back and forth with Adam—that love didn't have to mean suffering.

It could mean this: sitting on the living room floor after a catastrophe, taking care of each other because it felt good to do so.

I thought about a lifetime of evenings like this with the two of them, allowing the dream to unravel like a velvet carpet before me. We would coordinate our jobs so that we didn't have to be apart for longer than a handful of weeks at a time, and when we weren't working, we could split our time between my place in New York City and Adam's perfect Carbon Beach house. Linnea would flourish in her career and attend her own premieres, where Adam and I would just be her two very willing accessories. Adam's career would be unaffected by his open love for both a man and a woman, and in tandem at that. I would be inspired to write even more screenplays now that the stale pain around my heart had come loose in the cool tide of Adam and Linnea's presences back in my life.

I held that precious, impossible dream in my heart for as long as

I could hold my breath, before I exhaled a future that would never be.

Hope, I had to remind myself, was its own poison.

So why did I keep willingly drinking it down?

CHAPTER TWENTY-THREE

ADAM

We fell asleep tangled together like puppies.

It was mostly my fault, too.

Linnea had still been reeling from her mother's episode and I wanted to shelter her with my body and soul, so I tucked her into my side as if I could shield her from the world where we lay. Even though it was foolish, it made me feel better.

It was instinct that had me reaching for Sebastian with the arm I laid my cheek on, extended up over Linnea's golden hair with my palm open.

He didn't hesitate to curl around Linnea's back, one arm draped over her waist and the other meeting mine on that pillow, his thick fingers twining tightly with my own.

When I woke up hours later, it was even worse.

My morning wood was trapped by Linnea, who had rolled on top of me in her sleep and lay draped across my body, her face pressed into my bare chest, her riot of waves half in my face and splayed across my arm. Sebastian was pressed up tight against my side, his arm still draped over Linnea's back, his mouth tucked into my neck, breath hot on my pulse point.

I was smothered in them and for one exquisite moment, I luxuriated in it. The peppery warmth of their combined scents, the feel of them both trusting me, drawn to me, in their sleep. I wanted to marinate in this feeling of contentment so I would never forget it.

Instead, I realized what had woken me.

Miranda stood in the doorway to the kitchen with her hair mussed and her robe cinched tightly around her body. There was a clearness in her eyes I recognized even in the shadows of the curtain-drawn room.

"She won't like this," she said.

I didn't have to ask who she was speaking about.

Savannah had been on my mind since the moment Linnea called me breathless with panic to say the paparazzi had staked out her house. It should have been beneath my ex-wife to call the tip in, but Hank had been a popular call when he lived in London years ago, and Savvy wanted to tip off the press to our whereabouts.

Could she have done it now? Jealous in the wake of bumping into Linnea and me at Nobu?

I wanted to think the best, perhaps because I was spending too much time with a sunbeam of a woman and a star of a man, but my weary, rancid heart suspected I was right.

As soon as I had confirmation from Boone's team, I would act.

And Savannah would find just how little warmth I retained after the dissolution of our marriage.

Without another word, Miranda shuffled into the kitchen, and I heard the click of the stove turning on.

I figured Linnea would not have been pleased if Miranda burned the house down while I cuddled with her and Sebastian in bed, so I carefully slipped out from their bodies and went to supervise Miranda.

I wasn't much of a cook, having neither the time nor the desire to do so, hence Bruce. So, I was relieved when I rooted through the freezer and found a box of Eggo waffles. Miranda watched me with keen eyes as I set about popping them in the toaster, grabbing syrup from the fridge, and cutting up ripe mangos from a bowl on the counter.

"You seem to be feeling better this morning," I ventured casually.

She sniffed and tugged the robe tighter around her. "My mind's like Swiss cheese. Even when I 'feel better,' it's hell because I know it won't last."

My gut cramped with sympathy I was surprised to feel toward Miranda, who had always been a slightly ditzy, irritating figure in my life as Savannah's best friend. Even though her voice was still light and airy, a steeliness had emerged behind her words that was new. Degenerative illness left its mark on everyone involved, and I could sense Miranda's bitterness as if it lingered in the air.

I didn't blame her.

"I'm sorry this is happening to you," I said honestly, as I washed my hands of mango stickiness and then rested my hips against the counter to face her. "You and I were never close, but I hope you know I'm here for you. And Linnea."

She scoffed, her features twisted up into something ugly. "Linnea, maybe."

I shrugged slightly. "Linnea loves you, and I care about her so, yes, I am here for you, too."

"The girl just feels guilty that I'm sick," she mumbled, staring at a torn hangnail. "I wasn't a good mother or anything."

"Maybe not," I agreed because I had no sympathy for her in that regard. "But you did something right to raise such a good woman, even if it was to give custody to her father. She won't abandon you."

Something about my word choice seemed to resonate with her because tears pooled in her lower lids, and she glanced sharply away from me. Her mouth tightened in an effort to keep the emotions locked down.

"She never comes to see me," she whispered.

I knew without asking that she meant Savannah.

"She has never been brave enough to deal with the ugliness of life," I said plainly. "You know her well enough to know that."

Miranda shrugged tightly and huddled deeper within her robe. "I miss her."

"Sometimes, I miss her, too," I admitted. "But then I'm grateful she's gone because it left room for me to let new, better people into my life."

"Like Linnea."

"Yes," I agreed easily.

"You'll leave us both when you see what this is like." She indicated herself with a trembling hand and sneer before it collapsed into a pout. "What I'm like."

"I had a front-row seat last night," I noted mildly. "And I'm still here. In fact, this morning, I'm going to move you and Linnea into my house with me. It's time that someone looked after you *both*."

Miranda's gaze snapped up to mine, and her hand moved to cover her mouth as if she could hide her shock and relief from me. The tears in her eyes spilled over, splashing over her hand and the laminate table.

It had been a long time, before last night, since I had consoled anyone, but I found myself stalking across the kitchen to crouch before her, pulling Miranda forward with a gentle hand on her shoulder so her forehead was pressed into my shoulder. One of her hands clutched my bicep with a shakiness that spoke of weakness and her desire to grip me even harder than she was able to. As if she was worried I would disappear.

"Don't leave us like everyone else," she begged with a broken whisper.

"I won't," I promised, and I meant it.

When I glanced up from our embrace a couple of minutes later, Linnea had stood in the doorframe, her hair a tousled cloud around her drowsy face. The expression on her face was worth painting, and I wished I had the talent to translate it to a medium that could never expire.

Because it was beautifully trusting. As if she knew I would do everything in my power to protect and care for them both.

It had been a very long time since anyone had depended on me for more than just a salary or a stellar acting performance, and I found the responsibility filled me up like sunshine.

"I won't," I said again, this time for her.

And when she smiled at me, I had to blink away the sunspots.

Linnea took over with her mother after that, hustling her back into her room to bathe and dress because the movers would arrive in just over an hour, and there was a mass of things to do before then. Seb woke up and ambled into the kitchen, shuffling his feet with his eyes half closed as he went instantly to the coffee pot I had brewed and helped himself. He'd made a face at the contents, complaining in a thicker-than-usual Italian accent that drip coffee was *schifoso*. Disgusting. We ate standing up in the kitchen, discussing the particulars of the day as we got the Hildebrand/Kai women moved in, and I loved the casual intimacy of it.

It felt like we were, once more, on the same page. The awkwardness was gone, but not the angst, which lingered on the back of my tongue like a bad aftertaste. Things were not truly resolved between us, not when I wanted him with a fierceness that clouded my judgment, not when I could not have him, just as I could not have had him before.

Having Sebastian meant giving up *everything* I had ever worked for.

It meant the same for him, whether he wanted to acknowledge it or not.

It was romantic to think about sacrificing everyone for a loved one, but it was something only done in films and novels. Not in real life when the stakes were staggeringly high.

Or so I told myself as I stared at his mouth while it moved sensually around the words he spoke and at his strong, tanned hands as they moved through the air, highlighting his speech.

Moreover, while he had expressed interest in being friends once more and seemed just as attracted to me as I was still to him, he hadn't said anything about wanting the kind of love and commitment he'd yearned for a decade ago. We had both changed so much since then, maybe he didn't yearn for a love that moved the stars and the sky the way he once had.

But I seriously doubted it.

And a small, greedy, *dastardly* part of me wondered why he might not want it with me anymore even though I *knew* I didn't deserve it after how I had treated him.

I told myself to be grateful to have even this with him, sipping coffee once more in the morning together and talking about our lives as if it was our right to know everything about each other again.

It was enough.

It had to be.

Of course, it wasn't.

Chaucer arrived with the moving crew promptly at ten in the morning, holding her tablet in hand and wearing an earbud to communicate with whomever she needed to speak to over the course of the move. She was frightening in her efficiency, coordinating the burly men, Sebastian, Linnea, and me until everything was designated for my Carbon Beach house, a storage unit we'd rented out, or a donation to the local wildfire survivors' charity.

Within eight hours, Miranda was settled in the guesthouse with her most essential items and three nurses who eased Linnea's nerves by answering her many, many questions.

Linnea herself was set up just down the hall from my room in a guest room that I realized was woefully generic until it was cluttered with boxes of her belongings and swathes of cloth she used to make her colorful dresses and, apparently, scraps of lace and satin lingerie, the sight of which left my mouth dry. I texted Chaucer to clear out one of the other bedrooms so Linnea could have her own design studio here, and then emailed my friend Jensen, who was the creative director at St Aubyn Fashion House, to see what kinds of equipment I needed to order for her.

Sebastian stayed with us for the most part, helping without complaint, flirting with Miranda, who inexplicably thought he was an old paramour named Clark, and teasing Linnea out of her anxiety about changing things so drastically for her mother.

He was a saint, and it only reminded me how much of a sinner I was. How good these two beautiful humans were and how unworthy I was of their friendship. I clung to my gratefulness that they were here, in my orbit, at least for now, and banished my own self-hatred to the attic to haunt me again some other time.

Bruce made dinner for the three of us, which we ate outside on the terrace under the pergola. They both coaxed me into laughter, as if it were a game to see who could make me smile the most, but the worst part was the touching. Sebastian's hand squeezing my shoulder, Linnea's grip a little too high on my thigh, watching as Seb swept away a smear of tomato sauce from the lower corner of Linnea's pouty lower lip.

By the time we had finished, I was so hard it hurt, and I knew if I didn't get away from them, I would savage them both on the patio table, consequences be damned.

I thought a night of sleep would slake my thirst—and a furious session with my fist, a bottle of lube, and my vivid fantasies of them both—but I woke up with an erection that was almost purple it was so hard and aching.

Sebastian had gone home the night before, thank God, but Linnea was asleep under my roof and even running on the treadmill for an hour and then doing a ninety-minute weightlifting session did not diminish the restlessness in my limbs that compelled me to go to her.

So I spent the rest of the morning locked up in my office, taking meetings and checking in on my various business interests before things closed down for the weekend. I also posted a donation link in my Photogram account to a Frontotemporal Dementia charity and included a quote from Linnea's speech to the media on her front lawn. Mali texted me to say it was a brilliant idea and that the media were loving my defense of my girlfriend.

It made me grit my teeth because that was not the reason I did it, even though the entire reason I was even with Linnea was to boost my reputation.

I had a bloody brutal headache after that.

It was the Critics Choice Awards the next day, so I would be forced to spend time with Linnea then, but I was determined to take the day to dismantle the desire that had grown monstrous inside me after spending over twenty-four hours with her and Sebastian.

If I couldn't get a grip on it, I told myself, by the end of the day, then I would go to the club and find relief that way.

It made me uneasy to think of touching anyone other than Sebastian and Linnea even though we weren't exclusive or even together in a concrete way, but I figured directing a nonsexual scene would release some of the tension so I could get some sleep.

It was with that in mind that I finally ventured out of my office to grab water and something to eat for a late lunch. I realized I was practically tiptoeing around my house, trying to avoid Linnea, and told myself to stop being such a prat. The kitchen was empty, but the floor-to-ceiling accordion doors were open to the terrace, where I caught a glimpse of Linnea cutting through the pool on a brisk front crawl. I dropped ice into a glass, poured some homemade lemonade, and let my feet take me closer to the edge of the room where I was half hidden by a pillar with a full view of the saltwater lap pool.

Linnea moved with the ease of a lifelong swimmer, cutting through the azure water with nary a splash. It was mesmerizing, the rhythm of it and the sight of her at home in my house.

So I didn't realize she was getting out of the pool until it was happening, her bare shoulders emerging bronze and glistening, her golden hair slicked away from her striking features.

I forgot to breathe.

Even though I had kissed that luscious mouth and had my fingers in her tight, wet pussy, I had yet to see Linnea naked or anything like it. We had meant to go surfing together again, but time hadn't permitted, so I hadn't even witnessed her in a swimsuit until now.

The sight of her in the tiny yellow bikini should have been illegal.

I was hard so suddenly, it made my teeth ache.

Water sluiced down her caramelized skin and long, shapely limbs, gathering in the narrow gap between her heavy breasts and trickling in a line over her flat belly to the nearly transparent fabric of the small triangle covering her mound. When she hit the deck, she turned to walk away from me toward a lounge chair covered in a towel and arrayed with a fashion magazine and cracked-open can of bubbly water. It gave me an unmitigated view of her tight, round arse and the sway of her hips.

Jesus Christ, I was just a man and she? She was a bloody goddess.

I watched with my heart beating in my throat as she flopped to the chaise lounge, one leg on the tile and the other up on the cushions so that the ribbon of fabric between her legs was bared to me.

"Get it together, man," I muttered to myself even though my feet were cemented to the floor, and I found myself reluctant to blink.

Just as I was gathering the strength to break away and retreat, swiftly, back to my office, Linnea's hand swept from between her breasts to the top of her groin and played under the top of the fabric.

My mouth lost all moisture.

Her eyes closed as she lazily touched herself beneath the fabric, rolling fingers over her clit and down to her entrance.

I inched forward until I was leaning against the pillar. If she opened her eyes, she would see me, but I couldn't find it in me to care.

She groaned, a sound tinged with frustration, and moved her long, nimble fingers to the ties at her waist, undoing them so that her bottoms fell away to reveal her bare pussy, glistening wetly under the sun.

I rolled my forehead against the cool pillar and groaned softly under my breath.

My God, how was I supposed to resist the temptation?

Linnea arched her back as she dipped a finger inside herself, and the unraveling thread of my control finally snapped.

I stalked out from my hiding spot toward where she lay.

Her eyes opened slowly, completely unsurprised by my appearance.

I wondered if she had known all along I was watching, the little minx, and decided I didn't care. If she wanted to goad me, I would show her just how dangerous a game I liked to play.

I sat on the lounge chair across from her with my forearms braced on my thighs, my glass dangling between my legs, and I studied her.

A flush spilled from her cheeks down her throat to her chest, even her nipples pinked.

"Just what," I asked in a low, sinuous growl, "do you think you are doing, Linnea Kai?"

"Thinking about you," she said seamlessly, her legs working restlessly as she dragged a finger over her clit.

"Were you?" I murmured.

She nodded, trapping her lower lip between her teeth before saying, "And Sebastian."

"Ah," I crooned, completely lost to the heathen side of myself as if I had been possessed by another spirit, one that did not care about legal obligations or emotional consequences. Only about sex and sin. "And what were we doing in these fantasies?"

"Touching me. Touching each other," she breathed, her lids so heavy I could barely see through her lashes to the violet centers.

"Show me how we were touching you," I told her, sinking into that cool, calm place where everything felt under my control. "I want to watch you touch yourself while you tell me how Seb and I would please you."

A small sound like a truncated whimper escaped her parted lips as she cupped both of her breasts through her wet bikini top, her nipples clearly defined beneath the thin fabric.

"You both have big hands," she rasped. "Whenever I look at them, I wonder what they would feel like on my breasts and tweaking my nipples."

"Pinch them," I ordered her, leaning back on my hands in the seat as if I had all the time in the world to impassively watch her perform for me. "Harder."

She gasped as she obeyed me, her back arching slightly off the chaise.

"Pull the fabric aside."

Her fingers fumbled in their haste to do so, pulling the wet material to the outside of each breast so they were plumped together and framed by the yellow fabric.

My mouth watered, and I had to flex my hands around my glass and the edge of the chair to keep from touching her. Restraining both of us, though, was half the fun.

"So pretty," I praised, watching as the flush on her chest deepened. "What do you suppose Sebastian would say if he could see you now? Touching yourself while you thought about him."

She licked her lips. "I think he would come over and offer to touch me himself."

"Do you?" I drawled.

"Yes," she said defiantly. Even as she continued to writhe, she pulled and pinched at her reddening nipples. "He would, even if you won't."

"Why, Linnea Kai, are you trying to make me jealous?" I suggested in a low hiss as I got up from my chair and abruptly sat on the edge of hers just beneath her hip. My hand found her long, elegant neck and wrapped around it just tightly enough to feel the air move through her throat. "Because I have to warn you, the thought of Sebastian's rough hands on your lovely skin does nothing but arouse me."

She pressed up slightly into my hold on her neck, her pupils blowing wide until her eyes were mostly black. My girl liked to be choked.

My cock throbbed beneath my zipper, choked, too, by the fabric.

It was a good thing I liked a little pain as well.

"If he were here, I would have him get on his knees for you," I continued almost conversationally as I watched her breasts heave and her legs churn restlessly. "I would dig my fingers in that thick black hair and press his handsome face to your pretty pussy until you came again and again on his tongue. Until you begged us both to stop because you couldn't stand to come anymore. Would you like that, sweetheart?"

"Yes," she hissed, her eyes flying open to meet mine with surprising intensity. "And after I used his mouth, I would want to watch you use it too."

My hand flexed around her neck reflexively at the thought.

It had been too long since I had the pleasure of sliding into Seb's talented mouth, but I could still remember the awed, reverent look in his eyes when he took me straight down to the root. As if he wasn't complete until he was filled up with me.

A rough groan rumbled through my chest.

Linnea grinned at me, a sly, ultra-feminine expression. "I don't just want the two of you for me, Adam. I want the two of you for each other."

I thought of Savannah without wanting to, remembering how she had always wanted our dalliances to be about her as the center spoke of the wheel. My therapist had suggested that she had used my bisexuality as an excuse to divulge her need to be worshipped by younger, attractive men in order to validate her worth.

No matter the reason, her subtle maneuvering had only proved to deepen the roots of my internalized homophobia. I knew it, and struggled with it like Peleus wrestling the ever-changing shape of the goddess Thetis, but I had yet to conquer it.

I was making progress, though, and hearing that Linnea wanted Sebastian for me, too, was a balm I hadn't known I needed.

I bent forward before I could regulate myself, sealing my mouth to hers. She tasted of lemonade and Linnea, a potent mix that drugged me. I ate from her mouth and slid my free hand between her legs where one of her own was playing in the obscene wetness of her folds. Pressing my fingers over hers, I directed her to touch her clit, playing with it almost roughly.

She keened into my mouth, hips juddering as pleasure seared through her.

When I tore myself away from her sweet mouth, she glistened gold with sweat and sunshine, just shy of naked in a way that somehow was even more erotic than true nudity.

"I am not supposed to touch you," I growled. "But how am I supposed to resist everything that you are? Even when I close my eyes or turn away from you, I can feel your light like sun on my skin."

"You don't have to resist me," she coaxed, tangling our fingers together tightly and arrowing her hand deeper between her legs so that we could press inside her wet heat in tandem. She cried out, eyes squeezed shut, as I curled our fingers into her front wall and rubbed. "You never had to resist either of us. We're yours, you just have to open your eyes and accept it."

"You can't speak for Sebastian," I countered, but I didn't stop touching her, didn't curb the impulse to dip my head and suck a swollen nipple into my mouth.

"If you let him, he would tell you the same," she pushed.

I kissed her then to shut her up because I couldn't stand to think any more about the impossible promise of Sebastian Lombardi, let alone combined with the temptation of Linnea.

At this moment, it was just the two of us.

My future *wife* and the woman who was beginning to consume my soul.

"Linnea," I breathed against her damp lips as I cradled her delicate throat in my hand. "For now, let this be about us."

Her eyes were wide, so soft and tender a violet blue they seemed like crushed flower petals. "Okay," she breathed. "You and me."

"Yes," I said as primal satisfaction roared through me. "You are mine."

"I signed on the dotted line," she quipped, but her sassiness was undercut by the churn of her greedy hips grinding against my hand.

In retribution, I tweaked her clit between our fingers, and she shuddered.

"A contract is not enough," I growled, thrumming her thumb against her clit while our tangled fingers fucked into her obscenely wet cunt. "I would write my name on your skin, bite it into your neck, tattoo it onto your soul so that every inch of you was made mine in a way that would never fade."

"Not even in three years?" she whispered, even as her eyes started rolling back into her head and her breath hitched.

"Not even when our bodies turned to dust," I vowed. "Now, come for me, pretty little thing, and show me just how glorious you are when you come apart."

I squeezed my hand just a little bit tighter around her neck and ground my thumb into her swollen, slippery clit. Her gasp was thready as it escaped from the pressure in her throat, and her whole body went tight as a wire a moment before she shuddered over into a climax that made her groan and writhe.

I pinned her still with my hands, driving her pleasure higher and higher until she let out a soundless scream and squirted. Riveted by the wet flood of her cum over our hands, I pressed harder against the front wall of her grasping pussy and watched as she drenched herself.

"Fuck," I cursed hoarsely, so aroused my vision swam. "Such a good girl squirting for me like that. Coming all over our hands like a good little slut."

"Oh my God, oh my God," she chanted in a warbled murmur, eyes shut, head arched back into the cushion, legs juddering. "I can't, I can't."

"You can," I hissed, eeking out the last of her climax with a relentlessness that edged just shy of painful.

I could tell she enjoyed my ruthlessness by the weak moan that trembled through her throat under my grip.

When she lay panting and boneless, I carefully slid our wet hands from her pussy and used the edge of her towel to clean them before gently dabbing the terry cloth over her cum-slick thighs. I wanted to get on my knees and clean her up properly with my tongue, or better yet, have Sebastian here to do it for me, but years of control kept me from caving in.

She was utterly still as I tended to her but for her heaving chest and the hand she kept loosely circled around my wrist as if she was afraid I would let her go.

Tenderness filled me to the brim, threatening to split the seams of my skin.

More than making her come like that, so hard she was almost afraid of it, I loved that she trusted me to take care of her. It was a vulnerability I found difficult to admit to myself, so it meant all the more to have someone gift it to me.

I stroked her neck with the fingertips of my clean hand and traced up to the shell over her ear and the curve of her cheek. Her eyes fluttered open, slumberous and dark as Italian plums as she regarded me from under her lashes.

"What do I have to say so that we can do that every single day?" she murmured in a ravaged voice.

My own chuckle startled me, and another fierce tide of something warm and bright, like love, surged through. On its heels, fear swiftly followed.

Nothing good had ever come from me falling in love.

Why would it be different now, falling in love with a woman who was contractually obligated to be mine?

It occurred to me with a suddenness that felt like a ham-fist to the chin that I didn't want to marry Linnea Kai because I had to.

I wanted her to be Linnea Meyers because she wanted to bear my name and make it mean something pure and honest again. Because she wanted to be my partner and advocate in this life and the next. Because she adored me, the too-old-for-her curmudgeon with a closet full of skeletons and fears almost as big as the love in his heart.

I wanted her to *want* to take me on, not because she needed money for Miranda's care, not because she wanted a career in Hollywood, not because she was a bleeding heart who—God forbid—felt badly for me.

If I were the moon, as Sebastian had so often inferred, I wanted her to be the sun reflecting light and warmth into my cold, dark life. I wanted her to give me the strength to pursue joy again, even if it came with consequences.

Just as I had feared she would from the moment I saw her, Linnea Kai had brought me back to life, and Christ, it was painful, but it was also bloody exhilarating.

Because I had found the will to desire things again.

I had remembered how to dream.

With her, even Sebastian's impossible universe didn't seem so out of sight.

I was standing before I realized it, stepping away from her as if backing away from a predator.

"Adam?" she said softly, totally unselfconscious, sprawled naked and cum-soaked on the chaise. "Why are you looking at me like that?"

I swallowed thickly and heard myself speak as if from underwater. "Like what?"

"Like I scare you," she said softly as she sat up.

Even though she did not reach for me, I could sense she wanted to.

And if she touched me now, when everything I felt was seconds from bursting out beneath my stretched-tight, fragile skin, I didn't think I would ever be the same again.

I took another step away, cleared my throat, and shoved my hands in the pockets of my linen pants.

"Wanting what you cannot have is terrifying," I admitted with a smile that felt flat on my face. "Sometimes dreaming hurts."

"It doesn't have to," she insisted, leaning forward earnestly. "If you're brave enough to believe in them, they can come true. Miranda told me all my life I wasn't good enough to act, and today, the Oscar-winning director Georges Gallegos called me to offer me a part in his next project. For years, I've fantasized about being bent into shape with rough hands and cool words by a man powerful enough to take care of my needs in the bedroom and the real world. When I needed your help with Miranda, you called in the cavalry and rode in like a white knight. Today, when I needed to be broken apart by pleasure to get out of my own head, you dismantled every thought until all I could hear was your voice and all I could see was you."

She sucked in a deep breath. "Wanting something so badly it hurts doesn't mean it will end in more pain. Especially when what you want—who you want—feels the very same way about you."

"We've known each other for six weeks," I countered. "You do not know me well enough to say that."

She shrugged slightly, but her gaze was narrow with intensity as she pinned me in place with it. "I might not know the details, but I know the shape of your heart, Adam Meyers. People have fallen in love with less."

"Don't speak of love," I hissed. "You swore to me when we started this, you would not fall in love with me."

She cocked her head, completely unruffled. "Funny, I don't remember you promising to do the same."

"I'm going out," I declared as alarm bells trilled in my head. "Don't wait up."

"Where are you going?" she asked, and I could hear her get off the chair as I turned around to head back into the house.

"Out," I bit off the words. "Just because we live together doesn't mean I have to report all my doings to you, Linnea."

"You're mean when you're scared," she singsonged like the brat she was. Always pushing me, always prodding for weakness so she could wrench it open and kiss it better.

Well, not this time.

If she touched me again, I'd come apart.

Want pushed against my skin like an infection, bloating and ugly, just waiting to split the fragile flesh and ooze into the open.

I kept forgetting why I couldn't have her, him, them.

And then, something would remind me by kicking me in the bloody teeth.

"Stay," Linnea asked as she followed me through the kitchen to the foyer where she watched me tug on a jacket and toe into a pair of loafers without bothering with socks. "You can't be going anywhere good looking like that."

"You want to know where I'm going?" I growled through my teeth, spinning toward her and taking the three large steps between us so I could wrap my hand around her throat again. "I'm going to a club so I can slack some of this relentless thirst you and Sebastian have cursed me with."

"You don't need to leave the house for that," she said calmly, but her eyes were bright with daring, and she leaned hard into my grip around her neck.

"I do," I gritted out. "This situation is rapidly devolving into something without rules and boundaries. Something that could hurt us all."

"I don't think you can stop it now," she said quietly. "You and Sebastian, Sebastian and me, maybe even the path that brought us here to the three of us now, it all started a long time ago."

"Do you know why Oscar Hampton is coming after me now?" I demanded as poison bubbled up my throat and over my tongue. "Because I was lonely after Sebastian and Savannah left, and I ran into Oscar at a club in London whilst I was visiting. He knew about my bisexuality, about how Savannah and I used to be."

I closed my eyes as memories swept through me like ghosts, leaving nausea and goose bumps in their wake.

"I just wanted a friend." I forced the words through my tight throat but didn't look at her. "I just wanted to be seen for a moment after feeling invisible for so long even in front of the masses."

"And he took advantage?"

I nodded slightly. "It was a mistake. I was deep into my drinking stage, and he took advantage of that. I hardly remember the evening, but I woke up naked in a hotel room with Oscar smiling beside me. I told him once was more than enough, after I was sick in the toilet. He seemed fine with it. Only, a few weeks later, he called asking for a favor."

Linnea made a humming noise of realization. "He started blackmailing you."

"Yes." It felt good to talk about it with someone other than my publicist, agent, and manager. "I didn't even realize at first." My laugh was rough enough to hurt my throat. "Only when he asked to be production designer on my latest Jonathon Cross film and I told him it wasn't possible did he start threatening me."

"How long?" she whispered.

I opened my eyes to see her beautiful face suffused, not with pity as I'd feared, but rage.

"Seven years," I told her. "Ten months ago, when I was signed on to play Anton Daventry in the spy films, I drew a hard line and told him no more."

"And he told you he had a sex tape," she filled in the blanks. "So all this started."

"All this started," I agreed, realizing my hand on her throat had softened, my thumb pressing lightly against her pulse to feel it pound steadily against my skin. It was wildly soothing. "Everything I've ever wanted, Linnea, has ended brutally. Perhaps, if I keep myself from loving you, from loving him, I can keep that taint from you both."

"Adam." She exhaled my name and reached up to touch my jaw with her fingertips so gently, I wondered if she thought I might break. "That's not how life works, honey."

"It's how my life works," I said unequivocally. "I've had thirty-nine years to test its effects, and I won't risk it now. Not with you."

"What if I want to take the risk?" Linnea said, stepping closer so she could palm my own throat, brush a thumb over my rabbiting pulse point. "I may be younger than you, Adam, but I know how hard life can be. I've had blood on my teeth for a long time, and I'm not afraid to take one on the chin for you when I have to. A little hardship isn't enough to drive me from your side. Not now, and especially not if you give me your trust."

"If I had known how lovely you were when Sebastian suggested this arrangement, I wouldn't have brought you into my mess," I told her honestly, ignoring her plea.

Instead, I reeled her in by the neck and pressed a kiss on her forehead before releasing her and turning toward the door.

"Don't wait for me," I said.

And I meant don't wait up, but I also meant don't wait for an old, broken man to change his mind.

Linnea didn't say a word, so maybe she finally understood me.

It should have made me happy, probably, but as I closed the door without looking back, I felt sick enough to lose the contents of my stomach in the bushes beside the garage.

CHAPTER TWENTY-FOUR

LINNEA

"Are you sure about this?"

I tore my gaze from the rare rainy skies of Los Angeles out the window to look at Sebastian in the driver's seat. He was wearing black jeans that skimmed his powerful, long legs and a crisp white dress shirt with black buttons undone to the top of his chest. It should have been a professional outfit, but the way the Italian wore it was distinctly sinful. He looked exactly like a man who could convince a holy saint to sin with a flex of his full mouth into a seductive smile and the shine of his golden gaze.

It was exactly what we were banking on, really, so I was glad he had come to play.

I was similarly dressed in a fairly conservative wrap dress, a color of bruised blueberries that almost exactly matched my eyes. A pair of stilettos were on my feet, the same gold as Seb's irises. Beneath the fabric though, I wore a creation that had taken me weeks of careful hand sewing to bring together. Italian lace was extremely delicate, as was the silk I used to accent the plum-colored corset and thong set. I fiddled with the clasp where the stockings connected to the garter belt through the slit in my dress and watched as Seb's stare slid to my legs before jerking back to watch the road.

Was I sure about this?

The plan I had concocted in the thirty seconds it took me to locate my phone after Adam left and call Sebastian to come over wearing something sexy. I wasn't even sure it would work until I hunted down Chaucer in her office in the basement and asked her very pleasantly to tell me where the hell Adam's sex club was. She was Adam's number one, his manager but also his assistant, friend, and secret keeper.

I was shocked she told me without hesitation, typing the address into the map app on my phone.

She'd shrugged at my look of astonishment and offered blandly, "If Adam won't look out for his own happiness, someone should."

I wasn't sure if she meant herself or me or both of us, but it didn't matter.

She was right.

I would force happiness down Adam's throat if I had to, which was basically what the plan consisted of.

Showing up at Bacchanalia Sex Club with Sebastian in tow in order to seduce our reluctant Brit into *finally* giving this a chance.

Us.

Together.

"Yes," I said, and my voice was sure. "Are you?"

It was a more complicated question for Sebastian, I knew. He and Adam had so much history between them, years of stagnated pain that was just starting to properly heal now that they were addressing it. But I knew Sebastian in a way I was only beginning to know Adam. We had been friends for a very long time, and even though it was over distance, our postcards often served as diary entries.

I wanted a love, *he'd written me once,* that moved the stars and the sky. I thought I found it a long time ago, but maybe I was wrong.

Only half wrong, I thought, or maybe hoped.

To see Seb and Adam together was to believe in soulmates.

I didn't think Savannah deserved to be considered in that equation, but I desperately, wistfully hoped I might be.

Sebastian's hand found my thigh, skirting up the thin nylon stocking until he reached my bare skin bisected by the garter. When I looked up at him, his face was cast in the red of the stoplight, his expression raw with hunger.

"I have never wanted anything so much in my life," he said honestly, accent thick. "I have always been willing to work for what I want, Linnea. But if this is to work with Adam, he needs to be willing to fight for us, too, *lo capisci?*"

"I know," I agreed. "But I think he needs us to take the first steps. To prove we're here even when he tries to push us away."

Seb made a broken noise in his throat, hand spasming on my thigh. "I went when he told me to the first time. I won't make this mistake again. I am older and wiser, and I have you."

"I make a difference?" I asked, trying to be playful as if the question didn't mean anything to me.

"Without you, I think, Adam and I would still be strangers who used to love one another," he answered.

I chewed my bottom lip and picked at a hangnail. "You know, if this love story is about you two and there isn't room for me—"

"Do not continue," Sebastian ordered, lifting his hand to press it over my mouth. "*Dopo la pioggia, arriva il sole.* After rain, the sun arrives," he translated. "You are our sun, Linnea. Do not doubt that you are vital. I'm beginning to think you were made for us."

"And Savannah?" I asked because I had to.

Sebastian had loved her for a very long time, in a way that Adam didn't seem to share.

If we were going to convince Adam to take a chance on us, we couldn't afford a ghost muddying things up.

Seb's hand returned to the wheel with his other one and squeezed hard enough to squeak. "That," he said somberly, voice deep, "is done."

We pulled in front of an ornate gate blocking the entrance to a long driveway in Brentwood, of all places.

"This is it?" I asked as Seb lowered the window and pushed the intercom.

When a voice asked for the password, Sebastian spoke the Latin phrase Chaucer had given us.

A bene placito.

At one's pleasure.

Fitting for a sex club, especially one whose clientele included the rich and famous of Hollywood's elite.

Chaucer had contacted the manager for us, but it still took over an hour for her email to respond with the requisite forms that Sebastian and I had to fill out to be allowed into the club, even for the night. Without Adam's consent, he couldn't sponsor our evening, so Sebastian had reached out to someone else.

His brother-in-law, Daniel Sinclair.

He'd blushed when he made the call, but Sinclair only treated the favor with cool professionalism without requesting any messy questions.

Without me asking, Seb had explained, "My family isn't exactly vanilla. Sinclair is fairly infamous in BDSM circles. I try not to think about it too much."

The gates swung open, and Seb pulled the Lamborghini up the manicured drive until we reached a circular driveway in front of an enormous Tudor-style mansion. A woman wearing leather hot pants and a corset with a matching leather chauffeur's hat waited for us, opening my door and then walking around to take the keys from Sebastian.

Another woman waited at the entrance with a silver tray of champagne, wearing a sheer black mini dress with white frills like a very naughty maid's costume.

I swallowed thickly at the sight of her round curves spilling out of the deep collar.

Sebastian's chuckle was smoky in my ear as he took my arm and tugged me into his side. "You look very flushed already, Linnea. Are you ready for what we might see tonight?"

"I'm ready for what we might do," I corrected, because even though I was wildly excited to enter this sordid domain, I still felt like a coltish, overeager teen who didn't quite belong.

"Outdoor clothing is banned beyond this point," the woman told us after handing over the champagne. "There are lockers in the antechamber just through here. When you've disrobed, I will take you inside. Please pick a mask from the selection on the wall as we value our clients' anonymity here."

Sebastian led me into the beautifully appointed change room, empty of people but filled with the rumbling bass of music I recognized as Glass Animals.

"Have you ever done this before?" I asked, suddenly needing to know.

"No," he assured me, guiding me deeper into the room. "Adam had a club he frequented in London, but Savannah didn't like to play in front of others, and I never thought to ask to go along. This is a first for me, too."

"Does it turn you on?" I asked.

"You turn me on. In any place or time, even when it's inconvenient. Now, let me help you with this," Seb murmured as he shifted behind me and twisted my hips until I faced a floor-length mirror. "I've been dying to see what you have under this dress since you opened the door for me."

A violent shiver scoured through me as he planted a flat hand in my belly and used the other to slowly tug at the sash tying the dress closed around my hips. He looked so powerful towering over me, so much taller even than my five nine height that I felt uncharacteristically dainty pressed against him. The low lights limned him in gold, casting his features in shadows so that he seemed almost sinister.

I shivered again and leaned my weight back against him.

"That's my girl," he murmured, pressing his lips into my hair as the sash finally pulled through the knot and unbound.

I watched his eyes, azure gold in the lamplight, as my dress gaped open to reveal the intricate lingerie I'd designed myself.

His sharp inhale sounded almost painful.

"*Dio mio, sei incantevole,*" he muttered in husky Italian before remembering to translate. "My God, you are enchanting."

His hands traced the path of the high-cut plum-purple panties from my hips to the apex of my thighs, then fiddled with the bow at the top that dipped down to expose a V of bare skin on my pubis. Trailing his rough fingertips up to my belly button, he feathered his touch over the points of lace that draped down to touch the sides of my hips and then up to the center point of my ribs where boning plumped up my breasts until they raised obscenely over the cups, my nipples one heaving breath away from exposure.

"If I was not touching you, I would think you are a dream," he told me in a ragged voice as he cupped my breasts through the delicate fabric, rubbing his thumbs over the points of my nipples. "What beautiful wrapping for Adam's gift tonight."

I trembled at the possessiveness and praise.

"Will he reward me, do you think, for giving him something so lovely to play with?" Sebastian murmured, dragging his mouth from my ear to my neck, where he sank his teeth into my skin. He laved the small hurt with his tongue. "Should I leave my own mark so he knows who the present is from?"

"Yes," I breathed, tipping my head to the side as if my spine had dissolved.

"*Si,*" he echoed, before closing his mouth over my flesh and sucking hard.

I gasped, my knees weakening at the dual sensation of pain and pleasure that arrowed down my chest and sank into my low belly. Sebastian banded one arm under my breasts to keep me on my feet and sucked harder.

When he lifted his head, the bruise he'd left behind was very nearly the same dark purple as the lingerie I wore for them.

"My turn," I suggested, already twisting to Sebastian and raising on my toes in my heels so I could reach his neck.

Without hesitation, he lowered his head so I could sink my fingers into his rumpled black waves and fist them tight while I left my own vicious love bite on his throat.

When I stepped back, we were both breathing heavily.

"Pick my mask for me," Sebastian asked, smoothing his hands down my sides as if he could not stop touching me.

He spun me by the hips to face the wall of masks, and I hummed as I surveyed the hundreds of options. It only took a moment to pick one for him, though, and he laughed when I walked over to pluck it from the hook.

It was a black velvet mask with a spray of what looked like *real* diamonds across one side of the eyes that resembled the Milky Way. The rich color brought out his golden eyes and deepened his swarthy allure.

Without saying a word, he reached around me to secure my own mask, a delicate gold affair with a blazing sun in the crest of the forehead.

As he secured the ribbons around my head, I tipped forward to snag one more from the wall. It was pale silver and pockmarked like the surface of the moon and fitted in the shape of the same one worn by the Phantom of the Opera.

"He'll be wearing one already," Sebastian reminded me. "But I agree this is perfect."

"The sun, the moon, and the stars," I told him, spinning so I could press my body against the length of his. "Now, all you need is love enough to move them."

Seb made an inarticulate noise in the back of his throat, slid a hand into the back of my hair, and lowered his mouth to mine. This kiss was slow and sensual, a lead-up move that left my thoughts fuzzy around the edges and my thighs pressed together to stem the ache between them.

"*Trottolina,*" he murmured against my damp mouth as he stroked a hand along my jaw. "I am tempted to keep you in this room and ravage you myself. If you want to include Adam, we should leave while I have the will to do so."

Female satisfaction curled through me. "I want you with or without him. I always have," I confessed, taking his hand and pressing it between my thighs so that he could feel the dampness already gathered there. "I just happen to think the three of us together makes sense, somehow, more than just the two."

"Oh, I agree," he growled, cupping me hard through the lace and nipping at the love bite on my neck again. "How do you want to play this?" he asked me, and I loved that he was letting me set the stage.

Sebastian wasn't a total Dom like Adam, but he had a dominant streak that ran parallel with his submissive one, and it felt like a gift to be given the reins.

"Speaking of gifts," I said coyly, feeling inspired. "Do you think that woman has a pen and paper hidden anywhere in that little dress?"

Sebastian's answering grin was sly. "I'm sure we can find out."

CHAPTER TWENTY-FIVE

ADAM

Bacchanalia was not my favorite club, but it was serviceable.

I much preferred Club Dionysus in London now that it was under new management, with its large exhibition space and a beehive of small, private rooms filled with kink-specific equipment.

Or maybe it was just that, even with masks at Bacchanalia, the club was too filled with people I knew to be thoroughly enjoyable.

I sat alone in a small black velvet booth sipping scotch while I watched a Domme punish her male sub over a spanking bench on the main stage when yet another person stopped in my periphery to chat.

"Sod off," I growled, done with niceties for the night after a dozen others had come by to talk shop while I was clearly trying to brood and let off steam.

"Excuse me, sir," one of the barmen apologized. "I only came to deliver a note."

I winced at my rudeness and slipped a fifty-dollar bill onto his tray before I took the heavy card stock from it. "I apologize for my shortness."

The slim man just ducked his chin and retreated from the table, leaving me to my scotch and the envelope.

I kept my eye mostly on the stage as I opened the note, expecting to see a summons from John-Julian, the proprietor, perhaps, or an invitation from a couple playing in one of the rooms even though I wasn't known for my participation. Sometimes couples just liked to show off, and I was often a willing voyeur.

But this was not from some random couple.

Lord Meyers,

A gift awaits you in Private Room C. Please wear the mask hanging on the door before you enter and do not come unless you are ready to play. Be prepared to pay a toll for the honor.

Xoxo,
S&L

AS IF I WAS IN ANY doubt of who had written the message, along with an old-fashioned bronze key, there was an enclosed Polaroid photo of a man and woman on their knees with their heads bowed. One dark and masculine, one blond and feminine, both collared with red string that ended in paper tags that I could barely make out read *For Adam Meyers's Use Only.*

I hissed as my cock hardened too fast in my trousers, the length of it crushed against my zipper, my head light from the rush of blood down south.

Fuck *me.*

They had found a way into my club.

Into my dirty sanctuary.

And trussed themselves up like fat Christmas geese for me to devour.

I closed my eyes so tight stars burst beneath my lids, and I fought to breathe through the tightness of desire in my chest.

Was there any way I could resist this summons?

Any way to say no yet again when all I wanted was the two people waiting for me on their knees in Private Room C?

No.

Absolutely not.

My resolve died a quick, bloodless death on the seat of the black velvet booth as I held a photo of Sebastian and Linnea marked with my name in my hands.

They wanted me enough to risk coming here, to put themselves wholly into my hands, to pursue me even when I did not deserve them and told them as much again and again.

Enough was enough.

I might not ever *deserve* their goodness, but maybe, if I worked hard enough, I could earn it over time.

Friendship, it seemed, was not enough for any of us.

And even though I had no bloody idea where any of this could go for the three of us together, I was willing to admit Linnea was right.

We were on a path together now, and only an idiot would turn his back on walking through life with two people like them.

I stood before I had even opened my eyes, the photo and card secured in my hand, but my scotch forgotten on the table.

"Ah, Meyers," someone said, stepping into my path as I started across the main room to the hall leading to the private room on the right.

I neatly moved around him without stopping and increased my pace until I was almost speed walking.

The only thought in my head was them.

Sebastian and Linnea.

Waiting for me.

Beckoning me.

Daring me to be my basest, rawest self.

By the time I reached the door to Private Room C, my heart was hammering inside my chest, my blood hot enough to sear me from the inside out. A mask hung beneath the gold plaque naming the room, and I laughed soundlessly at the sight of its moon-like texture.

I slipped out of my plain black mask and into the moon's embrace before I fitted the key into the lock and turned the door open under my palm.

Without looking deeply into the shadows of the low-lit room, I closed the door behind me, breathed in deeply to collect myself, and then turned to face my lovers.

The room was themed like a harem, everything jewel-toned and draped in swathes of silk fabric, layered in deep, lush pillows. The bed was enormous and built into the floor to the left, while the right showcased a beautiful spanking bench, a wall of impact implements and toys displayed like glassware in a dining room, and a St. Andrew's Cross with red velvet padding.

But I noticed all of that only in my periphery because my total focus was centered on the two bodies kneeling in front of a low bench facing the door. Their heads were dipped toward the floor just as in the photo, their hands palms down on their spread and bent knees.

The handwritten tags lingered in the hollow of both their throats.

For Adam Meyers's Use Only.

On the left side of either throat, a love bite blossomed like a dark rose, a signature they'd signed onto each other for my benefit.

Fuck, they were glorious.

Perfect and depraved.

And *mine* if I was brave enough to let myself have them.

"What pretty presents someone left for me," I drawled as I came deep into the room and walked a circle around them.

The room was utterly silent, with not even a hint of music to distract from the quiet sound of our breathing.

I stopped in front of Sebastian and took the tag between my fingers.

"For my exclusive use," I pondered aloud, pressing my foot gently against the front of Seb's trousers along the ridge of his hardening cock. "What might I do to you, Sebastian?"

To my surprise, he tipped his head back to stare up at me with glittering eyes, a small, wolfish grin widening under the edge of his black velvet mask. "Whatever you want, Adamo. You just have to earn it first."

My brows raised into my hairline. "Oh, and how might I do that?"

"We're here," he said, signalling Linnea and himself. "We want you. I want you. And friendship has never been good enough to quench the hunger I have for you. Ten years later and I am still starving for everything you have to give me."

"Sebastian." I said his name because in moments when words didn't suffice to describe the enormity of my emotions, only his name could come close.

"I need you to prove you want me the very same way," he declared, bold and brave even on his knees at my feet. "I need you to show Linnea and me that we aren't the only ones willing to fight for what is between us."

"And what is between us?" I dared to ask.

"An impossible universe," he said solemnly.

I swallowed thickly as I reached out to run a thumb along the strong, stubbled line of his jaw until it rested on the crest of his full lower lip.

"I don't want to hurt you again," I confessed and then dug deeper so the words tasted bloody on my tongue, excavated from my very bone marrow. "I don't want to hurt myself again."

"Then don't," he said simply. "I understand the score. I'm not eighteen and naive anymore. I know I will never walk down the beach holding your hand, telling everyone the moon is my lover. But I can still feel pride knowing you are mine, even if I cannot touch you as I wish in public. Having you in any way is better than not at all."

His eyes were luminous, lit from within by the eternal flame of his faith and optimism. He made my heart ache with a powerful beat, strong enough to crack open my ribs and fall out of my chest to get close to him.

"Do you agree?" he asked.

I swallowed once, twice, fighting past the fear instinct, the memories of losing my mother, Juliet, in a car crash as a boy, finding Gregory in bloody bathwater, seeing Bryce killed in action after starting to fall in love with him, watching Sebastian walk out of my life during my panic attack, waiting for Savannah to leave me, realizing Oscar Hampton had my neck in a guillotine...

Those "zombie" years after Sebastian and Savannah left, when I'd been weak enough to let Oscar back into my life, had been one long slog of drudgery, shame, and regret with nothing but acting to punctuate my life with glimmers of contentment.

Since Sebastian and Linnea had re-entered my life, none of those things had ceased to exist, but my sense of gravity had adjusted. It was easier to stand tall and have the courage to want and wish again because I had their light to guide me out of those dark memories and moments.

Love made the pain of living worthwhile.

That was what they had been trying to show me and tell me for the past two months.

I just had to reach out and accept the hearts they held out on their proverbial sleeves, and I would be a much richer and happier man than I ever had been before.

Of course, it didn't mean Oscar would stop trying to sabotage my career or that it would be easy to come out to the public as a bisexual man, let alone one in a throuple. It didn't mean my father, who barely talked to me as it was, wouldn't throw a fit if he found out his son liked to suck cock. It didn't mean I would get to play Anton Daventry, the legendary British spy, a role I had lusted after since I was just a lad watching films for the first time at my father's knee.

But it meant I had people at my back who would soothe me through the hurts and cheer me through the successes.

It meant I wouldn't be alone, not ever again, so long as I trusted them and gave them reason to trust me in turn.

I used my hand on Seb's face to encourage him to stand.

He went willingly, unfolding to his full height, eye to eye with me and toe-to-toe. His physique was that of a swimmer, long and lean with the broad shoulders and narrow waist that made my mouth water.

"How can you trust me again after what we've been through? I want to be worthy of you, I want your forgiveness, but how can I earn it after all this time?" I asked because I knew he hadn't forgiven me. Not really.

How could he when I forced him out of my life and didn't speak to him for ten years after?

Sebastian studied me, his mouth pressed flat, but his eyes, always the windows to his shining soul, were bright.

"You want my forgiveness?" he drawled in an especially fragrant Italian accent. "Get on your knees and open your mouth."

I had never been on my knees for another man.

Not in all my years of dalliances or in my training as a Dom at clubs in Britain.

It had always been a hard line for me, something that seemed to trigger my feelings towards being kept under my father's thumb as a boy.

But this?

This was as different from that as night and day.

It was still hard to slowly drop to my knees on the carpeted floor, my gaze locked with Sebastian's.

Beside us, Linnea watched with a riveted gaze behind her golden mask, her heavy, aroused breathing causing her nipples to peek over and back under the lace of her corset. I was tempted to give her my attention because I didn't want her to feel left out when this was about both of them, but this moment was important to Sebastian and me.

I had to remember that Linnea said she wanted us not just for her, but for each other.

Sebastian stared down at me, a dark Adonis with his sleeves rolled up to expose corded forearms and his chest exposed indecently by the buttons undone almost to his naval. My mouth watered, and arousal warred with the mild discomfort of being in a submissive position.

He stepped closer, sliding both large hands into my hair to give it a little tug. My eyes drooped nearly closed at the sensation, my dick hardening in my trousers.

"Can you feel how hard I am for you?" Sebastian asked, adopting the same conversational tone I often used. "What's your safe word?"

"Lunatic," I said, the same one he'd picked so many years ago.

"Linnea," he said. "Do you want your own?"

"No," she whispered, eyes fixed on us as if we were a solar eclipse. "Lunatic is perfect."

"You should know," Sebastian continued. "I'm clean and so is Linnea. She's also on birth control."

"I'm clean," I said and my voice was a thick rasp. "Linnea and I were both tested as a requirement of our contract."

He grinned. "And you say you never intended to fuck her. It's fascinating how easy it is for you to lie to yourself, Adamo."

Yes, I agreed, but I had never been able to lie to him and I was finding it just as impossible to do so with Linnea.

Seb pulled me forward by the hair so that my open mouth skirted the thick bulge of his erection through the fabric. I was drooling so much, it saturated the wool, leaving a wet stain along the length of his dick.

"Do you want to take out my cock and take it down your throat?" Sebastian asked me. "I bet you want me to fuck your face until your throat aches, and you start to cry. Has anyone ever fucked your mouth like that before, Adamo?"

"No," I rasped as he pressed my cheek tight to the heat of his cock. "Never."

"Maybe Linnea and I should just trade you back and forth for a while," Sebastian pondered. "I could come down your throat and she could come on your tongue and then we would both eat each other's tastes out of your mouth."

"Fuck," I cursed, and I realized I was trembling slightly, from lust and from an edge of anxiety.

It didn't feel natural to submit, even to Sebastian, but that was part of the excitement, too. That I would act against my natural instincts to be good for him. I wasn't sure how long it could last, but I was determined to show him I could sacrifice for him, even in this small way.

"Open my trousers," Sebastian told me, his hands at his sides as he watched me obey with molten-yellow eyes.

I undid his belt and slid it through the loops with a snap, setting it beside me for later when I was back in control. Then his fly, the zipper lowering tooth by tooth over the lewd bulge of his erection beneath the fabric. I pulled him through the gap in his boxer briefs and the parted pants, his hard cock thick and long, curving just slightly upwards as if showing off the rounded head flushed with blood and limned in precum.

My mouth watered.

"God, but I missed this cock," I said, curling my fingers around the base and rubbing my opposite thumb over the slit, dipping the tip just inside it.

Sebastian hissed, his fingers going to my hair. "Suck it, show Linnea why I've jerked off every night for ten years to the thought of your mouth and hands on me."

Linnea's moan was loud in the quiet room, spurring me on to put on a show for them both.

Just because I disliked being on my knees did not mean I disliked having a fat dick down my throat.

I opened my mouth over his broad shaft and sucked him down in one smooth glide.

He cursed in Italian, hands tightening almost brutally in my hair.

I didn't care.

The only thing in the world that existed for me was pleasing that beautiful dick and showing Linnea this side of our world, convincing her we were worth risking everything.

"Come closer and watch," I pulled off his shaft to tell her, a string of spit connecting my lips to the head.

Linnea's beautiful face was flush with want, and she crawled to my side without hesitation.

"Put your hand on his throat," Sebastian suggested darkly. "Feel how deep he can take me."

She pressed her long fingers around her neck as I slapped Seb's heavy cock on my tongue and then closed my lips around his veiny shaft, slowly descending to the root so she could feel the indecent swell of it beneath her hand.

"Fuck, that's gorgeous," she praised, her hand squeezing just a little to test us both.

Sebastian groaned, and even though I was the one on my knees, it was me who wrested control of the blow job. I started a steady pace, up and down, mouth sloppy so that spit dripped down his balls and sucking sounds filled the room. Linnea held my throat through it all, occasionally flexing to take away my breath, to add tension to my throat's hold on Seb's already indecently thick cock.

My own dick throbbed in my trousers, and after a few minutes, Linnea seemed to take pity on me.

"Can I play with his cock?" she asked Sebastian, already shifting to palm me through my fly with her free hand. "I want to see it."

"It's big," Sebastian warned. "It might not fit in your little hand."

She trembled against me, but took his warning as approval and deftly undid my trousers to reach inside and yank out my erection. The sweet relief and the touch of her palm for the first time around my shaft made me groan around Seb in my mouth.

"Jesus," she murmured as she tested her grip, smoothing it down my shaft, rubbing a thumb on the underside of my head, tracing a vein from root to tip. "Isn't it enough you're both gorgeous? You have to be hung as well."

Sebastian's laugh ended on a moan as I hummed my endorsement of her touch around the base of his length.

Linnea touched me then as I had never been touched like it before, as if a simple hand job was the apex of sexual pleasure. She paused only to spit lewdly on her palm, rolling it over my head to collect precum before setting a brutal pace, jacking me with brief forays into playing with the slit in my head. Each time her fingertip slid inside it, my hips jerked and precum boiled out of me, slicking her firm, almost punishing grip for an easier glide.

Sebastian's dick in my throat and Linnea's hand on my cock might have been the sexiest thing that had ever happened to me, and I had done a lot.

But it was their conviction that undid me.

They fucked me like nothing else existed but this.

Like using me and giving me pleasure, alternatively, was their sole purpose on this earth, and nothing short of world destruction would pull them away from this moment.

God, I had never had a hope of resisting their dangerous temptation.

"Do you want to fuck him, *trottolina mia*?" Sebastian rasped. "Do you want to feel that thick cock fill you up?"

"More than anything," she said immediately, squeezing my base as if to test the girth she would have inside her.

"Take off your panties and climb into his lap," Sebastian ordered thickly. "I want to watch you fuck while I use both your mouths."

"Oh my God," she whispered almost to herself, shaking as she pulled away from my shaft to shuck her delicate lace thong before practically throwing herself in my lap.

Done with being passive, I clamped one hand over the curve of her hip and traced the other over the hairless crease of her groin down to the place where she was wettest. A groan worked through my throat along with Seb's dick as my fingers played at her drenched entrance.

Sebastian pulled out and fisted his cock, holding it so he could trace the wet tip over Linnea's dropped open mouth.

"Do you want to suck him?" I asked her as I pinched and rolled her clit. "You told me you like to be used. Show us how true that is."

Without hesitation, she closed her full, pink lips around his head, eyes meeting mine as she took him inch by inch down her throat. Her eyes glossed with tears at the effort, cheeks hollowed, throat bulging and breath stoppered up in her lungs.

"Good fucking girl," I crooned, wrapping my free hand around her throat lightly to feel them the way she had done with me. "You look even more beautiful with him in your mouth than I thought possible."

"You thought of this," Sebastian repeated, almost triumphantly, and when I looked up at him he looked every inch the conquering warrior, strong legs braced, thick cock curving like a flag as he pulled it from her mouth. "You fantasized about us."

"All the damn time," I admitted. "You haunt me. Both of you."

"Not anymore," Linnea corrected. "Touch me, we're real and here in the flesh for you to use."

I was used to Sebastian's filthy mouth, but that Linnea had one as well and it was almost too much bear. So I was grateful when Seb pushed his dick between her lips, occupying her so that I could focus on her pretty pussy in my lap. Her slick ran down my hand to my wrists, her hips gyrating desperately.

I couldn't wait to be inside her, so I didn't.

Her entrance kissed the head of my cock, so tight I hissed. It would be work to open her up around my shaft, but I thought our girl would like the stretch and burn, so I cupped my hands around her shoulders and pulled her inexorably down, down, down my length.

She groaned, eyes squeezed shut, mouth overfull with Sebastian and cunt overfull with me.

"Exquisite," I told her. "Bloody fucking perfect taking us both like this."

"Perfect," Sebastian agreed, his hips twitching with the effort to hold back from roughly fucking in her. "Both of you. I dreamed of this, and it still wasn't as good as this."

"It never is," I agreed as I hit the end of her with a jolt and pulled her off my cock slightly, using her like a sex doll.

She leaned into my hold as if she wanted to be puppeteered, needed me to take her however I saw fit. Her eyes were wide and burning on mine as she sucked Seb off.

"Do it," she gasped as he pulled out, and she wrapped a hand around his spit-slick base to jack him off while she spoke. "I want you both to let go and fuck me. Don't worry, I can take it. I *want* to take it. Every big. Stunning. Sexy. Inch of you both inside me."

She pressed Seb's leaking dick to her mouth, painting her lips in his cum before licking it off.

Sebastian and I locked eyes, sparks leaping between us as we silently agreed to take her apart.

"Brace yourself, sweetheart," I told her in a low voice that rumbled out of my chest. "And remember you asked for this."

She closed her eyes, tipped her head back, and opened her mouth wider for Seb's cock on her tongue. He pushed into her with a low, shuddering moan, one hand in her hair and the other diving into mine. The simple connection arrowed pleasure down my spine, where it burst into flames in my groin.

The way she gave herself over to us was one of the most beautiful, vulnerable things I had ever witnessed, and we took full advantage. The wet glug of her throat around Seb's shaft and his heavy breaths peppered with Italian curses were the only sounds as we fucked her from either end. The depravity of the moment, fucking each other without restraint, using her sweet, snug cunt for the first time, watching her breasts sway in my face, seeing Sebastian's face screwed up with the pleasure of her talented mouth was too much.

I was done.

Done with the chains binding me to my own self-hatred and regrets.

Done with castigating myself for needing this, a man and woman, *this man and this woman*, carnally and elementally. It was what I was made for, sex like this, where three bodies merged into one and pleasure was the only ultimatum. This place Sebastian and Linnea made safe and free for me to just be *me*. Exactly who I was, sinful and depraved and woefully in need of loving.

And here they were loving me.

Forcing me to take their tenderness and carnality and loyalty, even though I had tried so desperately to force them away.

Here they were asking me to love them because all they wanted to do was love me in return.

It was no longer a question of whether I was brave enough to let this happen.

It had happened.

Courage or no courage, I had fallen into the dark abyss, and instead of finding death at the rocky bottom, I had found only acceptance in their open, eager arms.

They knew me, the good, the bad, and the terrible, and they still wanted more.

Seemed to *need* me even.

And at my core, I was a man who longed to be needed.

My heart beat so hard inside my chest, it threatened to split me open as I fucked into Linnea and then, greedy for more connection, pulled Seb out of her mouth to slide him into my own. Undeterred, Linnea leaned closer to lick around his shaft as it disappeared between my lips, and then, when I pulled him to the end of my tongue, we kissed around his head, tongue lapping over each other and over him.

A bone-rattling groan overtook Sebastian.

"When you come," I told him, cupping Linnea's cheek as I fed his shaft into her mouth and then back out again into my own, pausing to taste him before handing him off to her again. "I want you to do it on both our faces."

"*Madonna santa*," he cursed. "I would love to see you both covered in my cum. Take off your masks."

I had Linnea's undone with a single tug to the ribbon at the back of her head and ripped mine off to toss it into some forgotten corner.

"Yes," Linnea echoed, jacking his shaft as I closed my mouth over his tip. "I can't wait to see Adam's handsome face dripping in your seed."

"Jesus," Seb and I swore simultaneously as Linnea took him into her throat once more and ground down onto my cock, her pussy milking me expertly.

I reached down to rub a thumb over her clit, and the first touch to the engorged bud sent her over the edge in a sharp orgasm that rolled through her like an electric shock. She spasmed around my dick so hard I had to grit my teeth to keep from coming, focusing on driving her higher and higher until her eyes rolled back in her head and she groaned madly around Sebastian's head lodged in her mouth. I used my other hand to jack his base, my fist tight and pace fast, just on the edge of too much until, on the heels of Linnea's orgasm, he broke.

He pulled out of her mouth as I pumped him, the first lash of hot cum falling across her open, swollen lips and into her mouth. Linnea lifted her hand over mine, closing it around my fingers and his shaft to angle the second shot at me. His taste exploded on my tongue as I opened for it, the salt and musk flavor enough to puncture my control and send me head over arse into my own climax.

My cock kicked inside Linnea's cunt, flooding her with so much cum I could feel it bubbling out from my shaft as I bucked up into her greedy grip.

Another jerk of his cock and Seb was splashing across Linnea's cheek and chin, then my lips and chest. I had forgotten just how much he could come, the sheer volume overwhelming as his seed dripped from Linnea's pretty face and mine.

It felt right. God, so fucking right, to have his cum on my skin and Linnea's around my shaft as if I had been re-baptized in the sacred art of Domination and submission, of ménage and unrestrained, totally trusting sex.

It wasn't a lie to say that I felt reborn.

Sitting there with a lap of sweet sunshine and one hand curled around the hairy thigh of a man who had always been my North Star, I knew that no matter what happened, my fate had been sealed.

For as long as life allowed me to keep them, these two were mine.

CHAPTER TWENTY–SIX

SEBASTIAN

I woke up with my cock in someone's wet, hot mouth.

My eyes peeled open to see who was sucking me, only to be met with the sight of Linnea's pussy lowering onto my mouth, her thighs straddling either side of my head. The sweet scent of her cunt hit me like a drug, and I groaned as I automatically opened my mouth to take her clit between my lips.

Stubble abraded the inside of my thighs as Adam lowered his talented mouth all the way down to the root of my cock, where he swallowed hard so that his muscles rippled along the length of my shaft.

"Fuck," I cursed into Linnea's folds, turning my head to sink my teeth into her inner thigh. "What a way to wake up."

Her laughter was breathless as she fisted a hand in my hair and started to ride my tongue in earnest.

"It's important to start your day with a good breakfast," she teased.

laughter turning into a breathy moan when I sucked hard on her clit.

"You'll come on his face before I let him come down my throat," Adam ordered imperiously from between my thighs, rolling my balls in his palm before he gave them a brief tug.

"What about you?" Linnea asked, rocking her hips harder as I used my fingers to roll her clit and my tongue to fuck into her entrance.

"Oh, I intend to come on both your very pretty faces," Adam told her darkly as he jacked my dick and then lowered his mouth to my hole.

Unhappy with the angle, he lifted my hips in his hands, shoved my legs back with his broad shoulders, and hummed happily when my ass was exposed to his talented tongue.

I groaned long and loudly into Linnea's pussy as he worked me open and left me sloppy with spit.

"Fuck me," I told him, muffled by Linnea's wet pussy.

I sucked her clit and thrummed it with my tongue until her hips stuttered and her breath hiccoughed.

"No," Adam said, twisting two fingers inside me just a little cruelly, so I felt the stretch and burn even though they were drenched in his spit. "Not unless you make Linnea come in the next thirty seconds."

I redoubled my efforts, reaching up to twist Linnea's diamond-hard nipples between my fingers, sucking against her clit with hard pulls and lashes of my tongue until my chin was covered in her leaking juices.

"Oh my God, can I come, sir?" she begged Adam as her hands turned to claws in my hair, and her hips juddered over my mouth. "Please, I want to see you fuck Seb. I want to come, and I want to watch you split him open."

My cock jerked so hard I was afraid I was about to come from her dirty words alone.

"Mmm, not yet," he cautioned. "Hold it for me."

She panted, her hips shivering as she fought to control herself. I knew his sharp reprimand would only fuel her higher. Our girl liked a slice of humiliation alongside her praise kink.

"Sorry, sir," she breathed. "Or should I say, my Lord?"

"Cheeky," he scolded, but there was no heat behind it, and I had a feeling he might have even been smiling. "If you can sass me, clearly Sebastian isn't doing a very good job."

At the prompting, I gave her no quarter, tugging on her sensitive breasts and sucking rhythmically at her clit until she cried out, her nails digging into my scalp, her head thrown back to the sky.

"Adam, please!" she shouted.

"Since you beg so nicely," Adam said with quiet, intractable authority. "You can come for us."

Her scream was almost soundless as her pussy flooded me with cum, the sweet tang of it like ambrosia on my tongue. Making her orgasm was so arousing that I found my balls drawing up from Adam's tongue on my rim and Linnea's cum in my mouth.

"*Cazzo*," I cursed, pressing the word into Linnea's slick thigh. "Adam, I'm going to come, too."

"Lick her clean and come for me then," Adam suggested blandly.

His affected coolness and haughty boredom had always been such a fucking turn-on, and combined with the addition of his fingers sliding into my entrance, I was a dead man.

The climax ripped through me as if someone had cleaved out my spine. My body arched involuntarily as my cock kicked, sputtering cum all over my abdomen until Adam reached out to close his mouth over my tip and suck down my seed.

I was cursing in Italian, a mumbling litany I was hardly aware of, as I floated on a sea of warm pleasure.

"God, you taste good."

Linnea's voice drew me back to earth enough to peer through one eyelid at her as she exchanged open-mouthed, almost sloppy kisses with Adam. I groaned long and low as I watched them swap my cum over their tongues, Adam's hand around her throat to hold her still while he fed her my seed. My softening cock twitched valiantly on my stomach, fighting to reharden.

"You two are criminally sexy," I muttered, flopping an arm over my forehead as if I couldn't handle it even though I made sure it didn't obstruct my view of them.

Adam pushed Linnea away with his grip on her neck and got off the end of the bed to stand proud in his naked glory. He was carved from pale gold marble, his hair and stubble shades darker than his skin, the trimmed thatch at the base of his wide, wide cock even darker than that. My mouth watered as he fisted that weapon of a cock, stroking up until a bead of precum hung from the tip. Linnea and I both quivered like dogs waiting to be released into the hunt.

He let the moment draw out, pulling along his shaft in long, strong strokes that made me feel dizzy even as I lay down.

"Get on your knees for me, beauties," he said finally.

We moved as if off the starting line of a race, swiftly throwing ourselves off the bed at his feet in our haste to get our mouths around that dick.

Linnea pressed her entire side into mine, one palm over my hairy thigh, nails digging just slightly into my skin. To anchor herself, I thought, and loved it.

After such a short time of playing together like this, we already moved in harmony, reading the subtle cues and physical sensations before voice even needed to be given to commands.

It was as if we had been made to come together like this.

"Open your pretty mouths for me," Adam demanded coldly,

staring down at us like a god, like someone just as likely to smite us as to reward us.

I was close enough to smell him, that earthy, salt-tinged musk of an aroused cock and dripping precum.

Moisture pooled in my open mouth as I tipped my head back slightly to present for him.

Linnea did the same.

"So good for me," Adam praised, reaching out with his free hand to hold her mouth open so he could slot his cock inside in one smooth thrust.

He pulled out and shifted to me to do the same, his grip strong on my jaw as he leveraged his thick cock between my lips and over my tongue.

Back and forth he went, fucking us each with one smooth stroke before moving to the other. Drool spilled from the edge of my open mouth and down my neck. The wet sounds our lips made as he thrust inside were obscene and underscored by the slight groans and whimpers we made as he used us.

I never could have known I would love it so much, a big cock in my mouth, a rough hand at my jaw, a pretty girl watching me take a man's dick deep inside me.

But it lit me up like a fucking Christmas tree.

I was hard so quickly I felt like a teenager again.

He fucked us like that for a long time, until my jaw ached and my thighs quivered. Precum dribbled from my cock and pooled around my balls.

"When we have more time," Adam told us casually, only a tightness beside his eyes speaking to the force of his restraint. "I'm going to put you both on your knees and fuck you like this. Linnea's sweet little cunt to Sebastian's tight arse. Back and forth, back and forth. I'll use you like that for hours until your little holes are red and puffy and filled with my cum. Would you like that, my beauties?"

"Please don't make us wait," Linnea begged as Adam drove his cock over my tongue. "I want to walk the red carpet feeling the ache of you between my legs. And I am desperate to see the two of you fuck. The idea of Sebastian bent over for your big cock makes me mad with want."

Adam paused before pulling out, pressing so deeply I couldn't breathe. I looked up at him as I struggled to hold him to the root and saw his face flushed with desire.

He caught me looking and slid a hand into the back of my hair. "Would you like that, Sebastian? Feeling my cock in your ass as you walk the red carpet separately from us? Knowing even if you aren't beside us, you. Are. Ours."

"Yes," I croaked, throat ravaged from his cock.

Adam hummed as he considered it, checking his Audemars Piguet watch. "We only have two hours until the hair and beauty people get here. Not as much time as I would like… but how can I resist you two? Crawl to the couch and rest your forearms on the cushions."

Jesus, it was demeaning and sexy as hell to crawl behind Linnea, watching her ass sway and her leaking pussy peek between her thighs.

We assumed our positions as Adam went into the bathroom and came back with a collection of things he placed somewhere behind us. We had all showered before falling into Adam's bed together last night, and he had cleaned me thoroughly, inviting Linnea to watch as he did, so I didn't worry about arching my back and presenting my hole to him.

His hand fell sharply against my cheek and, based on Linnea's muffled cry, hers too.

"Stunning," he praised us, rubbing away the sting of the spank.

"Now, I'm going to put this vibrating egg in your greedy pussy, Nea, while I work on opening Sebastian. When I'm ready to fuck you both, I'll use a new condom every time I switch back and forth until I'm ready to come."

"Come inside Sebastian," Linnea asked, twisting to look at me as Adam moved behind her and started rubbing a vibrating toy against her folds. "I want to know your cum is leaking out of him while he walks the red carpet."

"Jesus, you filthy girl," Adam praised.

"You like the idea," I confirmed, a little awed by how much she loved Adam and me together.

"I love it," she agreed, a high flush on her cheeks. "I can't wait to watch him fuck you."

I pressed my thumb to her mouth, and she sucked it inside without hesitation. A hiss worked through my teeth as she swirled her tongue around it. She was an absolute vision like this, on her knees, pinked with desire, hair mussed from our hands, every inch of her golden-tanned curves exposed to our gaze.

She gasped as Adam pushed the toy inside her but continued to fellate my thumb as Adam moved back to me and bent to fix his mouth to my hole.

Fuck, I loved how much that man loved to rim me.

He didn't bother teasing me, sucking and licking at me for a few moments before he started to finger me, first one, then two, then three, scissoring inside me to loosen me for his big cock.

I trembled, on the edge of coming even though I'd just orgasmed. I hadn't had my ass played with by someone other than me since London, and I'd almost forgotten how intense the sensations could be, gut swooping and toes curling.

Something smooth and cool pressed against my rim alongside his fingers before he pulled them out and slotted the toy inside me. It was long and curved, a dildo that vibrated as he flicked a switch somewhere behind me. The curling shape pressed into my prostate, and I couldn't help the involuntary hump of my hips as he kicked up the power.

"There you go," Adam crooned. "I can't leave either of you empty, now, can I?"

I twisted my neck so my head rested on my hands, and I could watch as Adam knee-walked behind Linnea, planted a hand on her lower back to arch her sweet ass higher, and then pulled out the toy.

"Suck on that," Adam told me, handing the pussy-slick toy to me before he fisted his other hand in Linnea's hair and slammed into her to the hilt.

She cried out, eyes squeezed shut, breasts swaying as she braced herself against the couch to meet each punishing thrust. Watching Linnea take her pleasure was one of the most beautiful things I would ever witness. She was so unabashed, so curious and easily aroused by anything either of us did to her or each other. She was a glutton at a feast, and she had zero inhibitions about enjoying herself.

It was fucking intoxicating.

I sucked the toy between my lips, trying not to focus on the thump of the other toy inside me as it drove me relentlessly towards climax, so I could watch Adam's torso clench into clean lines of striated muscle as he fucked into Linnea, to witness the unguarded desire ravage his handsome face.

This could be enough, I thought dazedly, even without the love and romance and flowery declarations.

This could be enough to sustain me for the rest of my life.

Linnea cried out as she came, spasming around Adam so hard he groaned long, low, and almost pained.

"Good girl," he praised, smoothing a hand down her side and

then slapping her rounded ass so she keened again. "Good girl coming around my cock."

He slowed his thrusts and then pulled out, opening his palm toward me, so I handed him the now-clean toy. He pushed it back inside her swollen folds, clicking a remote so that it turned on, and Linnea shivered at the sensation.

He bent to kiss her bum cheek and then moved toward me, his cock flushed almost purple and visibly throbbing. His fingers wrapped around the base and squeezed.

"You want this inside you?" he asked darkly.

My tongue swept over my lower lip. "*Cazzo*, yes."

"I won't fuck you gently," he warned. "I want to rail you into this couch until you can't feel your knees."

"Yes," I agreed. "Please."

He pulled out the vibrating toy inside me, a little cruelly so I hissed through the sensation. His thumb rubbed over my loose hole, dipping inside and stretching the rim.

"I love seeing you fucked open like this," he murmured almost to himself.

He plucked a condom wrapper from the ground, tore it open with his teeth and deftly rolled it onto his cock before coating it in lube.

A moment later, his lube-wet tip pressed against me, and my head dropped between my shoulders as he drove inside me.

It had been years since I had taken a cock, and even the occasional play with a dildo could not have prepared me for the punch of that wide prick inside me. My lungs seized up and I instinctively tried to pull away, seeking relief from the mind-crushing pressure blurring into overwhelming pleasure with every passing second.

"Uh, uh, uh," Adam scolded me, hands tight around my hips. "Don't run from me. You can take this. I know how much you love to be spread open and impaled. Let Linnea watch me fuck you stupid."

"*Cazzo*," I cursed as my body shuddered with an overload of sensation as he worked himself thrust by thrust deeper inside me.

I struggled to find an anchor before I spiraled off into oblivion.

"Fuck," I cursed in English, my fingers curled into the cushion, my hips twitching as I fought to take that beast of a cock. "*Dio mio,* Adamo, you are too thick."

"You can take it," he urged, sliding out to the very tip slowly and then driving back inside me.

He reached around to grab my tender, swollen cock and thumbed the wet head. "You want to come again, already, don't you?"

"Yes," I gritted out as I pushed back into his thrusts, feeling the hot zing of pleasure unfurl at the base of my spine and arrow into my groin.

"Too bad," he growled, bending over my back so he could bite into my shoulder. "This is about me, not you."

I panted at the declaration, unfairly turned on by being used.

"One day, I'll keep you and Linnea tied up to my bed to be used whenever I please," Adam fantasized as he ground his hips into mine and pulled back on my hips until he was deep enough I saw stars.

My brain started shorting out with pleasure, and I bit my tongue to keep from groaning so he wouldn't notice how close I was.

But this was Adam.

He noticed everything.

"No, no." He clucked his tongue as he chastised me and swatted my ass hard as he pulled out. "Not yet. Don't be greedy."

I panted, trying to find my equilibrium as he shed the condom and rolled on a new one to fuck Linnea. She was whining, a low, almost constant, stream of sharp air from between her lips as her hips shuddered. I wondered if the toy was constantly making her come and decided that yes, that was something Adam would do.

Death by orgasm for her and death through denial for me.

Madonna santa, he was a depraved genius.

He slid back into her with a low growl, palming her ass cheeks as he set a brutal pace, watching as they jiggled with each thrust.

"Fucking gorgeous," he told her, discarding the toy on the floor between us. "I could fuck you for days."

"Yes," Linnea said as if that was the best idea she had ever heard. "I don't know what I did before you both started fucking me."

We both laughed, and it felt good to laugh while we played. I couldn't remember if we had done that much with Savannah.

"I'm going to make you come one more time, sweet girl," he coaxed her even though she groaned when he palmed her pussy around his driving cock. "I know you're so swollen and achy, but I think you can handle one more for us, can't you?"

"If you want me to, sir," she breathed, and I watched Adam's jaw tick as he fought to hold back from the lust that one word unleashed in him.

"She's such a lovely slut for us, isn't she, Sebastian?" he drawled, smoothing his hands down her flanks as if she were a prize-winning horse. "Can you believe she's ours?"

Ours.

The word seared through me.

I wanted it to be true so much, it made my teeth ache.

We were lovers, yes, and friends, but someday soon, they would be *married.*

And I would be the odd man out again.

As if sensing my turn of mood, Adam studied me for a moment buried to the hilt in Linnea, and then slowly pulled out, hushing her protestations.

"I have a better idea," Adam said slowly as he moved behind me, discarding the used condom and rolling on another. He coated his shaft with lube, the slick sound familiar and sexy. "Linnea, crawl between Sebastian and the couch. Let him bury his desperately hard cock inside you."

She scrambled to obey, her long limbs uncoordinated for a moment before she managed to slip between me and the couch. I gathered her in my arms, lifting her so she hovered over my cock, her cum-slick thighs trembling. I looked over at Adam for permission and loved his rapt expression as he watched us.

"Go on, fuck her," he commanded, fisting his own cock as he sat back on his heels and watched us.

The feel of Linnea as she slid over my cock was pure heaven, a hot, wet, sucking glide. She was so swollen she seemed impossibly tight, and she spasmed around me as I hit the end of her.

"Fuck," we breathed at the same time.

"Can we move?" Linnea asked, her voice high with need as she struggled to hold still on top of me. Her hands made up for her hips' stillness, tunneling through my hair to hold me close.

"Not yet."

I almost choked on my groan when Adam slipped behind me and notched himself at my entrance. He grabbed me by the hip and slid his other arm around my waist to trail his fingers around my wet cock inside Linnea's pussy.

"Hold still, Sebastian, while Linnea and I fuck you," he told me, the first signs of his control cracking in his rough voice.

A second later, he was inside me, so big he stole my breath.

"*Cazzo*," I cursed as my body shuddered with an overload of sensation, and I struggled to find an anchor before I spiralled off into oblivion.

"Be good for us," he coaxed, currying my side the way you'd soothe a spooked horse. "Open up for me so I can use your sweet, tight little arse."

I sucked in a deep breath and forced myself to sink into it, him inside me and her around me.

Only then did they move, a gyration of hips, a short glide as they acclimatized me to being pulled apart, atom by atom, with teeth-aching desire.

The dual sensations of having my ass and cock stimulated made electric shocks pulse through my body, each shift of Adam's and Linnea's bodies like a lightning strike to my nerves.

Italian curses leaked from my mouth, spilling between us as my lovers used me, fucking back and forth, up and down, harder and harder.

"You aren't allowed to come until we do," Adam told me flippantly, but the hand wet with Linnea's juices traced my abs up to my nipples and twisted one between his fingers. "But we're going to make you break that rule, aren't we, sweet girl?"

"Oh yes," Linnea agreed, smiling wickedly at me as she rolled her hips up and down my painfully hard cock, as sinuous as the waves rolling into the shore.

The visual of her long body in my lap glossed in sweat and bronzed from the sun, her pale breasts swaying in my face as she lifted her arms to hold her hair away from our sweaty limbs was almost too much to bear.

And that was without the heat of Adam at my back, his punishing hands on my body, his filthy voice in my ear.

"You should be fucked like this every day," he told me in a low, throaty purr. "Every inch of you used for our pleasure and every inch of us for yours. Next time, I want to watch you top Linnea, see what your beautiful brain can think up for her with a bit of silky rope and some nipple clamps."

"And a blindfold," I huffed out as he ground himself inside me, and Linnea ground herself down on me.

I thought I was coming apart, each particle of my being humming and vibrating.

Was this nuclear fusion?

What would happen when I finally detonated? Would the pieces of me scatter so far and wide I would never recover?

I didn't care, even as the looming orgasm almost terrified me.

My hands curled into Linnea's plump ass as I held on for dear life.

"Come for me," I told her, unable to stand a moment more. "*Vieni per me, trottolina.*"

I bent my head to capture one of her nipples in my mouth and gently bit down.

Her shout punched through the air and she slammed herself to the root of my cock, her pussy clenching like a fist around me as she flooded me with cum.

Fuck, I loved that she could squirt.

"*Merda*, Adamo, I have to come," I begged, moisture pooling behind my lids as I struggled not to come, my entire body taut with the strain. "Please, fuck, let me come inside her pussy. She's milking me."

Adam shocked me by pulling out, but before I could protest, he was back, pressing his hot cock back inside me, and I realized he had taken off the condom.

"Come inside her while I come inside you," he bit out, his fingers bruising on my hips as he fucked into me. "Wanna feel you clench around my cock as you stuff her full."

"*Cazzo!*" I ground out as Adam's fat cock hit my prostate, and Linnea's cunt sucked hard around my aching shaft.

A moment later, I lost myself to pleasure completely.

The world whited out as my senses overloaded, and all I felt was the heat of a climax cleaving me in two. Vaguely, I was aware of Adam's own shout as his dick kicked inside me, flooding me with his own cum. Less distantly, I was aware of burying my face in Linnea's sweat-dampened breasts as I moaned and twitched as if in death's throes.

I had never come so intensely in my life.

It took me a while to come back to myself, and when I did, it was because Adam had pulled out to play with his cum as it leaked from my hole.

"Keep it inside you, Sebastian," he scolded lightly, fucking his seed back into me with his fingers. "Linnea wants to know it's leaking out of you in a few hours when we walk the red carpet and you win yet another award for *Waking Nightmare*."

"I can't wait to celebrate your win," Linnea murmured as she traced her mouth down my neck, licking up a bead of sweat and sucking a lazy kiss over my hammering pulse point. "I hope I'm in your acceptance speech. 'And to my brilliant, beautiful Linnea for bringing light into my life.' Doesn't that sound good, Adam?"

"It does," he agreed easily, and their rapport warmed me almost as much as the orgasm had. "I will accept acknowledgement, too."

"You will?" I asked, my voice threadbare from shouting through my climax. "Publicly?"

Adam chuckled, a self-satisfied sound that should have been arrogant, but I found wildly endearing. "You're such a smart man, Sebastian, so you can imagine my feeling of accomplishment when I am successful in fucking you stupid. Of course, you can acknowledge me. Not as your lover, but I have always been and will always be your friend."

My heart did that thing where it jumped and dropped simultaneously.

Good enough, I scolded myself.

But my greedy, overlarge heart would never stop yearning for more even though it hurt. Being an eternal optimist and romantic was rough.

"*If* I win, I'll consider mentioning you both," I allowed. "If it means sexual favors in my future."

Adam's and Linnea's laughter twined together like a gorgeous orchestra, lovelier than any of the classical music Savannah had played so often in the Rolls-Royce.

"Oh, I think we can manage that," Adam agreed, wrapping his arms around us both in a hug from behind that made my heart soar. "Anything for our marvelously talented screenwriter and award-winning actor."

"Anything," Linnea agreed.

And honestly, I thought they meant it, at least in the moment.

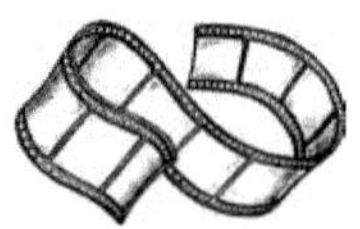

IN THE WEEK SINCE LINNEA AND I had confronted Adam at Bacchanalia, I had been living a dream. Oh, it wasn't the impossible universe Adam and I had once spoken of, but it was so close I could find no fault in the ways it wasn't perfect.

I basically moved into Adam's Carbon Beach house with Linnea, keeping most of my things in Adam's closet alongside his own and some of Linnea's, even though she had her own bedroom and wardrobe across the hall.

The Critics Choice Awards arrived the day after our reckoning, and while I got ready for the event with Adam and then got to see the vision he and Linnea cut together in his midnight blue suit and her violet-blue gown, I was left to take my own limo to the event and then walk the carpet alone.

I was seated at a different table from them, with cast members from *Waking Nightmare* I should have been happy to spend time with after so long apart. Instead, I found myself sneaking looks across the room at the future Meyerses all night.

Linnea made Adam laugh often, which soothed some of the ruffled feathers. He had told me a long time ago that he never liked award shows. Their pomp and circumstance were too inauthentic and self-aggrandizing for the upper crust, former military Brit, so he bore them with an inner stoicism and facade of charm that got him through most of his life without issue.

It made me happy to see Linnea charming him out of his shell as easily as she seemed to captivate everyone else at their table, including the infamously irascible older actor, Bob Granger, who, at one point, seemed to be having his palm read by my girl.

"You seem distracted," my costar from *Waking Nightmare*, Winona Kelly, leaned in to murmur to me.

She was shockingly gorgeous, with black hair and pale blue eyes that made her even more striking against her lovely pale skin. We had slept together once or twice before costarring together, but she had since married a famous boxer who scowled at me from her other side as she got a little too close.

I shot him an innocent grin.

"Girl trouble?" she continued, waving off her husband as if he weren't a two-hundred-and-fifty-pound brick wall with a serious glower. "Please don't tell me it's Savannah Richardson."

I barked out a laugh, surprised by her comment. "Is it such an open secret I had feelings for her?"

"Had?" she pressed, thin brows raised. "Good riddance. That woman is as cold as the sunken *Titanic*."

I laughed again as I shook my head. "You know, I should introduce you to Linnea Kai, I think you would be fast friends."

"Oh? The new girl on the block dating Adam Meyers? She's everywhere in the media right now, poor thing. Did you see the mess with her mother?"

"I was there," I said, my voice freezing so she would understand I was not about to gossip about it. "Linnea is one of my oldest friends."

"Interesting. Did you set them up?"

I studied her for a beat too long, so she laughed, opening her hands innocently. "You know I'm not going to do anything with the information, Seb. I'm just being nosy because I'm Welsh. I grew up in a village where everyone knew everyone."

"I guess Hollywood isn't that different," I quipped.

She grinned. "No, it isn't. In any case, it's nice to see Adam smile. I'd almost forgotten how handsome he can be when he isn't frowning."

I had been happy when we were interrupted by Andrea, who took me to the bar during a commercial break to talk with a few bigwigs about optioning *The Dream & The Dreamer*. Hightower Studios and its head, Damien Rivens, were interested but dragging their heels finding space for the film on their roster.

Tate Richardson caught me on the way to the bathroom during another break, cornering me with a knitted brow and a thick finger pointed at my face.

"Seb, my boy, what is this I hear about you shopping a new script around town to everyone but me? I would be hurt if I wasn't so sure this had to be some kind of mix-up."

I fought the urge to wince. No matter how complicated my feelings were for his wife, I liked Tate. He was an uncomplicated man who had taken me into his life not just because Savannah had asked him to do so, but because he genuinely seemed to enjoy my company.

"I did give the script to Savannah," I said carefully. "But I didn't think it would be a good fit for you."

"Anything written by you is a good fit for us," he insisted, clamping a meaty hand on my shoulder. "You're practically family, Sebastian, come now. I expect you to email me a copy tomorrow before noon. You'll give us a fair crack at it just like anyone else, I'm sure."

"We do have interest from a few studios," I admitted. "It could get expensive."

In a multiple offer situation, the screenplay would go to auction.

It was a profoundly *good* thing for a screenwriter, but not so good for me as a person, given that Richardson Productions had deep pockets and the Richardsons themselves were deeply motivated. They did not like to lose, especially when they felt they had a right to win.

"There is no price too high for a chance at a Sebastian Lombardi original," Tate declared, moving his hand from my shoulder to my neck for a squeeze. "You can count on Richardson Productions winning that bid."

Happily, I was saved from continuing the conversation by the music heralding everyone back to their seats for the final round of awards for the night.

I sat at my table of peers and costars, feeling oddly bereft and alone as I waited for the nominees for Best Actor in a Drama to be called. My gaze floated over the many gorgeous faces to land on the only two I really cared about in the room.

Linnea was looking at me, her eyes widening when they caught mine. She lifted her phone and wiggled it a little in my direction.

I pulled my cell from my pocket and found waiting notifications.

A new group chat had been created and named with only three

emojis: a sun, a moon, and some stars.

LINNEA

I've always wanted to fuck a Critics Choice Award winner._

ADAM

You have fucked a Critics Choice Award winner._

ADAM

Two of them._

LINNEA

It's different when it's a fresh win. Sebastian can hold his award while we suck him off, and if he doesn't drop it, he can come._

ADAM

Well, if that isn't incentive to win, I'm not sure what is._

ADAM

Break a leg, Sebastian._

LINNEA

We're rooting for you!_

I swallowed thickly as I rubbed my thumb over the screen. Such silly texts, really, to mean so much to me. I could barely breathe past the feeling of happiness filling my chest like helium.

So when they called my name as the winner some minutes later, I was already beaming ear to ear when I stood, kissed Winona on the cheek, and climbed the stairs to the stage.

I always prepared a speech because it was bad luck not to, but most of them were fairly standard. Thank the organization, thank the studio, and the cast and crew of the movie, especially the director and my costars. Then, move on to my beloved Mama and sisters.

Only this time, I ended with something significantly more enigmatic than I ever had before.

"And finally, to the people who remind me to never stop

dreaming, even when those dreams seem impossible. I have always had a relentless and dangerous optimism in my heart that has encouraged me to pursue wild opportunities and unlikely outcomes. Yet here I stand today holding an award for a career everyone told me would never be mine. I'm happy to continue to prove my naysayers wrong and to keep dreaming of impossible universes."

As the crowd erupted into applause, it was Adam and Linnea whom I sought out in the darkness. Adam lifted his glass to me, waiting for me to find his gaze. Linnea did a fist pump that made my wide smile deepen so it cut almost painfully into my cheeks.

That night, they proved they sucked me off until I dropped the award to the floor, but because I was a winner, they still decided to let me come.

We were busy, the three of us, so we spent most of those days apart from each other. Linnea no longer worked at the restaurant, but she spent a lot of time in the guesthouse with Miranda or working on designs in the studio Adam had created for her out of a spare room. She had landed a guest appearance on a popular sitcom that filmed in LA over the course of three days at the end of the week, and she laughed when I insisted on taking her to the production lot the first day to show her around.

I had podcast interviews, live interviews, a spot on a late-night show, and a shoot for Saint Aubyn cologne at El Matador State Beach, while Adam continued to prepare for his role as Anton Daventry, which was set to start filming in mid-March.

Even though we didn't spend the days together, we found each other at night.

I liked to cook, so I often helped Bruce whip up something for dinner or teach him some of Mama's recipes. Linnea would wander in next, usually in low-slung sweatpants and a teeny top that left acres of skin exposed beneath the bottom of her breasts and the base of her smooth stomach. We would chat until Adam ambled in, usually wrapping up a phone call or email on his cell.

Aside from acting, he also owned a stake in a popular winery in Sonoma and various other lucrative business holdings. Though he didn't speak to his father and step-mum, I knew his vast fortune was what kept them in comfort in their manor home in Cornwall.

Only when we were settled around the dining table outside on the terrace did we pick up the script for *The Dream & The Dreamer* to review the plot and conduct informal table readings. They helped make the story come alive in a way I couldn't have fully imagined when I first wrote it during those fevered few days. It became even clearer that Adam and Linnea had become my muses, and there was something almost scary about that, scarier than being their lovers.

A man and his muse were sacred, but often fraught with complications.

As evidenced by the very plot of *The Dream & The Dreamer*.

I tried not to think of it as a bad omen.

Savannah called me three times and texted me a dozen more.

I only read the first one.

SAVANNAH

The Dream & The Dreamer is Oscar bait, Sebastian. Absolutely amazing. Call me back so we can talk production.

THIS MORNING, AFTER THE THREE OF us fell back to sleep in post-coital exhaustion, I woke to Adam's hand on my face. My cheek had been pressed to his chest, one arm and leg slung over his body while Linnea did the same on his other side. A small part of me wanted to document every one of these small in-between moments, because I knew how quickly things could change.

"Morning, Sebastian," he murmured, rubbing a thumb along the roughness of stubble on my jaw.

"*Buongiorno*, Adamo," I echoed in Italian. "What's on your mind?"

"I'm going to marry Linnea," he told me in a hushed murmur.

It was absurd to be shocked by the statement.

Of course, I knew this.

It was in their contract.

Linnea had even mentioned that they'd moved up the timeline so they would probably need to get married in the next few months.

Oscar Hampton was a *figlio di puttana*.

However, the idea of them getting married triggered a primal response in my brain even though I tried to rationalize it away.

Adam and Savannah had been married.

They had brought me in to save their marriage and look how that ended up.

Linnea and Adam were only contracted to be married for three years.

What happened to them when those were up?

What happened to me?

"Will you go with me to buy the ring?" Adam's voice jarred me from my spiralling thoughts. "I want you to have a say in it."

"Why?" I asked before I could curb the vulnerability of the question.

Adam's gaze turned wary, and he examined my face for a moment before responding. "In public, I might walk alone with Linnea, but in private, we are three. I thought that was what you wanted?"

I blinked up at him, taking a moment to steady myself with the sight of his familiar, handsome face. The creases beside his eyes and mouth had deepened over the years, a smattering of silver threaded through the gold at his temples, but those green apple eyes and the firm, full mouth were the very same.

Had I ever stopped loving him? *I wondered.*

It didn't feel like it.

"It is," I confessed.

"Then you'll go with me to pick out her ring," he declared, smoothing his hand up into my hair to pull me closer for a kiss that started as a brush of lips and devolved quickly into something deeper.

Even in the morning, he tasted so fucking good.

"I picked out the Patek Philippe for you all those years ago," Adam told me, keeping me close so his verdant eyes were all I could see. "Savannah didn't know what it was we were giving you. That was a mistake. I don't want to make the same one now. This ring…I feel like it should be from both of us?"

"What are you saying?" I asked as my heart hammered so hard I thought I might be sick.

"I'm saying you are a part of this. Of me," he clarified. "Ask me how often I dreamed of you."

"How often?"

"Every day. It didn't stop when I opened my eyes in the morning, either. I saw you everywhere I went. I even bought this house because I imagined you here," he murmured. "I could see you as clear as day in the kitchen, out by the pool in those tight black shorts you like to wear, here in my bed with the moonlight on your skin."

I watched him swallow hard and mimicked the gesture. He was saying so many things I had waited for years to hear him say, so why was my heart racing as if I was being chased?

Had some part of me been infected with his pessimism? Because I couldn't stop thinking about how it had all ended so horribly for us before.

"I want to be with you both," Adam continued, holding my gaze so intractably I could not even find it in me to blink. "However we can. Marrying Linnea will make it safer to spend so much time together."

Bile rose on the back of my tongue. "Are you marrying her because of Oscar and the rumors or because you want to?"

I noticed Adam's free hand was in Linnea's masses of golden hair, and it stilled at my question. She was deeply asleep, her mouth lax and slightly open as her lids fluttered with a dream only she could see.

Dio mio, she deserved more than a marriage of convenience.

"I want to marry her," Adam said finally, and his voice was ironclad. "Not just for the reasons we signed on the dotted line for. I wouldn't ask you to go with me to pick out a ring if this—*she*—didn't mean more to me than that."

"I'm sorry," I said because I could tell I had offended him. "I can tell you care about her."

Love felt like a forbidden word.

I had said it once before to him, and I wasn't sure I had it in me yet to say it again.

Even to Linnea.

Even though that stomach-flipping, heart-galloping, gravity-redefining feeling was, by any other word, love.

The kind of love that rearranged galaxies.

"Let's go get our girl a ring," I said.

And the smile that Adam gave me in return was brighter than any diamond we saw that day.

WE DIDN'T GET HER A DIAMOND.

Of course, we didn't.

Our sunshine girl was brightness and color, vivacity and spirit. Nothing so cold, clear, and staid as a white diamond.

And one stone didn't seem right either.

Not when it was coming, ostensibly, from two men.

We visited four jewelers before realizing that nothing was right for Linnea, but fortunately, at the fourth, the jeweler suggested we get something custom-made.

Adam asked if he could have it done in twenty-four hours.

Even though it had been a very long time since I was a poor boy in Napoli, the cost took my breath away for a moment.

We agreed the wedding ring, a two-stone affair that would nestle on either side of the single gem on the engagement ring, could wait. We both wanted me to be there when she saw that one, the ring that represented us both.

Afterward, we drove back to Adam's house, but instead of going inside, we took a walk on Carbon Beach. Technically, it was open to the public, as all beaches in California had to be, but most people didn't know the access points, so it was still a very private stretch of sand, mostly inhabited by the insanely rich and famous.

"How are you going to propose?" I asked as we shucked off our shoes and walked in the damp, hard-packed sand right by the waves.

"I had a very public idea," Adam admitted, "but I have a private one, too. I thought I could do both."

I wanted to ask again if the publicity was that important, but I had already insulted him enough for one day.

As always, he seemed to read me anyway. "I thought I would do it at the Oscars," he admitted. "On the red carpet."

My mouth dropped open in shock, which Adam seemed to find

hilarious.

"It's just…you've never been much for public displays of affection," I tried to explain. "Even with Savannah."

"I do wonder if that was more of Savannah's influence," he said, scuffing his toes in the sand. "Linnea is very open with her physical affection, and I find myself enjoying it immensely."

I fought the urge to reach for his hand, the fantasy of holding it while we walked down the beach a long-ingrained dream.

"Do you think she would hate it?" Adam asked. "I already made some calls, but I could change the plan. I want her to…" He sighed and rubbed a hand down his chin. "I want her to want to say yes."

"Honestly? No, I think she would laugh and find it delightfully over the top," I said with a chuckle as I rubbed my stubbled jaw. "Your team would love the photo op, too."

Adam raised a cool brow at me. "They would. Something can accomplish two things at once. Someone with experience in a ménage might understand that."

He startled me into chuckling. "Touché."

"It's why I'd like to have a more private moment, too. One I'd very much like you to be part of."

I gave in to the impulse to bump my shoulder into his, and when I did, Adam rewarded me with that small, tender smile he used to give me in London. It still had the ability to stop my heart in its tracks.

"What did you have in mind?" I asked.

CHAPTER TWENTY–SEVEN

LINNEA

Preparing for the Critics Choice Awards had barely prepared me for the Academy Awards. This was Hollywood's shining award ceremony, the one to be nominated for and seen at. Sebastian was being nominated for Best Actor, and Adam was presenting for the category of Best Picture. They had to be primped and prodded by a team of makeup artists, fashion stylists, and hairdressers, but they were still done long before I was.

Five women were working on me, one for my nails, another for my hair, one for my makeup, and two more for styling with one specializing particularly in jewelry. Adam had rented a number of options from Tiffany's for the evening based on three dress options the stylist had okayed from my designs. I knew as soon as I saw the enormous yellow diamond pendant at the end of a sleek yellow gold choker that I had to wear the gown I'd labored over for the past week. It was a golden-yellow silk gown with a flowing A-line skirt and a bodice constructed of carefully overlapping and hand-stitched swathes of delicate fabric that resembled flower petals.

Even Eleanor, the stylist, clicked her tongue as she helped me step into the fragile silk and fastened it at my back. It fit like a dream, hugging and emphasizing the nip in my waist and drawing subtle attention to my leg through the slit of the dress and the roundness of my breasts above the bodice.

"I was skeptical when Chaucer told me you were wearing something you designed yourself," Eleanor explained. "But you look absolutely gorgeous and completely one of a kind."

I beamed at her because a compliment from an A-list stylist was as good as gold. "Thank you, that means a lot."

"The hair helps," Joey, the hairstylist, added with a cheeky wink as he carefully patted a few stray hairs down with an eyebrow brush coated in hairspray.

"It does," I agreed, because he had coaxed my wavy, often unruly hair into perfect retro Hollywood-glam waves that gleamed just a few shades lighter than the dress.

"If I didn't love you," Rozhin said from where she sat on the bed in "my" room, though I hadn't slept there in over a week, "I would punch you for looking so damn stunning. You'll give normal women everywhere a complex."

I laughed, tossing a cotton ball at her over my shoulder. "So dramatic. Are we sure you aren't the wannabe actress?"

"There is no 'wannabe' about it," she corrected, standing up to come just behind and beside me in the full-length reflection of the mirror. I towered over her in my five-inch heels that would put me at eye level with Adam and Sebastian. "You're a bona fide celebrity now, honeycakes. Dating one of the hottest men in Hollywood and being… friendly with another." She paused to let me fill in the blanks, but I skittered my gaze over the crew of beauticians who had started to pack up around us, and she took the hint. "Your episodes in the hottest comedy on television are airing in a few weeks, you've been cast in a Georges Galagoes film, *and* Sebastian has promised you a leading role in the first film he's written since *Blood Oath*."

She sighed heavily. "Soon, I'll just be a footnote in the life and times of Linnea Kai."

"Never," I promised, tugging her into my side for a hug. "I don't know how I would have made it through those first few months in LA without you, Ro. You're stuck with me for life."

She hummed but hugged me back briefly before stepping away to look at Miranda, who was seated in a wheelchair in the corner by the window. She had been quiet, but fairly lucid for the first couple of hours we were getting ready; even excited that I asked the nail tech to do her nails. However, now she had zoned out. It made my heart ache to see her stare vacantly into the distance, but I reminded myself I was doing all I could for her.

She seemed to be thriving as much as she could living in the guesthouse, which was much more spacious and well-appointed than her own house, and with the lovely nurses, Bituin, Jasmine, and Reyna.

That alone would have made my arrangement with Adam worth it.

But I never could have known how much happier it could make me.

My pussy still ached from Adam's and Sebastian's fucking earlier that morning, and I relished the phantom feel of them inside me. Just thinking about Adam's cum inside Seb as he readied himself to walk the red carpet, *to win* an Oscar, was enough to make a flush spill down my chest.

But it wasn't just the earth-quaking, life-altering sex.

Even in my wildest fantasies I couldn't haven conceived of how right it felt to be with them both, to submit to their pleasure and my own. It was easier than it had any right to be, too. But I had spent so many years taking care of my dad and uncles, and then Miranda, that giving up control to two men I could trust felt like *peace*.

Although, that was everything I had ever dreamed of and more.

It was the fact that Adam and Seb ran lines with me for my episodes on *Family Sentence*, that they made time to go surfing with me when they could in the morning, and that Adam was actually almost as good as Seb, a fact that blew us both away because he had kept his surfing habit secret from us, or that we tried to watch one of our favorite movies when we had a minute, and last night, Sebastian had tried to teach us some Italian while we watched *Cinema Paradiso* with subtitles. It was that Sebastian visited with Miranda, and Adam took time out of his afternoon one day to drive with me to Mrs. Ramirez's house so I could introduce her to her favorite actor of all time.

It was simply that they were the best men I had ever known, and that included my beloved Dad and uncles.

It wasn't that I could overlook their flaws, which were myriad and obvious, but that I found them so much more compelling because they were complicated creatures.

No one knew that Adam Meyers woke from nightmares about his time in the Royal Air Force with the crowned Prince of England, Arthur Whitley-Fairfax, and the death of his uni flatmate, Gregory, which he reluctantly told me about one morning when he woke me by shouting his name.

No one knew he loved to listen to jazz music while he went for his runs, and that a signed album from Miles Davis was one of his cherished possessions. That he could rattle off statistics about the English Premier League and, in particular, his favorite team, Kings Cross United, at the drop of a hat.

No one knew that he had such an enormous heart, his capacity for love seemed to scar him.

No one but Seb and me.

Sebastian pretended to be more of an open book than the Brit, but there were things no one would have thought to think about him based on his public persona. That he was just a little pretentious about food, with a heavy bias for all things Italian being highly superior to anything else. That he called one of his sisters or his mother almost every day to check in and chat, and he often seemed a little melancholy afterwards, as if he couldn't breathe for missing them. That he was ticklish on the bottom of his feet and laughed like a hyena when you brushed your fingertips there, or that he talked in his sleep, murmurs of Italian and English blended in an indecipherable mix.

The intimacy of knowing these two great and famous men in all the little ways, the most poignant ways, made me happier than securing that role in the Georges Gallegos film, happier than Eleanor complimenting a dress I'd poured my sweat and tears into for weeks, happier, even, than surfing at Ho'okipa Beach Park in the winters on Maui.

It felt like such a gift, almost a miracle, that not one but two extraordinary men would trust themselves with me.

It felt the same to know I could trust myself with them.

Because we might not have exchanged words of love, but I knew that was what this was.

Love.

Love so bright and warm that it felt as if I'd swallowed pure sunshine.

I wasn't used to holding back. My personality, for better or worse, was candid and passionate to the extreme, so it was hard to curb the frequent impulse to tell either of them that I loved them. That they had changed my life, and I was happy I seemed to be changing theirs.

Impulsive, I might be, but Sebastian and Adam had too much

baggage for that. They were still finding their footing with each other on a seriously cracked foundation, and we were still figuring out what the three of us even meant.

We didn't talk about it, but like blind men in an unknown room, we were groping our way toward each other.

I could wait.

At the very least, I had three years to work with, but my greedy heart hoped for much, much more.

"I better go," Ro said, as the crew started to say their goodbyes and filter out the bedroom door. "I have a shift tonight."

"Okay," I said, but I held her a little tighter.

In the whirlwind of the last two months, Rozhin had been my constant, and I suddenly felt like a child who'd been told to give up their comfort blanket.

She laughed as she pulled herself away from me. "You'll be wonderful tonight, Lins. Don't worry about anything. I have it on good authority that Adam will make this a night to remember."

"He makes every night feel that way," I confessed, twisting to face her as she started for the door, adjusting the train of my gown as I moved. "Lately, things have felt just…too good to be true."

"Hey!" she snapped, knocking a fist against her head. "Knock on wood, Jesus. Don't jinx yourself."

I rolled my eyes but laughed as she meant me to. "Okay, okay, I'll just try to enjoy."

"I know you don't get this," she said, stepping closer to take one of my hands, "but you deserve to be happy. This isn't about luck, this is about the hard work you've done to be a good person who deserves good karma, to be the best actress you can be, to be the sort of woman a man like Adam fucking Meyers could fall in love with."

"Oh, I don't know about love," I said, waving away her words as a blush warmed my cheeks.

Ro's eyes gleamed. "Well, I guess we'll see about that. Break a leg, knock 'em dead, may the force be with you, and all that jazz. Call me tomorrow for a complete debrief."

"I will," I promised.

"Do you want me to take Miranda back to the guest house?" she offered, already moving towards my mum to take the handles of her chair.

"I love you," I told her, because I seemed overstuffed with the emotion and needed a safe place to vent some of it.

She grinned as she pushed Miranda to my side and accepted my kiss on the cheek before waiting for me to do the same to mum. "We love you, too."

The moment they left, my gut twisted into knots.

I moved to pick at a hangnail and cursed myself, clasping my hands behind my back as I twisted to face the mirror again.

"Just who do you think you are?" I asked the admittedly beautiful girl in the mirror.

"My future bride," a familiar, crisp British accent sounded from the doorway behind me.

I angled myself in the reflection to see Adam, and I put my hand to brace myself against the frame of the mirror to steady myself.

He was an absolute vision.

The suit he wore was a deep charcoal that was almost black, a stark contrast to his crisp white shirt, which was unbuttoned at the throat. There was a vivid yellow silk pocket square in his breast pocket that exactly matched my dress and brought out the emerald green of his eyes. He had his hair pushed back from his forehead with product in a manner that only highlighted his masculine beauty, his strong features, and dark brows, as well as the dimple in his square chin. He looked exactly like a movie star should, almost otherworldly and so beautiful I had to blink away sunspots.

"I could certainly be convinced to marry you if you agree to wear that to the wedding," I said, going for playful and failing because my voice was too breathy.

Damn, he looked incredible.

For a moment I felt sixteen again, watching Adam and his wife leave with Miranda and Bobbi for one of their glamorous events in London. That I was the woman here with him now was utterly surreal.

He chuckled as he pushed off the doorframe and stalked toward me, that predatory gait that made my thighs clench even though I'd already come multiple times that day.

Knowing how skilled he was with his hands, his cock, his sinful mouth, and that depraved, devious mind only proved to amplify his beauty tenfold.

I would have sunk to my knees if it wouldn't ruin the lines of my dress.

His grin was wicked, as if he could read my mind as he came to a stop behind me.

The sight of us together in the mirror as he slid an arm around my waist took my breath away. And suddenly, being on his arm didn't feel so surreal anymore. We looked perfect together, so golden we seemed to glow.

"Look at you," he murmured, eyes raking over every inch of my reflection. "Just look at you. I'm not sure I knew a woman could captivate me the way you do."

I arched a brow. "You've been married and dated your fair share of actresses and models."

"Which means I am an authority on the matter," he countered coolly. "So you should believe me when I say I have never in my life seen a more striking woman. You will be the envy of everyone on the red carpet."

"You like the dress, then," I said with a pleased little smile.

"I like you in anything," he corrected. "But seeing you in your own art is especially appealing, I have to admit. You look ravishing."

"Thank you," I said, because his praise felt like cool rain flushing out the lingering toxicity of Miranda's biting criticisms in the past.

He pressed a kiss to my head and then reached for the jewelry box left open on the chest of drawers. "Allow me to help you with these."

I swallowed thickly as he carefully swept my hair off my neck and looped the cold gold necklace across my throat so that the ten-carat, yellow diamond gleamed in the hollow between my collarbones. Once done, he helped secure the matching cluster of yellow and white diamonds in my ears.

"Your hands are bare," he murmured, taking them in his own and smoothing his rough thumbs over my knuckles.

I curled my fingers into fists. "None of my rings felt good enough to wear tonight."

I'd bought most of them from consignment shops and at markets. Only the pearl piece from my friend in Hawaii was worth anything, but it didn't quite go with my dress.

Adam raised each hand to press a kiss to the back of both.

"You could wear those sweatpants that cling to your hips and one of those cut-off tees you like, and you'd still surpass anyone there tonight," he assured me with his particular brand of cool authority that made you believe everything he said. "Are you ready to go? Sebastian is waiting in the living room to see you before he takes off."

"Yes." I reached out for the tube of lipstick that the makeup artist had left for me to add to my clutch, along with a mini powder puff and a travel vial of my perfume. "I want to give him something before we leave."

"Good idea." He frowned. "I hate that he has to go by himself."

"He's taking Giselle," I reminded him. "But I know what you mean. There's nothing for it, though."

And truly, there didn't seem to be.

I was marrying Adam to keep him from public scandal. Arriving at an award show with a woman and a man on his arm would truly change everything about his life and career for the better. After years of blackmail from Oscar Hampton, he deserved some peace.

Even if I felt Sebastian deserved our love in the shadows *and* the light.

An impossible universe, Seb called it, and I thought he might be right.

"Speaking of Sebastian," Adam said as he escorted me down the hall toward the living area. "Brace for impact."

"What?" I asked, but I was immediately distracted by the sight of our Italian standing in a puddle of sunlight spilling in through the floor-to-ceiling windows.

The beams turned his eyes to liquid gold as they rose to lock on us, the color utterly arresting against the depth of his tan and all that raven-black hair that waved a little long over his ears and spilled over his forehead. He had grown out his usual stubble so that it was almost a short beard, the inkiness contrasting with the soft texture of his full pink mouth.

The dark to Adam's light and just as utterly magnificent.

"How do you say breathtaking in Italian?" I asked Seb.

His mouth twitched. "*Mozzafiato.*"

"*Sei mozzafiato,*" I told him in my best Italian.

"*Bella come il sole,*" he returned, and I knew enough Italian to translate that before he did. "Beautiful like the sun."

His suit was as dark as tar, the velvet blazer sleekly tailored to his tapered waist and broad shoulders. The only spot of collar was a light grey button-up, and I was grateful it wasn't black because otherwise my idea might not have worked.

If I was feeling particularly whimsical, I might have said Adam and Seb, as they came to stand together before me, looked like day and night, and I, in my dress, the sunshine between them.

"We both have something for you before we leave," Adam told him, pushing me gently in the back so I stepped into the circle of Sebastian's waiting arms.

He grinned down at me. "A present?"

"Yes," I murmured, suddenly shy. "If you don't want me to do it, you can just say so, but I wanted to mark you as mine before you go out there. I didn't like that you were alone and so far from us at the Critics Choice Awards, that there was no way to look over and know just with a glance you were ours."

Sebastian's throat worked around a hard swallow, and his pupils dilated with lust as he held me just a bit closer. "I can tell you right now that I will like whatever idea this is. I want to be marked as yours just as you want to mark me."

"Good," I breathed, smiling wide. "Because everyone will know you're taken if I do this. But only you, me, and Adam will know by whom."

I only had to tip my head forward, thanks to my sky-high heels, in order to take the edge of his collar in one hand to steady it so I could press my vibrantly painted rose-pink lips to the pale fabric. I'd had the makeup artist apply the pigment liberally with exactly this in mind so when I pulled away, I was satisfied to see the distinct print of my mouth on his shirt.

"There." The word rumbled out of me like a purr. "Now everyone will know there is a lucky lady in your life who is allowed to kiss you however and whenever she wants."

Sebastian stared down at me with a wealth of words written in those gold eyes. His mouth worked for a moment as if he had forgotten how to speak, but then it flexed into such a gorgeous smile I almost forgot my own name.

"I knew this suit was missing something," he teased, but there was a seriousness to his gaze that made me swallow as he pressed our foreheads together. "There is nothing better than belonging to someone."

"Someones," I corrected impishly.

He chuckled and pulled back so he could smile at Adam beside me. "Someones," he agreed.

"Well, she stole my thunder," Adam quipped as he stepped closer to us, pressed along Sebastian's side. We both watched as he pulled a watch from his pocket. It had a slightly worn leather strap, but the watch was gold, with a copper-pink dial and a moon and stars design inked in gold and navy blue. "Only fourteen of these were made, and my mother's father had one of them. It is from the 1940s, and it's the only thing I have left from him."

He stared at the watch as he held it between us as if transfixed by it.

His voice was quiet when he next spoke. "It's on loan," he told Sebastian as he finally raised his gaze to the other man. "Until the day you feel comfortable wearing the other Patek Philippe I once gave you. I wanted you to have something of myself with you tonight. It's not quite holding your hand myself..." he joked lamely and shrugged one shoulder.

Sebastian's fingers trembled ever so slightly as he raised his hand to take the watch. "Adam, if I still had that Patek, I would wear it now.

But"—he winced—"in a fit of rage, I returned it to Savannah when I first saw her in New York with Tate a few months after things ended."

Something like heartbreak followed swiftly by rage surged through Adam's expression. "Well, it wasn't hers to keep. I bought that for you."

"*Mi dispiace*," Sebastian said, reaching out to cup Adam's neck. "It was wrong of me, but I was hurt."

Adam's jaw clenched, but he shook off his anger relatively well and jerked his chin at the watch currently in Sebastian's free hand. "I'd like to see it on you tonight when you win your second Academy Award."

Seb lifted his hand toward him so that Adam could fix it to his wrist. It was oddly erotic watching him, and I realized I might have some kind of bondage kink. I was discovering all sorts of new and wicked desires in the company of Adam and Seb.

"Now, you're ours," I announced, leaning forward to brush my lips over Seb's. "Inside and out."

Sebastian chuckled lewdly at my innuendo, but there was pure, almost boyish joy as he smiled at us both and looped his long arms around our shoulders to bring us in for a three-way hug. It could have been awkward, maybe, to hug with an extra person, but we fit together like puzzle pieces, as if we'd been carved into shape for exactly this purpose.

I had never been a big believer in fate, but standing in Adam's living room in his and Sebastian's strong embrace, I thought back to that day on Croyde Beach in Cornwall and wondered if this wasn't exactly where life had intended us to end up.

CHAPTER TWENTY–EIGHT

LINNEA

My leg wouldn't stop jittering as the limousine inched closer to the front of the receiving line at the Dolby Theatre, where the Academy Awards, more colloquially known as the Oscars, were held each year.

Adam's big hand found my jumping limb and squeezed tightly enough to quell the movement.

When I looked over from the window, he was studying me.

"Nervous?" he asked. "You didn't seem so at the Critics Choice Awards."

"No," I agreed, "but they didn't seem so…iconic."

Adam's mouth flexed into a little smile. "This is much of the same, just on a grander scale. I'll be honest, all the award shows are dull as hell. Not enough bathroom breaks, too many egos in one room, and an absurd amount of droning on in the speeches. Adrien Brody once spoke for over *five* minutes."

"Wow, you really paint a picture," I drawled. "And to think I was excited."

"I think you'll enjoy it," Adam said with that coy smugness I had once found so annoying and now couldn't help but find charming. "I'll make sure of it."

"Oh, and how will you do that?" I asked, curling into him as he tugged me closer so I was basically in his lap. It would probably wrinkle my dress, but I wanted to be against him more than I cared about a few wrinkles. Besides, Chaucer was in the front with the driver and I thought she might have a portable steamer in her Mary Poppins-esque tote.

"You do know I'm a world-famous movie star with connections everywhere?" he asked haughtily.

I laughed and watched as his mouth edged into that little grin.

"Okay, well, I trust you," I said, already feeling much more relaxed as I snuggled into his side and took one of his hands between my own to fiddle with his long, blunt-tipped fingers. God, even they were gorgeous.

"Linnea," he called after a moment, slipping his hand out of mine to use it to tip my chin up so I was staring into his intense gaze.

"Mr. Meyers," I teased.

His lids lowered just a little, further proof if I needed it that he loved being called that.

"How do you feel about being Mrs. Meyers one day?" he asked, and suddenly, the car felt like a confessional, a sacred space for secrets and whispered prayers.

Mrs. Meyers.

It was strange to think of the title as belonging to me instead of Savannah, whom I had known as Mrs. Meyers for most of the time I'd been acquainted with her through Miranda.

And there was no mistaking that I hated Savannah.

She had squandered the incredible love of two men who deserved someone who would move heaven and earth for them.

Yet the idea of being Linnea Meyers?

Adam's wife.

His partner.

Of standing beside him as his witness through life, as his sword or his shield or his pillow to rest his weary head?

I loved the idea of that.

And it had very little to do with my obligations through our contract.

Adam deserved to have someone in his life who would fight for him. Even Sebastian hadn't fought, though he had only been freshly nineteen and forced out by Adam's chilling dictatorial ways.

I resolved as I sat pressed into his warm side, that I would fight for Adam until he no longer deserved my love.

And I honestly couldn't see that happening.

Ever.

So I turned deeper into his embrace and looked full-on into his perfectly handsome face, straight into those haunted green eyes.

"I'm not sure if, in this day and age, a woman *has* to take her husband's last name," I said lightly, just to mess with him because he was a man who needed to be teased and often. "But I love the sound of being Linnea Meyers almost as much as I love the sound of being *your* wife."

"Even if I were to rip up the contract between us right now?" he dared with a raised brow and narrowed eyes.

He wouldn't, of course, but it meant something that he wanted to test my feelings.

It implied that he had feelings of his own.

"Well, you made me swear I wouldn't fall in love with you," I reminded him. "But as you promised no such thing, I could probably be convinced to stick around, even if you didn't need me to salvage your reputation anymore."

"Oh, I need you," he murmured, his gaze like a caress along my face. "I need you in ways I did not know I could feel need."

"Take what you want," I offered. "I'm here and I'm yours."

His mouth was on mine before I had even finished speaking, his hand fixing my face in place so that he could eat desperately at my mouth. I groaned, pressing into him, opening my mouth for the savagery of his kiss.

It would absolutely ruin my makeup, but that's why I had a touch-up kit in my clutch.

"We're here, snoggers," Chaucer called through the now open partition. "Save some of it for the red carpet, please. Adam, you've completely ruined her lipstick *and* her hair. Can you keep your hands to yourself for even a moment?"

"It wouldn't be a carpet without Chaucer reprimanding me for something," Adam muttered out of the corner of his mouth.

I giggled as I whipped out the compact mirror and lipstick to repair the damage, and Adam used the edge of his pocket square to wipe off the transfer to his own mouth.

"Not exactly my color," he said dryly, then watched me laugh again before pressing his lips quickly to mine again.

"Enough of that," Chaucer snapped, but she was smiling. "Get out of this car and go be fabulously pretty for the evening and woefully bored."

"Will do," Adam said cheerily as someone opened my door and offered a hand to help me out. "Wait, I'll do that."

He left the car from the other side before I could insist I was fine to get out of the car myself, and then he was suddenly pulling the door open farther and reaching in to help me smoothly to my feet. His arm braced me as flashing lights exploded across my vision.

He had learned to avoid the flares a long time ago, but I was still momentarily blinded by the chaos of cameras. We had to make our way slowly through the crowds of cars and arriving celebrities, escorted by an event planner and a security guard, until we reached the security screening area. It was a part of the carpet they didn't show on TV that was decidedly unglamorous as they checked ID tags, X-rayed bags, and passed us through metal detectors.

Once we were done with that, Adam took my arm again and we stopped at the edge of the red carpet entry.

"I know I already briefed you and you've done a short version at the CCAs, but first we have the step and repeat wall for photos. We'll have most taken together, but a few apart. Then there are the more traditional media outlet interviews, the fan section where we can sign autographs and take some photos for the masses or just blow through with a few waves, and the social media zone where we might be asked to participate in content creation." He paused to make a face, which made me laugh because it was well-known that Adam abhorred social media. Given the extremity of his fame and the blackmail Oscar had been holding over his head for almost a decade, I couldn't really blame him. "Finally, the photo bridge where they'll shoot your marvelous dress in a three-sixty camera, and then we can actually move into the theatre."

"I got it," I assured him.

"It will probably take us close to an hour to run the gauntlet," he warned. "And we'll be stopped by some of my mates and acquaintances along the way. If it gets to be too much, just say your safeword and I'll extract us from the situation."

I grinned. "Adam, I've got this. I know these events aren't your favorite, but honestly, I'm new on the scene and I'm actually fairly excited to be walking the red carpet at the Academy Awards with *the* Adam Meyers."

He scoffed lightly at my teasing, but a little pleased smile remained tucked into the folds of his mouth. "Well then, prepare for battle."

It wasn't exactly battle, but it was a kind of oddly organized, overwhelming chaos. People screamed Adam's name desperately from the fan bleachers, and photographers shouted their directions as we posed in front of the step-and-repeat wall. Adam allowed them to take a handful of photos of both of us separately before he collected me with a possessive arm around my waist, shocking me by curling me deeply into his side and slightly over his arm in a backward bend.

"Adam." I laughed breathlessly even as I steadied myself with my arms around his neck.

He grinned, a wide, boyish expression of real joy, and then he kissed me.

The explosion of flashes from cameras blinded me even with my eyes closed.

His tongue parted my lips and dived deep, plundering me with a deliberate thoroughness as if we were in the privacy of his home and not in front of thousands.

When he finally parted from me, my knees were weak and my lips were swollen. He didn't move far, righting us but staying close enough to rub his thumb under my mouth to capture the smudged lipstick.

"I think you might need to reapply," he murmured, eyes dancing.

"What has gotten into you tonight?" I asked, but there was no reprimand in my tone.

To be so publicly claimed resonated somewhere deep in my soul.

The idea that a man who was so accomplished, so wonderfully talented, and beneath it, almost terribly tender and sweet could want to claim me?

My heart turned over in my chest, that sensation of a dream coming true that was almost painful.

"You, Linnea," he said somberly. "The sunbeam lighting my lonely dark."

I slid my hand up to cup his face and said, "I have waited a long time for someone to say my name like that."

"And how do I say it?"

"Like a poem and a prayer," I admitted. "I only knew it was possible because of the way Sebastian has always spoken *your* name."

Adam gripped my chin in his big hand so delicately it made me shiver. "You are his poem, I think, and my prayer. I did not even know I wished for you before you showed up."

This feels like love, I thought, my heart galloping like something wild and free across the plains of my chest. This feels like what I always thought love should be.

One of the event volunteers ruined the moment by approaching to nudge us out of the photography line and into the gauntlet of reporters waiting with eager eyes to interview us as a couple for the first time.

Adam took my hand, threading our fingers together, and led me forward, giving me a moment to fix my lipstick before we made our way to the first interview.

"Adam," a smartly dressed man with deep auburn hair and perfectly preserved features greeted my date with a warm clap on the back. Ellis Foster had been the host of *Entertainment Extra* since I was a girl, but he didn't look a day over thirty. "And the lovely Linnea Kai."

"Hullo," Adam said in a cheerful British way that drew my skeptical gaze.

Why the hell was he so happy?

Of course, we had started the day with a brilliant play that I could still feel in my swollen pussy and the peaks of my sore breasts, but I was surprised it buoyed him enough to enjoy the event. He had been his usual curmudgeon self at the CCA unless I was teasing him.

"I'm honored to be the first to interview you two," Ellis continued. "First, tell me who you're wearing."

"Tom Ford," Adam said, pulling me into his side. "But only because Linnea did not have time to create something for me herself."

Ellis's grey eyes widened comically as he took in my dress. "Are you implying she made this gown herself?"

"She did," I quipped, smoothing a hand over the ruffled edges of the handsewn silk. "I've been making my own clothes since I was a girl."

"It's exquisite," Ellis declared, still a little shocked. "I think this is the first time I've seen an actress wear one of her own creations on the red carpet."

"Linnea is one of a kind," Adam said proudly.

Warmth suffused my chest and stained my skin pink. "I have to be in order to beguile The Great Adam Meyers."

Adam chuckled. "You could beguile me in a paper sack, and you know it."

I shrugged one shoulder, winking at Ellis who watched the exchange with the eagerness of a reporter who knows he's captured gold.

"How did you two meet?"

"Believe it or not, we've known each other for a long time. Her mother is an old family friend. But it was my good mate Sebastian Lombardi who set us up. I owe him an extravagant gift for that, remind me, will you, Sunbeam?"

I blinked at the intimate use of my nickname. "I think he mentioned wanting the original Triumph Thunderbird motorcycle from Marlon Brando's *The Wild One* the other day."

Adam rolled his eyes. "Why that man feels the need to collect cinema paraphernalia is beyond me."

"You are both obviously good friends with the Italian," Ellis said, probing for more information. Adam and Seb hadn't been seen together in the media since gossip stirred in the tabloids ten years ago, leading to their breakup. "I think I saw a photo of you and Seb on surfboards recently."

"He's more like family," I said firmly, raising my brow like Adam to level Ellis with a cool look.

"I see," he said, nodding slowly. "And do you think he has a chance to sweep award season by clinching the ultimate prize of Best Actor tonight?"

"Unequivocally," Adam stated on top of my, "Of course."

"Well then, I hope you're right. I happened to love *Waking Nightmare* even though it gave me nightmares." Ellis mock shivered and then turned over his shoulder to hold his hand out for something from one of his aides. "Before you move on, I believe Adam wanted to give you these."

I frowned as Ellis handed me a huge bouquet of golden orchids. My gaze snapped up to Adam, who watched me with a self-satisfied smile.

"What are these?" I asked softly, sticking my nose in the petals.

"I simply wanted to surprise the love of my life with flowers," he told me imperiously.

I had to grin at him. "So you had Ellis Foster deliver them on the red carpet."

"When will you understand, Nea, that with me anything is possible," he teased, leaning forward to brush his mouth over mine.

Even Sebastian's impossible universe? *I thought but didn't say.*

Instead, I followed him to the next reporter, a stunning woman in a vibrant fuchsia dress that made her dark skin glow. She asked us some standard questions before she got derailed by Adam's unusually flirtatious banter with me.

"You seem happy, Adam," she said, a little gently as if she couldn't believe it.

It hurt to know that his pain had been so obvious for so long.

"I am," he told Imani. "For a long time, the only thing that brought me joy was acting. Now, I have someone who reminds me how to live for myself instead of my characters."

Imani and I both swooned in tandem.

At the end of the interview, Imani handed me another bouquet, this one a massive array of daisies.

"How did you know I love daisies?" I murmured as I accepted the flowers and tucked them into one arm along with the orchids. "Miranda tried to shame me out of loving them. She said they're cheap and they smell bad."

Adam shook his head at her antics as we walked to the next interview. "You have daisy designs on that white sundress you've worn a few times and on that lingerie I peeled you out of on Thursday. Not to mention, they suit you. They're happy flowers."

After the next interview, the reporter asked, "Is Adam romantic, Linnea?"

I laughed as I tipped my head at the flowers. "Wildly so, yes. Not just by giving me flowers but by showing up for me whenever I need him."

Adam turned his head to kiss my hair, his arm secure around my waist where it had settled most of the evening.

"What is the most romantic thing he has ever done for you?" Amy Liu asked, a mischievous look in her eye.

"I haven't done it quite yet," Adam stepped in to say before I could. "But now seems as good a time as ever."

"What?" I whispered as Adam led me to the right where a tall stage at the edge of the carpet obstructed my view of what perched on top. "What are you doing?"

"Going against my own orders," he said mildly as he helped me up the stairs, "and begging you to fall in love with me."

I stopped dead at the top of the treads, blinking madly at the small, white stage arranged with dozens and dozens of flower arrangements of the same florals I held in my arms. Petals scattered over the glossy floor, and a trio of string musicians started to softly play "Feeling Good" by Nina Simone.

Until that moment, I never realized how fitting the childhood song was for my relationship with both Adam and Sebastian.

Speaking of the Italian, he stepped forward from where he had waited with the musicians to take the flowers from my arms.

"You knew about this?" I whispered in a hiss as he leaned close.

His grin was a quick flash, like the green light as the sun sets over the horizon. "You think he could plan something this romantic himself?"

He stepped away, giving Adam the floor.

I had only a moment to wish he could be at the center of this with us before Adam captured my entire attention, the axis of gravity for my whole universe.

He took my hand to lead me to the center of the small stage, then pulled me into his loose embrace. Vaguely, I was aware of cameras flashing, but the stage was tall enough that they couldn't get a good angle on what was happening between us. A public moment, a bold declaration, but still somehow intimate.

"Adam," I said, a question and trembling plea.

"You make me love the sound of my name," he murmured,

pushing his hand into the side of my hair to cup my face. "You make me love a lot of things again. Before you, I think I'd entirely forgotten how to dream and desire. I only knew yearning and angst."

"What are you doing?" I asked because hope and love were threatening to burst through my skin like a supernova, and I wasn't sure I could contain it.

I needed to know if this was really what it seemed to be and *why* he was doing it in this manner.

We had spoken about simply going down to the courthouse to get married, done between one day and the next for the press to find out after the fact even though Mi Cha and Rachel wanted a big white wedding for us.

What we had was a business arrangement, so why was Adam looking at me like a blind man seeing the sun for the first time?

"I'm asking you to be my wife," he murmured, bringing his other hand up to my face so that I was framed by him. His long-lashed eyes were as serious and intent as I've ever seen them, filled with something I had never witnessed before.

I thought it might have been hope.

"I'm asking you for permanence because I think, in both our lives, that has been lacking. I don't want to marry you for three years, Linnea. I want to marry you for however long you'll consent to have this old curmudgeon in your life and, maybe one day, in your heart."

"Are you serious?" I breathed on a giddy, almost panicked laugh.

I brought my hands up to secure his wrists, needing an anchor.

"Deadly," he said. "You happened to me like a sunrise, casting light and warmth over the dark, cold shadows of my heart. I have been lonely for a very long time, and I think you have, too. I don't want that for either of us ever again. I want you, Linnea, without a contract, without an expiration date, until the end of time if you'll have me."

A sob fell from my mouth, and I caught it with one hand as Adam dropped to his knees slowly before me and reached into his blazer pocket. The ring he brandished was the color of sunlight, an enormous oval that glowed like he had managed to harness the sun from the sky and pour it into a diamond for me.

"You know I don't get on my knees for just anyone," he said playfully, but I could see how it masked the terror in his eyes. "But I would spend my life on my knees in front of your altar, worshipping you as you should be worshipped. Linnea Kai, my sunbeam, will you do me the incredible honor of being my wife?"

"Yes!" The word tumbled out of me as I fell forward inelegantly into Adam's waiting arms.

He laughed as I pressed my mouth to his and ate the sound of his tongue until it turned into a groan. When he lifted a leg to brace himself better, he sat me on his thigh, and I gave myself over to kissing him.

My future husband.

For the first time, the idea of marrying Adam didn't feel like some surreal plot twist in a Hallmark film.

It felt real, something I could hold in my hands and my heart.

I pulled away only when I felt his fingers sliding the ring along my skin. When I blinked down at my hand, the yellow diamond winked at me.

"It's stunning," I breathed.

"Sebastian helped me design it and the wedding ring," he said quietly, pushing my rumpled hair back from my face. "It's as much from him as from me."

Hope bloomed so large in my heart that it threatened to choke me.

"Really?" I whispered through my tight throat.

"Really," he repeated. "I am not the only man enamored with the girl with ocean eyes and a sunrise soul."

"I wish we could go to him," I said, even as I pressed closer to him.

"Later," Adam promised. "I have a very private after-party planned for us all."

"Adam," I said, gathering breath to tell him the truth crushing my heart. "I l—"

His hand muffled my mouth, and he smiled at my wide eyes.

"Hold that thought for later," he requested. "I want to be inside you after you tell me those words for the first time."

I laughed, tipping my head back so his hand released my mouth, and I could express my joy to the heavens. My gaze caught Sebastian's, who stood with a cluster of actors and reporters on the stairs of the stage watching us. He winked and raised his hand to press it over his heart.

And I wondered if it was possible to die of happiness.

CHAPTER TWENTY-NINE

SEBASTIAN

"You love them."

I yanked my gaze away from the future Mr. and Mrs. Meyers holding court over at their table on the other side of the room to look at my sister Giselle.

She looked positively gorgeous in a midnight-blue dress that made her grey eyes look like silver dollars and emphasized the unique shade of her dark red hair. I felt a pang for not giving her my full attention this evening, but it couldn't be helped.

Adam and Linnea were getting married.

And even though Adam had made me a part of the planning, of the moment by asking me to help pick out the engagement ring for her, I felt surprisingly hollow sitting across the theatre from them.

I was so distracted by my melancholy that it took me a moment to process her comment.

'Giselle," I said on a quiet hiss. "We are surrounded by gossips, be careful what you say."

"Okay," she said, but her mouth curled into a sad little smile. "You don't have to say it, but I can see it plain as day."

I scoffed but didn't try to refute it.

I was shocked the entire room couldn't see the love shining from my eyes every time I looked over at the golden-haired couple who had stolen my heart.

"What happened to Savannah?" she asked quietly.

I sighed. "I do not know if I have the kind of heart that can ever stop loving someone once that love is given freely. Part of me will always love her, but she doesn't feel the same way. As I was waiting, two people came along and made it clear that I was waiting out of habit. That if I just turned my head away from Savvy, I might find something better."

Giselle hummed, trailing her fingers over the stem of her wineglass. "I don't know Savannah well enough to speak much on her feelings. Though, over the years, it's become obvious to all of us that she loves you in her own way. But maybe this is better…can they love you where she couldn't?"

Absently, I rubbed a hand against my aching breastbone. "As much as they're able, maybe, given the circumstances."

"Is that enough for you?" my sister asked, because she had known me my whole life and understood better than most what a voracious heart I harbored.

"I don't know," I murmured, shocked to admit it even to myself. "I hope so."

Giselle leaned into my side, her familiar lavender scent washing over me like a cleansing balm. "The Lombardis have never chosen the easy path in life or in love, but as someone who has made it out the other side to the happily ever after, I can promise you, the struggle is worth the reward."

I caught the bright edge of Linnea's laugh over the crush of ambient noise and followed it to the source, seeing her with her head thrown back, Adam's arm around her waist so snugly, she seemed bound to him.

My throat ached with the need to be with them.

"Will you excuse me for a moment?" I asked Giselle, taking advantage of one of the commercial breaks to go to the bathroom for a moment of much-needed solitude.

I only offered up nods and smiles to my friends and acquaintances as I weaved through the tables to the back of the room and waited for security to open the doors for me. The hallway and restroom were mostly empty this close to the end of a commercial break. If I did not hurry, I would have to wait for the next one to be let back into the ceremony.

"*Menomale*," I said, thanking God for the quiet.

I braced my hands on the sink basin and breathed deeply for a few beats before running my hands under cold water and pressing them to my cheeks.

Could I live in the shadows forever, loving Linnea and Adam from a distance in public and carefully, always carefully, in private?

What of my own dreams of marriage and children?

Unbidden, images of a small daughter with Linnea's Italian plum-purple eyes and my dark hair running with a little boy with Adam's green gaze and dimpled chin flashed through my mind's eye.

My gut cramped with longing.

Yes, I thought, as I stared down at Adam's grandfather's watch, as I looked at the kiss stain I'd been questioned about ad nauseum by reporters tonight, I could endure anything if it meant those quiet moments of loving them both.

I'd been born and raised both a lover and a fighter because I had been taught if you were not willing to fight for love, then it wasn't real.

And I was willing to do anything to protect Adam and Linnea, even if it meant living half a lie.

Resolved and eager to end this interminable evening, I twisted to leave the restroom and go back to the ceremony.

Only to find someone leaning in the doorway with their arms crossed.

I hadn't seen Oscar Hampton in ten years, and even then, it was only once, at Pinewood Studios, when he had warned me off Adam and Savannah.

Still, I would never forget his narrow, almost pretty features and the slim, elegant lines of his body. Once, I had been jealous of him, of how he seemed to be Adam's type.

I now had the evidence inside my sore ass that *I* was more to his taste than any other man before or since I'd entered his life.

"Well, if it isn't Sebastian Lombardi," Oscar drawled in his posh British accent that was somehow grating where Adam's was lyrical. "You've come a long way since being the lowly chauffeur. That's what working on your back will get you, I guess."

"I suppose you should know," I retorted, crossing my arms over my chest as anger sank sharp teeth into my spine. "I do not think you want to be caught alone with me, Oscar. I have never thought of myself as a violent man, but that was before I knew that you were holding Adam over a barrel."

"I wondered if you were sleeping with him again," Oscar continued like I hadn't spoken, a smug aura about him as if he knew something I didn't. Foreboding tasted metallic on the back of my tongue. "Tell me, does he still fuck like a dream?"

"*Vaffanculo,*" I cursed him in Italian. "Watch your fucking mouth before I break it."

"Oh, Mr. Tough Italian Guy," Oscar mock shivered. "I shouldn't be surprised. I've heard the rumors about your sister Elena's husband, and his father, Amadeo Salvatore."

"Be very careful when you speak about my family," I warned him, eyeing the cameras in the corners of the room.

If I hit him first, he could press charges. I needed to keep my cool even though my Latin blood boiled me from the inside out. For the first time in my life, I thought I might have the capacity to kill a man.

"It is *you* who should be careful with me," Oscar corrected, putting his hands in his pockets as he shoved off the wall and strolled toward me. "I am the one holding the stick of dynamite, after all."

"You can speak to the press all you want about Adam's sexuality, but it's your word against his. You might make a few headlines, but now that his romance with Linnea is the talk of the town, I doubt any of your accusations will have a lasting impact."

Bitter fury flashed across his face, and I wondered how anyone could ever find him good-looking with such an ugly heart.

"If only it was conjecture," Oscar sighed. "Alas, I have irrefutable proof." He paused to let that sink in and then leaned closer with a wicked grin. "Would you like to see it?"

"A selfie in the back of the Rolls-Royce hardly counts as evidence," I told him coldly.

"Too true," he agreed easily, fishing his phone from his pocket and fiddling with it for a moment before he raised the screen to me. "But I think this does, don't you?"

The video played without sound, but it didn't need it to be utterly damning. Naked, Oscar sat on top of Adam who lay flat on his back in some generic hotel room with his eyes closed and his hands loosely clasped over Oscar's rolling hips.

They were fucking.

Jealousy and fury raged in my gut and for one horrifying moment, I thought I might throw up right there on the floor.

I had seen Adam in the throes of passion many times, but never like he was in the video, loose and almost sloppy in his movements, his eyes slumberous with something like sleep or drink and not bone-deep satisfaction.

"He did not consent to that," I lashed out, grabbing the phone and throwing it to the floor where it cracked neatly in half.

Not nearly good enough, I stomped on the remaining pieces until the screen was in smithereens and the body was completely warped.

Oscar just watched me with his hands in his pockets again, head cocked. "You know, I have copies of that everywhere. You just ruined a perfectly good phone."

"I will ruin your *cazzate* life," I roared, reaching out to fist my hand in his shirt and lift him to his toes. "You will wish you had never been born, you pathetic excuse for a man. I will throw everything in my power at you, including Dante and Amadeo Salvatore, if you think you can release this to the public."

"I'm not afraid of you. You are not the only one with powerful friends," Oscar said, meeting my eyes for a moment before darting away from the no doubt feral look in mine. "And you don't have to be afraid of me releasing this film if you do exactly as I say."

My fingers were numb with the strain of holding him aloft, so I dropped him to his feet and snarled into his face, "I'm not doing a fucking thing for you."

"Oh, I think you will," he disagreed with a meek little shrug, opening his palms as if he couldn't help but be a *figlio di puttana*. "If you don't, I'll send this little video teaser to all the major outlets and upload the full thing to Porn Central. Hey, maybe having a sex tape will do his career good? It worked for Paris Hilton and Kim Kardashian."

"Fuck you," I said, spitting at his feet.

"Oh, that's right." He snapped his fingers. "This proves Adam is *gay*, not a good look for Hollywood's leading man and the next in line to play the famous womanizer Anton Daventry, is it? I remember Adam telling me all about his dreams of one day donning the famous tuxedo as Daventry."

"Why are you doing this?" I had to ask. "Did he hurt you so badly?"

Oscar waved the words out of the air. "Yes and no. I thought I loved them both, but I realized they were just using me. Why shouldn't I use them, too?"

"That's psychopathic," I accused, shocked that there were people like this in the world. "You would ruin his career for that?"

"I would do it for pleasure," he said with bared teeth. "But money's better."

"What do you want?" I gritted between my teeth.

"Twenty million dollars," he said, as if asking for spare change to buy a coffee.

"You think I have twenty million dollars?" I asked, incredulous.

I had been a movie star for a decade and I made that much on on my last film, but I had also spent the first five years of my career setting my family up with houses, cars, and careers. I had savings, but not as much as one might think.

"Nice try, hotshot. I know you made ten mil on *Waking Nightmare* and twenty on *Black On*. You can afford me."

"This is fucking extortion," I ground out. "What makes you think I'd pay your hush money?"

"You love him," he said simply. "You always have, I think. It's disgustingly obvious. And I have it on good authority that you'd do anything for the ones you love."

My pulse pounded so hard against my ribcage I thought I heard the crack of bone breaking under the pressure.

"If I do this, you'll delete the video," I said.

"Oh, I think I'll keep a copy just in case, but I'll sign something swearing never to release it," he promised, and at my skeptical look, he laughed. "You can have your lawyer draw something up, and I'll sign it in blood. Just get me the twenty million dollars."

A muscle spasmed in my jaw as I ground my teeth together. I couldn't think of a way out of this other than to do what the sniveling little weasel wanted. And if I could shield Adam from this, I would take any chance at that, even if it meant keeping a sordid, awful secret from him forever.

"Fine," I grunted. "I'll have my lawyer draw something up."

"Excellent," he crowed, clapping his hands.

Behind him, someone knocked at the door, and I realized Oscar had locked it behind me.

"Just one more thing," he singsonged. "And you have to understand, this is a pivotal part of the deal."

"What?" I bit off like a curse.

Oscar rolled to his tiptoes to smile in my face. "You break up with Adam and Linnea."

CHAPTER THIRTY

ADAM

I hardly remembered the rest of the Academy Awards ceremony, but for the moment, the only man I'd ever loved took the stage to accept his Oscar for Best Actor.

He ended his speech by looking over at the table where Linnea and I sat, and even though I knew he couldn't really see us through the stage lights, it felt as if he was looking directly into my soul.

"Finally, to two people who put me back in touch with my soul. The brilliant and beautiful Linnea Kai and my old friend Adam Meyers. No matter what happens, thank you for reminding me what's important."

In the wake of our engagement, Seb's words received a resounding round of applause and some hooting and hollering.

It took forever to get out of the theatre after the show ended because everyone wanted to congratulate us. In the end, I was almost growling and snapping at people, with Linnea making excuses for me by calling me a "grumpy goose."

God, she was ridiculous and lovely, and somehow, *mine*.

As soon as we got into the car, she was straddling my lap with her hands in my hair and her mouth fixed to mine. She tasted of the lemon sparkling water she liked to drink, and her complicated oceanfront, rose-garden scent consumed my senses.

"Congratulations, you two," Chaucer said, laughter in her voice. "Linam is the number one trending hashtag on social media right now."

"Huzzah," Linnea said dryly without looking over her shoulder. "Chaucer, be a dear and put up the partition or else you and the driver are going to get an after-dinner show."

I knew Chaucer well enough to cut off her saucy remark before she could make it. "Chaucer, partition up *now*."

The whir of the screen rising was my answer as much as her soft chuckle was.

"Where are we going now?" Linnea asked me, carding her hands through my thick hair as if it were the golden fleece.

"Sebastian is meeting us at the house," I told her. "For our private celebration. There is something I want to do first, though."

"I hope it involves orgasms," Linnea suggested with a coquettish smile.

I laughed, feeling as if I'd swallowed the sun. "Later, yes. But now, I'd like to get something back that should have been Sebastian's all along. I gave you a ring tonight, but I'd like us to give him something, too."

"Because he belongs with us," she said, as if it were as easy as that.

"Yes," I said, the word thick in my mouth. "Because he belongs with us."

"Okay, let's get it," she said, leaning down to kiss me again as if she couldn't help herself.

Her physical response to me was unlike any woman's I'd ever

known. Even though Savannah had loved sex and submission, she had also always been wary, even a little ashamed of her own predilections. Linnea didn't have a drop of shame or pretense in her body. Everything she felt was expressed in her face or her voice, in the flush of her body and the way she placed it in my care.

It was fucking addictive.

We made out in the back of the limousine like teenagers as it plodded through the after-ceremony traffic and finally took off toward Brentwood. Only when we pulled into the driveway beside the gate intercom did I find the resolve to stop kissing her.

I traced a thumb over her swollen lower lip and looked into her twilight-sky eyes. "You've heard Sebastian and me talk about an impossible universe before."

"Yes, one where you can be together in the light as well as in the shadows."

I nodded. "I gave him a Patek Philippe Celestial watch ten years ago in London. It felt like a pledge that I would always try to love him the way he deserved to be loved, even if I couldn't do it openly." My heart rattled in my chest like something old and broken as I remembered the look of betrayal in his eyes when I'd told him to leave. "I broke that promise, but I'd like to make it again and mean it this time."

"Do you think he'll really stay with us?" she whispered, as if speaking it too loudly would make the hope disappear. "That we could be enough for him like this?"

"I hope so," I said, and then corrected myself. "I plan to make it so. Between the two of us, I think we can keep him filled with enough love to endure any of the pain that will inevitably come from hiding what we mean to each other. We aren't the first people to hide their love for fear of repercussion, and we won't be the last."

Her nails scratched lightly over my scalp. "Do you think, maybe someday when we're older and you've done five Daventry films, and Sebastian's won another Oscar or two for his screenwriting, that we could say fuck it to all things Hollywood and retire into obscurity to be the three of us as we were meant to be?"

I hadn't allowed myself that fantasy. It seemed too impossible to imagine. We had so many obstacles to endure and years to weather before that seemed like a possibility, and even then, we'd have to live with the idea that our life's work might be judged as poor just because we loved in an unorthodox manner.

Still, my heart raced as if toward that future.

"Maybe," I allowed even though fear was metallic on the back of my tongue. "But first, let's focus on convincing Sebastian that he is part of our forever, too."

"You're going to ask for the watch back," my clever girl surmised, twisting to peer through the window at the huge Tudor monstrosity through the gate. "I don't love the idea of you speaking to Savannah, but I guess you want to go in without me."

"She can be cruel and jealous. It's better if I don't rub her face in the fact that I have moved on to a much younger, much better woman." I pressed a hard kiss to her mouth and then forgot why I wasn't kissing her thoroughly again for some long minutes.

"Are you going to buzz in or will I die in this limo?" Chaucer called from the front seat.

Linnea laughed against my lips and slid off my lap to take my hand.

"Buzz us in, Chaucer, we'll behave."

"I'll believe it when I see it," she grumbled, but a moment later the gates swung open and we were ascending the drive to the house.

"Weren't the Richardsons at the Oscars tonight?" Linnea asked.

"Tate was. I saw him speaking to Sebastian and Andrea at one point, no doubt pressing his case for buying the rights to *The Dream & The Dreamer*." Linnea and I had already signed a contract that said we were a nonnegotiable part of the package, alongside Andrea as director and Sebastian as the other lead. No matter where the film was optioned, the three of us would be working together.

It was almost too much to ask for, the idea of collaborating on a film written by the genius man I loved with my other lover. Too many good things coalesced into one, making me wary of the inevitable bad stroke of luck life liked to throw my way when the going was just getting good.

"Savannah is at home," Chaucer said as the partition between us opened. "I texted her. You can go on in, Adam."

Linnea's grip on my hand tightened as I made to pull away, and when I looked into her face, I was surprised by the glower there.

"Do not let her hurt you," she demanded. "She doesn't know you anymore, and I'm not sure she ever knew how to put you first. I know she has the ability to say things that cut to the quick, but remember, I know the shape of your heart, and I know it's worth it. She doesn't get to touch that, even to hurt you. Not anymore."

"My fierce protector," I praised her, warmed through to my cold heart by her loyalty. "Don't worry about me. I'll be back in a moment."

She nodded tightly, kissing the hinge of my jaw before releasing me, but I could feel her gaze even through the car windows as I crossed to the front door.

It opened before I could knock, and Savannah appeared in a silk negligee and matching robe undone over top. I blinked at the familiar sight because I was fairly sure I'd bought her that set for an anniversary years ago.

Her hair was worn loose, the big curls unraveled slightly from a long day, and her makeup was slightly smudged beneath her eyes.

"Come in," she said in an unreadable tone, closing the door the moment I crossed the threshold.

"Good evening, Savvy," I said, leaning forward to brush a kiss against her cool cheek.

She still smelled of Chanel and the powder she dusted across her face.

For a moment, I was thrown back to those years when she was the center spoke of my life.

"What are you doing here? I imagined you'd be celebrating your upcoming nuptials with Linnea Kai."

Ah, there it was, that razor's edge of bitterness and envy.

"Do you have a problem with Linnea I don't know about?" I asked calmly. "Because if not, I urge you to watch your tone when you're speaking about my future wife."

Her grin was twisted like hot metal, and she hugged her arms around her chest. "She's the daughter of a slut, a woman who got pregnant too young and gave her baby away to be raised by uncouth idiots in Hawaii. She's déclassé, entirely too young for you, even given your current midlife crisis, and it is only a matter of time before she'll ruin your life. Trust me, Kais are like that."

"Trust you?" This time, it was my voice poisoned with bitterness. "The woman who vowed to love me for the rest of our lives, who left me after Sebastian was gone, and married another man six months later? You know a mutual friend of ours sent me photos of you and Tate while we were still married. How does infidelity feed in to your definition of class, Savvy?"

"Don't speak to me like that in my own house," she snapped.

"Then don't speak to me about ruining a life," I returned coldly. "For years, you left me ruined. I couldn't even trust myself. You made me feel fundamentally unlovable, did you know that?" Old wounds broke open in my chest and oozed pus. "Did you ever even love me?"

Her mouth thinned. "Don't be ridiculous. You were always so dramatic."

"It's called passion," I told her. "And I lost it for years, but I found my way back to it thanks to Linnea Kai, who has more class and grace in her little finger than you do."

She sniffed, her equivalent of a scoff.

"And thanks to Sebastian," I continued cruelly, because Linnea had been right, Savannah still had the ability to cut me through to the bone, and I wanted to hurt her, too.

She had always loved Seb more than me, I'd thought, and the flash of almost animal pain and fear in her eyes spoke to that truth.

"You've taken up with him again," she said, the words almost wooden, falling between us to the marble floor with a hollow clang.

"I never stopped loving him," I admitted, and fuck, it felt good, like an exorcism. "It was you I should have told to leave, never him."

"You know he came here a few weeks ago," she said, a little sneer in her mouth. "To beg me to be with him again. He never stopped loving me. He didn't speak to you for a decade, but he couldn't bear to have me out of his life for more than a few years. If he had to choose, we both know who he'd pick."

"Do we?" I asked softly, putting my hands in my pockets and rocking back on my heels, suddenly wary of her and this game, yearning for the freshness of Linnea's vibrancy to erode the old cold sweeping through my chest. "Obviously, you turned him away. Seb might be loyal, but even he has his limits, Savannah."

"Not for me," she said, tipping her chin at the haughty angle so she could look down her nose at me from her inferior height. "I'm his *duchessa*."

And I'm his impossible universe, I thought, but didn't say because I didn't want her to have any further part of us.

She was in the past where she belonged, and I wouldn't think of her again as soon as she gave me what was owed to us.

"It's no matter, now," I said. "You're married to Tate."

"And you're engaged to Linnea Kai. How is that any different?" she seethed.

"If we lived in a different world where love in all its shapes and sizes was considered sacred and beautiful, I'd have my ring on Sebastian's hand in a heartbeat." I paused and stepped closer to look down at her with cold scrutiny, seeing through her for the first time in a long time. "What's your excuse?"

She trembled slightly with frustrated rage, glaring at me as if I were the enemy.

Even though I thought she was cruel and unkind sometimes, unable to love me the way I'd needed, I was still shocked she could look at me that way when there had once been love and marriage between us.

"I came here for Sebastian's watch," I said, done with this play. It was a bad script and a shoddy role. "If you could fetch it, I'll be on my way, and I won't bother you again."

"Sebastian's watch," she repeated dumbly.

"The Patek Philippe Celestial. I know he gave it to you years ago when he saw you with Tate in New York. I was the one who bought it for him, and I'd like it returned to me."

"Why? It's just an old watch."

Apart from the fact that "old watch" was over six hundred thousand dollars, it had sentimental value for all of us, *I'd thought. That Savannah could refer to it as something so diminished soured my gut.*

"Who are you?" I asked. "When did you become so cold?"

She hugged her robe tighter over her chest as if she felt a draft and shivered. "Don't presume to know me anymore, Adam."

"Excellent, then you do the same," I suggested. "Please, do fetch the watch, and I'll be off. It's late, and I have things to do."

"Tell me why you want it," she insisted.

I rolled my eyes but the words burst out of me because I was still angry with her, and the man I'd been with her who had let Sebastian slip away for ten fucking years. "Because it was a promise! A promise to love him in a way that rearranged the universe so that we could be together forever, no matter the obstacles between us. You never should have taken it from him."

"He *gave* it to me. He didn't want it anymore." She said "it," but she meant "you."

"Things change," I said.

Or they didn't, because I had never stopped loving Sebastian. Knowing we had both existed under the same moon kept me up at night and yearning for the phantom touch of his hands against me and his Italian-soaked voice in my ear.

Now, he was back, by some miracle.

A miracle called Linnea Kai, who had somehow managed to bridge the gap over troubled waters so Seb and I could find our way back to each other again.

"I sold it."

I blinked as I came back to the conversation. "Excuse me?"

Savannah shrugged and studied her nails, her own enormous diamond glinting in the light from the chandelier overhead. "I sold it a few years ago. A friend of mine mentioned he was looking for a Celestial, and I offered it to him for a good price."

"You're not serious?" I asked quietly, a dangerous thread of fury in my tone.

I thought, for one moment, I might throttle her.

"I am. Rupert Meinhardt. Lovely fellow."

"You really are heartless," I breathed, shocked by it even though I had no reason to be. "How could you?"

"All of that was in the past, and that stupid watch was something between you and Sebastian that I always felt left out of," she admitted with narrowed eyes. "You were always trying to keep him for yourself."

"No, that was you," I said, running a weary hand over my jaw. "How could I ever have thought polyamory would work when you can't even properly share yourself?"

"I don't engage in that anymore," she said, as if it were beneath her.

I had to get out of there before I spiralled any further.

"Text me his number and then delete mine," I told her, moving toward the door. "And Savannah? I hope to God I never see you again."

I closed the door on her surprised face, breathing through my mouth in an attempt to calm my anger before I got into the car with Linnea.

It didn't work.

I slid into the back seat and barked, "Drive."

"What happened?" Linnea asked, pressing herself along the line of my body.

The feel of her unraveled some of the knots in my chest, and I turned to bury my nose in her hair as if the scent of her could burn out the remnants of Chanel lingering like smoke inhalation in my lungs.

"She sold it."

Linnea tensed against me, then muttered, "What a bitch."

The laugh startled me as it exploded from my lips. I curled her into my embrace as humor moved through me, so fucking grateful for her I finally understood why Tom Cruise would jump on Oprah's yellow couch and shout that he was in love. I wanted to tell the world how fucking lucky I was to have this woman in my life.

"We'll find another way to show him," she promised, canting her head to kiss the dimple in my chin. "But I'm sorry that's lost to you both."

"For now." I had every intention of hunting down Rupert Meinhardt and using bribery, coercion, or force to get that bloody watch back.

And use it to convince Sebastian that he was always meant to be mine.

CHAPTER THIRTY–ONE

SEBASTIAN

I went back to the hotel to shower and change after the award show before heading over to Adam's. I also needed to call Elena, and I couldn't do that where he or Linnea could over hear.

"Oh, *patatino*," Elena murmured through the phone after I explained the situation. "I am so sorry."

I huffed a weak laugh and rubbed my hand through my wet hair. "Yeah, yeah, me too."

"Are you sure you want to do this?"

"No," I said instantly. "It's not the money. It's…"

Could I stand to lose Adam again?

Could I bear not to have Linnea's light in my life?

My dream had been within my grasp, grazing my fingertips, only to have it be pulled so cruelly away from me, ripped to pieces and scattered in front of my very eyes.

"It's losing them," Elena finished for me. "Giselle told the family that she's lovely. Like sunlight, she said. And Adam? Well, you've always spoken about him like he hung the moon in the sky."

I laughed because she had no idea how on the nose those comments were.

"I feel as if someone reached into my chest and tore out my heart," I confessed, tears clogging my throat. More than Mama, Elena was someone I had gone to for advice. Mama was the shoulder to cry on, but my eldest sister was the one who would pick up a sword and fight for me.

"I'll make this contract so ironclad, Oscar Hampton will be obliterated from the face of the earth if he so much as breathes a word of the sex tape to anyone."

I exhaled a sharp chuckle. "Have I mentioned you are beautiful and terrifying?"

"It's a well-earned reputation," she acknowledged. "Have I mentioned you are loving and deserving of the whole world? I'm not sure Adam and Linnea were that for you, but if they were, I am so sorry, Seb."

"I recovered from heartbreak once before," I joked lamely, but God, this felt different.

Adam seemed different this time, older and wiser, more willing to consider the options than act in a blind panic. Linnea made it different, us and the situation. She wouldn't want to let me go. My girl was a fighter just like a Lombardi.

"Come back to New York when this is done," Elena suggested. "Come visit Rora and the twins, they miss their *zio* Sebastian."

She meant she missed me, and she wanted to be the one to watch over me protectively as I grieved.

"I might go to England to see Cosima," I mentioned even though the thought hadn't occurred to me until just then.

She was due with triplets any moment so she couldn't come to me, and I found myself desperately needing the solace and intimacy of my twin sister. She would understand everything without me having to find the words for the bloody massacre in my chest. She would tuck me up in one of those opulent bedrooms in her British manor home and lavish me with tea and treats and so much attention that I'd never feel alone even in such an enormous house.

I needed that more than I needed Elena's sharp watchfulness or Mama's mothering or Giselle's quiet company and understanding.

I needed Cosima to smother away the loneliness yawning open in my chest like an insurmountable crater.

"I can take some vacation time," Elena suggested. "I'd like to be there to meet the babies when they come."

"Okay," I said quietly because I wanted that, too.

Years ago, we hadn't been able to stand each other, but love had changed Elena just as it had changed me, then and now.

"Will you be okay?" she asked.

"No," I admitted on a raw laugh. "But they're waiting for me, now. At least I have tonight to say goodbye."

It was 4 a.m. in New York City, and my big sister had answered the phone on the first ring. She hurt for me, and it was obvious when she said, "Call me when it's finished. No matter what time, *d'accordo*? I'll be here."

"*Ti amo, sorella mia*," I told her as tears burned my eyes but didn't fall.

I love you, my sister.

"*Insieme sempre*," she responded, together always.

It had been our safe words as children when we needed to hide from the mafiosos circling our father, Seamus, like carrion crows.

In moments like this, it felt like a hallelujah.

Even when I felt like I was staring down the barrel of gun,

knowing I wouldn't be spending the rest of my life with the people I loved, I had a reminder that I'd never be truly alone.

THERE WERE CANDLES EVERYWHERE, but since it was California, even though it was only early March, they were flameless vessels with battery-powered ambient light. Strewn across the sand at the base of the narrow beach in front of Adam's property, they illuminated the night like stars fallen from the night sky above.

They spilled warm golden light on the two golden-haired beauties lounging on a black velvet blanket on the sand. They seemed like something from a fever dream, skin glowing, limbs tangled and undulating slowly like the waves rocking softly into the shore, their naked bodies alternatively hard and lush, perfect as usually only exists in the imagination.

But they were here.

They were real.

And they were waiting for me.

None of us said a word as they unclasped their bodies and rolled to their knees to wait for me to approach. As soon as I was in their reach, they disrobed me as if it were part of a sacred ritual, kissing every inch of skin they uncovered, smoothing their hands along the curves of muscle in my arms and legs, testing the weight of balls and the heft of my thickening cock.

Only when I was naked did they push me to the blanket. I settled between Adam's spread legs, my back against his chest, his erection flush across my spine, while Linnea climbed into my lap. Sandwiched between them, their hearts beating on either side of my chest, I almost started to cry.

It felt like something holy. A kind of love that transcended language and was spoken only through flesh and blood and bone.

"I wanted to tell you this under the moonlight," Adam said into my ear, rubbing his nose into the hair over my temple and pausing to breathe deeply, as if my fragrance was a drug he could get high off. "I wanted to hold you skin to skin while I told you the truest thing I've ever known."

His arms wound around me, one diagonally across my chest to rest his palm against my heart, and the other banded over my hips as if he wanted to fuse us.

"I love you, Sebastian," he said directly into my ear as if he didn't want any space between us to sully it. "I loved you then and I love you now in a way I know in my bones and marrow I'll never stop. I live a half-life without you, and I never want to experience that pain again. I wish I had the watch to give you, to show you how serious I am, but maybe one day I can give you a ring."

He sucked in a deep breath that I mimicked because I had forgotten to breathe until just then.

"I told you once that I would love you until the end of time, and I meant it," Adam continued. "I still want your impossible universe. Only now, Linnea had reminded me that it doesn't have to be impossible. One day, maybe years from now, I'm going to put a gold ring on your finger that matches your eyes, and you, me, and Linnea will exchange vows on the beach and vow to love each other forever even though we already have and always would." He swallowed thickly. "I hope one day, when we can walk away from the fame and film, we can have a family with children who look like you and never stop moving like our *trottolina*. I have this mad hope in my heart that you want that with me, with us, too. But even if you don't, you have always been my North Star, lighting up my life and leading me along the right path, the truest one to happiness. My Polaris."

"I don't want there to be an us without you," Linnea added, stroking her hand down my neck, pressing forward so her breasts were crushed against my chest and Adam's arms, her legs twined around my back and Adam's hips so we were as conjoined as three could be. "I think I fell in love with you at sixteen before I ever really knew you because I could see your heart in your eyes, and it spoke to me in a way no one ever had before. Most people never find their soulmates, and somehow, I've been lucky enough to find two."

She pressed her forehead to mine, and I swallowed my heart as it tried to leap up my throat and go to her. I raised my hands to cup her face and smoothed my thumbs over her cheekbones, trying to find the words under the crushing grief in my chest.

To be given the gift of these two hearts, knowing I would have to break them in the morning, was damnation befitting Dante's ninth circle of hell.

"*Seite il mio universo*," I told her in Italian. "You are my universe. Both of you. The moon and sun that redefine my sense of gravity. No matter what happens, please, promise me—swear to me—you know I love you both madly and eternally."

Adam made a pained sound in his throat a second before he was moving up and flipping out from under me to press me down to the ground by the shoulders so he could kiss me. Only Linnea was already there, her tongue in my mouth. We made room for him there, kissing each other in a way I had never done before, sharing breath and tongue and nipping lips until our bodies were warm and slick with sweat. Their hands wandered over me, tracing the same skin they had touched earlier, testing the firmness of my abdominals, squeezing their fingers around my cock until it was sheathed in their touch. They aroused me so sinuously, I was close to coming before I even realized how they'd done it.

I blinked dazedly up at the moon in the starry sky as they lowered their mouths to my groin and took turns sucking my dick, and I thanked whatever God might have ruled the heavens that I could have this.

Even if it was just for a night.

Then, unwilling to miss the sight of two golden heads laving my cock, I tipped my head down to watch them take their pleasure from sucking me. Adam held me by the base and offered my flush, plum-purple tip to Linnea, who sucked on it like a lollipop, swirling her tongue to suck up the leaking precum, paying special attention to the tender underside of the head.

"*Cazzo*," I cursed softly as she pulled off, shared a salacious, open-mouthed kiss with Adam, and then used a hand in his hair to force him down on my shaft.

He took me to the root in one easy move, his throat swollen with the length of me. I watched and felt as he swallowed around me and fought the urge to jerk my hips up and choke him.

"It's okay," Linnea soothed. "You can fuck his face."

"Jesus," I hissed as I carefully thrust into his throat. Linnea held his head steady as I slowly picked up the pace.

My cock made obscenely wet noises as it tunneled over his tongue and into his throat again and again. Linnea reached down to roll my balls in her hand and then spat on her fingers before trailing them over the seam of my scrotum to my hole beneath. Her face was suffused with lust as she rubbed them over my rim, dipping just the tip of her finger inside me.

Adam pulled off my cock only long enough to grab a bottle of lube by his hip and hand it to Linnea. "Stretch him open for me."

My hips canted at the thought, and Linnea smiled wickedly as she coated her fingers in cool lube and reached back between my cheeks in earnest. Adam resumed sucking on my cock as Linnea's long, narrow fingers slid inside me. I hissed as she twisted them, rubbing against my wall until she found my prostate, banging against it almost clumsily before she found a rhythm that made me writhe.

"God, you're sexy," she breathed as she watched me with low lids. "I'm leaking down my thigh watching Adam suck you while I fuck you."

I cursed viciously in Italian.

"That's it," she encouraged, wedging another finger inside me so I hissed at the stretch and burn. "Take everything we have to give you."

A shiver of embarrassment to be laid out like this and fucked by a woman's fingers only heightened my arousal. It felt wrong in a way that was decidedly right, and I fucking loved it.

"Good girl fucking him for me," Adam praised in a cock-ravaged voice as he slurped off my cock and watched Linnea finger fuck me. "Let me show you what he likes."

He moved a hand between the cheeks to place it over Linnea's, parting her fingers slightly so he could reach inside me at the same time. A long, low moan of a dying man escaped my throat as Adam's thick fingers slid inside me alongside hers.

"There, see how he likes to be filled up," Adam said in that conversational tone that made me fucking wild. "Does that feel good, sweet Seb?"

"*Che cazzo, si*," I moaned.

Adam laughed coldly. "You know you've hit the right spot when he forgets to speak English."

I swore again as my hips pumped desperately against their thrusting fingers. I didn't know how many were inside me anymore, but the stretch of fullness made the backs of my teeth ache and still I wanted me.

When they pulled out of me in tandem, I let out a growling protest that made them both laugh breathless.

"Hush, Sebastian, or I won't give you what you want," Adam scolded me, then picked up the lube and handed it to Linnea again. "Get me wet enough to slide right inside him."

Linnea shivered, fingers trembling as she coated Adam's bludgeon of a cock in lube, working her hand along the shaft almost reverently.

"You're so big. I can't believe he can take this in his tight hole," Linnea murmured.

"It's a snug fit," Adam agreed, "but he likes to struggle to take it all. Don't you, Sebastian?"

"Fuck, yes," I agree through my teeth.

"Put me in," Adam told Linnea, who had her tongue between her teeth, cheeks flushed to crimson as Adam maneuvered between my thighs, and she guided his broad tip to my worked-open hole.

"All the way in to the root," he instructed so she kept hold of my shaft as he started to work himself into my narrow channel.

I grunted as he drove into me stubborn inch by stubborn inch until finally, Linnea's fingers let go of his base, and he was seated to the hilt inside me.

Stars spun behind my closed lids as I adjusted to the brutal intrusion. For a moment, I couldn't find room to breathe around his girth, but then I remembered to sink into the sensation, and Linnea's clever fingers found my cock, coaxing it with a few strokes into fullness again.

A moan ripped from my throat as Adam worked his hips, slow thrusts out to the tip and hard drives that lashed my prostate like a match to a strike pad.

"Sebastian can't seem to stay quiet," Adam mused, the sweat beading along his hairline the only outward sign of his Olympian restraint. "Sit on his face for me, Sunbeam, and shut him up."

Linnea gave my dick one last, lingering stroke, dipping the tip of her finger into my slit to play with the bubbling precum there, before crawling up my body and swinging her long legs over my face. The scent of her pussy made my mouth water, but the sight of the wetness leaking down either side of her thighs made my cock twitch helplessly on my stomach.

"*Deliziosa*," I praised, before dragging my tongue through her sweet slickness. "Delicious."

"Sit on it, Linnea," Adam reiterated. "I want him to suffocate in that pretty pink cunt."

She ground down on my tongue, facing Adam so that she could watch him fuck me as she started to ride my face the way he rode my ass.

It was nirvana, a pleasure so intense it felt like there was pure lightning in my veins and thunder rolling through my hips, threatening to split down the middle.

Adam shifted, hooking one of my legs over his arm for a deeper angle that had me gasping into Linnea's swollen folds. I could breathe as I sucked on her clit, channeling some of this restless, burning pleasure into making her come.

"Do you see how much he loves this?" Adam kept up his almost businesslike conversation with Linnea as he took me apart with his wide, brutal cock. "How he jumps like *this* when I hit that spot inside me. Do you see how his cock is drooling all over his abs?"

Thick fingers smeared through the cum trails, and I knew by the sounds of sucking that Adam had offered them to Linnea.

"Doesn't he taste divine?" Adam asked darkly. "Do you like having his cum in your mouth while you come in his?"

She gave a sharp little cry, and I thought he might have been playing with her sensitive nipples because seconds later, she flooded me with cum. I lapped it up like a man dying of thirst, sucking on her labia, drilling my tongue straight into the source to lick up every last drop.

"Good girl," Adam praised her and then, his hand palming my throat and squeezing, he told me, "Good fucking boy."

"Lean over and clean up this sloppy cock," he commanded Linnea, and a moment later, she was bent over, her tongue rolling over my precum-glossed head and shaft.

She followed the trail to my groin, cleaning it with long, moaning licks before rolling her tongue along my head. I had never had head before the way Linnea sucked cock. It was clear she loved it, her lips sensitive, an oral fixation making her groan as she slid me to the back of her throat and swallowed me down to the root. I could feel her cunt leaking copiously as if nothing turned her on more than fucking me into her throat while Adam pegged my prostate like he had been built to do nothing else.

My bones vibrated like a tuning fork had struck them, every inch humming and thrumming, every atom bumping together like I was seconds from exploding and losing everything I was to this nuclear pleasure.

"Please, please," I begged, unaware I was even doing so.

"Hush and be a good boy," Adam told her firmly. "Don't come yet. I'm busy using this hole. Linnea is busy sucking your dick, and she likes to see me fuck you, don't you?"

"Yes," she whispered, her voice rough from taking my dick. "I fucking love watching him take you. He was made to be fucked."

"He was," Adam agreed proudly, running a proprietary hand down the inside of my thigh to raise my other leg over his shoulder.

A flare of embarrassment worked through me at being held open like that and held steady so I could take every inch of his shaft exactly how he wanted me to take it. But the twinge of shame only highlighted the desire, like kerosene on a bonfire.

"I'm going to fuck you so often this arse will always be ready for my dick," Adam continued. "I'll just have to fuck my fingers into Linnea's juicy cunt and coat myself in her cum before driving inside your loose hole whenever I want to. Bent over the kitchen island at breakfast so I can make you scream loud enough that even Bruce and Chaucer will know you're being fucked. Tied to my bed when you wake up, already filled with me, and Linnea's tight heat wrapped around your dick as we both use you to come."

"*Merda*, Adam, I'm going to come," I warned him as the fantasies scrolled across my active imagination. I couldn't unclench my teeth or breathe too deeply, or I would spill down Linnea's throat.

"Not yet. You can take more. Let us play with you."

I felt as if I was already climaxing, a rolling, bone-rumbling orgasm that would never end, even though I couldn't breathe properly, and I would probably die smothered in Linnea's gorgeous pussy.

"I-I can't take it," I ground out, arching into Adam's brutal thrusts, each one sparking hot shards of pleasure up my spine. "I'm going to come. I have to. *Cazzo, Adamo, per favore.*"

"There it is, the Italian," he stated triumphantly. "Okay, boy, you can come for us. Linnea, if you spill a drop, we'll have to punish you. Drink it all down."

"Fuck," I roared into Linnea's inner thigh as Adam swiveled his hips, rubbing the crown of his thick head against my prostate until my mind burst into light and my cock exploded down Linnea's tight throat.

She hummed as she swallowed everything I had to give her, emptying my balls into that tight, vibrating squeeze.

The orgasm wouldn't end, every one of my muscles clenching and releasing so hard I couldn't think or breathe or do anything but come and come. It was almost horrifying, an existential dread that I would lose myself to the pleasure, every atom combusting into dust. But this was the way I would have chosen to die—one last play with these two, filled with their taste and scent and touch.

And then Adam was fucking me harder, ruthlessly pegging me so that my legs shook, and my cock kept spitting dribbles of cum when I thought I had no more to give, and it seemed truly as if this was how it would end. Tears pushed against my closed lids and leaked down my cheeks, and I wasn't sure if it was from the blinding heat or the heartbreak that already cracked my soul in two.

"I'm going to fill this gorgeous, tight arse full of cum," he growled. "And when it starts to leak out of you, Linnea is going to fuck it back inside with her fingers. Maybe she'll even want to eat me out of this swollen hole."

Linnea panted through her own orgasm as she licked a weak spurt of cum dribbling down the side of my shaft and rode my tongue, spilling sweet cum into my mouth that I swallowed down like ambrosia.

I could have luxuriated in the peaceful, thoughtless high for the rest of my life, tangled with the two bodies that had become, in two short months, my new gravity.

But Adam wasn't done yet.

"Flip around and get on your knees," I heard him tell Linnea from my floating subspace.

The exactingness of his tone, that ironclad authority, sent a fission of new tension down my spine. I cracked open my eyes to see Linnea straddling my face, hovering over my face as she raised her ass to show Adam her swollen, drenched cunt. I watched as he pushed three fingers into that snug heat almost brutally, wedging them inside her and curling them into her front wall in a way that made her keen like an animal.

"Do you see how greedy she is, Sebastian?" Adam asked me as his fingers squelched in that juicy pussy, the sound lewd and mouth-watering. "She came twice on your tongue, but it's not enough, is it, Linnea? You need something big and hard stretching out this eager little cunt."

"Yes," she said, shivering and bucking her hips back against him.

My mouth hung open as I panted, relishing the front-row show of Adam ruthlessly fingering her. He slipped another finger into her entrance, twisted them deeper, and rubbed a thumb over her cum-slicked asshole.

Linnea's head dropped between her shoulders, and she cried out, the sound almost pained but utterly desperate.

My cock twitched and started, slowly, to fill.

"Do you need to be filled up, sweet thing?" Adam crooned. "Tell me."

"Yes," Linnea moaned as I turned my head to lick some of the cum up her thigh where it had leaked nearly down to her knees. "I want to be so full of cock I can't breathe."

A shivery sharp inhale and then a long, bone-rattling moan. I could see that Adam's thumb was inside her hole, lubed only by the copious amounts of her cum turning the place between her thighs wet as an oil slick, his fingers filling her up in both places.

Adam looked down at me, caught the way I had to lick away the drool that pooled to the side of my mouth, and his grin was a terrifying and beautiful expression. To see him in full Dominant mode, to watch the way his calculated eyes took every inch of us in and computed how best to turn us inside out was a thing of absolute wonder.

"Do you want inside her, Seb? I think you deserve it by being such a good plaything for us just now."

I had to be careful because he could be mean in this mood. Make me tell him that I wanted nothing more than to slide my hardening dick inside Linnea's sweet holes only to have him fuck her in front of me and forbid me from touching her myself.

"Only if you think I deserve it," I told him. "Sir."

Arousal rolled over him, blowing his eyes to black, his breath hitching in his lungs as he continued to play Linnea with his fingers like a maestro. He ignored her cries and juddering hips as if it wasn't about her pleasure, and I could tell she loved it because her knees were shaking on either side of my head.

"Come, help me take her apart," he said.

My hands were around her hips, yanking her back down onto my tongue before the last word was even spoken, licking around the stretch of Adam's fingers inside her. When he drew them away from her pussy to focus on her ass, I didn't need his instruction to fold my own fingers inside her, one, then two, then three, then four until she gasped and came suddenly on a cry like her own pleasure scared her.

Above me, Adam worked open her ass.

"Hush now," he told her, petting her hip as if soothing a horse as she cried out mindlessly through his climax. "Sebastian and I are going to fill you up. I know you're desperate for it but hold still while we fuck you open with our fingers first. We're both big for these little holes, and it's going to be hard for you to take us to the root, but you will just to please us, won't you?"

"Yes, sir," she panted, humping shamelessly back against us. "Please, please, please."

"It's time for us to claim you as ours," Adam continued darkly as he pushed another finger inside her, three in her ass and four in her cunt. We moved our wrists in tandem, fucking in one hole and out the other. "Ours for today, tomorrow, and the rest of time. Our sweet, eager little slut. If all it takes is our fingers to make you come this hard, what will you do impaled on both our cocks?"

My dick was so hard, it ached again, spitting cum like drool into my belly button. Adam reached down with his free hand to circle his fingers around the base and squeezed almost painfully.

"Sebastian is rock-hard at the thought of fucking this swollen, open pussy. Do you want to put him out of his misery?" he asked her.

She seemed beyond words now, just a shivering, quaking mess of wet flesh and a racing heart.

Adam laughed darkly as she hummed with approval, and roughly pulled out of her ass. She made a disconsolate sound that he ignored as he tugged her hips down, releasing my fingers from her sucking heat.

He kept hold of my cock with one too tight fist and held Linnea up over it with one strong hand, lining us up and rubbing me back and forth through her swollen folds. Back and forth like a hypnotist with a pendulum, lulling us both into an aching kind of surrender to a friction that wasn't nearly enough.

We both knew not to beg.

"My lovely toys," Adam murmured as he played us against each other, his voice finally rough and raw with lust.

And we were.

His to play with, to use, to fuck open however he saw fit.

How had I ever believed I could live without this?

How could I go on knowing I would never have this again?

Adam forced the impending doom from my thoughts by suddenly impaling Linnea on my cock. My hips jerked, driving even deeper into her pussy, which was so swollen that only the second thrust took me to the hilt. Linnea cried out, her hands flying to my chest where her nails cut perfect half-moons into my pecs. The sparks of pain turned to fire as they trailed to my groin.

Before either of us could adjust to the sensation, Adam was bending Linnea in half over top of me, pressing her head down by a hand around her neck so he could climb between my thighs and unceremoniously press the tip of his wide shaft into her ass.

I could feel the movement of him driving ruthlessly deeper, inch by inch, filling her so full that there was no room for me to move. Linnea's face beside mine was flushed crimson and slicked with sweat, her blond hair damp with it, lips puffy from biting them to hold in her moans, from sucking my cock.

She was gorgeous.

Perfect.

As given over to the pleasure and experience as I was, as Adam was.

There was no coaxing her out of her shell to enjoy this hedonism with us.

She was born to take us inside her, to make us wild enough with lust that we lost touch with our humanity and fucked her like dogs in heat.

That she so obviously loved it, crying out in euphoria as Adam worked his impossibly big cock into her ass, alongside mine in her pussy, proved what I had already known.

She was perfect for us.

Honest and gorgeous and voracious for pleasure in a way that meant I knew we would never get tired of this. We could fuck in this iteration and any other permutation for the rest of our lives, and it wouldn't be enough.

This intimacy, this feeling of being wholly connected to another person, mind, body and soul.

I pressed my mouth to hers and tasted her tongue as her cries fell onto it.

"Good girl." I praised her as my hands gripped her hips, linking with Adam's on one side as he held tight. "Let Adam open your tight ass."

"He's s-so fucking massive," she whimpered, trying to press away from the intrusion on instinct.

We held her still to take it.

"*Brava ragazza*," I praised. "Good girl taking us both. Don't you want us to be balls-deep in you? Don't you want us to fill you up with cum?"

Her moan rattled through her chest, and she found the will to seal her mouth fully over mine, lashing me with her eager tongue.

I took that as a *yes*.

"Fuck her with me, Sebastian," Adam ground out as he fucked the last inch of his dick inside her and ground against her ass.

The feel of him through the thin wall separating us made me dizzy, but as we both pulled out to the tip, dragging slowly through her clutching heat, I found I couldn't breathe.

"Let's take her apart," Adam instructed.

And we did.

Back and forth, ebb and flow, drive and pull.

Nothing existed but this timeless act, the instinctive drive to fuck my lovers until my sense of self dissolved in the flames of our passion and I was reborn as something other.

Something that was wholly theirs.

The stars seemed to glow above us, pinwheels of brightness in the dark sky, the moon a witness to the sacred way we took each other apart.

Linnea came, and we didn't stop for even a second.

When she came again, Adam pressed her deeper into my torso so our sweat-slick skin slid together and he could reach our mouths. He kissed her and then kissed me, her on the instroke, me on the outstroke.

This is it, I thought as Linnea's sixth orgasm tore through her, and Adam ate the cry from her lips, *this is why I'm alive*.

"Come for me," Adam told me as he broke from Linnea, feeling my hips stutter in our rhythm. "Come for her. I want us to brand her from the inside out with our cum."

That was all it took.

One last thrust and I was breaking apart, melding with her, with him, until I felt I could hear their individual heartbeats, their names sweet as honey in my mouth as I shouted through the climax.

When Adam came moments later, he pulled out of her ass to do it, holding Linnea down on top of me, pinning me in the process so that he could jack off onto the place my cock still spilled seed into her pussy. The splash of his hot cum against my balls and the nearly swollen, closed clutch of her cunt made Linnea and me both climax a little harder.

I held her close as she shivered in the comedown, peppering her face with kisses because her breath was ragged, and I knew how hard it was to get back into your own skin after subspace took you spiraling to the heavens. Adam's big, rough hand gently massaged his cum into her pussy, working it up inside her along my softening cock, over my balls and taint before he collected the semen he'd earlier pumped into my ass that had leaked out and fucked it softly back inside me.

"Wow," Linnea breathed when Adam finally stopped his smug playing and rolled to the blanket beside me, taking her by the hip to land her carefully between our bodies. It was only then I realized she was crying, soundless tears dripping down her beautiful cheeks.

I cupped one, rubbing my thumb through the salty trails. "Are you okay, *trottolina, amore*? Was it too much?"

She shook her head fiercely, and her eyes, when they pierced mine, were bright with tears and bone-deep contentment. "It was perfect."

"Yes," Adam agreed on a long sigh, holding her from behind and reaching up above her head for my hand. The moment I gave it to him, he twined our fingers. "Paradise, I think, isn't so much a place as it is a person." There was a smile in his voice as he added, "Two people who redefine my universe. Nothing feels so impossible with you."

"I love you both," Linnea said softly as if her throat couldn't bear the weight of the words. "So much, it scares me."

"It scares me, too," Adam admitted, raising on an elbow so I could finally see his beloved face. "I could end entire galaxies with what I feel for you."

"There's no need for that," I murmured in a threadbare voice as reality rushed back in and I remembered this was the last time I would hold them like this, love them like this. Just as we began, we were already ended. The tragedy of it threatened to eat me alive. "I just want you to love me enough to create one universe. That impossible universe where we can be together."

It was cruel to say so when I knew that future was already dead in the water, but my words lit those two pairs of eyes, one verdant green and the other the color of purpled twilight, with so much love I could feel it on my skin like sunlight.

Linnea drew her fingernail across the skin over my heart, biting deep enough for me to hiss. I didn't object, though, watching her concentration as she drew one circle through another and then another, all three overlapping almost like a bastardized Venn diagram.

"The three of us," she told me, pressing her palm to the small heart, her gaze hot on my face, tears cooling on her cheeks that made me realize I had tears on mine, too.

"One day," Adam vowed, leaning over Linnea to press his own hand over hers on my heart, his expression reverent and solemn as if taking vows before a congregation. "One day."

And only I knew that day would never come.

CHAPTER THIRTY–TWO

SEBASTIAN

Sunrise came too early, spilling pale tangerine light over the shimmering waves and touching my toes like a warm kiss. It did little to heat the coldness emanating from my heart turning my body to ice where I lay enfolded in the bodies of my lovers. I had the morbid thought I would have liked to be entombed like this, after death, in a tangle of Adam's and Linnea's limbs until we all turned to dust.

This morning felt like a death, so I took a moment to lie in my coffin and remember all of the beautiful moments that had led to this. Seeing Linnea for the first time in so long in a yellow sundress in the middle of the interview that threw me back into Adam's orbit. Realizing that the girl I had considered one of my best friends since she was sixteen was now a woman I could easily fall in love with. Showing up at Adam's house and pretending that I didn't ache every time he looked at me or breathed or moved. Concocting the scheme that, in hindsight, had been more than a little selfish, my subconscious last-ditch attempt to bring me closer to Adam, to heal hurts in him and Linnea that weren't mine to heal.

They would treat each other well, I knew, and their grief over losing me wouldn't rip them apart the way it had done with Adam and Savannah. Instead, it would knit them closer, Linnea's clever hands sewing them together in a way I was sure could not be undone.

If I let her, I knew she would do the same with me.

I had to get up before they woke.

But we had turned to each other so much in the night, my body was sore in ways it had never hurt before, and every atom of my being resisted the idea of moving out from under their warm, heavy bodies.

Only the thought of saving Adam and Linnea from Oscar eventually got me moving.

Because if the sex tape released, it wouldn't just impact Adam, but Linnea, too. The speculation around her being his beard or her being stupid enough to marry a gay man—because bi-erasure was alive and kicking—would hurt her career and their relationship.

I held my breath as I maneuvered away from them, and then froze when Adam cracked an eye open to regard me with sleepy confusion.

"I have to use the restroom," I lied, and the words hurt coming up.

He grunted, curling around Linnea. "Hurry back."

I closed my eyes a second after his closed and fought back the sob that lodged in my throat. Giving in to one last impulse, I leaned forward to kiss Linnea's forehead and then found Adam watching me from one squinted green eye.

"I love you in any universe," I told him before kissing him lightly as if I would do as he said and hurry back.

"I love you in this one, my Polaris," he replied firmly, cupping the back of my head to bring me in for a harder, longer kiss. The nickname scored through me as deeply as the kiss did. "If you aren't back in ten minutes, I'll drag you back here. I intend to have you both again when the sun is properly up."

"Yes, sir," I agreed with a lopsided smile and then waited until his hand dropped and he closed his eyes to get up and collect my clothes.

I dressed beside them but for my shoes and then slowly climbed the wooden staircase built into the cliffside to reach the house. It was empty and dark inside, too early even for Bruce to be in the kitchen or Chaucer to be up for her endless errands. I collected my belongings from Adam's spacious suite as quickly and quietly as I could.

The streets of Los Angeles were quiet, too, as I drove back into town toward the hotel I'd barely used in the last week. Blurry-eyed and hollow-souled, I left my car with the valet and shuffled into the elevator.

I thought about calling Elena and decided I would do that after I booked flights to England and got a few more hours of sleep.

So I wasn't prepared to open my hotel door and find Savannah Richardson sitting on my bed.

I rubbed my eyes hard to erase the vision, and when that didn't work, I merely stared at her.

"Hello, Sebastian," she said softly, hands clasped in her lap, face devoid of its usual makeup.

In fact, her hair was pulled back at the crown in a kind of ponytail, the short ends escaping at the bottom, and her outfit was a subdued cashmere knit set in stone that she normally wouldn't wear out of the house. She looked…soft. Soft and sad. A half-erased sketch of the person she usually was.

"What are you doing here?" I asked, and my voice sounded strange in my ears, almost combative.

I guessed I was at the end of my very long rope.

Her smile fell flat on her face, and she gestured to the suitcase I just now noticed huddled in the corner of the suite.

"I left him," she whispered. "I left Tate."

I blinked, suddenly unsteady on my feet as if I had been hit in the head.

I wondered if perhaps I had.

Because this was too surreal to process.

"*Scusa?*" I asked, forgetting English.

"I left Tate," she said again, more firmly this time as she tilted her chin up to meet my eyes with steely determination. "For you."

"For me," I echoed.

"For Christ's sake, Sebastian, *yes,* for you," she snapped, then smoothed a hand over her disheveled hair. "Of course, for you."

"I don't think there is any 'of course' about it," I protested. "I asked you weeks ago to be with me, and you showed me the door."

Cazzo, that seemed like such a very long time ago.

I had been holding on to her ghost for so long that it hadn't even felt like a death when I'd given her up because I had already mourned for years.

It was different with Adam. I hadn't been able to speak to him for loving him and being unable to have him. Living without him had been like breathing through an open wound because I'd loved him with a part of my soul Savannah had never seen fit to reach out for.

I had never been able to reconcile the loss of Savvy because the trauma of leaving the Meyers had felt so monumental, and she was an easier substitute as a part for the whole. She'd been easier to love, in a way, easier to fantasize about a future with because she was a woman, and I'd always been attracted to women, but also because she'd done it. She'd left him! Which seemed like the logical first step in being with me. So I'd never understood how she could have done that and not come to me.

I could never reconcile that hole blown through my heart, and I'd thought it would remain empty forever. But I couldn't have known Linnea would rise in my life like the sun in the east, utterly eradicating the long shadows cast by my troubled past, and that I would grow to love her the way I did. I couldn't have ever dreamed, even in my impossible universe, that the way I'd love Savannah would be a mere shadow of the way my heart was devoted to Linnea.

Just because she was the only thing that had ever made sense to me didn't mean that she was the only thing to exist.

I couldn't ever have conceived how loving Linnea could open the door to loving Adam again, when I'd thought it was forever closed and locked to me.

Yet none of that mattered now.

Because Oscar Hampton had closed the door on that future for me.

Fury writhed like snakes in my gut. I just wanted Savannah to leave so I could go to bed and cry in peace like a real man.

I knew now that she had never loved me.

Not like Adam did in ways enormous enough to terrify.

Not like Linnea did, as if I was as elemental to her as the stars in the midnight sky.

Polaris, Adam had called me last night.

Their North Star.

"Savvy," I said, voice weary. "If you're having problems with Tate, you should work through them. He loves you, and he deserves a chance to fight for you."

"And don't I deserve a chance to fight for you anymore?" she countered, standing up to stalk to me and poke a finger into my chest. Her indignation and passion shocked me out of my stupor slightly. "Why do you get to make grand declarations and not me? I just *left my husband for you*, Sebastian. Do you understand what that means?"

"Do you?" I countered, brows raised.

"It means I love you," she shouted, shoving two hands into my chest and pushing hard enough to rock me back on my heels. "I love you, you fool, and I have since I met you even though it's screwed up my plans."

My laugh was a series of empty shell cases pinging to the floor. "And it hasn't disrupted mine? If you are here to make me feel guilty, I won't have it. All I have ever done is try to love you and be good to you."

"You have been," she said, suddenly so gentle it almost gave me whiplash. Her big, blue eyes were wide with sincerity. It occurred to me that though she was eighteen years older than Linnea, in so many ways she seemed more immature. "I don't care what it does to my plans or my life. I don't care about any of it anymore. I have to have you."

"Is this because of Linnea and Adam?" I asked because I knew she had a feeling I was involved with them again.

Her mouth thinned for a moment before her eyes limned in tears. "It has to do with this," she declared, pulling something from her pocket.

My watch.

The Patek Philippe Celestial the Meyerses had given me in London.

My fingers shook slightly as I took it from her and flipped it over to read the inscription on the back.

For the man who wants to move the sun and the stars.

When I looked up at Savvy again, I felt a hairline fracture in my already broken heart, just a crack for her to wedge into, one hammered there by long-lost hope.

"That watch was a promise," she told me earnestly, taking my numb hands in hers, the watch between our fingers, "to love you in a way that rearranged the universe so that we could be together forever, no matter the obstacles between us. I wanted to give that back to you so you would know I meant it this time. I want us to be together no matter what it takes. I want to be your *duchessa* again. I want to love you again."

My universe felt as though it had been flipped on its head. I couldn't make sense of what was happening in the wake of grief I felt leaving Adam and Linnea, but a part of me that had existed for ten years reared its retired head and looked at Savannah's proposal with eager eyes.

This was all I'd ever wanted once, for a very, very long time.

And in the wake of losing Adam and Linnea, was there room to find solace with an old love? Could we mean anything to each other again?

The whisper of an eighteen-year-old boy who spoke in my own voice whispered, *yes.*

Even though my shattered heart screamed no.

They would never forgive me for taking up with Savannah again.

But maybe that wasn't a bad thing?

How else could I convince them that what we were was over than to move along with the one woman they couldn't stand?

They had to believe I was done with them. At least until I could try to figure out a way to fuck Oscar over without him fucking *them* over. And they were both too loving, too eternal to take my leaving lying down.

I stared at the watch and thought about the kind of love that moved the sun and the stars.

The kind of love I had for them.

"Okay," I told Savannah as I shifted my wrist for her to put the watch on me. "How do you feel about a trip to England?"

The End For Now.

Sign up for my newsletter to receive the **epilogue!**
The Stars & Their Sky comes out December 2025! Add it to your TBR
here.

Need to vent?
If you want to stay up to date on news about new releases and bonus
content like extended epilogues, JOIN MY READER'S GROUP,
Giana's Darlings on Facebook!

If you loved Sebastian's story, make sure you check out his siblings'
stories starting with Giselle in *The Frenchman*!

Meet Sebastian's sister, Giselle, and her enigmatic billionaire in The Frenchman!

Is a week of passion enough to warrant changing my life forever?
He was the most beautiful man I'd ever seen.
An enigmatic French businessman with auburn hair, blue eyes, and an intensity that stirred something deep inside me that hadn't previously been woken.
I wanted him instantly.
And for some reason, he seemed to want me too.
Only, he wasn't mine to have.
Older, wiser, and infinitely richer with a sophisticated girlfriend back home and no time for a holiday, yet that was exactly what Sinclair proposed.
A seven day, no-strings attached affair on the warm, sultry shores of Cabo San Lucas, Mexico.
I was innocent, naive in the ways of men, but I didn't care.
I had to have him regardless of the consequences.
Even if it meant losing my heart in the process.

THE FRENCHMAN

Rain pounded against the steaming tarmac and the force of the wind slapped each drop against the oval window beside my head so that the grey of the runway, the rolling clouds and the Vancouver skyline blurred into one. The rain calmed my nerves, and I closed my eyes to better hear the tap and whistle of weather outside the tin machine that had – somewhat precariously – carried me from Paris to Vancouver in just fewer than seven and a half hours. We were deplaning a third of the passengers and then refueling to make the last leg of the journey to my final destination, Los Cabos, Mexico.

I took a deep breath and tried to focus on my happy place while the economy passengers filtered off the plane. The flight was necessary and after twenty-four years of travelling, I should have been used to the bump and grind of air travel.

In theory, I was. Before every flight, I waited calmly in the endlessly snaking line to check my bags, greeted the attendant with a genuine smile and agreed that yes, I would have a pleasant flight. It wasn't until I was on the plane, secured in my seat by the tenuous hold of the belt, that the fear kicked into supercharge. I was intensely grateful to my younger brother Sebastian for loaning me the money for the first class flight. At least now, if the plane went down, I would have a bigger seat to cushion the fall.

"You still look a bit green, *cherie*." The middle-aged gentleman beside me leaned forward and offered me his unopened water bottle. "The worst is over, though. I hope someone is picking you up in Mexico, you are in no shape to drive after all of…" He waved politely at the remaining travel sickness bags the flight attendant had passed to me twenty minutes into our flight.

I managed a weak smile for Pierre. He was a fifty-year-old bachelor, quite distinguished really, with steel grey hair and cunning brown eyes. And maybe, under different circumstances, he would have propositioned me. As it was, he had offered to pay someone to switch seats with him when he discovered how sick I was. Failing that, he had settled in with relatively good grace and lectured me on the tricks of international trade law to distract me. Everything considered – I had managed to drool on his Hugo Boss blazer while I dozed between throwing up – I was grateful to him.

"No, but I'll catch a taxi to the resort." At the moment, I wasn't looking forward to my enforced vacation. All I wanted was to step off the plane back in my familiar Paris and slip into the small wrought iron bed in my studio apartment in *St-Germain-des-Prés*.

Pierre nodded and shot me a sidelong look. "Are you going to be alright now?"

He was getting off now to visit his daughter and newborn grandson. He didn't like North America, and I got the feeling he was lingering just to eke out a few more words in his native tongue before switching to English.

I nodded meekly but before I could respond the deeper voice of someone behind us spoke, "If you will allow me, I think you are leaving her in capable hands."

I opened my eyes when Pierre nudged me indelicately with his elbow and cleared his throat. Immediately, I blinked.

The man who stood before us dominated the entire aisle. His dusky golden skin stretched taut over his strong features, almost brutally constructed of steeply angled cheekbones and a bladed nose. I had only the vague impression that he was tall and lean because his eyes, a deep and electric blue like the night sky during a lightning storm, held me arrested. The way he held himself, the power of his lean build, and the look in those eyes reminded me of a wolf, caged within the confines of civility but eternally savage.

"I'm sure she would be delighted." Pierre sent me a barely concealed look telling me to pull it together.

I smiled hesitantly at the gorgeous stranger, aware that I was a mess of clammy skin and melted makeup. "I'm fine, really."

He nodded curtly, his eyes devoid of any real sympathy. "You will be."

Pierre hesitated, his eyes searching my face for reluctance. I smiled at him and took one of his hands between my clammy palms. "*Merci beaucoup pour tu m'aides. J'espere que tu passes un bon temps avec ta fille.*"

I was rewarded with a broad grin before he hastily collected his things and moved towards the front of the plane. I watched him go instead of focusing on the stranger as he took Pierre's abandoned seat, but after a few moments with his eyes hot on my face, I turned to him uneasily.

His thick hair was the color of polished mahogany and curled, overlong, at the base of his neck. My fingers itched to run themselves through the silken mass but instead, I smiled.

"There really is no need to look after me, Monsieur," I continued in French. "I am quite well now."

I squirmed in my seat when he didn't immediately reply. "It's silly really, I've been afraid of planes since I was young."

"Oh?" He crossed his hands, and I noticed that he didn't wear a watch, that his fingers were long and nimble. The freckles on the backs of those strong hands surprised me and I found them strangely appealing. I wanted badly to dig into the bag before my feet for my sketchpad.

Because I was uncomfortable, I nodded empathetically. "I was four when we moved to Puglia for a year and I don't remember the logistics of the move very well, but I remember the plane." I looked at him from the corner of my eye and he nodded encouragingly, his hands steepled in front of his beautifully drawn lips. "It was with some budget airline and the plane itself was barely held together by rusty bolts. I think the captain might have been drunk because we dropped and dipped the whole way through."

"Which airline?" His voice was silky and cool, like the brush of a tie against my skin.

"I don't remember now." I frowned at him. "Why?"

He waved my question out of the air with those deep blue eyes still intent on my face. "Tell me more."

Those are magic words to hear from a man, I think. It unfurls something hidden deep within a woman, something that is habitually scared and insecure. *Tell me more.* It was somehow intimate to hear those words, even from a stranger, *especially* from this stranger.

"My father was in debt so we were basically fleeing." I shrugged but the sharp ache of terror still resounded in my chest when I thought of my mother's despair, my brother's desolation. "Maybe I had caught the flu, or maybe I was scared, but I spent most of the flight losing the contents of my stomach. Needless to say, it wasn't a pleasant trip. Since then, I've travelled a lot, but the feeling never goes away."

"Ah, but flying is a pleasure." He did not smile, and I had the sense he rarely did, but his eyes grew dark with pleasure. "Close your eyes."

"Excuse me?"

"Close your eyes."

I pressed myself to the back of my chair when he leaned into me slightly in order to reach the button on my armrest. My chair tilted back, and I found myself looking up into his lean face, his shoulder still warm against my front.

"Close your eyes," he repeated firmly.

I swallowed twice before doing so. I didn't know his name, where he came from, anything personal to mark him with. But somehow, it was thrilling. To be in the hands of a perfect stranger, to trust him enough to surrender my sight, to allow him to make even the simplest decision for me.

So, I hardly flinched when a blanket covered my chilled feet and was pulled up under my chin. His fingers, ridged with slight callous, brushed against the tender skin of my neck as he tucked me in.

"You are flying," he said quietly, but it felt as though he spoke the words against my ear. "And if you relax, let every muscle loosen, and breathe deeply, there is nothing more soothing than being in the air."

Instead, the pit of my stomach coiled, and I found myself wishing that I was another kind of person, someone who flirted with handsome strangers, who would lean into that firm mouth and take it without a qualm.

"We aren't in the air," I pointed out. "We are in a machine made out of metal that has no business being in the sky."

"Ah, it is the machine that frightens you." I wondered where he sat, if he remained leaning over me. "Let it be a bird then, a swan."

"Okay," I mumbled, suddenly exhausted. "But only because swans are mean."

I smiled at his husky chuckle but fell asleep before he could say anything else.

WHEN I WOKE UP, IT WAS to the delicate tapping of rain against the window and the brisk click of fingers on a keyboard. Deeply rested and disorientated, I moaned and stretched myself across my seat before righting it. Blinking away sleep, I looked up and met the searing eyes of my stranger.

"You had a good rest," he noted, and for some reason, I flushed.

He was even more handsome than before, if that was possible. In the darkening night, his hair was mostly black, kissed red by the artificial overhead lights. He seemed like some creature of the night, something dark and too sexy to be true.

"Yes, thank you." We were speaking in English now and I couldn't remember if we had switched over before I fell asleep. His voice was smooth and cool, perfectly enunciated with just a hint of French charm.

"We land in twenty minutes." He watched my surprise and handed me a plastic cup of sparkling liquid. Our fingers brushed as he passed it off and a current of electricity made my grip on the cup shaky. Quickly, he righted it with his other hand and pressed both of my hands to the plastic. "You've got it?"

I nodded and flexed my fingers under his hold but he remained holding the cup, holding me, for a beat too long. He stared at me with a slight frown between his thick brows but I couldn't begin to discern if it was out of displeasure or surprise. I had never been so attracted to a man in my life, and I wondered if I was imagining the thickening tension between us. My tongue darted out to coat my dry lips and his eyes followed its path intently. Abruptly, his hands were gone and he was sitting back in his seat, his fingers flying on the keyboard of his Blackberry.

I blinked and slowly sank back into my chair. Obviously, I had misread the signs. I took a sip of the sparkling liquid and discovered with delight that it was Ginger Ale. Sipping it slowly to savour the sweet pop of bubbles on my tongue, I turned my attention to the early evening turning into twilight the color of a bruise outside my window. The sparkling lights of Los Cabos could already be seen ahead of us and instead of wondering about the intrepid stranger beside me, I focused on my excitement. I had one week of paradise before I met with reality in New York City.

After five years in Paris and only a handful of visits in that time, I would finally be reunited with my family. The last time we had all lived under the same roof I had been nineteen years old. My twin siblings Cosima and Sebastian had been the first to leave, Cosima when she was seventeen in order to model in Milan and Sebastian months later to England, with Cosima's money in his pocket and a fierce determination to become an actor. I had lived with my mother and eldest sister Elena after that before journeying to Paris.

I squeezed my eyes shut and refused to think about those years. It had been nearly five now since I had left our small life in Napoli to attend *L'École des Beaux-Arts* in Paris. Though I was close to my family, it had been good for me to spend these years apart from them. I was returning home to them a better person than I had been when I had hastily fled and I was both excited and anxious for them to see that.

"What are you smiling at?"

His question was faintly brusque, as if he was irritated with me. When I turned to him though, his eyes were on the glowing screen of his phone.

"I haven't been home in a long time, I'm looking forward to seeing my family again."

"Your husband?" he asked tersely.

I laughed, and it felt so delightful after hours of sickness and sleep that I laughed some more. He watched me with twisted lips, as if he wanted to smile but couldn't understand why. "Was that funny?"

"Oh, not really." I leaned forward conspiratorially. "But one needs a boyfriend to get married and I haven't had one of those in years."

"Now, that is funny." He put his phone back in his pocket and I felt a flash of triumph that he was once more focused on me. "It is incomprehensible to me that you would be single." His eyes sparkled as he leaned forward, and a lock of that overlong hair fell across his golden forehead. "Tell me, other than your obvious fear of flying, what's wrong with you?"

I laughed. "We're almost in Los Cabos, I don't have time to list all my flaws."

"I have a feeling there aren't many," he murmured and stared at me in that way I was discovering he had, of looking through me and at me all at once. "But perhaps it's better that you don't tell me. A woman of mystery," his voice was low and smooth, so captivating I didn't register the pilot ready the plane for landing, "is a seductive thing."

"You had better tell me about yourself then." I leaned back in my seat as the plane began its steep descent into the city. "You're handsome enough already."

His loud chuckle surprised both of us. It was husky with disuse and his expression, though inherently beautiful, was almost pained.

When the sound tapered off, it left him frowning. "What would you like to know?"

"Something repellent," I demanded cheerfully.

"Repellent? That's a tall order." Though normally I was uncomfortable under the eyes of another, those baby blues against my skin invigorated me and I beamed back at him. "When I look at you, I can only think of," his fingers found a lock of my auburn hair and he rubbed it between his fingers to release the scent, "Lavender and honey."

"Well." I cleared my throat. "Happily, we are talking about you."

His grin was wolfish as he leaned back in his seat again. "I make a very good living."

"Ah, you're one of those." His silver cuff links shone even in the dim light of the descending plane. "That helps, I'm more the starving artist type."

"Hardly starving." His eyes raked over my curves even though I wore a modest cotton shift.

Despite myself, I flushed. "No, but an artist all the same. Let me guess, you work with money."

"In a sense," he said, and his eyes danced. "Is this Twenty Questions?"

I laughed. "I haven't played that since I was a kid."

"Not so long ago."

"Long enough," I corrected and shot a look at him from the corner of my eye. "How old are you?"

"Thirty-one. I'm also 6'1 and I've broken my right arm three times." His small smile was a boyish contrast to his sharp, almost aggressively drawn features. I wanted desperately to trace the exaggerated line of his jaw and dip a finger into the slight hollow beneath his cheekbone.

"Twenty-four." I pulled the bulk of my wavy hair to one side in order to show him the tattoo behind my ear.

When I didn't explain its significance, he frowned. "What is it?"

"A mark," I said simply.

I jerked slightly when his fingers brushed over the swirled ink. "I like it."

"Thank you." My voice was breathy as I draped my hair once more over my shoulders.

"What brings you to Mexico? I take it your family doesn't live here." A finger ran down my arm lightly, highlighting the paleness of my skin.

"My family is much more exotic than I am." I thought of Mama and the twins with a slight grimace; years of hero worship were hard to completely eradicate. "My best friend booked the trip but couldn't make it. I was only too happy to take her place."

He nodded, his eyes intense as he contemplated me. The connection between us thickened and hummed like the air during an electrical storm. Disturbed, I shifted away from him to look out the window as we swooped low over the ground above the runway. Strangely, I did not feel my usual apprehension as the plane tentatively brushed the tarmac once, twice, before smoothly landing.

We didn't speak as the pilot came on the overhead system announcing our arrival and it was only when we came to a slow stop at the terminal that I turned back to him. He faced forward, a furrow etched deeply between his brows and his mouth was firm with concentration. I wondered what he thought of me, of this strange meeting.

Sensing my gaze, he said, "I've been trying to decide if I should see you again."

"What makes you think I would want to?" His eyebrow arched, and I gave into his silent reproach with a little shrug. "What's stopping you?"

The seat belt sign turned off, and we both stood at the same time, suddenly almost touching, the slim space between us charged with electricity the color of his eyes. He looked down at me, his deep chestnut hair softening the dangerous edge of his features. "I have never wanted someone the way I want you." His hand skimmed over my hip and sent a deep, throbbing shock through my system. "But I don't like the idea that you could very well change my life."

My heart clanged uncomfortably against my ribcage and though I desperately wanted to say something, I couldn't find the words to untangle the jumble of hormones and desires I had been reduced to. So instead, I watched a serious smile tilt one side of his closed lips as his eyes scraped over my face one last time and then, without a word still, he left.

Get the full book *now*!

THANKS ETC.

This entire trilogy has lived in my brain for well over a decade and I cannot properly describe how wonderful it feels to share Sebastian, Adam, and Linnea with you after all this time. I remember speaking with a friend years ago about the idea of changing the heroine between book one and two from Savannah to Linnea. "I wouldn't do it," they said, which was fair enough. I know readers get attached to characters, in fact, I wanted you to be attached to Savannah so that you would feel Sebastian's heartbreak at the end of The Moon & His Tides. I also wanted you to hate her a bit, for her haughtiness and ruthlessness. Savannah is a flawed character, just as Adam is, but I wanted them to contrast each other in this book to show the difference between what happens when someone learns to be brave enough to overcome their fears and what happens when someone allows their fears to rule them. Bravery is an essential element to true love, and Linnea has enough courage to not only love two very different men, but to bridge the gap of their troubled history and remind them how to find love with each other again.

I know the cliffhanger is a bit brutal, and you might rail at Sebastian for making the wrong choice, but nostalgia is a powerful poison, and not even our romantic Italian is flawless. It was his turn to make our blood boil. Brace yourself for The Stars and Their Sky, because shit is only just now about to hit the fan.

To everyone who makes my writing life flourish.

Jessica, my assistant and right-hand woman, thank you for being the most productive, proactive, supportive part of my business. Working with you feels like a miracle. You're the Chaucer to my Adam and I'm so grateful for that.

Georgana, my agent and publicist extraordinaire, thank you for always believing in me and loving me so fully. I am so thankful the world saw fit to throw us together because I can't imagine ever being apart.

Valentine, the black cat to my golden retriever, my Baby Darling. Thanks for being my bestie. For always making me laugh with your snark and sense of humor, for shopping with me and including me in your life. I love you.

Pang, thank you for being such a marvelous support and part of Team Giana.

Jenny from Editing4Indies, thanks as usual for taking my error riddled mess and polishing it to a high shine. I adore you.

Sarah Plocher, I don't know how many books we've worked on together now, but I am so grateful for each one. Your enthusiasm and support for my work means the world to me.

Sarah Gooch, my Aussie sister and soul friend, thank you not only for your work proofreading this manuscript but for your years of incredible friendship. Thank God my books brought us together because our friendship is one of the lights of my life.

To Najla and Nada Qamber at Qamber Designs for not only creating this gorgeous model cover, but also for always whipping up the most gorgeous edits and merchandise designs for my words!

To my beloved fellow Canadian, Cat at TRC Designs, for designing the stunning discreet cover of *The Sun & Her Burn*, formatting the gorgeous paperback, and for just being one of the most fabulous people ever.

To Vero, who is my Italian queen. Thank you for always helping with the Italian language and culture in my books.

My Bex, for being my girl and always cheering me on in whatever I endeavour to do. I love you to the moon.

To Jo, whose battle with Alzheimer's inspired me to write about Linnea and Miranda's relationship and struggles with Frontotemporal Dementia. You were one of a kind, a true matriarch and example of shining goodness, and you will be very missed.

My Darlings, who are my safe space on the internet and a place I can go every time I need a smile or a reminder that people care about the stories I tell. Thank you for being so positive and supportive all the time. I'm so in debt to you all for making my dreams come true.

To my Content Creator Team, thank you for being the best hype women ever! You make a world of difference in my career and it means so much to me.

Em, who runs @fansofgianadarling on IG, thank you for being my fangirl and ride-or-die supporter!

Brittany, years of friendship, ups and downs both professionally and personally, and there is no one in this industry I love and trust more.

Kandi, for inspiring me every day with your creativity, work ethic, bright spirit, and beauty. Thank you for being a soul sister.

To my girls—Fiona, Lauren, Madison, Armie, Bridget, Lisa—for being my real life cheerleaders and inspirations.

To my boys—Al, Devo, Kev, Sam, Spencer, Noah—for giving me the kind of friendship that makes me feel loved and accepted no matter what.

To my sisters, Grace and Beth, for being kick-ass inspirations and beautiful women who only ever support and love me.

And last but never least, my husband. I wake up every day filled with love and gratitude that I found my soulmate when I was fifteen. We've been through so much together, and I wouldn't change any of the trials or tribulations because it forged us like steel in fire. Loving you is the best part of my life.

OTHER BOOKS BY GIANA DARLING

The Evolution of Sin Trilogy

Giselle Moore is running away from her past in France for a new life in America, but before she moves to New York City, she takes a holiday on the beaches of Mexico and meets a sinful, enigmatic French businessman, Sinclair, who awakens submissive desires and changes her life forever.

The Affair
The Secret
The Consequence
The Evolution Of Sin Trilogy Boxset

The Fallen Men Series

The Fallen Men are a series of interconnected, standalone, erotic MC romances that each feature age gap love stories between dirty-talking, Alpha males and the strong, sassy women who win their hearts.

Lessons in Corruption
Welcome to the Dark Side
Good Gone Bad

After the Fall
Inked in Lies
Dead Man Walking
Caution to the Wind
Asking for Trouble

A Fallen Men Companion Book of Poetry:
King of Iron Hearts

The Enslaved Duet

The Enslaved Duet is a dark romance duology about an eighteen-year-old Italian fashion model, Cosima Lombardi, who is sold by her indebted father to a British Earl who's nefarious plans for her include more than just sexual slavery… Their epic tale spans across Italy, England, Scotland, and the USA across a five-year period that sees them endure murder, separation, and a web of infinite lies.

Enthralled (The Enslaved Duet #1)
Enamoured (The Enslaved Duet #2)

The Impossible Universe Series

Sebastian Lombardi has moved to London to pursue his dreams of being an actor while also providing for his family back in Italy by driving for a luxury car company. It's there he meets Savannah Meyers and her husband, Adam Meyers, who propose a scandalous deal, live with them as their lover and they'll make his wildest dreams come true.

The Moon & His Tides (The Impossible Universe Trilogy, #1)
The Sun & Her Burn
The Stars & Their Sky coming December 2025

The Dark Dream Duet

The Dark Dream duology is a guardian/ward, enemies to lovers romance about the dangerous, scarred black sheep of the Morelli family, Tiernan, and the innocent Bianca Belcante. After Bianca's mother dies, Tiernan becomes the guardian to both her and her little brother. But Tiernan doesn't do anything out of the goodness of his heart, and soon Bianca is thrust into the wealthy elite of Bishop's Landing and the dark secrets that lurk beneath its glittering surface.

Bad Dream (Dark Dream Duet, #0.5) is FREE
Dangerous Temptation (Dark Dream Duet, #1)
Beautiful Nightmare (Dark Dream Duet, #2)
Wildest Dreams Boxset

The Elite Seven Series
Sloth (The Elite Seven Series, #7)

Standalone
Serpentine Valentine (A Sapphic Medusa Retelling)

Coming Soon
My Dark Fairy Tale (A Mafia Romance) April 8th 2025

ABOUT GIANA DARLING

Giana Darling is a USA Today, Wall Street Journal, Top 40 Best Selling Canadian romance writer who specializes in the taboo and angsty side of love and romance. She currently lives in beautiful British Columbia where she spends time riding on the back of her husband's bike, baking pies, and reading snuggled up with her dog, Romeo, and her cat, Persephone.

www.ingramcontent.com/pod-product-compliance
Lightning Source LLC
Chambersburg PA
CBHW070336170726
48291CB00001B/65